THE
BLACKFIRE
BLADE

Also by James Logan

The Silverblood Promise

THE
BLACKFIRE
BLADE

The Last Legacy
BOOK TWO

James Logan

TOR

TOR PUBLISHING GROUP
NEW YORK

THE BLACKFIRE BLADE

A Tor Book
Published by Tom Doherty Associates / Tor Publishing Group
120 Broadway
New York, NY 10271

www.torpublishinggroup.com

Tor® is a registered trademark of Macmillan Publishing Group, LLC.

EU Representative: Macmillan Publishers Ireland Ltd, 1st Floor, The Liffey Trust Center, 117–126 Sheriff Street Upper, Dublin 1, DO1 YC43

The Library of Congress Cataloging-in-Publication Data
is available upon request.

ISBN 978-1-250-35065-7 (trade paperback)
ISBN 978-1-250-35066-4 (ebook)

Our books may be purchased in bulk for specialty retail/wholesale, literacy, corporate/premium, educational, and subscription box use. Please contact MacmillanSpecialMarkets@macmillan.com.

Originally published in Great Britain by Quercus/Hachette U.K.

First U.S. Edition: 2025

Printed in the United States of America

10 9 8 7 6 5 4 3 2 1

For my parents,
with love

Our story so far . . .

Lukan Gardova is a silver-tongued cardsharp, Academy dropout and—thanks to a duel that ended badly—the disgraced heir to an ancient noble house. Estranged from his reclusive, scholarly father—his only family—Lukan has spent seven years traveling around the Old Empire, drinking, gambling and wondering how to win back the life he carelessly threw away.

One night, after yet another card game that ended in a brawl, Lukan realizes he's being followed. He suspects an assassin sent by the Castoris—the family of the young man who Lukan killed in the ill-fated duel. Instead, he discovers that his pursuer is his father's steward, a woman called Shafia, who bears grave news: Lukan's father—an expert on the ancient, long-vanished Phaeron civilization-has been murdered by unknown assailants, and his study turned inside out. The killers were looking for something—but what? They only have one clue: a letter that Lukan's father wrote in his own blood, which contains three words: Lukan, Saphrona, Zandrusa.

The meaning of the first word is clear; the message was intended for Lukan. The second word—Saphrona-refers to the great city on the southernmost tip of the Old Empire—a place of commerce and powerful merchant princes. But the third word—Zandrusa—is a mystery. Might it be the name of his father's murderer? At Shafia's urging, Lukan swears a silverblood promise to travel to Saphrona to find the truth. It's too late for him to heal the rift between him and his father, but he hopes that unmasking the killers and bringing them to justice will offer some closure.

Lukan arrives in Saphrona a few weeks later and soon finds himself lost in the colorful chaos of the city's Plaza of Silver and Spice, where it's said anything can be bought—even a death, if one has the coin. Lukan, as it happens, doesn't have much coin—not that it matters, because no one he asks can tell him who, or what, or where, Zandrusa is.

Exhausted, Lukan takes a rest—only to find himself the target of a pickpocket. After catching the street rat in the act, he learns her name is Flea. In return for not handing her in to the guards—and for a few coins, because she's a sharp negotiator—Flea agrees to introduce Lukan to a man who might be able to answer his question. That man turns out to be Obassa, a blind beggar—or, as Lukan quickly realizes, a blind man pretending to be a beggar. Obassa reveals that Zandrusa was a Zar-Ghosan smuggler, who later became a merchant prince and adopted the pseudonym Säida Jelassi. Lukan's elation at finally learning the truth fades as Obassa informs him that Zandrusa was found guilty of murdering a fellow merchant prince and is due to be executed the following morning. Maybe. It all depends on Gargantua.

"Gargantua," Lukan learns the next day, is the name for the huge worm-like creature which serves as the official method of execution in Saphrona. Lukan and Flea join thousands of other spectators in the city's amphitheater and watch as three prisoners—Zandrusa among them—are chained in the "Bone Pit" and left at Gargantua's mercy. Flea tells Lukan that the creature is only allowed to claim one prisoner, with the others given a literal stay of execution. Lukan watches in horror, but is ultimately relieved as Gargantua chooses one of the other prisoners for her breakfast. Still, it's only a temporary reprieve—Zandrusa will be back in the Bone Pit in ten days, and if Lukan doesn't manage to speak to her before then, he'll never learn what link she has to his father. There's another problem: Zandrusa is locked up in the Ebon Hand—a Phaeron tower that rises from Saphrona's bay—which now serves as Saphrona's most notorious prison. Getting inside won't be easy.

At Obassa's suggestion, Lukan seeks the services of the Scrivener, who is said to be a master forger. Perhaps she can provide Lukan with the disguise he needs to infiltrate the Hand. But before Lukan can even speak with the Scrivener, he must win her trust—by playing the Pyramid game at Salazar's House of Fortune. The Pyramid is a Phaeron artifact that punishes players by inflicting them with illusions that feel real. Lukan plays the game with three other players, one of whom is Lady Marni Volkova, the scion of a powerful family in Korslakov, a city in the far north. The game doesn't go well; Lukan suffers two punishing illusions and is eliminated after blacking out. Still, he's proven his intent, and the Scrivener agrees to meet with him.

The meeting goes poorly; Lukan doesn't appreciate being tied to a chair, and the Scrivener takes umbrage with his attitude, but eventually they strike a deal, and she agrees to provide Lukan with the uniform and documentation he needs to impersonate an Inquisitor of the feared Saphronan Inquisition. Lukan hopes this disguise will enable him to infiltrate the Ebon Hand and speak to Zandrusa.

Lukan's stolen uniform and forged documents arrive a few days later and are just as convincing as he was told to expect. The guards at the Hand are certainly fooled, and Lukan eventually finds himself alone in a cell with Zandrusa. There he learns that his father and Zandrusa were old acquaintances, and that many years ago his father entrusted the merchant prince with a locked casket which she was instructed to give to Lukan should he ever come looking for her. Zandrusa still has the casket, but it's stashed at the Three Moons Counting House, and only she can access it—an impossibility, given her current predicament.

The only way Lukan will get his hands on the casket is by helping Zandrusa prove her innocence. The merchant prince claims she was framed for the murder of Lord Saviola, and that the real culprit is Lord Murillo—her political rival. She urges Lukan to speak to Doctor Vassilis, who tended to Lord Saviola's body—perhaps he noticed the same thing she saw: frost on Saviola's body, despite the heat of late summer. A sign that might somehow point to the real culprit. Lukan agrees to approach the doctor, and to this end

Zandrusa advises him to seek help from her steward, Magellis, at her estate. He might be able to help.

Lukan is a few steps from freedom when his luck runs out. The captain of the Ebon Hand requests an audience, and Lukan feels obliged to attend him. During their conversation, the captain sees through his deception, and Lukan is forced to escape the Ebon Hand by jumping out of a window. It's a long drop to the sea below.

Lukan reconvenes with the Scrivener, who offers her ongoing support, as well as the use of one of her safehouses. Lukan's next move is to visit Zandrusa's estate, and her steward Magellis, who informs him that Lady Valdezar-another merchant prince—is holding a soiree, and that Doctor Vasillis will likely be there. Magellis offers Lukan the invitation that Zandrusa received before she was incarcerated.

Lukan attends Lady Valdezar's gala, where he encounters General Leopold Razin, an exile from Korslakov who is seeking funds to raise an army to avenge a past injustice. The drunken general points Lukan toward Doctor Vassilis, who is very reluctant to talk about Lord Saviola's death, and makes a hasty retreat when Lukan pushes him too hard. Lukan then meets a genial merchant prince called Lord Marquetta, who in turn introduces him to Lord Murillo—Zandrusa's nemesis, and the man she believes framed her for Saviola's murder. Lukan takes an instant dislike to the man, and decides Zandrusa is likely right.

As Lukan is leaving, Doctor Vassilis emerges from the shadows and tells Lukan to visit him at the Collegium at midnight. Lukan does so, accompanied by Flea, and one of the Scrivener's men by the name of Hector. Lukan hopes to get answers, but instead he finds a dead body—that of Doctor Vassilis. Someone—Lord Murillo, Lukan guesses—must have learned of their meeting, and murdered the doctor to stop him talking. As they search the study, Flea discovers a secret space where they find the doctor's journal.

Back at the Scrivener's safe house, Lukan reads the journal, and learns that Vassilis also saw the frost on Lord Saviola's body, and suspected sorcery was involved in his murder. The doctor writes that soon afterward he was visited by masked intruders who threatened to kill him unless he reported that the merchant prince died solely from a knife wound. No doubt it was these same masked intruders who murdered the doctor at the Collegium, before Lukan could speak to him. But if so, why didn't they try to kill Lukan as well? They had the perfect chance, after all.

A moment later the back door crashes open downstairs, and Lukan hears fighting as Hector and another guard engage the intruders. Seems the doctor's murderers have come for him after all. Lukan goes to help Hector, but the fight is over too quickly, and instead he hides with Flea in a bolthole behind the fireplace. They hear the intruders—who all seem to be named after gemstones-moving around in the room beyond, but they remain undiscovered.

Eventually the intruders leave—taking the journal with them-and Lukan and Flea emerge from their hiding place. When Lukan goes downstairs, he discovers that one of the attackers—Topaz—has remained behind. During the confrontation that follows, Flea stabs Topaz in the leg and Lukan knocks him out with a frying pan. With half the kitchen on fire, thanks to a shattered oil lamp, they make their escape, dragging the unconscious Topaz with them.

While Lukan bears the brunt of the Scrivener's anger at the night's events, another one of her agents, Juro, is busy interrogating Topaz. Juro relays what he's learned: Topaz is a member of a mercenary group called the Seven Jewels, led by Madame "Diamond" Delastro. Topaz denies the group had any involvement in the murder of Lord Saviola, but admits to the theft of the Sandino Blade, a crime widely believed to be the work of Lady Midnight, so-called master thief and Flea's idol. Topaz claims not to know who the Seven Jewels are working for—their employer always wears a mask—but reveals the group is due to escort them tonight into the catacombs for unknown purposes.

Lukan and Flea hide out in Saphrona's cemetery and watch as the Seven Jewels escort a masked figure—Lord Murillo, most likely-into the designated tomb. When the gate is left unlocked, Lukan senses an opportunity. He confronts the guard—Amethyst—and engages her in a swordfight, which he seems destined to lose until Flea shoots her with a crossbow she took from Topaz. With Amethyst subdued, Lukan and Flea follow the rest of the group into the catacombs. They soon reach a chamber where the masked figure is talking with a woman Lukan identifies as Madame "Diamond" Delastro.

When the figure removes his mask, Lukan is stunned to see the genial Lord Marquetta—not Murillo, as he'd expected. More surprises follow as two more conspirators enter the chamber: Prime Inquisitor Fierro, head of the Saphronan Inquisition, and Pontifex Barbosa, the highest religious authority in the city. As they discuss recent events, Lukan wonders how they know so much about his movements—and gets his answer moments later when Magellis appears. It transpires that Zandrusa's steward is actually Lord Marquetta's agent. Sadly for Magellis, he's outlived his usefulness, and is murdered by Delastro at Marquetta's command.

As the conversation continues, Lukan learns that Marquetta is responsible for the murder of Lord Saviola, and that he deliberately framed Zandrusa for the crime. Both acts are part of his wider plan to start a new war with the Southern Queendom of Zar-Ghosa—an act he believes will usher in a glorious new age for Saphrona. The final part of his plan is to assassinate the Zar-Ghosan ambassador at the upcoming Grand Restoration—a ceremony meant to symbolize peace between the two cities.

The Pontifex asks Marquetta how he intends to murder the ambassador in front of the entire city. A sorcerous portal forms in the air in response, and three armored figures step through, wearing armor shaped respectively in the likeness of a wolf, a snake, and a kraken. Lukan stares in disbelief as Marquetta introduces the Faceless—legendary figures that have long faded into myth and children's stories. This, he says, is how he intends to murder the Zar-Ghosan ambassador in front of the entire city—the Faceless will perform the act for him with their powerful sorceries. In return he will give them the Sandino Blade, stolen for him by Delastro and her Seven Jewels.

The Faceless then detect Lukan's presence and summon a sorcerous wolf that chases him and Flea through the catacombs.

Lukan distracts the wolf to allow Flea to escape, and eventually ends up being captured by subjects of the Twice-Crowned King, the ruler of Saphrona's criminal underworld. After a painful interrogation, he's thrown in a cell. A while later, another prisoner joins him—Ashra Seramis, also known as Lady Midnight, who the Twice-Crowned King has been hunting for some time. Flea idolizes Lady Midnight and claims the master thief can walk through walls. The truth is that Ashra has a pair of Phaeron rings—the Rings of Last Resort-that can summon portals. She uses them now, and together she and Lukan escape to one of her safe houses.

There, Lukan tells Ashra all he knows, and the master thief joins with him to try and foil Marquetta's plan. Lukan reunites with Flea, but receives short shrift from the Scrivener, who terminates their agreement and refuses to help them. Lukan, Flea and Ashra are forced to watch as the Grand Restoration ceremony descends into bloody chaos-but not in the way Lukan expected. Instead of murdering the Zar-Ghosan ambassador, the Faceless possess her with their sorcery, and force her to murder Saphrona's Grand Duke and his twin sons. Lukan belatedly realizes it's a coup; Marquetta is seizing control of Saphrona.

In the aftermath of the assassination, Lukan and his allies are approached by Madame Delastro, who intends to cut her ties with Marquetta. She reveals that Topaz is her nephew and requests his safe return. Lukan agrees, but demands her help in obtaining the Sandino Blade. He's come to realize why the Faceless want it; the legends suggest the Faceless seek a type of rare purple crystals, and the Sandino Blade has one set in its pommel. Lukan believes that if the blade is in his possession, he can turn the tables on Marquetta. Delastro and her crew are due to transport the blade to the Ducal Palace that very evening, and she agrees to hand it over to Lukan. There's just one problem: Marquetta keeps the blade locked in a Phaeron casket, which can only be opened by pressing the glass panels in a specific order. Delastro doesn't know the sequence but reveals that Pontifex Barbosa does.

As unrest across the city explodes into violence, Ashra disguises herself as a courtesan and infiltrates the Pontifex's villa, forcing the sequence from him at the point of a knife. Meanwhile, Delastro delivers the Sandino Blade to Lukan, who is forced to beg for her protection when a large mob tries to storm the carriage transporting the blade. Ashra arrives shortly after the rioters have fled, and together she and Lukan successfully open the casket and take possession of the Sandino Blade. Delastro then transports the empty casket to the Ducal Palace, at Lukan's request. She has no idea that Flea has hitched a ride by clinging to the carriage's roof.

Flea successfully infiltrates the Ducal Palace. She learns that Marquetta is in the great hall, and finds a safe place to activate one of Ashra's Rings of Last Resort, opening a portal that Lukan and Ashra traverse to join her. Together, they enter the great hall through a secret passage and find they're just in time: the Faceless haven't yet appeared, while Marquetta—now Lord Protector-appears oblivious to the theft of the blade. The Pontifex and Prime Inquisitor are both present, as is Artemio, the chancellor, who is tied to a chair and gagged.

Soon the Faceless arrive through a portal of their own. At Marquetta's prompting, they kill the Pontifex and Prime Inquisitor—it seems the newly-minted Lord Protector is tying off loose threads. Marquetta then prepares to murder Artemio—a task he seems to relish—only to be interrupted by the Faceless, who demand their payment. Marquetta acquiesces, only to open the casket and find the Sandino blade gone.

Lukan takes this as his cue, and announces his presence. Marquetta is furious and orders the Faceless to kill Lukan and take what is rightfully theirs. The Wolf—who seems to be the leader of the Faceless—walks toward Lukan, as if to carry out Marquetta's command. But Lukan is gambling on something his father once told him: that the Faceless never take anything by force and will always trade for it instead. He offers the Wolf a trade: the blade in return for proof of Marquetta's treachery.

Marquetta attacks Lukan, but one of the other Faceless incapacitates him. The Wolf then gives Lukan an artifact that contains the Wolf's own memories of their dealings with Marquetta. The Faceless then leave through another portal, taking the blade with them, just before the ducal guard break into the room. The captain of the guard can scarcely believe the tale Lukan tells her, but his version of events is backed up by the chancellor, Artemio, not to mention the Wolf's memories, which Lukan is able to show her by using the artifact.

After a few days being interrogated by the Inquisition, Lukan, Flea and Ashra are released. Marquetta's treachery was confirmed by the Pontifex, who somehow survived the events at the Ducal Palace, and confessed to the entire conspiracy. Both men are in chains and a devastating war between Saphrona and Zar-Ghosa has been averted.

Lukan visits the now-vindicated Zandrusa at her villa, where the merchant prince presents him with the Phaeron casket Lukan's father entrusted her with—which only Lukan can open. When he does so, he finds a key inside for a vault at the Blackfire Bank, located in the city of Korslakov in the far north of the Old Empire. Ashra joins Lukan and Flea as they prepare for the voyage north, with one question on their minds—what awaits them inside the vault?

THE
BLACKFIRE
BLADE

1

JUST ONE DRINK

Thunk.

Lukan Gardova jolted awake and—for a blissful moment—couldn't remember where he was. Realization dawned as his eyes took in the cracked plaster of the walls, the moth-eaten blankets on the beds—and the crossbow bolt stuck in a wooden beam. He muttered a curse, and the wind rattled the nearby shutters as if in mocking response. *Korslakov. Of course.* He grimaced and rubbed at his arms. *As if this damned chill would let me forget.* He reached for the bottle on his bedside table, swore again when he realized it was empty.

Thunk.

"You already finished it," a girl's voice said. Flea stepped into the light of their solitary lantern as she crossed the far side of the room. "Just before you"—she gritted her teeth as she pulled her crossbow bolts free—"fell asleep."

"I didn't fall asleep," Lukan replied, working his tongue around his dry mouth. "I was just—"

"Resting your eyes," Flea said, mimicking his voice (and doing a good job of it, if Lukan was honest). "Sure you were." She aimed her crossbow at the beam, her tongue poking out one side of her mouth.

"Where's Ashra?" Lukan asked, realizing the master thief was absent.

"Out."

"Do you—"

Thunk.

"—know where—"

Thunk.

"—she went?"

"I dunno. Out."

"Out *where*?"

The girl shrugged as she went to collect her bolts. "She just said she wanted to have a gander."

"A *what*?"

Flea pointed two fingers at her own eyes, then pointed at the window. "A gander."

"A look about. Right."

"That's what she *said*, anyway." Flea smirked as she reloaded her crossbow—the small, sleek weapon could hold two bolts at once, though only shoot them one at a time.

"What does that mean?" Lukan demanded.

Thunk.

The girl swore under her breath, one of the many new curses she'd picked up from the crew of the *Sunfish* during their three-week voyage from Saphrona. "It means"—she said, adjusting her aim—"that maybe the real reason Ashra went out was to get away from *you*." Her second bolt was a blur as it shot across the room and bit into the wood, a hair's breadth from the first. Lukan had to admit that she was getting annoyingly good. Not that he would say as much.

"Or maybe," he countered, swinging his legs off the bed, "she got sick of listening to you shooting those damned things against the wall. Can't you give it a rest? There'll be nothing left but splinters at this rate."

"I need to practice."

"You spent the whole voyage practicing. It's a miracle you didn't sink the *Sunfish* with all the holes you shot in it. And an even bigger miracle Grabulli didn't demand compensation for the damage."

Flea flicked her little finger at him—a crude Saphronan insult he'd now grown used to—as she went to retrieve her bolts. Whatever the reason for Ashra's departure, Lukan didn't blame her for seeking solitude. *Goodness knows we've all had enough of each other after three weeks on that damned ship.* It was a miracle they hadn't strangled each other, forced as they were to share a small cabin for the entire duration of the voyage. They'd tried to give each other as much space as possible, but it hadn't been easy— tempers had flared on many occasions. *Mostly mine, looking back at it.* His initial amusement at seeing Flea and Ashra struggling with seasickness had worn off after the former had—accidentally, she claimed—thrown up in Lukan's hammock, and the voyage itself had offered little in the way of distractions. They'd seen a pod of dolphins on one day, and the tall fin of a black shark on another; Graziano Grabulli, the captain, claimed it was the same shark that had bitten him a decade before, but—as with most of his stories—Lukan took it with a hefty pinch of salt. The most exciting moment had been two weeks in, when a corsair ship was sighted on the horizon, and Lukan by that point was so deathly bored that he almost hoped it *would* attack, but the ship had instead slipped away into the deepening dusk. *Probably for the best,* he'd thought later that same night, as he stood at the prow sharing a cigarillo with one of the sailors. *Though it would have been fun seeing Flea skewering a few corsairs with her bolts.*

They were all relieved to finally reach Korslakov. The *Sunfish* had arrived on the evening tide just past the sixth bell, and dusk was already settling across the city and the Wolfclaw Mountains beyond. By the time Grabulli had finished arguing with a harbor official over berthing fees, darkness had fully descended, bringing a chill wind with it, and all Lukan could think about was having a hot drink, a hot meal and a hot bath—ideally all at the same time. Grabulli was able to oblige with the former, and offered them all a shot of steaming rum as his crew prepared the gangplank. Lukan knocked his back and didn't object to Flea doing likewise, though he did stop her from taking Ashra's drink as well after the thief declined it. Finally, Grabulli shook Lukan's hand, kissed Flea's, and sensibly offered Ashra nothing more than a smile and a nod, before sending them on their way with vague directions to what he claimed was a cheap but reputable inn. Lukan had spent enough years on the road to know that "cheap" and "reputable" mixed about as well as oil and water, but he couldn't be bothered to contest the point.

And so they'd ended up here, in a cramped room with only two beds and a pervading smell of damp, which cost about four times more than it was worth. Still, the food that had been brought up to them was passable, if you ignored the dubious meat it contained, and Lukan had managed to get a fire going in the small hearth, before he'd apparently passed out on one of the beds.

It would do for one night.

As for tomorrow night, who knew? If he opened his father's vault at the Blackfire Bank to find a mountain of gold and gemstones inside, then he would treat them to more luxurious accommodation. Sadly, he suspected the reality would prove far less exciting.

As Flea fired another couple of bolts into the wooden beam, Lukan reached for his father's key, hanging on a chain round his neck. The two gems set into the stylized "B" of the handle—an amethyst and a garnet—gleamed in the lantern light. He'd spent much of the voyage wondering what lay in wait for him in the vault—what his father could possibly have hidden there, and why. Would it somehow contain a clue as to the identity of his father's murderer? He felt his grief stirring deep inside him, a constant companion whose presence he was still growing used to. Most of the time it kept its distance, but now and again it would make its presence known, even if only briefly, like a cloud passing in front of the sun.

I'll find them, Father. I'll find whoever did this to you.

"You say something?" Flea asked, frowning at him.

"Hmm? Oh. No." He let the key fall back against his chest. "I was just thinking about tomorrow. The vault, and all that."

"What do you think's inside?"

"What did I tell you the last ninety-nine times you asked me that question?"

The girl adopted a look of mock concentration. "Normally something like, 'I don't know' or, 'How in the bloody hells should I know'—it depended how grouchy you were at the time."

"You try answering the same question a hundred times and see how you like it."

"Maybe it's a golem!" Flea said, with sudden excitement. The revelation that the alchemists of Korslakov could create and command automatons fascinated her. "You could tell it what to do!"

"I could," Lukan agreed. "Maybe I'd order it to clamp its hand over your mouth when you're talking too much."

Flea flicked her little finger at him again. "I want to see one," she declared, sliding her bolts back into her crossbow.

"So you've said," Lukan replied wearily, "many times now. And you will. Once we're done at the bank, we'll go and find one for you to stare at. And when you're finished, we could go and see the alchemists' tower, or the Glasshouse, or . . ." He trailed off when he saw the look of disgust on the girl's face. "Or we can give it all a miss. I just thought maybe you'd like to see a bit of culture while we're here."

"I just want to see a golem," Flea replied, turning her attention back to her crossbow.

And I just want to know what's in the damned vault. Now that they were finally here, he was impatient to learn the answer to the mystery that had been taunting him ever since he took possession of the key. The bank wouldn't open for business until the ninth bell of the morning, and the night stretched before him, already feeling like it was passing painfully slowly. The smart thing would be to bed down and try to get some sleep, but he was too agitated, his mind too restless; and in any case the concept of an early night was as unfamiliar to him as the city he now found himself in.

Instead, his thoughts turned to a tavern he'd spied earlier. It was only a few streets away. Surely a little nightcap wouldn't hurt? It would be remiss of him not to take the opportunity to taste Korslakov's famous vodka, and see some of the local color. After three weeks spent in a small cabin with Flea and Ashra, it felt like the least he deserved.

"I'm going out," he said, rising from the bed.

"Out?" Flea questioned, lowering her crossbow. "Where?"

"I don't know," he replied, mimicking her shrug of a moment earlier. "Out."

"Hilarious."

"I'm just going for a drink."

Flea rolled her eyes. "Of *course* you are."

"Just one drink. And only for half an hour." He picked up his heavy coat, which he'd bought in Saphrona with this trip in mind, though already he had cause to doubt its quality, given how the wind had knifed through it as they'd left the ship. *Seems you can buy anything in Saphrona except for a decent coat.* "Will you be all right here?"

Flea pulled a face. "I guess."

"Lock the door behind me."

"Oh, I was going to leave it wide open." She gave him a scornful look and turned away. "Don't get drunk," she said over her shoulder, as she fired another bolt into the beam.

"I won't."

"And don't get into a fight, 'cos I won't be there to save you." Flea turned, a hopeful look in her eyes. "Unless you want me to come with—"

Lukan shut the door in her face.

2

FIRST IMPRESSIONS

Ashra's first step into Korslakov had been inauspicious.

As she'd stepped off the *Sunfish's* gangplank, she'd slipped on a patch of ice. A gust of wind had knifed her as she struggled to keep her balance, and it felt as if the dark city that loomed around her was saying, *you don't belong here.* Taunting her.

Let it try, she'd thought.

Swiftly she'd regained both balance and breath. As she'd followed Flea and Lukan across the lamplit wharves, she recovered something else too: the elation that had been growing inside her ever since they'd sighted the distant lights of Korslakov earlier that evening. Elation at being free of the ship's narrow confines, Lukan's grating company, and the seasickness that had tormented her. But most of all, elation at placing an entire continent between her and the Twice-Crowned King.

It would take more than a little cold and darkness to steal that feeling from her.

The *Sunfish's* captain, Graziano Grabulli, had given them directions to what he claimed was a reputable inn, but the man was a rogue through and through (it took one to know one) and, while the inn was just as close as he'd promised, Ashra was unsurprised to find it was nowhere near as refined. Perhaps it was a matter of taste. Regardless, the room they rented would do for one night. Lukan managed to light a fire in the small hearth before passing out. Flea was content to sit on her own bed and fuss with her crossbow, but Ashra felt restless. She was keen to explore this strange new city, despite the frosty welcome it had given her. She'd never left Saphrona until deciding to take her chances with

Flea and Lukan on the *Sunfish,* and she could feel the lure of
Korslakov's unfamiliar streets calling to her. It wouldn't hurt to
familiarize herself with their immediate surroundings. Preparation was a thief's greatest tool, after all. So, after extracting a
promise from Flea that the girl wouldn't leave the room, Ashra
had slipped back out into the darkened streets on her own.

An hour later, she felt she had the full measure of the City of
Spires.

If Saphrona was like the sun, bright and warm and full of
promise, then Korslakov mirrored the moon: austere, cold and
shrouded in secrecy. The two cities stood at opposite ends of the
Old Empire, after all, Saphrona at its sun-kissed southern tip and
Korslakov at its bitter northern point. Yet the startling difference
still managed to surprise her. As she traversed the darkened streets,
Ashra felt as if she'd entered a different world entirely. Saphrona
never truly slept; music and laughter and shouts and screams all
carried across the red-tiled roofs well into the small hours. Her
home city had a restless spirit, a vibrant energy that felt like it
might tear loose at any moment.

Korslakov felt different.

It wasn't just the cold. It was the silence, which was broken
only by the odd burst of music or snatch of laughter that carried through open doors only to be snuffed out again. It was the
way the streets were almost deserted, long before midnight. It was
the way those citizens who were abroad held themselves: hooded
heads bowed, cloaked shoulders hunched, as if trying to pass un-
noticed. It was in the way the tall buildings of granite loomed, austere in the darkness, their high-gabled roofs frowning down at her.

Korslakov felt like a city holding its breath, as if scared to draw
the attention of the Wolfclaw Mountains that encircled it. The *Sunfish* had arrived on the evening tide, so Ashra hadn't properly seen
the mountains themselves, but she could sense their immensity by
how they blocked out the stars. They made the mountains that
rose behind Saphrona seem like mere hills. Their vastness stole the
breath from her lungs. Or perhaps that was the cold.

If Saphrona's identity was light and the clamor of life, Korslakov's was the darkness and the quiet of the grave.

Ashra hated it already.

But she hated how it made her feel even more.

With every twisting, darkened street, she could sense her elation of an hour before fading. A nervousness grew in its place; a creeping fear. She could guess at its origin. Ashra knew Saphrona like the back of her hand. After three weeks on the *Sunfish*, she could say the same of the ship, and that had lessened the uncertainty she'd felt at leaving the only home she'd ever known. But Korslakov was a mystery to her, as unfathomable as the depths of the ocean they'd just sailed on. And that made her anxious. She felt unsure and unprepared. Worse, she felt vulnerable in a way she hadn't felt since her mother's accident had forced her into a life of thievery.

She hated that feeling more than anything—more than the heavy coat that weighed her down, more than the brooding, unfamiliar city that threatened to swallow her.

Ashra paused by a tavern, took a deep breath of the cold air. Tried to take some comfort from the faint laughter and thump of a drum within. Signs of life in this dark place.

The wind gusted again, icy fingers tugging at her coat. Probing. Invasive.

She considered heading back to their room. Told herself the city would look different in the morning. That she would feel better.

But that felt like defeat.

And Ashra hated losing as much as she hated feeling vulnerable.

No. There was only one option.

To conquer the fear that was growing inside her, she would have to unmask the city's face and reveal its secrets. Which meant walking its streets and squares and alleys and thoroughfares until she knew them as well as those of Saphrona.

And she would start right now.

Fortunately, she'd come prepared. Captain Grabulli had been of limited use; he was full of entertaining stories about Korslakov, but precious little useful information. For the latter, Ashra had approached one of the sailors, a hard-bitten Korslakovan woman called Zoya, whose accent was so thick Lukan had joked you could strangle someone with it. Ashra had wished he'd test the theory on himself; just three days into the voyage she'd already started to tire of him. Zoya, for her part, had shown little interest in talking about her home city—"Dark. Cold. I like the sea more," was all she'd offered at first—but had eventually come round once she'd seen the glint of Ashra's silver. Over the course of an afternoon she'd told Ashra about the artificers and their technological marvels, the alchemists who hid away in their tower crowned by its great purple flame, and the ruling Frostfire Council, which convened in the throne room of the last king of Korslakov—whose skeleton apparently remained on his throne, with the dagger that killed him still lodged between his ribs. Even more helpfully, Zoya had sketched a rough map of Korslakov on some parchment. When Ashra had complimented her on the quality of her penmanship, the woman had shrugged and said, "I wanted to be an artist. Fate had other plans." Ashra could only nod. She knew only too well how capricious fate could be.

She recalled Zoya's brushstrokes now as she passed through a district of cobbled streets and well-appointed shopfronts, their wrought-iron signs casting shadows in the lantern light. This, she assumed, was Hearthside, the city's upmarket trade district. Any lingering doubt was dispelled as she caught sight of a street sign— THE AVENUE OF CHERISHED SILVER—which she knew to be a major thoroughfare. Ashra followed its winding course, eyeing the upmarket boutiques that catered to the expensive tastes of the aristocrats who lived in the Mantle. As she walked she caught the occasional glimpse of that exclusive district higher up the hillside, well away from the smoke of the foundries on the other side of the river. Purple-white flames—frostfire, Zoya had called it—glimmered in the darkness, lending the Mantle an otherworldly feel.

As if Korslakov didn't already feel strange enough.

Ashra followed the avenue westward until she reached the bank of the River Kolva. Her breath caught in her lungs—not from the cold, but at the sight of the alchemists' famous home—the Tower of Sanctified Flame—which stood across the water, some distance upriver. The frostfire that gave the tower its name burned in a great bowl at its summit, purple-white flames bright against the black sky.

She'd never seen anything like it.

Ashra stared at the tower for a long time, before turning her gaze to the district that spread around it. Emberfall, she thought, recalling its name. The home of Korslakov's famous artificers and machinists. Even now, with midnight approaching, the furnaces and foundries were aglow with industry. Fires also burned to the south of Emberfall, in the slum called the Cinders, which Zoya had described as Korslakov's most impoverished ward. The district to Emberfall's north, by contrast, was entirely dark. No firelight shone in those windows. No lamps illuminated the streets. That quarter of the city had once been called Ashwall, Zoya had told her, but had become known as Ashgrave following a deadly plague. When Ashra had pressed her for details, the sailor had become evasive, saying only that the entire district had been walled off. No one lived there now, she claimed, nor was anyone permitted entry.

No wonder it was so dark. The bright glow of Emberfall only made it seem more pronounced. The longer she stared at the darkness, even from the other side of the river, the more Ashra felt it looked back at her.

Doubt stole into her mind.

She turned her gaze back to the alchemists' tower. As she watched the purple flames, she wondered whether she'd made a mistake in coming here.

Suddenly she felt a very long way from home.

But that was the whole point. She'd chosen to come here, to this strange and unfamiliar city. Korslakov satisfied her need to get as far away from Saphrona as possible. The cold and darkness were small prices to pay to evade the clutches of the Twice-Crowned

King. Putting up with Lukan Gardova, however, was something else entirely.

She could have chosen differently, of course. Traveled alone, gone somewhere else that wasn't so damned cold. It wasn't as if she and Lukan had gotten along smoothly even before they'd boarded the *Sunfish*. The trials and tribulations of that voyage had certainly made her question her decision several times. But always, in the end, she decided that she had made the right choice. The knowledge that she had to leave Saphrona had unnerved her, there was no denying it. But doing so in the company of companions made the ordeal seem less daunting. Even if Ashra doubted she and Lukan could survive three days in a cabin together, let alone three weeks. In his defense, she was sure he felt the same.

Yet somehow, they had managed. Partly thanks to Flea's interventions, but mostly by trying to avoid each other as much as possible. Grabulli had occasionally joked about throwing Lukan overboard, and at times she'd wished he would. Still, in the end they made it to Korslakov without murdering each other. All that remained now was for Lukan to unlock his father's vault and discover what was inside. He'd claimed not to have a clue as to the nature of his inheritance, and for once she fully believed him. Her twentieth rule of thievery was to expect the unexpected—and that was especially true where Lukan Gardova was concerned.

Ashra tensed, suddenly alert.

Footsteps sounded behind her.

Two people. Men, judging by the heaviness of their tread. Approaching with intent.

She reached into her left coat sleeve, fingers grasping for the small blade strapped to her forearm. She slipped the knife free, and kept it concealed as she turned to face her would-be muggers.

"Evening, miss," the taller man said, a questioning note in his voice, as he touched the brim of his fur hat in greeting. "Everything all right?"

Ashra took the two men in at a glance, her instincts telling her they meant no harm. Not at present, at least. She studied the speaker, who was older than his companion, noting his red cloak and orange tunic, the latter bearing an insignia of a burning torch in yellow stitching. The second man—barely more than a youth, she realized—was similarly attired, and peered curiously at Ashra in the light of his lantern.

They were Sparks, Ashra realized, recalling Zoya's name for Korslakov's city watchmen. So named for their colorful uniforms— and, the sailor claimed, for their famously short tempers.

"Miss?" the speaker repeated, eyes narrowing under bushy brows. "Are you well?"

"Yes," Ashra replied, not releasing her blade. "I'm just . . ." She was going to say *out for a walk*, but realized how odd that might seem given how almost everyone else—at least on this side of the river—was probably abed. "Getting some air," she offered instead. "I've had a headache for much of the day."

"I see," the man said, his lie not as convincing as hers. "Your accent—are you new to the city?"

"I am."

"Well, I suggest you move on. Most of the riffraff are on the other side of the river"—the man glanced at the distant lights of the Cinders—"but we get the odd cutpurse lurking about in Hearthside."

"How distressing," Ashra replied dryly. "I'll be sure to watch out for them."

"It's the Rook you want to look out for," the boy piped up.

"Enough with that," his companion chided, shooting him a sour look.

"The Rook?" Ashra prompted.

"There's talk of a thief who prowls Hearthside, and even the Mantle," the man said reluctantly. "Some fool who wears a mask with the face of a bird or some such."

"And he has glowing yellow eyes," the younger man said eagerly. "I've heard that he often targets women, and apparently he can—"

"I said enough!" his companion growled, glaring at the other Spark until he lowered his gaze.

"My thanks for the warning," Ashra replied, "but I can look after myself."

"Of course," the older watchman said, dipping his head in apology. "Please ignore my companion here. The Rook's nothing you need worry about. Even so, I'd be getting home, if I were you." He touched his furred hat again and then dragged the younger man away into the night, muttering under his breath as they went. Ashra released her hold on her blade as she watched them go.

It was probably best to heed the guard's advice and head home—if their cramped lodgings could even be called that. At least there would be a fire. She shivered, suddenly realizing just how cold she was. She could barely feel her toes. She'd only explored a small part of the city, but it was enough to take the edge off her fear. For now, at least. That would have to be enough.

As Ashra started back toward the inn, her thoughts turned to her companions. Flea had been fussing over her crossbow when she'd left, while Lukan was likely still asleep. And if not, she hoped he was behaving himself.

The last thing they needed was him getting into trouble.

3

DOWN AND OUT IN THE CITY OF SPIRES

Lukan stumbled out of the tavern.

He immediately slipped on something wet and fell to the ground, banging his head against a barrel as he did so.

"Shit," he burbled, rubbing his temple as he fought his way to his knees, and then—eventually—his feet. The dark street tilted around him, the glow of lanterns streaking across his vision. "Shit," he muttered again, taking a lungful of the cold air as he hugged the barrel.

That flagon of black ale had been a mistake.

So had the three double shots of vodka before it.

And that was before he even considered the many drinks that had preceded those, most of which he'd already forgotten. "Only meant to have one," he murmured. That was true, at least. And he'd so nearly managed it; he was just one final gulp away from finishing his gin and making good on his promise to Flea. But before he could take that last swallow, he'd fallen in with a group of students celebrating a birthday, and someone had thrust a drink into his hand, and he'd thought, *well, what harm can it do*, and the tiny voice of reason that squealed at the back of his mind had fallen silent the instant a young woman had met his gaze with a glint in her eye and a smile on her lips. The rest of the evening was a blur: lots of drinking, lots of shouting, a bit of bad dancing, and the disappointment of seeing the woman fumbling with someone else in a dark corner.

So it goes.

Lukan eased himself off the barrel and took another lungful of air, hoping the rasping chill would sober him up, and feeling only regret when it did. He'd hoped to be back before Ashra returned from her own jaunt, but she was likely now warming herself before the fire and waiting for him with an expression sharper than her stilettos. Still, he'd endured plenty of those looks over the past three weeks. What was one more? A drink or five was the least he deserved after surviving an entire voyage in her company. *Perhaps I should tell her that.* Lukan snorted to himself as he started forward—and almost slipped over again. He gripped the barrel again and glared accusingly at the ground. Blinked at what he saw.

Snow.

A thin layer covered the cobbles. He was so drunk he'd not even noticed. He looked up, watched the tiny flakes falling in the light of a nearby lantern. It sometimes snowed in Parva, but only in the depths of winter, not at the arse end of the autumn. Still, it wasn't surprising that winter had come early to Korslakov. This was as far north as you could go and still find yourself in the Old Empire. Beyond the Wolfclaw Mountains lay the Clanholds, occupied by the clans with whom Korslakov had warred for centuries. The frozen wilderness held far greater dangers too, if his father's old map was to be believed. Lukan could still remember the inscription, scrawled in flowing script: *these be the unmapped lands of men that look like beasts and beasts that walk like men.* It was a load of nonsense, of course; old mapmakers loved that sort of cryptic annotation. On the other hand, he'd thought the Faceless were just a myth until he saw them in Saphrona. He shivered, and not from the cold. With luck he wouldn't see them ever again.

A distant bell tolled, and Lukan found himself counting the chimes, wincing as he reached the twelfth. *Midnight. Bloody hells.* Somehow he'd been gone for three hours. As he listened to the faint strains of the brass band coming through the tavern door, underscored by shouting and laughter, he felt an urge to nip back inside. Perhaps he could have a shot of whiskey—just to warm up, of course, before he attempted the walk home. Besides, he was so late that another quarter-hour wouldn't hurt.

Instead, the little voice of reason—previously drowned out by both the music and the drinks he'd been downing—finally made itself heard at the back of his mind. With a sigh, Lukan stumbled back toward their lodgings.

Two things quickly became apparent as he tottered through the dark streets.

The first was that he was lost. The inn they were staying at was only a handful of streets away, yet he'd somehow let his mind wander, and now he didn't have the faintest idea where he was. Secondly, the reason he felt so bloody cold was because he'd left his coat behind and was walking around like a fool in his shirt. If he hadn't been so drunk, he would have noticed sooner, but then the alcohol swirling in his stomach was also the only reason he wasn't curled up shivering in a gutter, so perhaps it evened out. He swore and reached beneath the collar of his shirt, his fingers curling round the cold metal of the key that hung from his neck on a chain. Losing that would really have ruined his night, and a whole lot more besides. But with the key safe, nothing else mattered. Except for finding his way back to the inn, of course.

He turned at the sound of boots crunching in the snow. A man was striding down the street, his head down, shoulders bunched against the falling snow.

"Excuse me," Lukan said, trying to keep both his speech and movements on an even keel. He failed miserably with the latter, and his inebriated lurch caused the man to give him a wide berth, his pace increasing. "Sir," Lukan called after him, "would you happen to know the way to . . . ah . . ." Lady's blood, he couldn't even remember the name of the inn.

In any case, the man walked on without a backward glance.

"Thanks for your help," Lukan muttered, rubbing his arms as he turned away. The warming effect of the alcohol was now wearing off, and he could feel a chill stealing over him. "It's fine," he told himself. "You've been in far worse situations than this." He might have thought of his recent encounter with the Faceless, or the narrow escape from the Twice-Crowned King's cell, but for some reason his mind—perhaps not as sober as he thought—picked out the time he'd been forced to flee a notoriously rough gambling den in just his underwear. Still, it was an apt recollection: that escapade had worked out all right. So would this. All he had to do was knock on a few doors. Surely someone would be kind enough to point the way. He grimaced as he became aware of another unwelcome sensation.

He really needed to piss.

Lukan ducked into a nearby alley illuminated by the light of a solitary lantern and fumbled at his trousers. He threw back his head and sighed as he relieved himself, only to fall silent as he spied a large, dark shape crouching on a windowsill above him. *Probably a stone gargoyle*, he thought as he looked down. The strange carvings decorated many of the buildings in Korslakov. But then he heard a scraping sound and glanced up again just as a small flutter of snow fell against his shoulder.

The shape was moving.

Must be a cat, he decided, as he laced himself up, only to pause as the shape leaned out over the windowsill, and he caught a glimpse of what looked like a beak. *Some sort of bird, then.* What it was doing up there was anyone's guess. Lukan didn't much care. He turned away, took a step back toward the street.

And grunted in surprise as something struck his back.

He hit the ground hard, his chin striking the snow-covered cobblestones. He tasted blood in his mouth, heard a ringing in his ears. *What in the hells . . .* He tried to rise, but the heavy weight on his shoulders wouldn't shift. He gasped as he felt something sharp—talons—digging into his shoulder. *The bird*, he realized with disbelief. *The bloody thing landed on me.* For a fleeting moment he imagined being pecked to death by his avian assailant, and almost laughed at the absurdity of it all. But then he felt a pressure round his neck as the chain he wore was pulled tight against his throat, and his humor vanished as he flailed hopelessly in rising panic. He thought the bird—or whatever it was—was trying to choke him, but then the chain snapped, and the weight on his back vanished.

Lukan rolled over to see that his assailant had retreated a few paces away. It wasn't a bird, of course, but a person wearing a cloak lined with feathers. The shape of a beak—a mask of some kind—protruded from the hood that covered its head, which was downturned as the figure studied the object that dangled from its talon-like hand.

Lukan's heart dropped at the sight of his key, glinting in the lantern light as it swung on its chain. He raised a hand to his throat, seeking to disprove the evidence of his own eyes. His fingers came away empty. *Shit.* A rush of panic forced him to his feet.

"Hey," he said, taking a step forward. "That's mine."

The figure looked up sharply, fixing Lukan with a glowing eye that burned yellow within its hood.

What in the hells . . .

Then it spun, whip-fast, and raced into the darkness of the alley.

Oh, shit—

Lukan ran after it, snatching the lantern from its hook as he passed. It swung in his hand, casting a wild light as he chased the thief through a series of narrow passages and alleys. His knee struck a barrel as he hurtled round a sharp turn, but he was so intent on catching the figure ahead of him that he barely felt the pain. Yet the thief was fast, and the distance between them was growing; all he saw now were glimpses of the birdlike figure disappearing round corners. Panic followed in his own frantic footsteps. He couldn't lose the key, not when he was so close to getting the answers he sought.

Lukan's growing fear receded as he twisted into another passage, only to find the thief standing in the middle of the alley. As he skidded to a stop, he realized why: a sheer wall rose beyond them, eight or more feet in height.

A dead end.

"All right," Lukan said, breathing heavily as he set the lantern down. "The fun's over. Give it back."

The thief tilted its head and raised Lukan's key, as if to say, *you mean this?*

"That's right," Lukan replied, taking a cautious step forward. "Hand it over and I'll forget this nonsense happened. Hells, I'll even give you a couple of coppers for giving me a good chase. What do you say?"

The figure regarded him, and again he caught a glimpse of a glowing eye within its hood. It seemed strange that a simple thief would bother with such theatricality. A few heartbeats passed as they stared at each other, then the figure shrugged and held out the key.

"Good choice," Lukan said, barely keeping the relief from his voice as he reached out a hand.

The thief whipped the key away just as his fingers were about to close round it.

"Hey," Lukan objected, but the figure was now racing toward the wall. "There's nowhere to go," he called after it. "So stop pissing about and . . ." He fell silent and stared in disbelief as the thief scaled the sheer wall with ease. Upon reaching the top, it turned and looked down at him. Slowly it raised a taloned hand and mimed doffing a cap.

Mocking him.

"You bastard," Lukan swore. "Don't you dare . . ."

The thief turned and vanished into the night.

4

COFFEE AND CONFESSIONS

Lukan was already on his fourth coffee of the morning by the time Ashra and Flea joined him in the inn's common room. They'd both been abed by the time he'd finally found his way back to their lodgings, but he could tell Ashra was awake; he could somehow feel her judgmental stare, even in the darkness.

The same stare she was directing at him now.

"Lukan!" Flea exclaimed, as she practically bounced onto the bench opposite him. "Have you seen the snow?"

"I've seen it."

"There was some on the windowsill. Look!" The girl held out a hand, which contained a rapidly melting snowball. "It's so cold," she added, with a grin.

"And wet," Ashra replied, gently pushing Flea's hand away from the table.

"Do they have cinnamon buns?" Flea asked, cupping the snowball in her hands, as if it was a precious jewel. "Or maybe I'll have a honey cake." She slid off the bench and headed toward the kitchen.

"Don't steal anything," Lukan called after her. "Make sure they put it on our tab."

The girl flicked her little finger at him as she scampered away.

"You were up early," Ashra said pointedly.

"Couldn't sleep," Lukan replied, taking a sip of his coffee. That was the truth; he'd slept fitfully, what little sleep he'd managed plagued by dreams of a bird with yellow eyes. The rest of the time he'd simply lain in the darkness, cursing his own stupidity. He'd slipped out of bed just after the fifth bell and had been brooding ever since, replaying the previous evening's encounter over and over in his mind, and dreading having to tell the others what had happened. But now that the moment had arrived, he didn't feel ready to face it. So he stared at his own reflection in his coffee, delaying the shame and embarrassment for a short while longer.

"That helping with the hangover?" the thief asked eventually. She knew something was wrong; it was clear from the slant of her eyebrows, the weight of her gaze.

"What makes you think I've got one?"

"I could smell the drink on you when you got back." Ashra wrinkled her nose. "Still can, in fact."

"Wait, you were *drunk*?" Flea said accusingly, as she rejoined them. Her chin was coated in sugar and a half-eaten honey cake had replaced the snowball in her hand. Lukan didn't want to know where *that* had ended up.

"You said you'd only have one drink," she continued, her eyes narrowing. "You *promised*."

"Lady's blood," Lukan swore, "don't you start."

"Why are you so grouchy?" the girl demanded, shoving the rest of the cake into her mouth and proceeding to talk around it. "I thought you'd be excited about opening the vault." She swallowed and sucked the sugar from her fingers, a sly grin spreading across her face. "Is it because you were hoping for some . . ." She made a series of exaggerated kissing noises.

"I think," Ashra replied, her gaze fixed on Lukan's throat, "that it's more serious than that."

Flea frowned at the thief's grave tone and glanced between her and Lukan. "Oh," she said, her eyes widening as she noted the lack of a key hanging from Lukan's neck. "No, you *didn't*."

"I did," Lukan admitted, staring at the tabletop.

Several heartbeats passed as they all tried to digest the admission, Lukan included. Even now, he couldn't quite believe it.

"So you lost your key," Ashra prompted.

"No," Lukan said, meeting her gaze, and wishing he hadn't when he saw how sharp it was. "It was stolen from me-"

"We've been here one night," the thief replied. Her voice held even more of an edge than her glare. "*One.* And you go and do something like this."

"Are you even going to let me explain?" he snapped back.

Flea sighed and rolled her eyes, as she so often had when they'd butted heads on their three-week voyage.

"Fine." Ashra folded her arms. "Explain." The tone of her voice made it clear there was nothing Lukan could say that would convince her that he hadn't been an utter fool. He could hardly complain; he'd spent all night trying to convince himself of the same thing, and had come up short every time. However he tried to spin the story, he always arrived at the same conclusion: the theft of his key was entirely his own fault.

"I was jumped in an alley," he said. "By a thief wearing . . ." He winced, almost embarrassed to say the words. They only made his story sound even more foolish. "Some sort of bird mask. And it had—

"Glowing eyes," Ashra cut in.

Lukan stared at her in surprise. "It did. How do you know?"

"I spoke to a couple of Sparks last night."

"Sparks?"

"City guards." Ashra raised an eyebrow as if to say, *you should know that.* "They told me a thief was working this side of the river. A thief who looked like a bird. They called it the Rook."

"The Rook," Lukan echoed bitterly. "Well, at least we know it's got a name."

"Tell us everything."

"Well, as I said, I was in an alley-"

"From the beginning," the thief interrupted. "Starting with your trip to the tavern." Her upper lip curled. "I'll bet that had a lot to do with what happened afterward."

Lukan made to object, but his protest died on his tongue. Ashra was right, of course. She always was. With a sigh, he recounted the night's events, lying shamelessly about the amount of drink he'd consumed, but otherwise sticking to the truth.

"Strange," Ashra commented, once he'd finished. "Why would the Rook take your key but not your coin purse?"

"Maybe because it was empty," Flea replied, "because Lukan spent all his coin in the tavern."

They both stared at him.

"That's not true," he insisted. "Most of the drinks were . . ." He was going to say *paid for by someone else*, only to realize that wouldn't help matters. Even if it was the truth.

"Were what?" Flea demanded.

"Never mind," he replied, picking at a splinter on the tabletop. "It hardly matters now."

"One drink," the girl continued, shaking her head in disgust. "That's what you said. And instead you had, like, a *hundred* drinks-"

"Not quite that many."

"-and lost the key!" She leaned across the table and punched his arm. "You idiot. How could you be so stupid? After everything we did to get it."

Lukan knew a punch was the least he deserved. He glanced at Ashra, expecting a stronger rebuke, but the thief—not one to lose her cool—merely regarded him with something close to disdain. Somehow that was even worse.

"Have you told the Sparks?" she asked.

"No," he admitted. "All I could think about was finding my way back here before I froze to death. Besides, I was, you know . . ."

"Shitfaced."

"Tipsy," he corrected. "I didn't think they'd believe me. If I'd known they were already familiar with the Rook . . ." He sighed. "Anyway, it's not like they'd have a chance of catching him."

"Him?"

"Her. It." Lukan shrugged. "Whoever the Rook is. The kid was fast. Scaled that wall like a bloody cat."

"You're sure it's a child?"

"Yeah. I mean . . ." He thought back to the encounter, realizing he'd only really seen the Rook in darkness. "It was small," he said eventually. "About Flea's size. Maybe a little bigger."

"I'm not small," the girl objected.

"It was faster too," Lukan continued, subtly moving his coffee mug out of Flea's reach so its dregs wouldn't be thrown in his face. "And it didn't speak the entire time, which is another factor in its favor."

Flea hissed under her breath and punched his forearm again.

"Be calm, *majin*," Ashra murmured, using the nickname she'd given the girl at some point during their voyage. Apparently it meant *little tiger* in the language of the Southern Queendoms. "Remember the fourth rule of thievery."

"Emotions make for poor allies," Flea recited through gritted teeth.

"Exactly."

"I'm going to get another honey cake," the girl muttered, glaring at Lukan as she slid off her chair.

"Why a bird?" Ashra asked, as Flea headed back to the kitchen.

"What do you mean?" Lukan replied.

"Why would a child thief wear a bird mask?"

"I don't know." Lukan rubbed at his temples. He could feel a headache coming on. As if the despair he felt wasn't enough punishment already. "Does it matter?"

"Maybe not. But I'm curious about the glowing eyes."

"I assumed it was some sort of alchemy. We're certainly in the right place for it. There must be all sorts of alchemical knick-knacks lying around Korslakov. The kid must have stolen it and decided to complete the disguise, taloned gloves and cloak and all the rest."

"Hmm." She drummed her fingers on the table. "So, what now?"

"I'll plead my case to the Blackfire Bank. I can't be the first customer to lose their key." Lukan drained the dregs of his coffee. "But before that, there's, um, something else."

"What?"

"I need you to buy me a new coat."

A light snow was falling as they left the inn half an hour later. *Looks like it snowed all night*, Lukan thought as they trudged through the thick white layer covering the cobblestones. Their slow progress wasn't helped by Flea stopping every few paces to scoop up snow to add to the ball she was shaping in her hands. Lukan had a nasty suspicion about her intended target, but that was the least of his concerns as a distant bell tolled to mark the tenth hour of the morning. He swore under his breath. He'd hoped to be at the Blackfire Bank by now. Every moment they delayed increased the chance of the thief beating him there and gaining access to the vault before he could report the theft of his key. *Assuming the kid realizes what they've stolen.* Even if they did, surely the bank's officials would be suspicious of a child possessing a key to one of their vaults? He swore again at the absurdity of it all, then a third time as he felt the cold already seeping through his boots. At least the new coat Ashra had bought him was keeping the chill at bay, though there was nothing *new* about it; he felt sure the musty garment was older than he was. He had no idea what long-dead animal's fur he was wearing, nor where Ashra had acquired it, and decided that on both counts he was probably better off not knowing.

Lukan hesitated as the street split in two.

"I think we go left here," he ventured.

"We go right," Ashra corrected, trudging past him. "And *then* left."

"Well, I'm glad you could understand the innkeeper's accent. He sounded like he had a bumblebee in his mouth."

"I couldn't. But I scouted this route last night." The thief shot him a look. "While you were getting drunk."

Ah, he thought glumly, *so that's how it's going to be.* He knew Ashra had been holding back at breakfast, couldn't escape the sense he'd escaped all too lightly. *Now I know why.* Instead of a solitary damning judgment, she clearly intended to show her disapproval with a succession of sharp looks and barbed comments that would continue for the rest of the day, and possibly beyond. *Wonderful.* Still, he couldn't deny he deserved it. "Where's Flea?" he asked irritably, turning round just as a snowball exploded against his shoulder.

"There's your answer," Ashra replied.

"Lady's blood," Lukan swore, wiping snow from his face as the girl joined them. "Did you *have* to do that?"

Flea shrugged. "Thought you needed to cool down."

"Very funny." Lukan aimed a swipe at her, which she dodged. "Here's hoping the coin-kissers at the bank have a similar sense of humor."

"You think they will?" Ashra asked.

Lukan snorted. "No."

Eventually they reached a wide thoroughfare lined by graceful trees with white boles and silver leaves. *Winterwood trees,* Lukan thought, recalling the desk of white wood that stood in the quarters of Captain Varga of the Ebon Hand. Such wood was highly prized, and the proliferation of these trees along this avenue suggested it was a place of significance—as did the bronze statues that stood at regular intervals, violet flames of frostfire burning in the bowls at their bases.

"This is the Promenade of Patience," Ashra said.

"I know," Lukan lied, feeling annoyed for not knowing that himself. The thief's effortless navigating of an unfamiliar city made his idiocy of the previous night even more glaring. He didn't want to have to admit he didn't have a clue where they were.

"Then you'll also know," Ashra continued, glancing at him, "that the Square of the Builder's Blood is halfway along the promenade."

Lukan made a vague noise of agreement.

"So why don't you lead the way?" the thief asked.

Lady's mercy, he thought, *this is going to be a long day.* "Fine," he muttered, glancing both ways along the avenue, hoping to glimpse some sort of clue as to the correct direction, and seeing none. "Come on, then," he said, opting to turn left. He walked five paces before realizing neither Flea nor Ashra was following. Swearing under his breath, he turned back. "On second thoughts . . ."

"We need to go right," Ashra replied.

"Of course. My head's still, um, rather foggy."

"And whose fault is that?"

"Look, do we have to do this?" he asked, irritably. "You've made your point."

"Have I? Let's see." The thief turned to Flea. "What rule of thievery did Lukan break?"

"Twenty-two," the girl replied quickly.

"Which is?"

"Preparation is a thief's greatest tool."

"Well done, *majin*." Ashra glanced at Lukan. "You're right," she said, as she started up the avenue. "I *have* made my point."

As they made their way up the Promenade of Patience, Lukan found his own supply slowly dwindling. Despite the night's heavy snowfall, the promenade was busy with activity. The tree-lined path they now walked was bustling with fur-wrapped citizens going about their business, while horses and carriages traveled up and down the wide road, hooves clopping and wheels rattling on cobblestones surprisingly clear of snow. Lukan idly wondered how they'd been cleared so quickly. He got his answer a moment later.

"Look!" Flea suddenly cried out, pointing. "Golems!"

There were three of them, all shoveling snow to the side of the road as a bearded man looked on. They stood close to seven feet tall, and each was the width of two men. As he stared at their iron frames, Lukan was immediately reminded of the antiquated suits of armor that he used to gaze at as a child, all overlapping plates and bulky joints. These golems looked much the same, yet there was nothing clunky about their movements, which were smooth and precise, almost human-like. *Incredible*, he thought, momentarily forgetting his impatience and frustrations as he felt an awe like that which was plastered across Flea's face.

"How do they work?" the girl asked the man, stepping toward him. "How do they understand what you say?"

"Step back, missy," he replied, not unkindly. "Dangerous for you to get too close."

For once Flea did as she was told, keeping her distance and then gasping with excitement as the nearest golem turned and looked at her, its eyes glowing amber behind its visor-like face. *Just like the Rook's eyes*, Lukan thought. *Interesting.*

"Back to work, number thirty-one," the bearded overseer ordered, giving the golem a tap on the shoulder with a stick he held in one gloved hand. The construct instantly obeyed, returning to its work and lifting a full shovel-load of snow with ease. It was little wonder they'd cleared the road so quickly.

"Thirty-one?" Flea echoed, a note of scorn in her voice. "You should give them proper names."

The man glanced at her, his demeanor less friendly than before.

"My apologies," Lukan said quickly, gripping the girl's arm. "We'll be on our way."

"He *should* give them names," Flea insisted, as he led her away. "Calling them by numbers is stupid." She grinned. "Weren't they bright, though?"

"Bright?"

"She means great," Ashra replied.

"I thought sharp was your word for that."

"It is." Flea sighed, as if irritated that he didn't yet possess an intimate understanding of the intricacies of the slang used by Saphrona's Kindred. "But bright means even greater." She slowed as she looked back at the golems, still shoveling snow as they'd been doing all night, and showing no sign of fatigue.

"Come on," Lukan urged, though he didn't begrudge the girl

her fascination. Now that he'd seen them, he was curious himself as to how the constructs worked, the rules that bound them, and what strange power it was that gave them life. *If you can even call it that.*

"Grabulli said that one golem is as strong as a hundred men," Flea said, finally turning away from the constructs.

"Grabulli is—" Lukan began.

"Full of shit," Ashra finished.

"I was going to be generous and say *not on speaking terms with honesty*," he replied, "but yeah, that too."

The captain of the *Sunfish* had plenty to say about golems, though sorting fact from fiction had proven difficult. He claimed once to have smuggled a construct out of Korslakov, a claim that Lukan doubted even more now that he'd seen the sheer size of the things. The golem had apparently woken up in the hold, broken free of its restraints and gone on a destructive rampage that had nearly sunk the ship. The drama only ended when the construct toppled overboard and disappeared beneath the waves. Grabulli claimed it was still trudging around at the bottom of the sea—a thought Lukan found strangely melancholic. After all, he'd spent many years walking in his own kind of darkness, with a great weight pressing down on him and no sense of purpose or direction.

"We're nearly there," Ashra said, gesturing to a smaller avenue that branched off from the Promenade of Patience. An iron sign bolted to a wall read To the Square of the Builder's Blood. "I hope you've got your sob story ready."

"Where's Grabulli when you need him?" Lukan replied. "If there's a man alive who could charm his way into a banker's black heart, it's him."

"You think?"

"Probably not. But I'd love to watch him try."

5

ONE KIND OF TYRANNY

The Square of the Builder's Blood was lined with grand buildings, though the Blackfire Bank was the most imposing of all, dominating one corner like a king looming over his courtiers. The bank was an impressive monument to commerce—or greed, depending how you looked at it—standing four stories tall and boasting an almost indecent number of sculpted cornices and lintels. It was the towering bronze statue that stood above the entrance, though, that caught Lukan's eye—a stern, bearded man, perhaps the Blackfire of the bank's name, whose gaze fell upon all those who dared approach and said *don't even think about asking for a loan.* No doubt plenty of would-be claimants turned away there and then, which Lukan imagined was the entire point.

"They used to build statues to emperors," he said. "Now they build them to bankers. We swapped one kind of tyranny for another."

"Is that how it felt?" Ashra asked, giving him a hard look. "Being born into wealth?"

"No, of course not," he said quickly, realizing too late the trap he'd blundered into. "I was just saying—"

"Living in your mansion, surrounded by servants?"

"It's hardly a mansion. And we only had two servants."

"You had guards though," Flea piped up.

"We did. Not that they saved my father from being murdered." He felt a twinge of guilt—one of the guards had also died at the hands of his father's killers—but his words had the desired effect, as both Flea and Ashra fell silent. "I can't help my background," he continued, "but I don't blame either of you for resenting me for it. And Lady knows I'd rather have grown up listening to aristos comparing the size of their chandeliers than having to fight for survival like you both did. All I'm saying is that I came to loathe the world I grew up in. The flaunting, the boasting. The obsession with status. I've seen first-hand how wealth corrupts."

"And we've seen how poverty condemns," Ashra replied, though her voice had lost its edge.

"I guess we're all ruled by coin one way or another," Lukan said, glancing at the frowning statue again. "Come on then, let's get this over with." He stepped toward the bank's doors, only to hesitate. "Hands to yourself," he warned Flea. "Got it?"

"Are those real gems?" the girl replied, staring past him to where two guards stood before the doors, resplendent in black sable cloaks and gleaming breastplates that bore stylized Bs, inset with garnets and amethysts. She blinked as Lukan snapped his fingers in front of her face.

"What did I just say?" he asked, ignoring the girl's scowl as he turned and approached the guards.

"Good morning, sir," one of them said, eyeing Lukan's sword. "Weapons are not permitted inside the bank. Please leave them in the cloakroom." Her gaze settled on Flea's crossbow and she raised an eyebrow. "All of them."

"Understood," Lukan replied, unsheathing his blade as Ashra did the same. The guards exchanged a glance as Ashra plucked all manner of blades from beneath her coat. *Not the most promising start*, Lukan thought, with a wince. He stepped past the guards, Ashra close behind him, only to pause and turn round.

"Flea," he prompted. "Let's go."

"Uh-uh," the girl replied, shaking her head. "I'm not handing over Nighthawk."

"Nighthawk?"

"Yeah." Flea held his gaze, as if daring him to pass comment. "All the best weapons have names."

"My sword doesn't."

"Your sword's a piece of shit," the girl replied, folding her arms. "That's what you said."

"You did say that," Ashra commented.

Lukan swore under his breath as one of the guards grunted a laugh. "Fine, stay here," he said, figuring that Flea getting bored and causing mayhem in the bank would hardly help his cause anyway. "Just . . ." *Don't steal anything,* he was going to say, but decided they'd made a bad enough impression already. "Behave yourself," he finished, waving the girl away.

Flea flicked her little finger at him and scampered off.

"We have a quarter-hour before she gets into trouble," Ashra said, pausing as she removed a blade from one boot. "Maybe less. That enough time to convince the coin-kissers to open your vault?"

"I doubt it."

"Then I'll stay here and keep an eye on her." She slipped the blade back into her boot. "Good luck."

"Thanks." Lukan turned toward the door. *I expect I'll need it.*

The Blackfire Bank's interior was just as grand as its facade, with a columned entrance hall giving way to a cavernous interior. Lukan paused on the threshold, stepping aside to allow a man through—an alchemist, judging by the blue and purple robes he wore. A copper circlet rested against his forehead. Lukan half-recalled Grabulli saying something about the value of the metal reflecting an alchemist's rank. He wasn't sure where copper sat on the scale. Not very high, he imagined. Maybe that was why the alchemist wore a sour look and swept past him as if he wasn't there.

"You're welcome," Lukan muttered, stepping into the bank's main hall.

Daylight filtered through a dozen barred windows just beneath the vaulted ceiling, but little of it reached the rows of desks far below where clerks scribbled away in their ledgers. A hundred lamps provided illumination, the candleflames reflected by the polished marble floor. Even so, shadows lingered between desks and in corners, combining with the scratching of quills to create a secretive atmosphere that did Lukan's nerves no good at all. Nor did seeing a couple of guards dragging a customer away, his pleas falling on deaf ears. By the time a clerk beckoned him forward, he was fidgeting like a priest in a bawdyhouse.

"Good morning!" the clerk said brightly, waving a hand at the two chairs before him. "Do take a seat." The man was younger than most of his colleagues, his manner suggesting he'd not yet been ground down by years of counting rich people's money and dealing with their fury when he came up a copper short. Lukan felt a sliver of hope. *Perhaps he'll be easier to persuade than his peers.*

"My name's Caspar Konstantin," the clerk continued. "And you, sir?"

"Lukan Gardova," Lukan replied, as he sat down. "*Lord* Lukan Gardova." He cringed inwardly, hating how he sounded like a self-important arse, but knowing that he needed every advantage he could get.

"Lord Gardova," Caspar echoed uncertainly, staring at Lukan's shabby fur coat.

"I just arrived," Lukan offered, cursing himself. He'd been so distracted he'd not even considered his own appearance. "All my clothes are still being conveyed to my lodgings."

It was a weak explanation, but Caspar was happy to grasp it all the same.

"Of course, my lord," he replied, bowing his head. "I trust you had an enjoyable journey?"

"Oh, yes," Lukan replied, recalling the countless hours spent watching Flea firing bolt after bolt into the *Sunfish's* hull. "Most enjoyable."

"Excellent." The clerk leaned forward and clasped his hands. "How may I be of service?"

"Well, as it happens, I'm actually in a bit of a bind." Lukan paused, affecting weariness. "Where to even begin . . . You see, Caspar—may I call you Caspar?"

"Of course, my lord."

"You're too kind. It began when my father was murdered."

The clerk's eyes widened and his mouth dropped open. "Oh—my condolences, my lord."

"Thank you, Caspar. It's been a tough time." That was true enough. "My father—Lord Conrad Gardova—was a customer of yours and held a key to one of your vaults in his name."

"Just one moment," Caspar murmured, opening his ledger to a particular page and tracing a finger down a list of names. "Yes, I've found him. Vault thirty-three."

"Indeed," Lukan replied, feigning recognition of the number. "The key was passed to me after his death, and I'm here have a look inside."

"Of course. It would be my pleasure to escort you."

"There's just one problem. The key was stolen from me last night, and I've no hope of getting it back."

"I see," Caspar replied, his tone suddenly wary as his gaze flicked again to Lukan's patchy coat. He cleared his throat, as if to shift the doubt that was forming there. "That's . . . unfortunate."

"I thought it best to notify you at once," Lukan continued, sensing he was already losing the man. "I feared the thief might try to gain access and steal what's inside."

Caspar consulted his ledger again. "No need to worry, my lord. No one has tried to access the vault this morning."

"That's wonderful," Lukan replied, feeling a rush of optimism. "I'd like to open my vault immediately, so how do we proceed? Presumably you have a spare key?"

"We do, my lord, but first we need to verify your identity."

"Of course." Lukan waved a hand. "Just tell me what to do."

"Are you known to any of the bank's governors?"

"Personally, you mean? No."

"Do you possess any legal documentation confirming your identity?"

"No."

"Ah." Caspar winced in apology. "In that case, my lord, you'll need to obtain such documentation before we can unlock your vault."

"But all paperwork relating to my title and estate is back in Parva," Lukan protested, his hope fading. "It'll take too long to sort out. I need to get in the vault now, not in six months."

"I'm sorry, my lord, but those are the rules."

"There must be another way."

The clerk glanced to his right, as if seeking the nearest guard, his smile increasingly forced. "I wish I could help, truly I do, but—"

"Listen to me, Caspar," Lukan said, lowering his voice. "I need to get in that vault, understand? Not tomorrow, not next week, not next month. Now. And I'm willing to grease as many palms, and kiss as many arses, as it takes—yours included." He leaned forward. "Do I have to kiss your arse, Caspar?"

The clerk swallowed. Wetted his lips. "Let—let me fetch the head banker," he stammered.

Lukan smiled. "You do that."

As Caspar scuttled off into the shadowy depths of the bank, Lukan sat back in his chair and listened to the sounds of scratching quills and lowered voices. The ambience brought back childhood memories of accompanying his mother to the Riverside Counting House in Parva. The proprietor, Claude Flambergé, was a large man with an even larger personality, known for his lacy cuffs, ludicrous ruffs, and for breaking into a falsetto at random moments. *What I'd give to see old Claude come tottering out of the shadows.*

As it happened, the head banker who finally appeared couldn't have been more different to the man from Lukan's youth. He was gaunt where Claude had been rotund, his expression hawkish instead of jovial, his movements brisk and not relaxed. Worse still, where Claude's eyes had twinkled with merriment, this man's gaze looked like it could strip meat from a bone.

Lady's blood, Lukan thought, trying not to squirm in his seat. *I'm screwed.*

"Lord Gardova," the man said, offering Lukan the shallowest of bows. "I am Zarubin, the head banker. I hear you've suffered a misfortune." The man spoke tersely, as if each word cost him a copper.

"I have," Lukan agreed. "As I explained to Caspar"—he indicated the clerk, who lingered behind Zarubin like an awkward shadow—"my father's vault key was stolen. I was jumped by—"

"The specifics don't matter," the man cut in, gesturing sharply. "The key is lost. To open your vault, you must prove your identity." He paused deliberately. "As Caspar has already informed you."

"My father was murdered," Lukan replied, his anger stirring at Zarubin's attitude. "I need to find out who killed him, and I need to know why. There could be answers in my father's vault. I *have* to open it."

"My condolences," Zarubin said, without sympathy, "but the bank's rules are immutable. You must prove your identity with legal papers."

"But my estate is in Parva. It'll take months."

The man smiled thinly. "Then I wish you safe travels."

"Lady's blood," Lukan swore, surging up from his seat. "That's it, then? No key, no papers—thank you very much, the door's over there, don't let it smack your arse on the way out?"

"Lord Gardova," Zarubin warned, entirely unfazed by Lukan's outburst. "I must ask you to—"

"My father is dead," Lukan interrupted, his voice echoing across the hall. "A clue to his murder could be lying in his vault, and you"—he jabbed a finger at Zarubin—"are happy to just let it sit there, locked away and gathering dust?"

The head banker nodded, but his gaze was over Lukan's shoulder. His nod wasn't a response, but an order. Lukan heard footsteps and turned to find two stern-faced guards approaching.

"Please show Lord Gardova out," Zarubin said, giving Lukan a final dismissive look before spinning on his heel and departing.

"Yes, off you trot," Lukan called after him, as the guards seized his arms. "Back to your lair built from debtors' bones and Lady knows what else." He didn't resist as the guards dragged him away. "Wait," he said, as they reached the entrance hall. "I need to fetch my sword." But the guards propelled him straight past the cloakroom, where an attendant stared at them with wide eyes as they passed. "Fine," Lukan added, as the doorway yawned before him. "It was a piece of shit anyway."

With a heave, the guards threw him out.

Lukan staggered, managed to hold his balance, only for his right foot to slip on a smooth patch of snow. He swore as his leg shot out from beneath him and he ended up on his hands and knees.

"I'm assuming," a voice said, "that it didn't go too well."

He glanced up to find Ashra standing beside him. "Whatever gave you that impression?" he replied sourly as he climbed to his feet. "Where's Flea?"

"Over there." The thief pointed to where the girl was shaping a large snowball, which Lukan suspected she would hurl at his back at the first opportunity.

"So what now?" Ashra prompted.

"I need to find the Rook."

"That could be difficult."

"It's just a thief in a mask." Yet even as he spoke, he recalled the figure's glowing amber eyes, similar to those of the golems they'd seen earlier. Just a coincidence, of course, yet the similarity lingered in his mind.

"Even if we find the Rook," Ashra continued, "we'll still have to catch him. Or her."

"We'll find a way."

"They had little trouble escaping you last night."

"That's because I was . . ."

"You were?"

Pissed, he was going to say. "Caught unawares," he said instead. "This time there will be three of us."

"You said the Rook was fast. Agile."

"It was. But let's see how quick they are once Flea's shot a bolt in their arse."

"Once I've shot a bolt in whose arse?" the girl asked, as she scampered over to them, cradling the large snowball in her arms.

"The Rook's," Lukan replied, eyeing the ball warily.

"Huh. So you didn't get in the vault?"

"No. Turns out it was guarded by a dragon that breathes bu-reaucracy instead of flames."

"Bureau-what?"

"Never mind. Good jokes are wasted on you. Both of you, come to think of it."

He pointed to the large snowball the girl cradled in her arms. "Don't you dare throw that at me."

Flea rolled her eyes and dropped the ball.

"Even if we do catch the Rook," Ashra continued, "there's no guarantee they still have your key. Chances are they've already sold it on."

"Lady's blood," Lukan snapped, rounding on the thief. "It's just endless negativity with you, isn't it?"

"It's called common sense," Ashra replied coolly. "And it's a pity you didn't show more of it last night."

"Ah, there it is. I wondered how long it would take you to stick the knife in. Lady forbid I have a drink or two after spending three weeks in a room with you."

"You had more than two."

"If you've got something to say, then say it."

Ashra's jaw tightened, as if she was fighting to keep the words behind her teeth. "Now's not the time," she said finally.

"Wonderful, we can have another row later, then," Lukan said, knowing he was being petulant but unable to stop himself. "You don't have to stay, you know. You can leave whenever you want." He flicked a hand at Flea. "It was her who wanted you to come along, not me."

"Do you want me to go?"

"No!" Flea exclaimed, stepping forward and grabbing Ashra's arm. "You're staying with us. I want you to stay. And Lukan does too." She gave him a hard stare. "Don't you?"

Lukan sucked in a breath, a dismissive response already form-ing on his tongue, only to hesitate as reason finally asserted itself. Ashra was right; he should have shown more sense. And while he and Ashra mixed about as well as cats and dogs, he knew that his chances of finding the Rook—and capturing the little brat—were far better with her at his side. *Hells, it would've taken me all day just to find the bloody bank on my own.* Besides, given how Flea was staring at him, he could expect far worse than a snowball to the back if he told Ashra to leave. "I do," he admitted eventually. "I want you to stay. I need your help."

"I can only help if you let me."

"I know, it's just . . . I have a different way of doing things."

"Oh? I hadn't noticed."

"Look, I know I can be a little rash—"

"A little?"

Lukan took a deep breath, forced down the anger that was threating to rise once again. "I'm reckless. I know that. But you don't need to keep pointing it out."

"I'll stop pointing it out when it's no longer getting you—us—into trouble. Deal?"

"Fine," Lukan agreed. "Deal." He thought he caught a flicker of relief in the thief's eyes, yet he also felt the weight of words unspoken, as he recalled her earlier comment: *now's not the time.* Clearly this conversation wasn't over. *Still, that's a problem for later.* "So," he said, looking to get back on an even keel. "How do we find the Rook?"

"Leave that to me," Ashra replied, already turning away. "I'll see you back at the inn."

"Do you want me to come?" Flea called after her.

"I can handle this, *majin,*" the thief replied. She looked back and made a subtle gesture to the girl, who gave a sign of her own in response. *Kindred cant,* Lukan thought. He'd seen Ashra teaching it to Flea during their voyage. And he had a feeling he knew the meaning of this exchange.

"Let me guess," he said, once Ashra was out of earshot. "You're to keep me away from any taverns."

Flea grinned. "Something like that."

Pity. Despite the role liquor had played in the loss of his key, a roaring fire and a hot whiskey with a touch of honey seemed the perfect way to wait for Ashra's return. Instead he'd have to find another way to spend the afternoon. "Come on, then," he said, turning back toward the Promenade of Patience. He took a few steps, then paused when he didn't hear the girl's footsteps following behind.

"Flea?" He turned. "Come on, let's—"

The snowball hit him full in the face.

6

THE COST OF PROGRESS

"Why are the flames purple?" Flea asked.

Lukan barely heard the question; he was too busy staring at the sprawl of Korslakov, which stretched out before them.

After leaving the Square of the Builder's Blood, they'd followed the Promenade of Patience as it gently rose through the eastern side of the city, curving upward toward the mountains. Eventually they reached its end, where it opened into a square even grander than that they'd left an hour before. A sign declared its name as the Square of Sacred Memories, and, while Lukan had no idea what that meant, he assumed from the imperious buildings bedecked with flags, and the heavy presence of guards, that this was the heart of Korslakov's government. The western side of the square had been left open, and they walked to its edge to take in the view.

Korslakov was a city of two halves.

The Kolva river was the dividing line, its sluggish, steel-grey waters separating the industry of the west from the affluence of the east. Or so it seemed to Lukan. What little he'd seen of Hearthside, with its bistros and boutiques, its wide avenues and well-kept buildings, contrasted strongly with the ramshackle sprawl of Emberfall across the river. Whereas Hearthside possessed the grand spires that gave the city its famous sobriquet, a thousand columns of smoke rose from Emberfall's forges and workshops.

But none rose as high as the Tower of Sanctified Flame.

The home of Korslakov's famed alchemists stood by the river on the edge of Emberfall, near the heart of the city. The tower didn't attract one's attention so much as demand it, the huge purple fire at its summit burning bright against the dark backdrop of the mountains. Even after the sights Lukan had seen—most recently the Ebon Hand of Saphrona—he found it hard to look away.

Fortunately, Flea was on hand to help him out.

Lukan grunted as the girl punched his arm. "The hells was that for?" he demanded.

"I said," she repeated, "why are the flames purple?"

"I don't know," he replied, rubbing his arm. "You'd have to ask an alchemist. Though I doubt they'd tell you, even if you pointed Nightshade at them."

"Night*hawk*," the girl corrected. "And I bet I could get them to talk."

"Perhaps. Though Grabulli said the alchemists are a secretive lot." What had the captain called them? *Grubby-fingered sulfur sniffers. That was it.* He'd claimed they rarely left their tower and didn't answer to anyone, not even the Frostfire Council. But then he'd also claimed that condemned criminals were sent to the tower because the alchemists liked to dine on human flesh, so it was hard to know what to believe, really.

"Is it sorcery, do you think?" Flea asked, staring at the purple flames. "Like what gleamers do?"

"No, alchemy is . . ." Lukan trailed off, realizing he wasn't quite sure. Korslakov's alchemists were famous throughout the Old Empire, and their globes—glass orbs that shone with light when touched—were highly sought after by those who could afford them. "It's a natural philosophy," he said, figuring that was as good an explanation as any.

"A natural *what*?"

Perhaps not.

"A natural philosophy," he repeated. "It's about trying to understand the laws of nature by experimenting with liquids and metals, and so on." He paused, recalling the frazzled appearance of the Master of Alchemy back at the Academy of Parva. "As far as I can tell," he added, "alchemy is mostly about making things explode."

"Explode? Why?"

"Because that seems to be the cost of progress." Lukan frowned as a thought occurred to him. "Hey, you remember those gloves that Ashra gave you? The ones coated in that black stuff that helped you stick to that carriage, back in Saphrona?"

"You mean Halikar's Grip?"

"Right. That was probably an alchemical substance."

"So alchemists make stuff to help people?"

"Um . . ." Lukan thought about the many galas he'd been to in Parva, where the number of alchemical globes were often used as shorthand to demonstrate an aristo's wealth. He shrugged. "Sometimes."

"I wonder how they make the golems," Flea said, looking back at the tower.

"Hmm," Lukan replied, thinking again of their glowing amber eyes. "Me too."

They stared out across the city for a while longer, before the girl, ever restless, turned and scampered toward the square's central feature: a huge, iron disc set in the ground, which—like the rest of the square—had been swept free of snow.

"What's this?" Flea asked as she walked along the disc's perimeter.

"I've no idea," Lukan replied wearily as he joined her. He was already tiring of the girl's incessant questions, and they probably still had several hours to kill until Ashra returned.

"There are pictures on it," Flea continued.

She was right, he realized as he looked closer; the disc was engraved with dozens of different scenes, some of them depictions of battle, featuring figures in antiquated armor—or no armor at all, but animal skins. *The northern clans*, he realized. It was then he remembered the square's name—the Square of Sacred Memories. "I think these are historical events," he said, intrigued despite himself. "They're telling the history of the city."

"Look at that one," Flea said, stepping onto the iron. "It looks like a golem."

"You there!"

Lukan looked up at the sound of the voice, to see a large man striding toward them. Several medals slapped against his coat as he walked.

Oh, shit. Lukan pulled Flea off the disc with one hand, and raised the other toward the stranger in contrition. "My apologies," he said, as the man reached them. "She didn't mean to walk on it."

"Yeah, I did," Flea muttered.

The stranger looked between them, his bushy white eyebrows bunched in confusion. "What in the bloody hells are you on about?" he demanded in a thick Korslakovan accent. "You can walk all over the medallion, for all I care. The best scenes are at the center, anyway. I always take a few moments to look at the scene of the Builder winning his first battle against those northern savages. Nearly brings a tear to the eye, don't you think?"

"Ah, well, I've not actually seen it—"

"Not seen it! Builder's balls, man, how can you not have seen it! The swearing-in ceremony happens right in front of it!"

"I'm sorry—what ceremony?"

The man stared at Lukan in astonishment. "When you swore your oath!"

Lukan shrugged helplessly. "What oath?"

"To protect Korslakov, of course!"

"I've not sworn any oath."

"Of course you have! All soldiers swear it."

"I'm not a soldier."

"Not a soldier? Hmph." The stranger tugged at his white walrus mustache. "I remember the face of every soldier who ever served under my command. Every single one. And I recognize yours, sir."

"I fear you've mistaken me for someone else," Lukan said, yet even as the words passed his lips he felt a flicker of recognition, and looked at the stranger more closely. The man was tall and broad-shouldered—no doubt once physically imposing, though Lukan had the sense his muscle had mostly run to fat. The great fur cloak and military uniform he wore—both of which, like their owner, had seen better days—made it hard to tell. But there was something familiar about the man, and his white fuzz of hair and drooping mustache . . .

Silence stretched as the two men stared at each other, both trying to recall where they'd seen the other.

Flea beat them both to it.

"You were at the Grand Procession!" she exclaimed. "You were
riding a donkey."

The man blinked at her, as if noticing the girl for the first time.
"I was!" he replied, offering her a bow. "And you, sir," he said,
pointing a finger at Lukan, "were at Lady Valdezar's gala! We
spoke in the garden. You were looking for that doctor . . . damn it,
what was his name . . ."

"Vassilis," Lukan offered, nodding as a memory surfaced of the
man standing before him being roaringly drunk. That same man
now grinned and thumped him on the chest with such force he
staggered backward.

"That's it!" the stranger exclaimed. "Doctor Vassilis! And as
for your name . . ." His white brows creased, "it was Lord . . . Ber-
trand! No, no." He raised a finger to forestall the answer forming
on Lukan's lips. "Give me a moment, I'll get it . . . Bastian! Lord
Bastien Dubois of Parva!"

"Impressive," Lukan said, and meaning it. Given how shitfaced
the man had been, it was a miracle he remembered their encounter
at all. He wondered if he should reveal his real name, but decided
that would only complicate matters. "I'm afraid, sir," he said instead, "that you have me at a disadvantage, since my powers of
recollection are no match for yours. I can only apologize."

"Nonsense!" The man seized Lukan's hand and pumped it vig-
orously, his grip strong as iron. "General Leopold Razin, at your
service."

"Yes, of course." The familiar name trigged another memory.
"You were seeking investment," Lukan offered, "or looking to
raise funds. Something about . . . an army?"

"Indeed," Razin replied, his smile faltering. "I was. But those merchant princes are all misers. Easier to draw blood from a stone. I left
Saphrona after the Grand Duke's assassination. Were you there?"

"I was."

"Terrible business." The general tugged at one end of his mustache. "The word is Lord Marquetta was behind it—did you hear?"

"I did." Lukan glanced at Flea, who had opened her mouth, and shook his head. The girl scowled but remained silent.

"What a wretched cur," the general continued, oblivious to the exchange. "Still, I expect he got what he deserved . . ." He paused as a distant bell tolled to mark midday. "Brandur's balls!" he swore, "I'm late for my appointment. They're trying to reduce my military pension again, the bastards, and I'll be damned before I let them take another copper from me. They've already taken everything else." He seized Lukan's hand and pumped it again. "Forgive me, my lord, but I must be about my business. A pleasure to see you once more."

"Likewise, General," Lukan replied.

Razin strode away, only to turn back to them. "Come to dinner tonight!" he called back. "My manse is in the Mantle, not far from here." He gestured eastward, toward the large mansions higher up the hillside. "Look for the Avenue of Unblemished Steel—and then the gate with the two bears! I'll see you at the seventh bell!" With a salute of farewell, he strode away.

"Lady's mercy," Lukan muttered.

"What's the matter?" Flea asked.

"I've no appetite for a social engagement, especially with a man I barely know."

"I like him. He's funny."

"I suppose he is," Lukan conceded, recalling the general hurling the drink Lukan had offered him into Lady Valdezar's shrubbery. *Hopefully there won't be a repeat of that particular incident.*

"So will you go, then?"

"I suppose so. It would be poor form not to." He frowned as a thought occurred to him. "Besides, he might prove useful. A man like him is bound to know important people."

"You think he could help us find the Rook?"

"Maybe. I don't know. Our best chance is that Ashra turns something up."

"I bet she will."

"I hope you're right." Lukan wished he shared Flea's confidence. "Come on," he said, turning back toward the Promenade of Patience. "We've probably got a few hours before she gets back. Shall we go and find the famous alchemical clock? Apparently, when it strikes the hour, these little metal figures come out and do a dance, and—"

"A *clock*?" Flea interrupted, her tone one of disgust. "A *dance*?"

"Fine." Lukan threw his hands up. "Forgive me for trying to show you a little culture. What do *you* want to do?"

"Play cards." The girl kicked at a mound of snow. "*Beat* you at cards."

"That sounds like a challenge."

"It is."

"You'll never beat me at cards."

"That sounds like a boast."

"It's a statement of fact."

"Yeah?" Flea grinned. "Wanna clink coin on that?"

"You still owe me three coppers from the last game."

"Do you?"

Lukan returned her smile. "Oh, yes."

As they made their way back to the inn, Lukan felt his mood improving with every step. Sitting beside a fire and fleecing Flea at cards was a far preferable way to spend the afternoon than tramping around in the snow. As his spirits rose, he dared to think that his luck might improve as well. Surely after the run he'd endured— his key being stolen, the bank rejecting his pleas and an undesired dinner invitation—he could expect his fortune to improve?

Fate had other plans.

The first sign that he was mistaken was Flea beating him at cards—not once, but three times in a row. He told himself it was due to a series of dreadful hands on his part, and that a serious player wouldn't have had the indecency to bluff as outrageously as the girl had in that final hand, but the truth was that he was off his game, and he knew it. His frustration was compounded when the innkeeper strode up to their table and claimed the number of honey cakes set against their tab (two) didn't tally with the number the girl had taken from the kitchen that morning (four). Furthermore, a kitchen boy insisted he'd seen her dump a snowball into a pot of soup. Flea denied it, of course, and as the conversation grew more heated she pulled out her crossbow and demanded to know where the innkeeper would like his new pie hole. It was all Lukan could do to stop the red-faced man throwing them out there and then.

It was shortly after this incident, with Flea grumbling because Lukan had offered the innkeeper half her winnings, that Ashra returned, and what little optimism Lukan still had fizzled out entirely. He knew immediately by the thin line of her lips that the thief's mission had been unsuccessful. He told himself she always looked like that, but the thief soon confirmed his suspicions. She was sparing with her words, as she always was, saying only that she'd made contact with Korslakov's Kindred, and that neither of the two main factions had any leads on the Rook. The Black Powder Boys wanted to recruit them, while the Silver Street Syndicate wanted to punish them for infringing on their territory. Neither of them had a clue who or where the Rook was.

This revelation cast a silence over them, with even Flea at a loss for words. Lukan stared into the fire for a long time, lost in his own thoughts, oblivious to the common room filling with conversation and pipe smoke, to the lengthening shadows and the barmaid lighting candles to ward off the darkness. Eventually, as the clock above the fireplace chimed to mark the sixth hour of the evening, he threw on his coat and strode out into the cold, heading for his dinner date with General Razin, who—inexplicably—was now his only hope.

7

A MAN OF IMPORTANCE

Lukan had no trouble finding his way to the Mantle.

Korslakov's most affluent district sprawled across the eastern hillside, its stately townhouses standing proudly—like ornaments on a mantlepiece, he realized—high above the smoke and flames of the city's industry.

Finding General Razin's home was proving more difficult.

"The Avenue of . . ." Lukan held his breath as he peered at the sign. "Sanctified Something." His breath clouded as he sighed. "Shit." So far, he'd found no end of Exalted This and Hallowed That, but no sign of the Avenue of Unblemished Steel. As he stood in the cold, pondering his next move, he wondered why Korslakov's streets and squares all had such grandiose names that felt at odds with its citizens' terse, gruff demeanors. Perhaps General Razin could explain. *If I ever bloody find him.*

As Lukan trudged down this new avenue, he caught glimpses of the distant forges across the river, casting the western side of the city in a hellish glow. The Mantle felt cold in comparison, with its frostfire lanterns of purple-white flames, and austere mansions looming behind high walls and wrought iron gates. No doubt it was far quieter too, though that was partly because he'd left Flea back at the inn. What he would give now for some of the girl's chatter to break the Mantle's imposing silence.

Lukan was halfway down the avenue when he realized he'd been there before, and that he was walking in circles. He swore and kicked at a pile of snow that had been neatly piled beside a gate. As he did so, he heard a distant bell tolling to mark the eighth hour. He swore again. Now he was late as well as lost. He kicked at the pile of snow again. "Stupid bloody piece of—"

"Sir?"

Lukan started at the voice, turned to find a man standing beyond the gate's bars, a small lantern in one hand and his other on the sword at his hip.

"Are you well?" the guard asked, in a tone that suggested if the answer was no Lukan ought to piss off and be unwell somewhere else.

"I'd feel a lot better," he replied, "if you might point me in the direction of the Street of Unblemished Steel."

A quarter of an hour later—with one wrong turn, and no more feeling in his toes—Lukan finally found his destination. The metal sign that bore the street's name was far from unblemished, being covered in spots of rust; an irony that on another day might have made Lukan smile. As it was, his good humor was in short supply. The sorry state of the sign was echoed by the street itself; the road had been cleared of snow, but all that did was reveal the poor state of its cobbles, which were illuminated by conventional flames in lieu of frostfire—if they were illuminated at all. At least half the street lamps were unlit, creating deep pools of darkness. The walls of the estates here were crumbling at the corners, the houses that stood behind them smaller and less imposing. It was an illusion of grandeur, Lukan realized; a street pretending to be more than it was, inhabited by people whose fortunes had faded. *No wonder General Razin lives here.*

A short while later he found the general's house, as evidenced by the weathered stone bears rearing on either side of an open gate. *This must be it*, he thought, though his relief was dampened by the sight of the overgrown grounds beyond, where the snow-covered shrubbery looked like it was trying to swallow the house at the center of the estate. No lights shone from the manse's windows, and the darkness was held back only by a solitary lantern hanging beside the front door. Lukan lingered by the gate, feeling a vague sense of foreboding, and wishing for the second time that night that Flea was with him, watching his back with Nightshadow, or whatever she called her crossbow. But it was just him, or nine-tenths of him at least, since he couldn't be sure his toes were still attached to his body. "Should've bought a new sword," he murmured as he stepped through the gateway. Instead, he drew a dagger and started toward the house, his boots crunching against the snow.

As he stepped into the lantern's feeble light, Lukan hesitated as he noticed the front door bore a series of scratches and deep cuts, the latter of which could only have been made by a bladed weapon. *Bloody hells.* He thought seriously about cutting his losses, even half turned back toward the gate, only to pause again. One lesson he'd learned from his years of traveling was that help could sometimes be found in unlikely places. While he had to admit that this place felt more likely to offer him a quick knife in the back than anything more helpful, he wouldn't know for sure if he walked away now.

Reluctantly Lukan turned back to the door, grasped the iron ring that hung from a bear's snarling face, and knocked three times.

A dog started barking furiously inside the house. *I guess that explains the scratches*, he thought, as the barking grew louder. *If not the blade marks.*

"Quiet, Ivan!" a deep voice shouted. "Enough, damn you!"

Lukan flinched as the door flew open, then stumbled back as a huge, furry shape leaped at him with bared jaws. A memory flashed in his mind: a sorcerous wolf, thrashing against a set of iron bars . . .

"I said enough!" the man bellowed, hauling the animal backward with a firm hand. "Sit, or you'll get no supper!" The dog growled low in its throat. "My apologies," the man said, stepping into the lantern light. Lukan was relieved to see it was General Razin, his impressive frame filling the doorway. "Ivan is like a damned soldier. Always tetchy until his belly's full." He nudged the dog with his foot. "Aren't you?"

Ivan growled again.

"Don't worry about him," the general continued, turning back to Lukan. "He's all bark and no bite." His bushy brows knitted. "Though he did once chew off a clansman's face." He shrugged. "Regardless, you won't be needing that."

Lukan followed the man's gaze to the dagger he held in his hand. "Oh," he replied, quickly sheathing the blade. "My apologies." He managed a weak smile and gestured at the dog. "I thought for a moment he was a wolf."

"Hah! You're not the first." Razin looked admiringly at his pet. "Korslakovan wolfhounds do tend to be more wolf than hound. Though truth be told, Ivan was the runt of his litter. He's a little on the small side." He turned back to Lukan, his gaze hardening. "You're late, Master Dubois."

"Yes, I had a little difficulty finding—"

"A soldier's never late!"

"I'm not a . . ." Lukan sighed inwardly. "I apologize for my tardiness, General."

"Don't mention it!" The man gave a wolfish grin of his own. "Please," he said, hauling Ivan away from the door, "come inside."

Lukan stepped into the darkened entrance hall and waited as Razin pushed the door closed.

"This way," the general said, stomping toward another door at the end of the hall. The welcoming glow of firelight spilled through from beyond. Razin paused on the threshold. "Go on in and make yourself comfortable," he said. "I'll join you as soon as I've given this beast his dinner."

As the general dragged Ivan away, Lukan stepped through into what he took for a drawing room. A large fire crackled in the stone hearth, illuminating the shelves, side tables and bookcases that lined the room—all of them empty. *Seems the general really has fallen on hard times*, he thought, noting the marks in the dust, left by trinkets and ornaments now absent. *No wonder he was trying to raise money in Saphrona*. Some artifacts remained, presumably the ones Razin hadn't managed to sell, or couldn't bring himself to part with: a suit of armor that looked far too small to fit his large frame, a warhammer hanging above the fireplace, a faded banner with a tear through its central motif. *Relics from his glory days*, Lukan mused. Their presence suggested a man clinging to his sense of identity. He felt sympathy for the general, but also a hint of despair. This was hardly the home of a man of power and influence. It seemed unlikely Razin would be able to help him, and he felt foolish for thinking otherwise. Perhaps he ought to slip away while the general was occupied, and cut his losses. But no, that would be terrible form, and his mother—Lady rest her soul—would be appalled at his lack of etiquette. Besides, he'd gone to so much trouble to find his way here that he might as well see what the evening held in store. A decent meal, if he was lucky. *And if not, well . . . at least it's warm in here.*

It was then that Lukan spied another curiosity: a huge beast's head mounted on one wall. A first he thought it was a wolf, but no, it was too big, the jaw too wide, the brow too heavy, and the eyes . . . He felt a flicker of trepidation. There was a gleam of intelligence in the beast's unseeing orbs, something that felt almost . . . *Human*, he realized, his own eyes widening as he realized what he was staring at. *Lady's blood, this must be one of the Skath.*

"Fearsome bitch, isn't she?"

Lukan turned at the sound of the general's voice from the doorway. "She?" he replied.

"Aye." Razin moved to Lukan's side. "Male skath are even bigger, if you can believe it."

Lukan wasn't sure he wanted to. "I've heard stories," he offered, recalling some of the tales he'd heard of these fearsome creatures of the Clanholds.

"Stories," Razin echoed in a disdainful growl. "Rumors, you mean, spread by quill-pushers who weren't even there." He shook his head, his jaw tightening. "No doubt you heard that these beasts walk like us. That they *think* like us."

"Well . . ." Lukan sensed a trap. "Something like that."

"Nonsense!" the general barked, causing him to flinch. "I've seen them, lad. Seen them with my own eyes. They're more than wolves, I'll give you that. They do walk on two legs, that's true enough. But that's where the similarities end. They're just animals. Savage. Feral. This one here"—he nodded at the head above them—"stole into our camp at night. Killed five of my soldiers before we took her down. One of them had just got married. Private Ostranova—I knew all my soldiers' names." He breathed a heavy sigh. "I had to tell her wife she was dead, and that we'd buried her where she fell because there wasn't enough left of her to bring home."

Lukan winced in sympathy. "That must have been hard."

"*Hard* is the soldier's lot, boy. Hours on parade in uniforms so stiff they could keep you upright if you fell asleep in them. Nights sleeping on frozen ground. Stomachache from terrible food. And countless hours of boredom punctuated by moments of terror." The general shook his head. "But by Brandur's balls, there's no better way to spend your life."

Lukan could think of many ways, as it happened, but thought it best to keep quiet. He could think of a number of ways he'd rather be spending this evening, too, yet he couldn't deny his interest was piqued by the general's story. He knew nothing of the clans and the Clanholds beyond rumor and the contours of his father's old map. "I imagine you've also seen many battles against the northern clans?" he prompted.

"I have," the general replied, his chest swelling with pride. "I fought in five campaigns against those tattooed savages."

Lukan's knowledge of Korslakov's relations with the clans was hazy, but he knew they'd been fighting for centuries, ever since Korslakov's northward expansion into the Clanholds, which were rich with gems and minerals and whatever it was that made men in expensive clothes rub their hands with glee. No doubt it was more complex than that. But probably not much.

"I had the honor of leading the last two campaigns," the general

continued, his tone wistful. "The first one was glorious. The liber-
ation of Longhorn Watch, the heroic rear-guard action at Needle
Gap, and then the King of the Crags himself kneeling at my feet—
mine!" He shook his head in wonder. "Days of glory, boy. Days of
glory."

Lukan wasn't sure there was much glory in stealing a people's
land and murdering them when they objected, but he thought it
best to keep quiet about that too. "And the second campaign?"

The general's expression darkened. "Best we don't talk about
that."

"My apologies," Lukan said, "I didn't mean to pry." But the
general didn't seem to hear him. The man's gaze was distant, as
if he was looking deep into the past, his fists clenched so hard
his hands were shaking, his knuckles white. "General?" Lukan
prompted.

Razin blinked, the tension leaving his body. "Drink?" he asked,
a grin splitting his white beard. He turned and stomped over to a
cabinet that stood against one wall, and opened the wooden doors
to reveal a selection of bottles that glinted in the firelight. "I might
not have much left, Master Dubois," the general said, sweeping an
arm at the sparsely furnished room, "but what's a man if he can't
offer a guest a decent drink?" He peered at the bottles. "You're
from the Heartlands, aren't you?"

"I am. Parva born and raised."

"The City of Songs," Razin commented, his lip curling. "You're
too soft, you Heartlanders. Too fond of music and dancing and
frippery. But you make bloody good wine."

"That we do."

Bottles clinked as Razin's thick fingers rummaged through
them. "I used to have a bottle of Parvan Red, but I think I sold it."

"What about Parvan Bronze or Silver? We make good liquor
and spirits too."

"No, but . . . aha!" The man triumphantly held up a bottle.
"I've got some Parvan Gold if that takes your fancy."

It didn't, really—Lukan's father had been partial to a brandy, but he'd never taken to it himself, preferring whiskey or gin. Still, the general seemed pleased at finding the bottle, and Lukan felt it would be remiss of him to request something else. "Perfect," he replied, forcing a smile.

Razin poured two brandies. "To your health," he said, as he handed Lukan his drink.

"And yours," Lukan replied, touching his glass to the general's. He took a sip, let the brandy sit on his tongue for a moment before swallowing. "Very smooth," he said appreciatively. "And far better than what they were serving at Lady Valdezar's gala."

"Ha! Quite. I didn't take to that green shit at all."

"I remember. You sprayed it into the bushes."

The general laughed, a great booming sound that filled the room. "I did! Brandur's balls, I was on the sauce that night. Only way to get through those tiresome evenings. Especially when all those perfumed princes denied me the coin I sought." His expression soured. "And my vengeance along with it."

"Vengeance?" Lukan prompted.

"Aye. Vengeance against Orlova. Against the Frostfire Council. Against them all."

Orlova. The name stirred a memory from their exchange in Lady Valdezar's garden. "You said something about Orlova stealing your victory," Lukan said, pausing as the general downed the rest of his drink, his fingers tightening round his glass. He sensed that to probe further would be like poking an angry bear with a stick, but he couldn't quite resist. There was an intriguing story here, he could tell. "What exactly did she do?"

"Orlova ruined everything with her damned scheming!" Razin snapped, with sudden ferocity. "My second campaign should have secured our control in the Clanholds for a generation, but she sacrificed it all on the altar of her own ambition. The Battle of the Black Ice was my victory, not hers! But the bloodbath at Cauldron Pass, no no no." He waggled a finger. "That was all her fault. I took the responsibility, of course. That was my duty, you understand? But it was Orlova's incompetence that caused that massacre. And sometimes I wonder . . ." He bared his teeth like a wolf. "I *wonder* . . ."

"What?"

For a moment it seemed Razin would share whatever thought held him in its grip. Instead he sighed and waved the question away. "It doesn't matter," he replied, forcing a smile. "What's done is done. It's over."

It's far from over, Lukan thought, though he kept silent. Whatever had happened on that second campaign haunted the general— had hollowed him out and filled him with a fury that had driven him to the other end of the Old Empire in search of the only cure: vengeance. *But vengeance for what?* It was a question that would have to wait for another time. Lukan felt a pang of sympathy for Razin as the general poured himself another drink. It was easy to imagine him stomping around in this very room, ranting about past injustices and drinking himself to oblivion every night. He'd assumed the general desired his company to regale him with war stories. Now he wondered if the man merely wanted a distraction from them. *In which case I'm happy to oblige.*

"I recently suffered some misfortune of my own," Lukan said. "I was robbed by the Rook."

"The what?"

"The Rook," Lukan repeated, already regretting mentioning the subject. "It's a thief who wears a bird mask with glowing eyes." He waved his own words away. "Forget it, it doesn't matter."

"Come to think of it," Razin replied, his brows knitting, "I think I did hear something about a fool in a bird costume."

"What did you hear?"

"Only that he'd robbed a few people. You say you were robbed as well? What did this Rook take? Nothing of value, I hope."

"My key to a vault in the Blackfire Bank."

Razin's eyes widened. "Oh. Oh, dear. That's most . . ."

"Unfortunate?" Lukan smiled without mirth. "Yes, it is. We've asked around, but nothing's come up. No one knows anything about the Rook or where he might be found. Perhaps you might know someone who could help."

"Me?"

"Yes. I hoped you might have some contacts, given your status as a man of importance." Lukan gestured at Razin, as if the general was in a smart uniform and not a stained, patched-up tunic.

The general barked a laugh and gestured at their surroundings. "Does this look like the home of a man of importance, Master Dubois?"

"Well . . ."

"No, it does not," Razin answered for him, a hint of venom in his voice. "I lost everything after that second campaign. Everything. My career, most of my pension. And then I lost my . . ." He trailed off, his brows knitting. "I've just remembered something," he continued, snapping his gnarled fingers. "The other night, when I was deep in my cups. Something Timur said . . ."

"I'm sorry—who's Timur?"

"My aide. Well, he was during our army days, anyway. Now he calls himself my steward. I had to let the other servants go—the cook, the maid. I couldn't afford to pay them. Nor can I afford to pay Timur, but he stayed regardless. He's a stubborn old goat, but I don't know what the hells I'd do without him."

"So Timur said something?" Lukan prompted. "About the Rook?"

"Oh. Yes. I forget what. One moment." Razin stomped over to the doorway. "Timur!" he bellowed in a powerful voice that Lukan could well believe once shouted orders on battlefields. "Your presence is required."

Footsteps sounded a moment later, and a small man entered the room. Lukan put him in his late forties; his dark hair was thinning but neatly combed, and he was clean-shaven save for a thin mustache, with a pair of small spectacles perched on his nose. "General?" the man inquired, giving Lukan a polite nod.

"Correct me if I'm wrong, Timur," Razin replied, swilling the brandy in his glass, "but didn't you mention the Rook the other night? That idiot in the bird mask, who steals things?"

"I did, General," Timur replied, with a bob of his head. "I relayed a story I'd heard that I thought you might find intriguing."

"I'm sure I would have, if I hadn't already drunk myself senseless." Razin gestured at Lukan. "Master Dubois here is one of the Rook's victims. He's seeking information. Tell him what you told me. Something about your niece, was it?"

"My nephew, General." Timur turned to Lukan. "My nephew works—worked, I should say—for Lord Grigor Baranov."

"One of the archons," Razin put in.

"I'm sorry," Lukan replied, glancing between them. "Archons?"

"The heads of the most powerful families in Korslakov, who all sit on the Frostfire Council," Timur offered. "There are five of them. Lord Baranov is one."

"So he's an influential man?"

"Very," Razin replied. "Wealthy too." He shook his glass at Timur, and drink sloshed over its rim. "Well, go on then!" he urged. "On with the story!"

"My nephew worked in Baranov's kitchen," Timur continued, with the calmness of someone used to such interruptions. "One morning, he was preparing the fires for the ovens. He went outside to fetch some wood—this was not long after the fifth bell, so it was still dark. As he turned back to the house, he saw a figure perched outside a window on the eastern wing. In his surprise he dropped one of the logs he was carrying, which caused the figure to turn and stare at him."

"And the figure's eyes glowed amber," Lukan guessed.

"They did. As my nephew watched, the figure—who he believed to be the Rook—opened the window and slipped through into the darkened room beyond. My nephew ran to the main gates and told the guards what he'd seen. One made for the house, the other ran to fetch the Sparks—a patrol had not long passed by. My nephew waited outside until they arrived. When they did, he followed them inside, only to find Lord Baranov most displeased to see them. He apparently waved away concerns about the Rook's possible presence in his house. When the captain of the Sparks suggested they search the eastern wing as a precaution, Baranov became agitated and ordered them to leave." The small man spread his hands. "Why would he do that if he had good reason to believe a thief was in his house?"

"Man's hiding something," Razin replied, draining his brandy. "All the bloody archons are."

"What's in the eastern wing of the house?" Lukan asked.

"I asked my nephew the same question. All he was told was that the eastern wing was off-limits and always kept locked. Apparently not even Baranov ever went in there. Otherwise, the other servants were tight-lipped. And they were right to be. When Lord Baranov found out it had been my nephew who had seen the Rook and alerted the guards, he gave him his marching orders. No warning or anything. Just told him to leave and not come back."

"A strange way to treat a servant who thought they were acting in their master's best interests."

"Indeed."

"It's a damned mystery, all right," Razin replied, pouring himself another brandy. "Though I can't imagine it's all that useful to you, Master Dubois."

"On the contrary," Lukan said truthfully, excited to be finally getting somewhere, "it's most helpful. What about Baranov—is there anything else you can tell me about him?"

"Strange man," the general replied dismissively. "Cold. Humorless. Though he wasn't always like that. Only since his bereavements."

"Bereavements?"

"Lord Baranov's wife, Lady Anya, died while giving birth to their son," Timur said. "And just a few months ago, the son—Gavril—died as well. Some sort of illness, apparently. He was only seven."

"Life hasn't been kind to him, then," Lukan said, feeling sympathy for the man. "Does Baranov have any other children?"

"A daughter, Galina. She's quite a bit older, nearly nineteen, I believe."

"I see." *Perhaps*, he thought, *if Baranov won't talk to me, his daughter might. Something to keep in mind.* "If I wanted to speak with Lord Baranov," he asked, "how might I go about it?"

"Well, he's something of a recluse. He doesn't take visitors and tends to spurn social gatherings. He rarely even attends council meetings. Galina often attends in his place." Timur's brow creased in thought. "Though come to think of it, my nephew did mention that Baranov will sometimes take an afternoon walk with Galina in the Gardens of Undying Grace. That might be your best chance."

"My thanks," Lukan replied. "This is most helpful." In truth, it was barely the shadow of a lead, yet he couldn't help but feel there was more to the story—something that might shed some light on the Rook.

"You're most welcome, Master Dubois."

"How's that venison coming along, Timur?" Razin asked, frowning at how little brandy remained in the bottle. Before the small man could answer, the general glanced at Lukan. "Venison sound good to you, Bastien?"

"Ah." Lukan winced. "About that."

"You don't like it?" The general looked appalled.

"No. I mean, yes—I do. What I mean is . . . Bastien isn't my name."

General Razin and Timur both stared at him.

Lukan managed a wan smile. "I guess it's my turn to tell a story."

8

THE RULES OF ARISTOCRATIC ENGAGEMENT

The Gardens of Undying Grace were well named.

There was an undeniable elegance to the domes of the Glass-house, said to contain flora from across the known world, which stood at the northern end of the park. There was a majesty too in the rows of winterwood trees that lined the circular walkways, spiraling around a great bronze statue of Brandur the Builder at the park's center. Under different circumstances—say, a beautiful summer's day, spent in the company of an equally beautiful young woman, and a bottle of Parvan Red—Lukan would have had himself a grand old time.

As it was, he was sitting on a stone bench and freezing his arse off.

For the third afternoon in a row.

On his two previous visits he'd had Flea for company, but today the girl had elected to stay at Razin's house with Ashra. The general, after dinner that first night, had been appalled to learn where Lukan and his companions were staying—he'd denounced the inn as "a bloody fleapit"–and had offered then and there for them to stay at his own townhouse, in a couple of the spare bedrooms. Lukan's acceptance of the generous offer (partly influenced by the general's impressive drinks cabinet) had been another point of friction between him and Ashra. The thief hadn't voiced a complaint, but he could feel her disapproval all the same. He sensed something else as well; a shadow behind her cool glances, beneath her clipped words. Something she was holding back—some accusation or criticism that would make an appearance at an inopportune moment, no doubt. He didn't much care, but for the fact that Flea had sensed it too.

That, he suspected, was why she'd stayed behind with Ashra. The girl claimed to have grown bored of messing about in the gardens, but Lukan knew better. Flea had noted the tension between them. Perhaps she was worried that, if she left the thief alone again, Ashra wouldn't be there when she got back. Lukan didn't much care either way—or at least told himself that he didn't— though it bothered him that the girl was caught in the middle. Not enough to actually do anything about it, though. Still, if Ashra had an issue with him, that was her problem, not his. He had bigger things to worry about.

Such as Lord Baranov's continued absence.

Lukan hissed a curse. *Another wasted afternoon.* Another three hours sat in the cold, studying every couple who strolled past. The same pang of frustration each time when they didn't match the description he'd been given. At this point he'd settle for a quick word with Baranov's daughter, Galina, in lieu of meeting the man himself. Timur said she walked in the gardens every day, even if her father remained at home. She'd likely walked past Lukan several times already and he'd not even realized. But how was he supposed to identify her? Many of the women walking past him were wrapped up so tightly only their eyes showed between their scarves and hats. Approaching them and asking if they happened to be Galina Baranova would only end with him being escorted away by the Sparks manning the gate.

Lukan swore again and jumped up from the bench, not willing to sit for a moment longer. He was done with waiting. Being patient and motionless was the kind of approach Ashra would take. He'd far rather be up and doing *something*, even if it was walking aimlessly.

So he did, venting his various frustrations under his breath, until he found himself at the center of the park, where the statue of Brandur the Builder stood. Thanks to General Razin's fondness for blaspheming using his god's name, Lukan knew the Builder had bloody hands, a frozen beard and iron balls. The statue, un-surprisingly, didn't appear to feature that last detail. Beyond this vague grasp of the deity's anatomy, Lukan knew precious little about Brandur. He'd been a mortal man, apparently, who founded Korslakov an age ago, and then somehow ascended to godhood. It sounded a bit woolly, now that Lukan thought of it, not to mention unfair. The Lady of Seven Shadows, for example, had sacrificed herself to save humanity from sin. What was laying a few stones compared to that? Regardless, the Builder, judging by his frown, didn't look too pleased to be standing in the middle of a garden. No doubt he'd prefer to be standing amidst the smoke and fire of the forges.

At that moment, Lukan realized he would prefer to be some-where else as well—namely back in Razin's house, standing in front of the roaring fire. Even if it meant putting up with Ashra's silent judgment.

Lukan turned toward the gates. Back to Razin's, then, to mull over the disappointment of another fruitless day. At least the general's drinks cabinet would help take the edge off his frustration. To celebrate their first night in his house, Razin had popped the cork on a bottle of spectacular Talassian rum, rich and dark with squid ink. Lukan was pretty sure there was some left. And after that, perhaps he'd have a bath before dinner—if Ashra wasn't already doing so. Razin's impressive copper bathtub was about the only thing they shared an appreciation for. Their efforts to inspire a similar enthusiasm in Flea had, so far, not met with success.

Lukan hesitated, the thought fleeing his mind as he caught sight of two people strolling along a nearby path. An older man and a younger woman. He felt a flicker of hope as he took in the man's appearance: tall and broad-shouldered, black hair swept back and a beard dusted with silver. *He certainly fits Timur's description.* Razin had given him different advice. "Just look for the most mis-erable man in the park," the general had said. Lukan had assumed he was joking, but this stranger's appearance suggested otherwise. His finely tailored clothes were a mix of blacks and greys, a match for his somber aspect. Despite his stature, the man seemed to draw in on himself, his head bowed and his shoulders hunched as he walked. *As if carrying an unseen weight*, Lukan mused. *Like the deaths of a wife and son.* He knew all too well how grief could hollow you out, and he was starting to suspect it was something that never left you, but which you had to learn to live with. It had been nearly two months since he'd learned of his father's death, and he still had moments where he felt it pressing down on him. A cold fist squeezing at his heart.

The young woman walking at Baranov's side—Galina, he assumed—didn't appear to share her father's burden. *Or perhaps her poise merely hides her turmoil.* Regardless, she walked with her back straight and head held high, her smile as she spoke a stark contrast to Baranov's grim expression. Lukan quickened his pace to meet them where their two paths intersected.

"Good afternoon," he said brightly, as he stepped in front of them. "My sincere apologies for interrupting, but do I have the utmost pleasure of addressing Lord Grigor Baranov"—his eyes slid to the young woman—"and his charming daughter, Galina Baranova?"

The man's iron-dark brows bunched, his frown carving deeper lines on his face. Displeasure glinted in his eyes. Lukan felt the force of his stare like a slap.

The silence stretched.

Lukan kept his smile in place. He knew how this worked. Korslakov might have been a very different city to Parva or Saphrona, but he suspected the rules of aristocratic engagement were the same.

"Father," the woman whispered, with a chastening glance.

Her companion remained silent.

The woman sighed and met Lukan's gaze. "You do," she replied, with a smile that accentuated her fine features. "Though you have us at a disadvantage, sir."

"I am Lord Lukan Gardova of Parva. Freshly minted, since my father only passed recently." He thought that fact might soften Baranov's disposition, bridging the gap between them. But the man didn't display as much as a flicker of sympathy.

"It's our pleasure to meet you, Lord Gardova," Galina replied, with a curtsey. "And our sincere condolences for your loss."

"Thank you; you're too kind. And the pleasure is all mine."

"What do you want?" Lord Baranov asked, his voice tight.

"Father," Galina murmured in admonishment, her smile faltering.

"My lord," Lukan replied, sensing he needed to move quickly. "I hoped to ask a question of you, if it please you."

"It does not."

"Please, Lord Gardova," Galina interjected, "do say your piece."

"You're too kind, my lady," Lukan replied, inclining his head. "I'll be succinct. A few nights ago, I had the misfortune to be accosted by the rogue commonly known as the Rook."

Baranov's jaw tensed.

"I'm sorry to hear of your misfortune." Galina's expression hadn't changed, but her tone was now guarded, as if she was wary of where this conversation was going.

"The Rook took something of mine that I seek to repossess." Lukan feigned reluctance. "And, while I don't hold with frivolous gossip, I understand that you have also suffered misfortune at the hands of this rogue. And so, I was wondering if you might know—"

"Good day," Baranov said curtly, stepping away.

"Please, Lord Baranov," Lukan replied, raising a hand, "I only seek information that might prove useful in—"

"I know nothing of the Rook. I cannot help you."

"Cannot or will not?"

Baranov stiffened. "I beg your pardon?"

"You heard me."

"You dare question me with such insolence?" The man's voice was cold, but a fire now flickered in his eyes. "Do you have *any* idea to whom you speak?"

"I know who you are," Lukan replied, careful to keep his tone mild. "And I know the Rook was seen entering your townhouse."

"That is none of your business."

"I understand that when the Sparks arrived you ordered them to leave. Why would you do that? Why would you not want their assistance in catching the Rook?"

"I said enough!" Baranov roared. Lukan took a step back, such was the depth of fury in his eyes. "One more word from you," the man said, raising a finger that shook with barely suppressed anger, "and I'll have you thrown in a cell." The man turned and strode away. "Come, Galina," he called over his shoulder.

"My apologies, Lord Gardova," the young woman whispered. "Father hasn't been the same since my brother died."

"I didn't mean to cause offense," Lukan said, with genuine sincerity. "And my deepest condolences for your loss."

Galina smiled. "Thank you."

Then she was gone, hurrying after her father.

What is he hiding? Lukan wondered, as he watched Baranov storming toward the gates, fists clenched at his sides. *Why has the mere mention of the Rook got him all riled up?* Three days of waiting for a moment of fraught conversation felt like a poor exchange, but the few words the man had uttered spoke volumes. There was a mystery here, and, if Baranov wouldn't give him the answers, he'd have to find them himself—or have someone else find them for him.

Lukan started back toward Razin's house.

Hopefully Ashra would still be there when he got back.

9

THE RETURN OF
LADY MIDNIGHT

Korslakov did share one thing in common with Saphrona.

Its guards never looked up.

Not that they would have seen Ashra if they had. Clad entirely in black, she was all but invisible as she perched on the wall of Lord Baranov's estate. The expansive grounds lay beneath her, swathed in snow. They were larger than those of General Razin, as was the manse at their center, which was built entirely of somber grey stone, its spires rising high above the surrounding lawns and hedges. Ashra couldn't imagine anyone wanting to live in such a joyless place, but Lukan had said Baranov was just as solemn as Razin claimed, so it was no surprise he spent his days stalking the corridors of such a place.

She could only hope she didn't encounter him while she did the same.

Still, the archon was just one danger among many. The night ahead promised plenty more.

Ashra wouldn't have it any other way.

That's what Lukan hadn't realized, when he'd returned from the park and sought her out earlier that afternoon. He'd approached her cautiously, aware of her discontent with him, even if he misunderstood the reason for it. He'd used the sort of fancy language he slipped into when he was nervous, as if afraid she would refuse his request. Not realizing how much she wanted this. *Needed* it. Ever since she'd watched the red-tiled roofs of Saphrona recede into the distance, a question had haunted Ashra's mind. Could she be as brilliant a thief in Korslakov as she was in her home city? She told herself that she could. That a master thief like Lady Midnight could ply her trade anywhere, with the same level of skill and finesse.

Now she had the chance to prove it.

One of the estate's guards appeared round a hedge, a smoking pipe drooping from his lips. Ashra counted silently as he strolled along a path. Embers flared in his pipe as he inhaled and coughed out a lungful of smoke. A few moments later he disappeared round the far side of the house.

"Two hundred and forty-seven," Ashra murmured, saying the words out loud as if to stop her lips freezing over. Similar to his nine previous rounds. So far, his quickest circuit of the house had been two hundred and thirty-nine heartbeats. More than enough time for her to climb up to the balcony where the Rook had been spotted. Or it would have been, if she was in Saphrona. Here, in Korslakov, the numbing cold would affect her limbs, slowing her movement and weakening her grip. The gloves she was forced to wear wouldn't help. It might take her several attempts to her land her grappling hook, and longer than normal to shimmy up the rope. Time she didn't have.

It was too risky.

Ashra's eyes flicked to the small door at ground level. Likely the same one Timur's nephew had used. Picking the lock would be no problem. She could always melt back into the shadows if needed, which wasn't a possibility if she was halfway up a rope. But it would also mean having to find her way upstairs once she was inside, which increased the risk. There could be more guards. More obstacles. Her eyes flicked back to the balcony. No, the door was the better option.

Ashra waited for the guard to reappear. She wasn't counting this circuit, but it felt like he was taking a lot longer than usual. Perhaps he was talking to the two guards at the front gate. Or maybe . . .

She hissed a curse.

Maybe the guard was changing. Which would mean another hour spent on the wall, watching his replacement's movements.

Another hour in the cold. She bleakly imagined Lord Baranov's surprise at finding a frozen thief on his wall in the morning.

But no—here was the same guard, ambling along with the same lack of urgency as before. Ashra gave a silent sigh of relief and shifted position, trying to work some warmth into her limbs as the guard strolled along the side of the house. She needed to make every moment count.

The guard disappeared round the far corner.

Ashra dropped from the wall and started toward the house, ignoring the dull ache in her limbs. She mouthed silent numbers as she flitted from snow-covered sundial to hedgerow to holly bush. She arrived at the door before she'd even reached twenty and crouched down to inspect the lock. It looked simple enough. Ashra opened the leather wrap containing her set of picks. "Twenty-five," she murmured, sliding a slender pick into the lock. "Twenty-six." She gently turned the pick one way and then the other. The lock resisted. She tried another one with a curved end. No joy there either. Nor did she have any luck with the three picks after that. "Two hundred," she whispered, forcing down her frustration. Had she lost her edge? No. This was just a tricky lock. She still had a couple of picks to try, but for now she had to retreat. Let the guard pass and then try again.

Sometimes backward was the way forward.

Ashra turned and searched for a suitable hiding spot, her gaze settling on a pool of darkness where two hedgerows met. She stepped into it, still murmuring numbers. The guard appeared just as she reached two hundred and forty-two.

It was only as he neared her that Ashra realized her mistake. She held her breath. Maybe the guard wouldn't notice.

But he did, and hesitated mid-stride. He held out his lantern and stared downward.

At her footprints in the snow.

Ashra cursed silently as the man glanced up, his gaze following the tracks toward her hiding place. How could she have been so stupid?

No time to answer that question now.

The guard drew his sword and strode toward her.

A lesser thief would have panicked. Broken cover and run. But Ashra's fingers were steady as she slipped a small metal sphere from a pouch. She'd already identified her target: a bronze statue of a stag that stood nearby. A tricky throw for most Kindred. Not for her. She flicked her wrist and the sphere shot through the darkness and struck the stag with a loud clang.

The guard flinched and glanced around. "Who's there?" he demanded, in a smoke-coarsened voice. "Show yourself!"

Ashra pulled the glove from her right hand and tucked it in her belt. She then fished a ring from a pouch, slipped it onto her index finger and removed the tiny leather sheath from its wicked point.

"Identify yourself!" the guard demanded, turning his back to her.

A mistake.

Ashra flew from the darkness, her fist raised.

The guard whirled at the crunch of her footsteps.

Another mistake.

The back of his neck was protected by his high collar, but now he presented his front to Ashra.

She took full advantage.

As the guard raised his sword, she leaped toward him and drove her fist into his throat. He choked a cry and stumbled backward, his lantern falling to the snow. He kept his feet though, and enough of his wits to step forward.

Ashra remained still.

"Who are . . ." he breathed, raising his sword. "You . . ."

Then he toppled like a statue.

Ashra caught him as he fell and eased him to the ground, his weight almost pulling her off her feet. She couldn't see the blood from where her ring had punctured his skin, but his sudden paralysis was all the confirmation she needed that the toxin was doing its work. Venom from the ghosthead jellyfish was expensive, but it worked quickly and incapacitated its victims for up to an hour without any serious side effects. Perfect for a jellyfish looking for a meal, or a thief needing to incapacitate a guard.

Still, how long before his absence was noted? How soon would one of the guards at the front gate come to investigate? And how quickly would he find his fellow guard lying unconscious beneath a hedgerow?

Too many questions.

The simple answer to all of them was: too quickly.

Best get moving.

Ashra dragged the guard—damn, he was heavy—into the darkness of her hiding place. Snuffed out his lantern and placed it beside him. Then she raced for the door, fingers reaching for the two picks she'd not tried yet.

The first failed like the others.

"Come on," she hissed as she tried the second pick. The lock replied with a metallic click. The door swung open.

She was in.

Ashra slipped through and closed it behind her.

Silence. Darkness. The cloying scent of herbs, mixed with the earthier smell of root vegetables. She must be near the kitchens. Ashra remained still, waiting for her vision to settle. To *see*. Anyone else would have seen little beyond the vague shape of a corridor, but Ashra could see the flagstones, the sacks piled against one wall, the doorways on either side of the passage.

She didn't have much left of the elixir that granted her what she called her night-eyes, and as such used it sparingly. It had been a gift from the Twice-Crowned King, another of their attempts to convince her to stand behind their throne. To be their champion. Their instrument. She'd kept the gift and rebuffed the approach, as she always had. Alphonse had warned her she'd pay a heavy price for all her refusals.

He'd been right.

Ashra stole silently down the corridor. She glanced through both doorways—storage rooms and pantries, nothing of interest—and entered the kitchen. The door on the far side opened into another

passage leading to the heart of the house. She passed a large din-
ing room and several other chambers whose purpose escaped her.
Why did the rich need so many rooms?

A moment later Ashra reached the entrance hall. Moonlight
shone through an oval window above the front doors, illuminating
the curves of the spiral staircases that rose upward on either side.
She paused, looking and listening for any sign of patrolling guards.

Nothing.

She moved into the hallway and stole up the nearest staircase
to the landing above, where she saw the door to the upper eastern
wing.

It was time to see what secrets Baranov was hiding.

Ashra turned the handle. Locked, as she expected. She crouched
and studied the metal plaque that housed the keyhole. Not promising. Simple keyholes meant simple locks. Keyholes surrounded
by significant metalwork were a different story. And the size and
shape of this plaque worried her.

But not nearly as much as the two holes to the right of the lock.

She swore under her breath. This wasn't good. But she needed
to be sure.

Ashra reached beneath her collar and pulled out a small glass
vial of liquid that hung from her neck on a chain. It produced a
faint greenish glow when she shook it. She'd commissioned the
glowglass from the same chemist in Saphrona who'd created some
of her other substances. Its light was weak, but enough to reveal
the skulls that had been engraved on the plaque, above the two
small holes beside the keyhole.

A drop-dead lock.

Exactly as she'd feared.

Lockteasers among Saphrona's Kindred spoke of such locks
in reverential tones. Ashra had never seen one herself, but she'd
heard the rumors. These locks were said to be highly sensitive and
difficult to pick. Worse, the slightest mistake would result in sharpened metal bolts shooting from the two holes and skewering her
eyeballs. Or jets of acid would melt her face. The defense mecha-

nism had several variations, from what she'd heard. It was hard to know which one was worse.

Ashra's instincts told her to walk away. But that would mean returning to Lukan and Flea empty-handed. It would cause them both to doubt her.

Worse still, it would make her doubt herself.

She let the glowglass fall against her chest. Took a breath.

And got to work.

"Tension is the key," she murmured—not one of her own rules, but that of the man who had taught her how to pick a lock. *Most folk think teasing a lock is all about kissing the pins in the right order*, he'd told her, in his dry rasp of a voice. *But it's not. It's about how tightly you squeeze the lock. Too much and the pins won't rise, too little and they'll just fall back down. It's all about tension, girl. Don't forget that.*" Those words had served her well over the years and she heeded them again now, sliding her tool that the Kin called a "squeezer" into the lock and gently turning it to exert a small amount of pressure.

Now for the pins.

Ashra slid her pick into the lock. She barely dared to breathe as she gently probed from back to front, counting the pins. Five. Damn. She'd been hoping for four. No matter. She took another deep breath, trying to slow her heartbeat, and gave each pin a light tap, seeking the one that resisted the most. The second, she decided. That one seemed marginally stiffer than the others. She nudged the pin upward and exhaled in relief as it clicked into place, the lock rotating slightly as the pin gave way.

One down. Four to go.

The next two pins gave her no trouble, both rising without complaint when she prompted them. The fourth proved a different story. Ashra went back and forth between the two remaining pins, tapping them with her pick. Both resisted with similar force. One *had* to be raised before the other. But which?

As she delayed, her anxiety grew. She could feel it building inside her, feeding on her indecision. Seeking control. "Never give fear a share of the spoils," she whispered to herself, even as her left hand started to tremble. She closed her eyes and took a deep breath. The slightest twitch of her hand could activate the defense mechanism. If she surrendered to her growing panic, it was all over.

She willed herself to calm, to stillness.

But her heart was going too fast. Her breathing was too shallow. In that moment she was a little girl again, terrified at the thought of picking her first pocket, but knowing too that she had no choice.

Nor did she have a choice here.

True, she might be able to twist aside and avoid the bolts or acid or flames that shot out from the holes. She might be able to escape with her life. But not with her sense of identity.

Not a trade she was willing to make.

"Death or glory," she murmured, repeating the tongue-in-cheek mantra Alphonse always recited when he was making a daring play at cards. Emboldened, Ashra swallowed her fear and gently probed the pins again. This time she felt that one of them resisted *slightly* less than the other. It wasn't a difference so much as the shadow of one. Certainly not enough to risk her life on.

She did it anyway.

Gritting her teeth so hard her jaw felt like it might crack, Ashra nudged the pin upward.

The lock turned a little more.

Relief surged through her, but she fought it down, forced the smile from her face.

Emotions made for poor allies. She focused on the final pin. This could still go wrong if she touched it with too much pressure.

She took a breath.

Tapped the pin.

And sighed with relief as the lock turned. The click it made was one of the sweetest things she'd ever heard. There was a deeper clunk too—the sound of the defense mechanism being disarmed. What it was, she would never know.

It didn't matter.

She was in.

Ashra put her tools away and gently eased the door open. The room beyond was dark. She slipped through and closed the door behind her. Time was of the essence now; she'd spent too long unlocking the door. It surely wouldn't be long before the guard's body was discovered. She needed to be far away when that happened.

Ashra stole forward, deeper into the room. It was spacious, its purpose unclear, the furniture within covered by sheets. Her eyes flicked around, from floor to wall to window, searching for anything of interest. Seeing nothing, she pressed on toward a door at the far end. This time there was no lock to contend with.

The door opened without a sound and she slipped through, closing it behind her. The purpose of this second room was not in doubt; as Ashra moved forward her glowglass illuminated a wardrobe, a chest of drawers, a dresser and a four-poster bed. A bedroom then, but whose? The wardrobe provided the answer, revealing a selection of women's dresses and gowns when Ashra looked inside. The dresser, likewise, was arrayed with a woman's accessories—a fine hairbrush of filigreed silver, a comb, pots of ointment and bottles of perfume. Not Galina's, Ashra decided— this bedroom wasn't in regular use. The dust that coated all its surfaces made that clear. Galina's bedroom was elsewhere. Which surely meant this bedroom had belonged to the deceased Lady Baranov.

Ashra paused as something flashed in her light. A silver frame on a bedside table. She picked it up and studied the painting within. A dark-haired man and an elegant woman stared back at her. Lord Baranov and his late wife, most likely. Both were smiling, their eyes bright. She set the painting down. Lukan had said Baranov was just as dour as Razin had claimed him to be, but this picture suggested he'd not always been that way. No doubt grief had changed him, the way it changed Ashra. But she'd managed to find a way to move forward. To make a break with the past.

Lord Baranov had not.

Instead, he'd preserved his wife's bedroom, as if by doing so he could capture her essence, could deny that she was truly gone. This was a sacred place to him. That was why the servants weren't allowed entry. Why he'd refused to let the Sparks investigate the night the Rook had been sighted.

But Baranov hadn't just lost his wife. He'd lost a son too.

Ashra opened another door, already guessing at what she would find.

She was proven right as her light illuminated a child's bedroom, much of the floor taken up by toys—a rocking horse with a mane of real horsehair, soldiers painted in red and gold, a wooden sword with a leather grip.

Gavril's room, preserved just like his mother's.

The velvet drapes at the window weren't fully closed, and revealed a balcony limned in moonlight. This was the room that the Rook had entered. But why had it come here? Ashra kept her glowglass away from the window as she approached the dresser set against one wall. Its drawers revealed nothing of interest, just neatly folded clothes. She moved to the empty table beside the bed and pulled open the solitary drawer.

A creased envelope lay within.

Ashra picked it up. There was no name on the front, just ashen smudges. Its seal of red wax was already broken. Within was a folded piece of parchment. A note scrawled in an untidy hand.

Mistress Izolde—
Construct frame now ready. Design amended as requested—
see sketch overleaf.
Please ensure prompt payment.

V. Z.

"Izolde," Ashra murmured, her gaze lingering on the name. Who was she? Not Baranov's wife, who had been called Anya, nor his daughter, who was named Galina. She turned the paper over to reveal a charcoal sketch of a humanoid figure, its features expertly drawn in fine lines, from its taloned feet, to its feathered cloak, to its birdlike features.

Her eyes widened.

She was staring at the Rook.

Ashra turned the page over and read the message again, sure she'd misread the words. But no, they were the same as before. Which could only mean one thing.

The Rook was a construct.

Lukan had admitted the possibility, on the basis that the Rook's eyes had glowed amber, just like the golems they'd seen, but he'd rejected the idea after seeking Razin's opinion. The general had insisted that constructs were subservient, unthinking, able only to respond to a series of simple commands. They didn't have free will, let alone the sort of mischievous personality Lukan claimed to have seen. There was no way the Rook could be a construct.

This letter suggested otherwise.

Another note, written in a more elegant hand, was scribbled beside the sketch:

My dearest G,

Isn't this wonderful! It's even better than I expected. I know that you're unsure about this course of action, but I hope this helps assuage your doubts. All my love, as always.

Izolde

"Izolde again," Ashra murmured. Who was she? Baranov's lover, perhaps? The obvious affection in her message suggested so. She turned the paper over and glanced at the initials beneath the first message. *V. Z.* Not much to go on. Whoever they were, they'd built the construct for Izolde. But why? Presumably it was related to the "course of action" she was referring to. And what was Baranov's connection to all of this? Why was this letter in his dead son's dresser? And why had the Rook been seen entering this very room?

Ashra had come in search of answers. All she'd found were more questions.

A shout sounded from outside.

She surged up from the bed and cocked her head, listening

intently. Another shout; the sort a man might give when he'd just discovered a fellow guard lying unconscious under a hedge.

Ashra slipped the sketch back into the envelope and shoved it into a pocket. She tucked her glowglass back inside her coat, crept to the window and eased the drapes back. The glow of a lantern immediately drew her eye—a figure stood by the hedge where she'd left the unconscious guard. Another man ran over as she watched, the two of them exchanging words, their faces grave. One of them glanced toward the house and Ashra flinched away, letting the drapes fall back.

Time to leave.

How, though? Quietly slipping out the way she'd come was out of the question now that the guards were aware of her presence. She toyed with the translucent ring on her right hand. A simple rub of her thumb and she'd be back at Razin's house in moments.

No.

She pushed the thought away, irritated at herself for even entertaining it. She'd named them the Rings of Last Resort for a reason. Her current situation wasn't desperate enough to demand their use. Not yet anyway.

Think.

It was hard to remain still when she knew the guards were closing in. When every heartbeat felt like another opportunity lost. But these knifepoint moments, when success and failure were balanced on the tip of a blade, were what separated the amateur thief from the professional. Where the former might panic and run into danger rather than away from it, the latter knew to remain calm.

So, Ashra stood still.

She breathed.

She *thought*.

And then she was moving, out of Gavril's room and across Lady Baranov's bedroom. Back through the door with the drop-dead lock and out onto the landing. She crept to the central banister opposite and above the main doors, knowing she was merely another shadow in the hall.

Any moment now.

The door opened as a guard stepped through, lantern held in one hand, sword in the other. Two more followed. They held a brief, whispered conversation, their faces caught between nervousness and bewilderment as they glanced around at the darkness. Men who thought the uniforms they wore would never demand any responsibility of them.

The guards split up, as Ashra knew they would, each one taking a course that she'd already guessed. One headed into the western wing while another took off in the opposite direction, heading toward the kitchen and passages that Ashra had traversed earlier. The third guard made his way up the staircase to her left, presumably to check on the safety of the Baranov family in the upper western wing.

As the guard ascended on one side, Ashra stole silently down the other. She paused on the lowest step, searching for any sign of the other guards, but both had vanished into the separate wings of the house.

The front door stood open. They'd not even thought to close it. Careless. She glanced upward to find the third man had disappeared. She was alone and unobserved. Ashra checked the envelope was still tucked in her belt, then darted across the entrance hall and slipped through the door.

She moved through the grounds, elation and relief rising inside her. She refused to acknowledge either. Moments like these were the most dangerous of all. Hesitation might have been a thief's worst enemy, but complacency was a close second.

The job was *never* over until it was over.

Ashra spurned the front gates for a grappling hook over the estate's wall, which she scaled in a few heartbeats. A backward glance revealed no signs of pursuit. She allowed herself a smile then, wondering why she'd ever doubted herself.

She still had it.

She was still Lady Midnight.

And then she was gone.

10

MONEY'S NOT ENOUGH

"Do you think there are more of them?"

Lukan started in surprise at Razin's voice, the first words the general had spoken in more than half an hour. He'd thought— hoped might be a better word—that the man had fallen asleep along with Flea, who lay slumped across Ivan. There were only so many war stories he could take in one evening. Especially three nights in a row.

"More of what, General?" he asked wearily.

"The Faceless."

Ah, Lukan thought. *Here we go.* He'd told Razin and Timur his whole story, that first night at dinner—starting with his father's murder, and ending with how the three of them had foiled Lord Marquetta's conspiracy. Neither of them had believed him of course, until he pulled out what he'd come to refer to as the memory stone: the black object the Wolf had given him, which contained the Wolf's own memories. Despite the many twists and turns of the story, and the many heroes and villains it contained, it was the Faceless that Razin always seemed to come back to. Lukan couldn't blame him. It wasn't every day you learned that creatures from a childhood myth were real. He knew all too well how that felt.

"Well?" Razin persisted. "Do you?"

"I don't know, General. I wasn't really in a position to ask." But he *had* asked if the Faceless were Phaeron, which the Wolf had denied, leaving him with a question of his own that had gnawed at him ever since. *If they're not Phaeron, then what the hells are they?*

"It's just extraordinary," Razin continued, swirling the rum in his glass. "To think the Faceless are real! And that you spoke with them!"

"Well . . ." Lukan wasn't sure that he had spoken with the Wolf so much as the masked figure had read his thoughts, but decided to let that detail slide. In truth, he preferred not to think of the chill that spread through his skull as the Wolf's mind connected with his own. Was that what had happened? Even now he wasn't sure. But he could recall the dislocating strangeness of it, which still wasn't half as strange as the visions he'd seen: the purple gem exploding in a white flash, the huge grey tentacles writhing through a crack in the sky. It was that second vision that kept him awake some nights. That he wished he could forget.

"Sometimes you're better off not knowing," he murmured.

"What was that?" the general replied.

Lukan hadn't realized he'd spoken out loud. "Nothing," he replied. He glanced at the translucent ring on his right hand—the twin to the one Ashra wore—but it remained dull. Which was good, of course, because if it glowed that meant Ashra was in trouble. Even so, he couldn't quite quell the trepidation stirring inside him, which had only grown stronger as the hours ticked by. He sighed and drummed his fingers on his chair's armrest.

"Problem?" Razin inquired.

"Just wondering where Ashra's got to." Lukan had been reluctant to involve the general in their illicit scheme—breaking into the house of an archon was no minor indiscretion, after all—but the man had responded with an almost childish enthusiasm, and seemed just as intrigued as them to learn what Baranov might be hiding. "I expected her back by now."

"I wouldn't worry, lad."

"I'm not worrying."

"No?" Razin raised a bushy eyebrow. "You've barely touched your drink, and if there's one thing I've learned about you in the past few days it's that you like your liquor almost as much as me."

"I just hope she's not run into trouble," Lukan replied, taking an obligatory swallow of his rum. He barely tasted it.

"Ashra will be fine, lad. That woman's a sharp one, eh? Eyes like a hawk. Sees everything, I'll wager. Bet she could steal up behind you, and you'd not even know it until it was too late."

"Like this?" Ashra said from the doorway.

Lukan and Razin both jumped.

"Brandur's frozen balls," the general muttered, staring at the rum he'd spilled all over his breeches.

"How did it go?" Lukan asked, springing up from his chair. "Did you get inside? Did you find anything?"

Ashra's cool gaze found his. "I'm fine. Thanks for asking."

"Oh. Sorry." He raised a hand in apology and tried to find the right words. "I'm glad you're safe."

"My," the thief replied as she stepped into the room. "That seemed like hard work."

"I'm happy to skip the foreplay, if you prefer."

"Of course you are."

"What's that supposed to mean?"

"What in the blazes are you two bickering about?" Razin demanded, his raised voice causing Flea to jolt awake. "You're acting like damned children." He turned to Lukan. "You—shut up. And you"—he snapped his fingers at Ashra—"give your report."

"Forgive me if I don't stand to attention," Ashra replied, kneeling to receive a hug from Flea.

"Was it dangerous?" the girl said as they parted. "Were there lots of guards? Lukan was worried." The girl shot him a sly glance. "He didn't think you could do it."

"I never said that," Lukan objected.

"You *were* quite anxious," Razin said, swirling the liquor in his glass. "Barely touched your drink all evening."

"That's a first," Ashra muttered.

"So did you make it inside?" Lukan asked, unsure about—and a little chagrined at—how he'd become the center of attention. "Did you make it into the eastern wing?"

"I did."

"And?" Razin leaned forward eagerly. "What did you find?"

"His wife's bedroom. And his son's. Both preserved as if they were still alive." Ashra held up a creased envelope. "And this."

"A letter?" Lukan replied, feeling a flicker of anticipation. "What does it say?"

"It's more about what it shows." Ashra unfolded the letter to reveal a charcoal illustration.

Lukan stared at the drawing, a memory stealing into his mind of the Rook peering down at him from the top of the wall, eyes glowing in its birdlike mask. His heart started racing. The illustration was the exact likeness. "The Rook," he breathed, reaching out a hand. "May I?"

When Ashra nodded, he all but tore the letter from her hands and moved to the hearth, where the firelight revealed every fine line of the sketch. There was a note written beside it, and he read the words eagerly. *Who's Izolde?* he wondered. *Did she draw the Rook? What's this course of action she's talking about?*

"Turn it over," Ashra said, as if sensing his thoughts.

Lukan did so and found another scribbled note. His eyes widened as he read the words. He turned back to the sketch, then read the note again. *Impossible.* "Construct frame now ready," he said, reading the words aloud. "Design amended as requested . . ." He looked at Ashra. "So the Rook *is* a construct?"

"Seems that way."

"But . . . that's not possible," he continued, trying to give shape to the thoughts racing around his head. "Constructs don't have free will. They can only follow orders." He looked to Razin. "Right, General?"

"Correct," the old man confirmed. "If you tell one of them to stand in the pissing rain for eight hours, it'll do so without complaint. It wouldn't even think to do otherwise. *Couldn't* think, for that matter. They're dumb as rocks. Nothing going on inside those tin heads of theirs. That's why we won't have them in the army. Too much of a liability."

"But if you told a golem to steal something," Ashra asked, "would it do so?"

"Hmm." Razin tugged at one end of his mustache. "I suppose it would have to. They're obliged to follow orders, though no one knows how those damned sulfur sniffers compel them to do so." He frowned. "You think that Baranov has instructed this Rook to steal from people? Why in the hells would he do that? He's one of the richest men in the city."

"Money's not enough for some men," Lukan replied, thinking of Lord Marquetta and his vision for Saphrona. He read the note beside the sketch again. "Who's Izolde?"

"A lover," Ashra said. "Judging by her words."

"All my love, as always," Lukan read, frowning. "Hard to imagine someone feeling this passionate about Baranov. The man's got all the warmth of those frozen balls of Brandur's that the general's always talking about."

"Eh?" Razin looked affronted. "I do *not* always talk about them!"

"Yeah, you do," Flea said from the floor, where she was playing with Ivan's tail.

"Do you have any idea who this Izolde character might be?" Lukan asked Razin.

The general thought for a moment. "Not a clue," he replied eventually, shaking his head. "There's no one among the aristocracy with that name. Besides, Lord Baranov was married to Lady Anya for twenty years, and I've not heard a whisper about him having any involvement with anyone else after she died."

"A secret affair then," Lukan mused. "Perhaps Izolde is one of his servants, or someone of lower social rank, and Baranov's trying to avoid a scandal."

"No," Ashra said firmly. "He's not."

"It's the most likely explanation."

"I was there. I saw his wife's room. Baranov's turned it into a shrine. I've been in temples that felt less holy. He clearly worshipped her."

"Perhaps in his grief he sought solace in the arms of someone else."

"No. He didn't."

"People are complicated. They're inconsistent. We're all stitched together from different feelings that contradict each other. It's possible for Baranov to be grieving his wife and having a fumble with the scullery maid at the same time."

"If that's all she was to him," Ashra countered, "a *fumble*, why is the note about the Rook addressed to her?"

"Because . . ." Lukan racked his mind for an explanation, determined not to let Ashra tear holes in his theory. "She was a distraction in more ways than one," he continued, seizing upon an idea. "Baranov used her as a go-between. With Izolde acting on his behalf, he removed any direct link between himself and the Rook."

"You're both missing the damned point," Razin said, knocking his drink back and slamming the glass down on the table beside his chair. "Why in the name of Brandur's frozen . . ." He caught himself, glanced at Lukan and coughed. "Why in the name of Brandur's frozen *beard* did Baranov commission a golem, just to order it to skulk around causing mischief? It makes no damned sense."

"Perhaps we should ask Baranov himself," Lukan replied. "Show him this letter and demand he explains himself."

"And reveal it was us who stole it?" Ashra asked. "Who broke into his house? Not a smart move."

Damn it, she's right. He chewed his lip. *There's got to be something . . .* "We could take them to the Sparks," he suggested. "I'm sure they'll be interested in hearing about Lord Baranov's involvement with a known criminal."

"The Sparks?" Razin snorted. "They're more likely to arrest *you*. For stealing confidential documents from an archon, you're looking at, hmm . . ." He poured the last of the rum into his glass. "A decade of hard labor." He shrugged. "If you're lucky."

"And if we're not?"

"Baranov will pull some strings and have you killed."

"Wonderful," Lukan muttered, glancing at the letter and briefly feeling the urge to hurl it into the fire. "We know the Rook is a construct. We know that Baranov likely paid for it and is likely giving its orders, even if we don't know why. And there's nothing we can do about it."

"Not necessarily," Ashra replied. "We know who created the Rook's body. Their name's on the note to Izolde."

Of course. Lukan glanced at the letter. "V. Z," he said, looking at Razin. "Those initials mean anything to you, General?"

Razin frowned. "Can't say they do." He turned toward the door. "Timur!" he bellowed, making them all jump. Even Ivan raised his head, looking disgruntled.

The small man appeared at the door. "General?"

"We've a letter here from a construct maker with the initials V. Z. Any idea who that might be?"

Timur thought for a moment. "It's likely to be Viktor Zelenko," he replied. "He's a master golem craftsman, one of the best in Korslakov. He supplied most of the constructs we used in the army."

"Makes sense that Baranov would seek his services," Ashra said.

"It does," Lukan agreed. "And I think we should have a word with Master Zelenko first thing tomorrow."

THE PRICE OF OBSESSION

The air rang to the sound of hammers.

Lukan felt as if they were striking the inside of his skull. He winced at a fresh stab of pain behind his eyes. Too little sleep. Again. Some habits were difficult to shake. At least he didn't have a hangover this time. A distant bell tolled—goodness knew how he heard it over the cacophony—and he counted along. Eight chimes for the eighth hour of the morning. Far too early, especially to be wading into the bustle and noise of Emberfall. Still, at least the heat from the furnaces kept the cold at bay.

"Careful," he warned, grabbing Flea's shoulder and guiding her away from the path of an oncoming horse and cart. The girl shrugged his hand off, not even lifting her gaze from the array of gilded clocks on a bench in front of a nearby workshop. "Don't get any ideas," he added, noting the way her eyes lingered on a small pocket-sized timepiece.

"I'm not gonna steal a *clock*," the girl replied, scowling up at him.

"Good."

"But if I see a shiny dagger—"

"You leave it exactly where it is." He knew she was teasing him but felt the need to make the point anyway, just in case she *was* being serious. With Flea it was always hard to tell. He supposed that was what made her a first-rate windup merchant. He winced and raised a hand to his temple as another stab of pain flashed through his skull. He'd stayed up after the others had retired to bed, staring at the sketch of the Rook in the dying light of the fire and hoping some insight might strike him. None had.

"You and early mornings," Ashra commented, without sparing him a glance. "Not really on speaking terms, are you?"

"We've never really got along," Lukan admitted. "But fortunately we don't meet that often. You, on the other hand, are positively sprightly for someone who spent half the night prowling about."

The thief had said little about her nocturnal adventure. He'd probed her over breakfast—partly out of interest, and partly because Razin would fill any silence with one of his war stories—but Ashra was sparing with the details. But that was how she was, always preferring to keep her business and thoughts to herself. Whatever had unfolded at Baranov's townhouse, the thief didn't seem any the worse for wear this morning. She was alert as always, her eyes never resting. It made Lukan nervous.

"Everything all right?" he asked.

Ashra didn't reply.

"Only," he continued, "I've seen shimmer addicts with more control of their eyeballs than you. What are you looking for?"

"Trouble."

"What kind of trouble?"

That earned him a scornful look.

"Got it. The knife-in-the-back, crossbow-bolt-in-the-face kind. But why? Baranov doesn't know we stole his letter. Unless there's something you're not telling me."

"It's not Baranov I'm worried about."

"Who, then?"

"You *know* who."

"Would it help," he said, trying to sound reassuring, "if I reminded you that Saphrona is a very long way from here?"

"Not far enough."

"You think the Twice-Crowned King will send someone after you?"

"I think they're already here."

Lukan glanced around, seeing only the hustle and bustle of industry—smiths at their forges, artisans in their workshops, and countless laborers, servants and patrons all going about their business. Sparks flew from anvils, steam hissed from pipes, and smoke rose from countless chimneys. And above it all, the tower of the alchemists loomed imposingly, purple flame bright against the steel-grey sky. Nowhere did Lukan see any sign of potential assassins. Which wasn't to say they weren't out there, of course. But he wasn't going to worry about such vague threats. Not when he had more immediate concerns.

"Maybe they are," he conceded. "But you know what I think? Let them come. You're among friends. They'll have to get through us first. You're safe here."

"Safe?" Ashra stopped abruptly, forcing Lukan to halt as well. "My father was murdered in his own house," she said, a sharp edge to her voice. "My mother was struck down by a wagon in the street. Safety is a privilege. Only those born into wealth don't have to worry about their well-being. The rest of us don't have that luxury. And we don't trust it when it's offered. We look after ourselves."

Lukan was taken back by both the volume and the intensity of her words. Once again, he felt the space that existed between them. It had always been there, a distance caused by their strikingly different backgrounds and personalities. But since they'd arrived in Korslakov he felt it was only growing wider. He didn't know how to bridge it, or whether he even wanted to.

"All I'm saying," he said, raising a placating hand, "is that we have your back. Isn't that right, Flea?"

The girl didn't reply.

Lukan turned to find that Flea was some way behind them, distracted by a workbench full of shiny metal implements. "Well," he shrugged, turning back to Ashra, "not *right* at this moment. But you get the idea."

"So *you* have my back?" Ashra replied, one eyebrow raised.

Lukan hesitated, sensing a trap. "I do. And your front too."

"Where's the nearest guard post?"

He blinked at her, uncomprehending. "The nearest—"

"Three streets back, on the western side. Do you know how to get back to the gatehouse we came through?"

"Of course," he lied, looking back down the street. "We take a left back there and then . . . um, we go right—"

"Left again." Ashra's lips thinned. "Which of the blacksmiths along this street do you think would be most likely to assist us if we were attacked?"

Lukan sighed. "I've no idea, but no doubt you're going to tell me."

"The one with the army tattoos all over his arms. He'll be no stranger to violence and is more likely to raise a sword in our defense if we ask for help." She tilted her head, as if appraising him. "This is the reality of growing up on the streets. You need to be aware of *everything*. Because the smallest detail could be the death of you." She stepped away. "I can look after myself."

"Fine," Lukan replied, feeling chagrined. "But it wouldn't hurt to just let your guard down from time to time."

"Like you did on our first night here? When the Rook stole your key?"

Lukan held the thief's stare and again felt the presence of words she hadn't said, a blade that she hadn't yet unsheathed. Not for the first time he wondered what she was keeping back, and why. Wondered whether he should force the issue. But a busy street near the heart of Emberfall wasn't the place for that conversation. "Fine," he said, raising his hands. "Point taken."

"Then let's stop wasting time." Ashra started forward. "Zelenko's workshop shouldn't be far."

As he watched the thief walk away, Lukan half-hoped an assassin or two would appear, if only so he could prove his point. Then his head throbbed again and he decided it was a complication he didn't need. Especially with Flea distracted. Lukan sighed and went to fetch the girl, who was now idling at another workbench.

". . . and that one?" the girl asked, pointing at a peculiar metal implement as Lukan approached.

"That's called a corkscrew, madam," the flustered trader replied, with the strained patience of a man who'd already fended off a dozen inane questions and was anticipating a dozen more. His eyes welled with hope as Lukan arrived.

"What's it for?" Flea asked, picking the corkscrew up and squinting at it. "Pulling out eyeballs?"

"It's for removing the cork from a bottle of wine," Lukan said, plucking the implement from Flea's hands, "as well you know." He placed it back on the workbench and gave the man a smile of apology. "However," he continued, grasping the girl's arm, "I'm sure we could make an exception for you." He guided her away from the table, surprised to find she didn't resist. "No more dallying. We've got work to do."

"I was done looking anyway," Flea replied, turning something over in her hands as they walked. Something shiny and metallic.

"For the love of . . . What is *that*?" he demanded.

"What's it look like?" She grinned and held up the corkscrew.

"You *stole* it?"

"Course I stole it," she shot back. "I'm a thief. Like Ashra."

"You're a . . ." He almost said *child*, but thought better of it when he saw the sharp end of the corkscrew, and the glint in the girl's eye. "Never mind."

Emberfall was just across the river from Hearthside, but it felt like a different world. If Hearthside and the Mantle were the respectable elder children of Korslakov, Emberfall was their wild younger sibling, possessed of a fiery spirit and a restless, ramshackle soul. The turning cogs and smoking chimneys and flying sparks were dizzying to look at, the cacophony of industry nearly overwhelming. Lukan glanced at Ashra, who was still watching for signs of trouble, and wondered how she expected to see it coming amidst the tumult and the countless people thronging the street and workshops. He couldn't help but feel any potential danger would be breathing down their necks before they even realized it was there.

As it happened, they reached their destination without running into any would-be assassins. Zelenko's workshop was exactly where Timur had said it would be, on the edge of a crossroads deep in the shadow of the alchemists' tower. Lukan remained oblivious, his focus instead on the tower itself, which rose high above them, even more impressive up close than it was from a distance, its crown of purple fire burning bright against the steel-grey sky. It was only when he bumped into Flea—receiving an elbow in the ribs for his trouble—that he realized they'd arrived.

Aside from a faded wooden sign—VIKTOR ZELENKO, MASTER ARTISAN—nothing about the building spoke to its owner's position as one of the city's foremost golem makers. The workshop looked much like all the others they'd passed. If anything, it was smaller and shabbier, its chimney soot-blackened, its wooden windows warped and peeling, its external pipes spotted with rust. Lukan found it hard to imagine the Rook's body being built in such a place, and even harder to think they'd get any answers from the man who had made it.

Still, they were here now.

There was just one problem.

"Locked," Ashra said, stepping away from the front doors. The tight line of her mouth mirrored Lukan's own frustration. Dragging himself out of bed at an ungodly hour and trekking halfway across the city, only to find Zelenko hadn't even bothered to show up to work, was not how he'd hoped this morning would go. He felt something brush his nose and glanced up at the sky. *And now it's snowing again. Brilliant.* "Maybe Zelenko's one of these mercurial genius types," he said, as much for his own benefit as anyone else's. "You know, the kind who doesn't keep to usual hours. Who prefers to burn the midnight oil."

"And who's allergic to daylight, like you?" Ashra replied.

Lukan shrugged. "Takes one to know one." He pointed at the doors. "I'll bet he's in there right now, asleep on a pile of drawings just like this one." He patted his pocket. "We just need to wake him up."

"HELLOOOOO," Flea called, cupping her hands round her mouth. "MASTER ZELENKOOOOO—"

"Lady's blood," Lukan swore, giving the girl a shove. "Not like that." He glanced around, caught sight of a woman watching them

from the doorway of a nearby workshop, her expression one of be-
musement as she polished something in her hands. "Wait here," he
said, ignoring Flea's gestured insult. "Morning," he said as he jogged
over to the woman. "My apologies for the disturbance. Can't take
her anywhere."

The woman's mouth curled in amusement. "She's got a good
pair of lungs on her, your little friend."

"She's got a good punch on her as well. We're looking for Viktor Zelenko." He gestured at the man's workshop. "Does he normally start work late?"

"No," the woman replied, her brow furrowing. "He doesn't. I
normally see the glow of his forge before I've even lit my own." She
shrugged. "He does take the occasional day off to visit his niece,
but he saw her just a few days ago." The woman pursed her lips.
"Perhaps . . ."

"Yes?"

"Viktor is . . . unconventional." She smiled in the manner of
someone well used to another's eccentricities. "He finds it hard
to concentrate sometimes, so he built himself some sort of helmet
that blocks out noise. Says it helps him think. Might be he's wearing it right now, which is why he can't hear you knocking. There's
a door round the back of his workshop that you might like to
try—he often forgets to lock it." She raised a finger in warning.
"Don't tell him I told you that."

"I won't. Thanks for your help."

"Anything?" Ashra asked as Lukan rejoined them.

"A door at the back," he replied. "And a helmet."

"A *helmet*?"

"I was right, Zelenko's the mercurial genius type. He grinned.
"As I said, takes one to know one." When the thief didn't reply, he
added, "I'll take your silence for agreement," and then turned to
Flea. "Ashra and I are going inside, which means we need you to—"

"No," the girl replied, shaking her head furiously. "I'm not staying out here. I'm coming too."

"But we need someone to keep watch."

"You do it, then."

"Lady's blood," Lukan snapped, his head throbbing once again, "just for once can you do what—"

"Why the hells is it always me?" the girl shouted.

"Because . . ." Lukan waved his hands, exasperated.

"Because you've got the sharpest eyes," Ashra said, her expression softening as she crouched before the girl. "The fastest feet. The keenest ears. You're the perfect spy, *majin*. And we need your help."

Flea scowled down at the ground. "Fine," she said grudgingly, though Lukan sensed she was secretly pleased with Ashra's praise. "I'll do it."

"Thank you." Ashra rose and glanced at Lukan. "Let's go."

"How'd you do it?" he asked, as they rounded the side of the workshop. "How do you convince her so easily?"

"Because I treat her as an equal. You treat her as a child."

"She *is* a child."

Ashra whirled to face him. "Flea's from the Splinters, like me. You grow up fast there. It's that or get left behind. Her childhood was stolen from her, just as mine was. She never knew her parents. Lost her brother. She spent her younger years watching people getting knifed over a heel of black bread. I'll bet you spent yours whining that your porridge was too hot."

"Too cold, usually." He raised a hand as the thief's expression darkened. "Just a joke. I take your point."

"Always a joke with you, isn't it?" Ashra leaned closer, her green gaze so fierce that Lukan almost took a step back. "Flea's not a child, no matter how she looks. She's seen too much. Her habits that annoy you? Be grateful for them. It's a miracle she still has a sense of humor after what she's been through. The Splinters stole mine."

"Really? I hadn't noticed." He knew it was a petulant response, but he was tired, frustrated and increasingly weary of this shadow game they were playing. He'd been waiting for the right moment. Perhaps this was it. "Look," he said, trying to sound reasonable and coming up short. "If there's something you want to say, then just say it."

Ashra regarded him in silence, but there was a hard gleam in her eye. For a moment he thought she might let loose the words she'd been holding back. But then her lips thinned and she mastered herself. "All Flea wants is your respect," she said evenly. "Don't deny it to her. She's more than earned it." With that, she turned and strode away.

"Another time, then," Lukan murmured under his breath, glowering at her back. She wouldn't be drawn, he knew. Whatever Ashra had to say, she would say it at a time of her choosing. Until then, all he could do was wait. With a sigh, he hurried after her.

He caught up just as they rounded a corner of the workshop and stepped into a yard full of crates, barrels and rusting construct frames, their metal bodies limned in snow. A back door to the workshop—practically falling off its hinges—stood ajar. Ashra eased the door open and peered into the gloom beyond.

"Hello?" she called. "Master Zelenko?"

"If he's wearing this helmet of his then he won't hear us," Lukan commented, slipping past her. The workshop's interior was cold and dark, the air heavy with the scent of metals, wood shavings and oil. Weak daylight filtered through broken shutters, revealing the dim outlines of workbenches set against the walls. Lukan approached a front window and pulled the shutters open. "Flea's still there," he commented, spying the girl sitting on an upturned crate on the other side of the street. He gave her a wave. Flea flicked her little finger in response.

Lukan turned away from the window and surveyed the workshop. His first thought was that it was a miracle he hadn't tripped or rolled his ankle; the floor was littered with scrap metal, rivets and nails, and even entire construct appendages—an arm, metal fingers forming a claw, lay just to his left, as if trying to grasp his foot. The workbenches were no less cluttered, while the walls were covered with tools hanging from nails, and pieces of paper bearing all manner of detailed charcoal diagrams—not just for constructs, but for a whole host of bizarre contraptions that Lukan couldn't make head nor tail of.

"A mercurial genius?" Ashra said as she peered at the pictures. "More like a madman."

Lukan approached a nearby bench where a large, round object stood. "This must be the helmet that woman mentioned."

"Doesn't look like any helmet I've ever seen."

Lukan felt inclined to agree. The object was tall and cylindrical, constructed from copper, with two circles of glass—presumably for the eyes—and a mouthpiece featuring a tube that was presumably to aid breathing. Carefully he picked it up, finding it was surprisingly light, and glanced inside at the soft, padded interior. "Yeah," he said, setting the helmet back down. "Madman is right."

"I'll check upstairs," the thief said, moving to a set of steps in one corner of the workshop. "You see what you can find down here."

"Fine," Lukan agreed, thinking it best not to argue. He glanced around the workshop and felt a stab of frustration. Unless Viktor Zelenko happened to be sleeping like the dead upstairs, they'd have to wait for him to return from wherever he'd disappeared to. He leaned back against a workbench, a sigh escaping his lips as he knuckled his eyes. It felt like all he'd done since arriving in Korslakov was wait for something to happen—for Baranov to appear, for Ashra to return, and now for Zelenko to—

"Lukan."

He froze at the sound of Ashra's voice, noting the edge to her tone. Whatever she'd found upstairs, it wasn't good. Lukan had a horrible feeling he knew what it was. The wooden staircase creaked as he took the steps two at a time, emerging onto an upper floor that was just as untidy as the workshop below. Ashra was leaning against a doorframe. Any lingering hope Lukan had was dashed by her grim expression. "In there," she said, thumbing at the doorway.

Lukan stepped past her and into a bedroom, though in truth it felt more like another workshop with a bed crammed in one corner. A man lay on the stained sheets, one leg tangled in the heavy blanket. Lukan knew it was Zelenko because the man looked exactly how he imagined a mad inventor to look: wiry limbs with oil-stained fingers, and a fuzzy mass of unruly white hair. The man's eyes were closed, and under different circumstances Lukan would have assumed the inventor was asleep.

The stab wounds in his belly suggested otherwise.

"Shit," he muttered.

"The blood's fresh," Ashra said, entering the room behind him. "This happened not long before we arrived. We need to leave."

"No."

"What do you mean, no?" The thief moved to his side. "You realize what's happened here?"

"Baranov discovered his letters have been stolen," Lukan replied, his mind racing through the implications. "He knows he's compromised, and killed Zelenko to stop him from talking."

"We need to go," the thief urged. "It's not safe here."

"We can't," Lukan said, staring at the man's bloody nightshirt. "Zelenko's our only lead."

"And now he's dead."

"There might be more letters. More correspondence. Something that directly implicates Baranov."

"Whoever killed him probably took them."

"Maybe. Or maybe they didn't find them."

"And you think you can?"

"I can try," he replied, irritation bleeding into his voice. "If you want to help, you can search up here. I'll look downstairs."

"Every moment we stay here puts us in danger."

"The sooner we find what we're looking for, the sooner we can leave." Lukan strode past Ashra and took the stairs two at a time, not willing to argue further. *It's Saphrona all over again*, he thought, recalling the night he and Flea—and Hector, Lady keep his soul—had found Doctor Vasillis sitting in his study with a slashed throat. Flea had saved the day on that occasion, locating the doctor's journal inside a secret compartment. He wished he could call on her intuition again now, but the need for her to keep watch was more important. He glanced out of the window. Flea was still across the street, huddled in her coat and looking miserable. Not to worry; he'd make it up to her later. Buy her a cake or two. The girl's sweet tooth was often the quickest way to brighten her mood. Besides, she couldn't talk when her mouth was full.

He turned and surveyed the workshop. Its untidiness reminded him of his father's study back in Parva. Zelenko's expertise may have been in metalwork and constructs, not histories and myths, but he saw the same obsession that had driven his father's work. And Zelenko had seemingly paid the price for that obsession, just as Conrad Gardova had done. He felt his grief stir deep inside him, but forced it aside. Now wasn't the time. Instead, he took a deep breath and began his search.

12

BETWEEN HAMMER
AND ANVIL

Excluded. Again.

Flea scowled and kicked at a mound of snow. Being forced to stand around in the cold was bad enough, but being asked to keep watch was even worse. The role of spotter, as they called it on the streets of Saphrona, was traditionally given to the youngest member of a thieving crew. When she and her brother Matteo had run with the Blood Rats, Flea had played the role many times, always envious of the older kids who got to do the fun stuff. She'd progressed eventually, moving on to be a runner and even a cutter. But now she was a spotter again. It wasn't *fair*. So what if she was a lot younger than Lukan and Ashra? She'd already proven herself, not least when she'd jumped onto that carriage and ridden it all the way to the top of Borja's Bluff. *And* she'd infiltrated the ducal palace without anyone noticing. Without her, they'd never have stopped Marquetta.

And yet here she was, tasked with keeping watch, as if all her escapades in Saphrona had never happened. As if they meant nothing. As if she was nothing but a *child*. Flea kicked at the mound of snow again, muttering all the swear words she knew under her breath. It took her a while; she knew a lot of them, including half a dozen from the Southern Queendoms that she'd learned from the nights she'd spent in Saphrona's Zar-Ghosan quarter. Her heart ached as she recalled that same place burning beneath the stars, sorcery flashing among the flames. Many had died on that awful night, the first victims of Marquetta's brief reign. But all her friends had survived: Misha the baker, Kalam the carpenter and Obassa the beggar, who she'd always known was really some sort of spy. She wondered what they were doing now. Misha and Kalam would be hard at work, while Obassa would be sipping tea and whittling away at his wood. The sun would already be high in a perfect blue sky, glinting off all the bronze domes across the city, and the market in the Plaza of Silver and Spice would already be swarming with people, all with purses ripe for the cutting . . .

Suddenly Flea was hit by a rush of longing for Saphrona so strong it stole her breath away. Which was silly, because how many times had she sat on Saphrona's docks, watching the departing ships and wishing she was on one of them? And now she was in Korslakov, at the other end of the Old Empire. And it was cold. That was her main impression, now that her initial excitement had faded. Cold and grey. She didn't think she'd even seen the sun since they'd arrived. Maybe that was why Korslakov's citizens seemed so miserable, hidden and withdrawn beneath their cloaks and furs. Not that she understood a word they said, when they did speak. It was all such a far cry from Saphrona, and it left her feeling adrift, like a fishing boat that had come unmoored from the pier. She missed her home. She missed the people. She didn't belong here. None of them did. And if Lukan hadn't gone and lost his key, they would have already left. Now it was anyone's guess how long they'd be stuck here. 'Til they froze, probably.

Flea swore again and stamped her feet against the cold, her eyes tracking across the churned snow and mud of the street, up to the smoking chimneys, higher still to the top of the alchemists' tower. Even the novelty of the purple flames was starting to wear off a little.

Flea turned her gaze back to the street. As she glanced down one lane, she caught sight of a sign outside a workshop that depicted a black hawk with its wings spread. An image that had become familiar to her. Flea studied her crossbow, excitement growing as she eyed the same design etched into one side of the weapon. Lukan had told her the crossbow had likely been made in Korslakov, though he liked to think he knew a lot about everything.

She bit her lip, considering. Glanced back at Zelenko's workshop. She'd only be gone for a few moments. It wouldn't hurt. She'd still be able to watch the street—she'd just be a bit further away, that was all. Decision made, Flea scampered toward the workshop with the black symbol. A table stood in front of it, displaying half a dozen crossbows. As she drew closer, she saw they were all larger than her own but shared the same sleekness of design, and were made from the same black polished wood. She was left in no doubt that whoever had made these had also made Nighthawk.

"Beautiful," a voice said.

Flea flinched in surprise and looked up to see a man standing before her, across the table. She'd not even sensed him approach. He was like no one she'd ever seen; he wore two braids in his hair, which was the color of fire, with a fringe that tumbled across eyes of startling green. His freckled skin was very pale. His smile was friendly, but she knew better than to return it. She'd seen plenty of these men before—men who preyed on young women, even girls. They always smiled at first, to mask their true intentions. She backed away as the man approached the table.

"I'm talking about the crossbows," the man added, gesturing at the weapons. His voice had a strange timbre to it. "Aren't they beautiful?"

"Oh," Flea said, feeling a rush of relief. "Yeah. They are."

"Maybe a bit large for you, hmm?" His smile was teasing.

"It's all right," she replied, raising Nighthawk. "I already have this one."

The man's eyebrows rose. "May I see?" he asked, reaching out a hand. Flea instinctively drew back; she didn't allow anyone else to touch Nighthawk. "A good markswoman is always protective of her weapons," the man said, with a nod of approval. "Please, I won't take it from you. As you can see," he added, gesturing again at the array of crossbows, "I have more than enough already."

Flea's trust wasn't easily earned, especially by a stranger, but there was something about the man's manner that made her feel at ease. Even so, it was with some reluctance that she handed her crossbow to him. "Did you make her?" she asked. "Nighthawk has the same hawk as the one on your sign."

"It does," the man agreed, rubbing his thumb over the symbol etched into the crossbow's flank. "But no, I didn't make this. Radimir did."

"Oh," Flea replied, her heart sinking a little. "Who is Radimir?"

"My husband. The finest bowyer in the Old Empire, and perhaps even the four corners of the world." The man grinned at her and, adopting a grand tone, continued, "No one makes crossbows that are as sleek, or as light, or as reliable. Each piece is a work of art, crafted with masterful skill and passion from the heart." He gave a little bow. "I am Matiss. Unlike my husband, my gift lies with words. He makes the crossbows, and I convince people to part with their coin. What about you—what's your name?"

"Flea."

"Well, Flea," Matiss said, turning Nighthawk over in his hands, "I don't remember selling this to you."

"I took it," Flea replied, feeling suddenly defensive. "From a man called Topaz. He attacked my friend Lukan, so I grabbed Nighthawk and shot him in the leg. Then there was a fight and the lantern smashed and the house went on fire . . ." She shrugged. "It doesn't matter. Nighthawk's mine now."

"To the victors, the spoils of war," Matiss replied with another smile, handing the weapon back to her. "Do you know how to use it?"

"Course I do," Flea replied, giving him a sharp look. "But . . . I only have two bolts. I did have three, but one of them . . ." *Ended up in the sea*, she was going to say, only to realize how that might sound. "Do you have more?"

"Of course. But Nighthawk here"—she liked that he said the name without the mocking tone Lukan used—"is a special case. She is lighter and smaller than most of the crossbows my husband makes, and as such she takes smaller bolts." He handed the weapon back. "I remember this piece and the man who commissioned it—Talassian, yes? Well, if I recall correctly, only six bolts were made for it."

"Oh." Flea's heart sank.

"But perhaps Radimir can make more," Matiss added. "Why don't we go and see?"

Flea hesitated, glancing back at Zelenko's workshop. She really shouldn't go with Matiss; she was meant to be keeping watch. Lukan and Ashra were relying on her. Yet the lane was empty, save for a few workers going about their business. Besides, what if she didn't get another opportunity? *The more bolts I have for Nighthawk, the more chances I have to save Lukan's life.* Pleased with her own logic—and telling herself she wouldn't be gone for long—she nodded. "Okay."

"Follow me." Matiss turned and led her into the workshop, a lightness to his step. Dozens more crossbows—some of them bigger than Flea herself—hung on the walls. "Arbalests," Matiss said, noting her interest. "Or at least that's what they're called in this Old Empire of yours. In my homeland, we call them bearkillers." His smile flickered.

"Your homeland?" Flea asked, curious.

"Aye. I was born in the Clanholds."

She couldn't contain her surprise. "You're a *clansman?* But . . ."

"I'm not a screaming savage with paint on my face and a wolf snarling at my side?"

"I wasn't going to say that," she insisted, though in truth the words she'd been reaching for weren't all that different. General Razin had told her all about the clansfolk, and none of it had been good. "Why are you here?" she asked instead. "In Korslakov, I mean?"

"Because my own people turned against me." The man's smile remained but now had a melancholic quality. "I was born to a clanswoman, but my father was a Korslakovan soldier. They met during one of the rare periods of peace. One night of illicit passion and nine months later I arrived. My mother tried to keep my father's identity a secret, because even during the peace such relationships were forbidden, but somehow it got out. We have a saying in the Clanholds—even the trees have ears. All was well while my mother lived, but she died young, and once she was gone the distrust the other clansfolk held toward me turned to malice, and then hatred. So, I left. I made my way south to one of Korslakov's forts and convinced the soldiers to take me in. I worked as an apprentice to the fort blacksmith, and eventually I made my way to Korslakov itself. And I've been here ever since."

"But do people here not hate you as well?" Flea asked, thinking again of General Razin.

"Why would they?"

"Because . . ." Flea shrugged. "I thought Korslakov and the clans were always fighting."

"They usually are. And it's true my mother's people hate Korslakov and its people, but then they have good reason. Their land was stolen by this city, and they want it back. But the people here—my father's people—they don't seem to care much about the clansfolk. Most of the ill will shown toward the Clanholds comes from Korslakov's rulers, not its commoners."

"My friend"—Flea thought it best not to mention her "friend" was the former general of Korslakov's army—"told me that clansfolk can command bears and wolves. Is that true?"

"And birds," Matiss said with a nod. "A rare gift, it is." He pointed to the engraving on Flea's crossbow. "The hawk is the symbol of my clan. Radimir stamps it on all his weapons. His little tribute to me." A shadow seemed to darken Matiss's eyes. "He has sacrificed a lot for my sake."

"What do you mean?"

"Despite the way my people treated me, I wish them no harm. Radimir used to supply weapons to Korslakov's army, but no longer. It has cost him much in silver, but he tells me he has gained something far more valuable." Matiss smiled and started toward a doorway. "Anyway, let me introduce you."

Flea followed him into another room, where a large man labored at a workbench, shavings dropping all around him as he filed a length of wood.

Radimir glanced up as they approached. He was broad-shouldered where Matiss was slender, his face more lined, and his cropped dark hair was dusted with grey. Instead of greeting his husband, Matiss made a rapid series of signs with his hands. Radimir's eyes flicked to Flea, then to Nighthawk, then back to Matiss, before he replied with some hand signals of his own. "My husband cannot speak, nor hear the words of others," Matiss told her. "He asks if he might hold Nighthawk, which he thinks is a good name."

This time Flea didn't hesitate. She felt a touch of pride as she held out the crossbow. Radimir took the weapon and turned it over in his hands, nodding to himself in silent approval. Then he placed the crossbow on the table and made another series of signs.

"He says he can make more bolts for you," Matiss translated. "Would six be enough?"

"Yes!" Flea replied, only for her excitement to fizzle out. "Only . . ."

"Only?" Matiss echoed, amusement touching his lips.

"I don't have any money," Flea admitted. "I mean, I have a few coppers, but . . ." She trailed off as the two men engaged in another exchange, their fingers moving so quickly she couldn't follow them.

"My husband says he will make them for free," Matiss told her, "but only if he thinks you shoot well enough to deserve them."

Flea grinned. "Just show me the target."

Nothing. Lukan tossed aside another piece of scrap metal and swore under his breath. Well, not *nothing*. He'd found plenty of items of vague interest—scribbled notes, detailed diagrams and various mechanical contraptions—but nothing relating to the Rook. He'd even found Zelenko's secret stash—a half-empty bottle of vodka and a small bag of bluish powder that he took to be shimmer, not that he had any interest in finding out. He'd tried the drug once back in his academy days, and that had been enough. The vodka was more tempting, but he decided that alcohol at this time of the morning was indecent even by his standards.

Lukan was sifting through some half-finished sketches when he heard the voices. He couldn't make out what they were saying, yet he knew they meant trouble; there was something in the cadence of the tone and the clipped words. He crept to the front window and peered outside.

Three Sparks stood in the street, unmistakable in their fire-colored uniforms. All wore grim expressions as they stared at the workshop.

Shit. He glanced around for Flea but saw no sign of her. *Where the hells has she got to?*

Lukan ducked back inside and ran to the stairs, dodging the metal detritus littering the floor. "Ashra," he hissed up the staircase, "the damned Sparks are outside! We need to—"

The back door smashed open, swallowing his words, and several watchmen swarmed into the workshop. It was a trap, he realized with dismay. Not content with murdering Zelenko to keep his secret, Baranov had decided to frame whoever had stolen his letters, guessing they would come to sniff around. It was a smart ploy. *And we walked straight into it.*

"Who are you?" the lead watchman barked, pointing a cudgel at him.

He considered giving a false name but saw little point. "My name's Lukan Gardova. *Lord* Gardova, I should say."

The Spark didn't react to the honorific. "Where's Zelenko?"

"Upstairs." Lukan winced inwardly, knowing how the next part would sound. "He's . . . dead."

The watchman gestured at the staircase and two other Sparks rushed forward, the wooden steps creaking beneath their weight as they ascended. *At least Ashra will know they're coming.* Not that it would help. As quick and nimble as she was, the thief would have no chance against two armed watchmen. *Maybe she's already escaped out the window.*

"Did you kill him?"

The watchman's question snapped Lukan back to attention. "No," he said, reaching for calm, as he knew how desperation would look. "We . . . I came here to talk to him. He was already dead when I arrived."

"So why are you still here? Why did you not report this immediately?"

"I was just about to when you lot came storming in, saving me the trouble."

"Zelenko's dead, Captain," one of the Sparks called down the stairs. "There's no one else up here."

Ashra must have escaped. Lukan masked his relief, which proved short-lived as the captain's expression hardened.

"Seize him," he commanded.

Lukan didn't resist, knowing it would only enhance the man's belief in his guilt. He winced as his arms were wrenched behind his back and manacles roughly forced round his wrists. "Take him away," the captain ordered.

Why didn't Flea warn us? Lukan wondered, feeling a burst of frustration as he was dragged outside. He glanced around but still saw no sign of the girl. He did see Ashra though, cuffed just like he was, her arms held by two guards. She met his gaze, the resignation in her eyes a match for his own.

"Flea?" he mouthed at her.

The thief gave a subtle shake of her head.

"Caught this one jumping out the window," one of her captors said, as Lukan and his entourage joined them. "Fought like a clanswoman. Gave Borys a bloody nose and left him on his arse."

"No, she didn't," Borys protested, though his red nose and the mud on his uniform suggested otherwise.

"This one was poking around the workshop," one of Lukan's captors replied. "Left Zelenko lying dead upstairs."

"I didn't kill him," Lukan retorted. "He was already dead when we—"

"Save it for the judge," his captor sneered, cuffing him round the head.

"Enough!" the captain barked as he reappeared. "Get them to the cells."

As he was dragged away, Lukan stole another glance at the street, still seeking an answer to his question. *Where in the hells is Flea?*

"Very good," Matiss said, with an approving smile as he picked up the toy soldier. "But can you hit it from . . . here?" He set the soldier down again on a workbench against the far wall and stood back. Flea squinted at the metal figurine. It seemed a long way away, further than anything she'd successfully hit before. Smaller too. But that didn't mean she couldn't do it. She raised Nighthawk, chewed her lip as she judged the shot, and glanced at the two men, who were watching intently. They were showing far more interest in her skill with the crossbow than Lukan or Ashra ever had. Flea turned her gaze back to the figurine, which she'd already hit three times out of three. Could she make it four? She took a breath, held it and squeezed the trigger.

The bolt flew across the workshop and struck the figurine, sending it spinning. Matiss whooped while Radimir grinned and punched the air. Flea smiled as well, her heart bursting with pride.

"Magnificent!" Matiss said, clapping his hands. "As fine a display of marksmanship as I've ever seen." He exchanged some rapid hand signals with his husband. "Radimir agrees," he added. "And says that if you're prepared to wait for an hour or two, he'll make your bolts—free of charge. What do you say?"

"Oh. I can't." Flea's elation faded as she retrieved her bolt. "I have to get back. I'm meant to be keeping watch for my friends."

"Keeping watch?" Matiss echoed, green eyes twinkling.

"They're speaking with Zelenko, the construct maker." Flea shrugged. "There might be people coming after them. Bad people."

"I see." Matiss set the toy soldier back on its feet and exchanged more hand signals with Radimir. "My husband says to return at your convenience. The bolts will be waiting for you."

"Thank you," Flea said, her elation returning. "I'll come back as soon as I can."

"Our pleasure," Matiss replied, as Radimir offered her a bow. "See you soon, we hope."

"I hope so too," she replied, and hurried toward the door, only to pause as she saw some crates stacked nearby. Colorful flames were painted on them in various colors. The lid of one had been removed, and several peculiar cylindrical objects poked out of the top. "What are those?" she asked.

"Fireworks," Matiss replied, as he joined her. "Imported all the way from the Mourning Sea. I thought it might prove a lucrative little sideline for us. Besides, this dreary city could use cheering up a bit." He glanced at her sidelong, a conspiratorial smile on his lips. "Perhaps you'd like a demonstration?"

Flea longed to say yes; she'd only seen fireworks once before, when the Archduke of Saphrona had married his second wife. The sight of bright colors exploding in the sky was imprinted on her memory. But she'd been gone long enough already. "Maybe next time," she said reluctantly, and, with a final wave, she departed.

The cold breeze clawed at her as she stepped outside, but for once she barely noticed, intent as she was on getting back into position before Lukan and Ashra noticed she was missing. How long had she been gone? She had no idea. But it couldn't have been that long. *And so what if they've already noticed?* she asked herself, feeling a spark of defiance. *So what if Lukan's angry? Serves him right for making me be the spotter when he—*

Flea froze.

She stared at the Sparks walking across the street up ahead. There were lots of them, bright in their orange and yellow uniforms.

And stumbling alongside them, their hands in manacles behind their backs . . .

"No," Flea whispered, her eyes widening in horror. She started forward, raising Nighthawk before her, only to hesitate as her street-honed pragmatism asserted itself. What was she going to do, shoot one of the Sparks? That would only end with her in manacles as well. With her heart sinking into her boots, Flea lowered her crossbow. *This is my fault*, she thought, as she watched the guards lead Lukan and Ashra away. *So I need to fix it.*

She ran after them, and closed the distance in a few heartbeats. "Lukan!" she yelled. "Ashra!"

Lukan twisted round, relief shining in his eyes. "Flea!" he called back. "Get back to Razin! Tell him we're—"

"Quiet!" the captain snarled, driving a fist into Lukan's stomach. "You," he added, pointing at Flea. "Come here."

Flea flicked her little finger at him.

And ran.

13

WE STILL KILL THE OLD WAY

"Well," Lukan said, as he glanced around the cell. "This is . . ." *An improvement on the last one*, he was going to say. And it was; for starters, unlike the cell they'd shared as prisoners of the Twice-Crowned King, there was a barred window, not to mention an iron pisspot, and—the height of penal luxury—actual beds (well, stone slabs) with thin blankets. But the words died on his tongue as soon as he saw Ashra's expression.

"Don't," the thief warned as she sat down on one of the beds. Her voice was as sharp as the blades the Sparks had taken from her. They'd taken all her other thieving implements as well, none of which did much to support their claim of innocence. Quite the opposite. They'd taken Lukan's sword—an old blade he'd borrowed from Timur to replace the one he'd lost at the bank—and his dagger as well, not to mention his coin pouch. *No doubt that'll be lighter when I get it back. If I get it back.* But worse, they'd taken the sketch Ashra had stolen from Baranov's townhouse. *And without them, we have nothing to link him to the Rook.* At least they'd not taken his mother's silver ring, the same one he'd sworn his silverblood promise on. He toyed with it now, twisting it round his finger, recalling the flophouse room in Torlaine, the words he'd spoken and the somber expression of Shafia, his father's steward. Had that only been two months ago? It felt like a lifetime. *Hold on*, he thought, feeling a flicker of hope. *If they let me keep my ring, then perhaps . . .*

"I don't suppose," he said, turning back to face Ashra, "that they overlooked your . . ." He gestured at his own ring. His hope died as the thief raised her hands, fingers splayed. All were bare.

"They took it," she replied, lowering her hands.

"Damn it," Lukan replied, glancing beyond the bars to the darkened passage leading aboveground, where their captors were likely rooting through their gear. Hopefully they'd overlook the translucent ring, which was far more valuable than all the other items combined. Flea had the ring's twin—Ashra had given it to her that morning as a precaution—but without the thief's own ring they couldn't summon a portal. *Which would have been rather useful right now.* He huffed out a breath and started pacing, ignoring Ashra's glare, unable to cast off the frustration and anger rising within him. *Bloody Baranov.* Not only had the man lied to his face, but he'd killed Zelenko and planned for Lukan to take the blame. *And I walked right into his trap. Like a damned fool.* And now he was being held on suspicion of murdering of a man he'd never even met. The one man who might have been able to give him some answers. He hissed a curse through gritted teeth, his fists clenched. The only answer that mattered now was how he'd escape this cell. But as he looked around—at the stone walls, the iron bars, the darkness beyond—no answer was forthcoming. So, he continued his useless pacing, not knowing what to think, not knowing what to say. In the end, he settled for just two words.

"Well, shit."

"That sums it up," Ashra replied. "Can you . . ." She nodded at the other bed.

Lukan obliged and sat down, the thin blanket offering little comfort against the stone slab. He took a deep breath, as if preparing to blow on the faint spark of his belief to coax it into life. "All right," he said, rubbing his hands together in way that said *I have a plan.* He didn't, as it happened. But he hoped someone else did. "Here's what's going to happen," he continued. "Flea will fetch Razin. The general must still have *some* influence, and the vim and vigor to go with it. When he gets here, he'll give the Sparks a piece of his mind. They'll be quaking in their boots. I bet he'll get us out of here in no time."

Ashra regarded him with the cool disdain he'd grown so used to. "Why do you lie to yourself?" she asked.

"I'm not lying to myself," he lied, irritated that she'd seen through him so easily.

"No? Then you haven't thought this through."

"I have, actually," he fired back, and that was true enough. He'd already decided the chances of Razin securing their release—through legitimate means, or otherwise—were vanishingly small. But he preferred to live in hope than accept his fate lying down. Passion before reason, and all that. "Razin will find a way."

"They found us with Zelenko's body," Ashra replied, her green eyes holding his gaze. "They found the murder weapon. They caught you rooting around downstairs, and me jumping out a window." She leaned forward. "How do you think that looks?"

"Not good," Lukan admitted.

"Not good," Ashra agreed. "They're going to charge us with Zelenko's murder. And there's nothing Razin can do about it." The thief sat back and folded her arms. "So don't fool yourself."

"Lady's blood," Lukan swore, irked by the edge to the thief's final words. "What would I do without your sunny disposition?" He sprang up from his bed. "Would it hurt you to be positive for just *once* in your life?"

"I'll be positive," Ashra replied, entirely unruffled, "when there's a reason to be."

"We're still alive, aren't we? Isn't that enough?" He waved a finger, as if he was writing something in the air. "There's always a way out," he quoted, throwing one of the thief's own rules back at her. "So, let's figure out what that is."

"The way out?" Ashra replied, a dangerous note in her voice. "The way out was when we found Zelenko's body. You remember what I told you."

Lukan's optimism withered. "You said we should leave."

"*That* was the way out. You didn't want to take it."

"Right, so it's my fault—of course it is. Never mind that Flea just vanished at the crucial moment."

"Don't blame her for your own lack of sense."

"If she'd paid attention, we wouldn't be stuck in here."

"If you hadn't got drunk and lost your key, none of this would have happened at all."

"Ah, there it is." Lukan smiled without humor. "I was wondering when we'd finally have this conversation. My only question is why you've been holding back. Flea just called me an idiot at the time and had done with it, but she's straightforward like that. At least I know where I stand with her. You, though?" Lukan grimaced and shook his head. He knew he was ranting but couldn't stop himself. "You hold everything back, and all I get are frosty silences and death by a thousand glares. As I told you earlier, if you've got something to say, then just say it. I've already apologized for losing the key—"

Ashra surged upward with such speed that Lukan stumbled backward onto his own bed. He was suddenly glad that the Sparks had taken her daggers, for if they hadn't he was sure she'd have one pressed against his throat now.

"This isn't about your damned key," she snapped, with fury that Lukan hadn't seen from her before. "It's not even about you. It's about Flea. It's about me."

"I'm not sure I follow," he replied, raising a hand, both to try to calm her and to protect himself in case she lunged at him. The anger shining in her eyes made it a possibility.

"What I'm saying," the thief said, her voice taut, "is that you act like we're not important to you. That our thoughts and feelings don't matter."

"What? No, that's not true-"

"You're doing it now," Ashra interrupted, her eyes narrowing. "Telling me I'm wrong before you've even let me speak. Dismissing my opinion because it's not what you want to hear." She stepped toward him, and in that moment she seemed to fill the cell, all tautness and sharp angles, and Lukan felt he might cut himself on her if she got too close.

"I'm sorry," he said, forcing the words out. "Say your piece."

"You only think about yourself," Ashra said. "You don't think about others. Only what you want."

"Perhaps you could elaborate," he replied, hating how churlish he sounded, but not quite able to stop himself.

"The night you lost your key," Ashra said, holding his gaze. "When you went out to get drunk. Did you think about how Flea felt, being left on her own in an unfamiliar city? Did you even think to ask?"

"I did, actually."

"And what did she say? Was she happy for you to leave?"

Lukan recalled the face the girl had pulled, and the reluctance of her response. "Not exactly," he admitted, "but she was fine on her own."

"Fine," Ashra echoed, practically spitting the word. "So she didn't tell you about the drunkard, then?"

Lukan felt his stomach drop. "What drunkard?"

"The drunk man who tried to force his way into the room while you were out. Who only backed off after Flea opened the door and pointed her crossbow at him."

Lukan could only shake his head. "She never mentioned him," he replied. "But I'm sure she's faced worse." It was a weak excuse, and he knew it. "Lady's blood," he added, heaving a sigh. "Why didn't she say something?"

"Because," Ashra said, with a touch of exasperation, "you'd just lost your key and were feeling sorry for yourself. Flea didn't want to rub salt in your wound. She's considerate like that." The thief didn't have to add *unlike you*, but Lukan could read it in her expression.

"I had no idea," he said, feeling a stab of guilt.

"You didn't," Ashra agreed. "You never do. Because you don't pay attention." She turned away, and Lukan fervently hoped that she'd exhausted her vitriol and would now give him a chance to lick his proverbial wounds, but then she spun to face him again. "When was the last time you asked Flea how she was feeling?"

He couldn't help but raise an eyebrow at that. "Seriously? She'd just roll her eyes at me if I did."

"When was the last time?"

"I don't know." He wasn't sure he ever *had* asked. It had never occurred to him to. *Damn it.* He supposed that was the exact point Ashra was making. "But she seems fine."

"She isn't," Ashra replied, almost scowling now. "She knows you and I don't see eye to eye. And she's worried that I'll leave, and she'll be forced to choose between us."

Lukan sighed. He'd guessed as much. Not that he'd tried to do anything about it. Another failure on his part. "She should have told me," he muttered.

"Would you have listened?"

"Of course."

The gleam in Ashra's eye told him he'd just walked into a trap. "The same way you listened to me when we found Zelenko's body?" she asked him. "When I *told* you we should leave?"

It took all Lukan's willpower not to look away. As much as he'd found the thief's frosty silences to be frustrating, he preferred them to this white-hot version of her. "*You* could have left," he tried, knowing it was futile. "You didn't have to stay."

"Not the point," the thief fired back, without missing a beat. "You only thought of yourself. What you wanted. What you needed. And your recklessness put me in danger, just as it did to Flea on that first night. *That* is why I'm angry with you. We both deserve better." She turned away and returned to her own bed. "Not that it matters now," she added, as she sat down.

Lukan ground his teeth as he searched for a response. He was angry at the accusations Ashra had thrown at him. But only because he knew she was right. He'd never seen the thief speak so passionately, nor string so many words together at once. She'd said more to him in the past few moments than she had on their entire three-week voyage.

And yet . . .

"You're right," he said, reaching for levity as he forced his anger down. "I'm not considerate enough. I don't pay enough attention. But nor am I completely oblivious." He found her gaze. "There's something you're holding back. Something you're not telling me."

Ashra didn't look away, but a shadow passed across her face.

I knew it, Lukan thought. "So, what is it?" he prompted. "Since we're airing our dirty linen, it's only fair that you—"

"Quiet," Ashra hissed, glancing at the bars. "Someone's coming." Footsteps echoed down the corridor. "Two people," she whispered.

A broad-shouldered Spark emerged from the shadows, carrying a tray, which he set down beside the bars of their cell. "Food," he grunted. "Water." He turned and waved an arm at a younger man who stood behind him. "Lawyer."

"I'm actually a clerk of the court," the other man replied, with a nervous titter. The Spark gave him a dour look and disappeared back into the shadows, his footsteps echoing back down the passage.

A distant door slammed.

The man cleared his throat and stepped up to the bars. "Hello," he said, pushing his small pair of spectacles up the bridge of his nose, only for them to slip back down. "My name is Misha Misko. Clerk to the Court of the Gilded Hammer. I understand I have the pleasure of addressing"—he glanced at a piece of paper—"Lukan Gardova?"

"*Lord* Gardova," Lukan corrected, hoping his title might carry some weight.

"Oh!" The man bobbed his head. "My sincere apologies." He turned to Ashra. "And you, madame . . ."

Lukan watched Misko as he spoke to Ashra, noting the way he fidgeted with a loose button on his coat, and how he constantly shifted his weight, like a child who needed the bathroom. There was a skittishness to his manner, an anxious trill to his voice. It made Lukan nervous.

"Well, it's, um, a pleasure to meet you both," Misko was saying, with the forced smile of someone stalling for time. "As you're aware, you're both being held on suspicion of, ah, murdering Viktor Zelenko." He winced, as if in apology. "I'm here to inform you about your trial."

"Will it be soon?" Lukan asked, glancing at Ashra. "Because at this rate we'll murder each other long before it starts."

Misko tittered again. "Well," he replied, wringing his hands. "Actually, your trial has . . ." He swallowed. "Already happened."

"What?" Lukan gripped the bars and pressed his face against them. "The hells do you mean, it's already happened?"

"It's over. The trial. The judges have already met. In private."
Misko was babbling, his voice increasingly shrill. "And they, um,
they decided . . ."

"*What* did they decide?"

"That you're guilty." His eyes flicked between them, and then
down to the flagstones. "Of murder," he added.

"The hells are you talking about?" Lukan demanded. "How
can the trial have already happened? We weren't even there!"

"All I was told was that the judges have passed their verdict."
He swallowed, his throat apple bobbing. "And that, um, you've
been sentenced accordingly."

"Sentenced to what?" Ashra asked calmly.

"Well, normally the sentence for murder is hard labor in the
mining camps, up in the Clanholds. There are worker shortages,
you see, and—"

"Sentenced to *what*?" Lukan demanded, though he already
knew the answer.

"Death," Misko said, his voice little more than a squeak.

The word struck Lukan like a punch to the gut, even though he
was expecting it. Misko was saying something else, hands splayed
as if in commiseration, but Lukan couldn't hear his words over the
rush of blood in his ears; the sound of his rising fury.

"This was Baranov, wasn't it?" he demanded, slamming the heel
of one fist against the bars and barely noticing the pain. "Look at
me, damn you!"

Misko met his gaze fleetingly before looking away again. "I
don't know . . ."

"The bastard's framed us for Zelenko's murder and has now used
his power to deny us a fair trial. To ensure we're found guilty. Executed." He practically snarled the last word. "Tell me I'm wrong."

"Please!" Misko replied, throwing up his hands. "I only know
what I was told!"

"Lukan," Ashra said, with an edge of weariness. "He doesn't
know anything."

As he glared at Misko, Lukan realized the thief was right. The clerk had played no part in this vindictive plot. He merely had the misfortune to be the messenger. "So when's our execution?" he asked, forcing a bitter laugh. "Do you know that, at least?"

The clerk nodded, looking even more miserable than before. "Tomorrow."

If their sentence had felt like a gut punch, this revelation felt like a chill breath on the back of his neck. "Tomorrow?" he echoed, all strength gone from his voice.

"At dawn," the clerk clarified.

Lukan felt his fury recede, a strange numbness stealing in to replace it. He locked eyes with Ashra, saw a flash of disquiet in her gaze as he sank down to his bed. He didn't know what to think, what to say. Everything was moving too fast. *How the hells has this happened?*

"How?" Ashra said. Her voice seemed very far away.

"I'm sorry?" Misko replied.

"How will they . . ." She drew a finger across her throat.

"Oh. Well, not like that." He tittered, as if it was amusing, only to cough into his fist as Ashra's gaze hardened.

"Please tell me," Lukan said, finding his voice, "that our execution won't involve a giant worm."

Ashra gave him a sharp look, as she always did when he joked in serious moments. But the thief didn't understand—had never understood—that his humor had always been a shield.

"A giant worm?" Misko replied, baffled.

"It's how they dispense justice in Saphrona."

"Oh! Well. No." Another nervous laugh. "Here in Korslakov, we still kill the old way." He frowned at his own words. "Um, that is to say, by hanging." He gestured to Lukan. "Though you, Lord Gardova, are entitled to choose the sword, if you wish."

"Marvelous," Lukan replied, with a snort. "Good to know my noble status entitles me to a no-nonsense decapitation, rather than pissing my britches as I swing from the gallows."

"You don't have to decide now," Misko said, as if this was some-how a good thing. "You can take your time to decide how you, um, want to . . ." He waved his own words away. "In the meantime, is there anything I can do for you? If you have affairs to settle, I can provide quill and ink."

"It'll take a lot more than that to settle my affairs," Lukan replied, thinking of the silverblood promise he'd sworn. *All that effort*, he thought, recalling the trials and tribulations he'd faced in Saphrona. *All that danger. And all for nothing.* Yet the sigh that followed caught in his throat as he recalled the pyramid game, and the Lady in Red he'd played it with. He remembered her coy smile and lack of nerves, but most of all he remembered what Juro had told him afterward. *Lady Marni is the daughter of Lord Fyodor Volkov*, the Scrivener's man had said. *The head of the Volkov family-one of the most powerful noble houses in Korslakov.* Lukan felt a flicker of hope as he turned back to face Misko. "On second thoughts," he said, "quill and ink would be appreciated."

"Let me get this straight," Ashra said a short while later as Lukan studied his letter, which was laid out on the stone bed before him. "You think this frilly will save us because you played the pyramid with her, and you felt"—she shook her head—"a *connection*?"

"That's right," Lukan replied, nodding to himself and signing his name with a flourish. He had a strong signature, had spent many lectures at the academy practicing it, just in case he one day wrote a play and became famous. He hadn't, of course, but, if there was ever a time that called for an impressive autograph, it was the let-ter on which his entire life depended—and Ashra's, whether she admitted it or not. "If we'd been in a bar," he continued, "I daresay the looks she was giving me would have led us somewhere more private. As it was, I was too busy having my balls tickled by an imaginary centipede to think about more intimate matters."

Misko shot him a bemused look from where he was lingering

in the shadows beyond their cell, only to look away again when Lukan returned his stare.

"Yet Marni didn't visit you after the game," Ashra pointed out.

"I imagine she was too busy enjoying her winnings."

"Or maybe she'd already forgotten about you."

"I like to think I'm unforgettable."

Ashra's snort told him what she thought of that. "We don't even know if she's back in Korslakov. She could still be in Saphrona."

"Lady's blood," Lukan swore, his anger rising in response to the thief's questioning. "I know you love to see the worst in things—"

"I'm being pragmatic."

"—but this is our one chance. So." He folded the letter and slipped it into the envelope. "Let's just be hopeful for once. Because if this doesn't work"—he glanced at Misko and lowered his voice—"we'll have to fight our way out, this time without your portal to help us. And I don't fancy our chances, do you?"

Ashra had no reply to that.

The hours passed slowly.

Lukan spent them pacing the cell, driven by a nervous energy, as he listened out for any approaching footsteps. Ashra had long since given up complaining about his restlessness. The thief sat cross-legged on her bed, her face a mask once more, but Lukan knew she was also listening for any sign that their salvation might be close at hand. At one point he paused in his pacing, convinced he could hear Razin's booming voice. He allowed himself to believe the general would appear at any moment, with an apologetic Spark cowering beneath his righteous fury as he unlocked their cell door. But it was always the hope that killed you. If Razin had pulled some strings and pled their case, it seemed to have fallen on deaf ears.

Nor did Lady Marni make an appearance.

As the daylight waned beyond their small window, Lukan's hope that she would intervene faded. It had been a small hope, admittedly. A little desperate, even. Yet he'd still felt there was a chance the Lady in Red would appear. That if she just lingered for a moment beyond their cell, he could convince her that, no, they *weren't* murderers, and that, yes, it *would* be worth her while to secure their release. And that she would then do just that. *Idiot.* How foolish that notion seemed now. *She probably threw my letter in the fire after reading it. If she even read it at all.*

Lukan ran a hand over his face as he turned to the window, watching as the darkness of evening descended. The last he might ever see. His stomach lurched at the thought.

"They're not coming," Ashra said, once the daylight had fled. Burning torches beyond their cell threw shadows across the stone walls. "Razin and Flea."

"Doesn't look like it," Lukan agreed.

"Neither is your Lady in Red."

"There's still time. She may have been out for the day and only just returned home. She could be sitting before a fire as we speak, with a glass of red wine in one hand and my letter in the other."

"You think?"

"Yes."

"What did I say earlier? About lying to yourself?"

"I'm not . . ." Lukan's retort died on his tongue. What was the use in even trying to deny it. He *was* lying to himself. It was far better than the alternative, which was to accept that they were going to die in a matter of hours. And that he was going to go to his grave without knowing what awaited him in his father's vault. Without knowing who murdered his father, or why. Without winning the justice the old man deserved.

Dying was bad enough. Dying without answers—with unfinished business—was even worse.

The Veiled Lady's priests claimed a paradise awaited Her most devout followers, and in that moment Lukan wished he believed it. Death wouldn't be so bad if it was merely a door to another place, where he might see his father again. Where he might get some answers. But he'd never believed the tenet, never seen it as anything other than a way for those same priests to line their collection plates. Not that he and the Lady had ever been on speaking terms anyway. No, nothing awaited Lukan but the endless dark. He gritted his teeth, the combination of regret and frustration and guilt scraping against his ribs like a jagged blade.

"I'm sorry," he said, the words passing his lips before he even realized they were there. He wasn't even sure who he was apologizing to. *It's a pretty long list, after all.*

"What for?" Ashra replied.

"Everything."

"Care to narrow it down?"

"Ah, there it is," Lukan said, turning to face her, a wry smile on his lips. "I knew you had a sense of humor." The thief regarded him silently as he crossed to his bed and sat down. "I'm sorry I landed you in here." He gestured at the cell. "That I didn't listen to you when you said we should leave Zelenko's workshop. And . . ." He waved a hand. "For any other indiscretions and offenses." He said the last part in a wry tone, but he meant every word. He only wished he could say the same to Flea. The girl loved to tease him about how many times she'd saved his life, but she wouldn't be saving him this time. And her reward for always having his back was to be left alone in an unfamiliar city. He could imagine her fury, and the black grief that would follow. It sickened him to know he was the cause of it. His only consolation was to tell himself—another lie, perhaps—that Razin and Timur would be there for her. Not that she needed their help. Flea was a survivor and could look after herself. That, at least, was no lie.

Ashra, for her part, gave no sign that she'd accepted his apologies, but nor did she reply with a glare or cutting barb. He supposed that was the best he was going to get. Perhaps it didn't matter. He'd said what he needed to say. That was the important part. What Ashra did with those words was her business, not his.

The night ground on.

Lukan spent much of it thinking of friends and enemies and

far-flung places, some made distant by geography, others by the
passage of time. He thought of his childhood; golden-hued in the
years before his mother died and plagued by shadows afterward.
Shadows that followed him into youth and adulthood. He retraced the rift with his father, memories so familiar they were like
well-worn cobblestones. He thought of his years at the Academy,
of Jaques and Amicia and the various adventures and escapades
they'd enjoyed until it had all ended in tragedy. He saw again—for
the thousandth time—Giorgio Castori's blood staining the cherry
blossom petals. Heard his father's bitter words, yet again: *you're
no son of mine.* Another familiar memory. Another familiar pain.
And then the restless years that followed: so many miles and places
and faces. Days spent trying to shed his old life like a snake sheds
its skin. Nights spent wondering how to win it all back. A thousand card games, drinks and bad choices. A life that was drifting.

Until Shafia found him and told him of his father's murder.

After that: fresh purpose, invigoration, the feeling of a chance
to make things right. The belief that he could, that he *would.* A belief that was now extinguished, his life soon to follow. Unless Lady
Marni deigned to show herself. *Or Ashra has a plan up her sleeve.*
The thief certainly looked like she might be plotting an unlikely
escape, the way she was staring intently into space, deep in thought.
But more likely she was just doing the same as him, thinking back
over the years and miles and trying to find some measure of peace.

Hopefully she was having an easier of time of it than he had.

At some point in the night, Lukan finally admitted to himself that
Marni wouldn't be coming to save them, and accepted he would
have to write a letter to Shafia, his father's steward. Writing to tell
the woman who had effectively raised him that he was going to die
on the morrow was every bit as hard as he expected it to be. Lukan
wasn't often lost for words, but the tip of his quill hovered over the
paper for a long time before he finally found the ones he needed.

And then, somehow, he slept.

14

A FASHIONABLE LATE ENTRANCE

Giorgio Castori had died on a beautiful spring day with a flawless blue sky.

Lukan wasn't so lucky.

His final day dawned grey and cold, bringing a sleeting rain that wasn't quite one thing nor the other. He shook his head as he stood by the cell's solitary window. *Not one thing nor the other. Not a bad way to sum up my entire life.* He'd been many things: son, student, gambler, swordsman, traveler. But most of all he'd been a failure, someone who'd had the fortune to be born into wealth (what remained of it, at least) and still found a way to mess things up. It was ironic that he'd finally found a sense of purpose and direction, only for this newfound vigor to lead him straight to his death.

If he'd had a spark of anger left, he might have slammed a fist against the wall, teeth bared against his impending demise. Fighting to the last against the dying of the light. But his fury had burned away over the course of the night and he was left with nothing but a sense of bone-deep regret. It was as if a veil had been pulled back, allowing him to see his life clearly for the first time. And what he saw was a lie. An illusion that he had created and convinced himself to believe in, because it was easier to claim the world had wronged you than accept that you were at fault. But now, he saw recklessness instead of courage. Arrogance instead of confidence. And instead of wit, he saw—actually, no, he was proud

of his silver tongue and anyone who judged him for that could go
to the hells.

But the wider point remained.

He wasn't the person he'd believed himself to be.

Amicia, his great love from his Academy days, had called him
a coward as he stood over Giorgio Castori's corpse. Ashra had
called him the same when he tried to hide at the bottom of a bottle
after the Grand Duke's murder. He'd denied her claim, just as he
convinced himself that Amicia was mistaken.

But he couldn't deny it now.

He'd told himself it was pride that made him accept Giorgio
Castori's challenge. That it was pride stopping him from recon-
ciling with his father. But it wasn't. He'd accepted Giorgio's challenge because he didn't want to look weak. He'd never offered an
olive branch to his father in case it was refused.

He'd let his fear rule him in the moments that really mattered.

Perhaps Ashra and Amicia were right. Maybe he was a coward.

Now all he could do was try to die bravely.

Should have gone for the sword, he thought darkly. He'd opted
for the gallows instead, reasoning that, since the the act of hanging would take longer, it might make all the difference. Perhaps
redemption would arrive in those precious extra moments as the
rope was placed round his neck. Now he wondered if it was just
cowardice again. A desperate attempt to stave off the inevitable.

Lukan swore under his breath, anger stirring once more, and
told himself that if he somehow survived the day he'd try to be
better. To be more responsible. More considerate. Less impulsive.
Hells, maybe I'll even drink less. Though he could murder a dram
or two of Parvan Bronze right now. A bit of liquid courage to help
him face what was coming. At the very least it might warm him up
and stop him from feeling the cold on the way to the gallows. He
didn't want people to see him shivering and think it was from fear.

"Seems Lady Marni didn't find you memorable after all," Ashra
said from behind him.

"I guess not," he replied, as he turned toward the thief. She sat perfectly still, eyes closed, her face the impassive mask Lukan had grown so used to. No pacing or brooding for her; if she had regrets, it seemed she'd made peace with them. *Calm and pragmatic, even at the end,* he thought, wishing he could feel the same. Seeing the thief radiating her familiar poise made him wonder whether he'd imagined her impassioned outburst the night before. But he hadn't.

And he hadn't forgotten what she'd said.

Nor the truth of her words.

"How are you feeling?" he asked, the question unfamiliar on his tongue.

Ashra's eyes snapped open, and her gaze locked with his. One corner of her mouth might've curved ever so slightly as she looked away; he couldn't be sure.

"I was hoping to see the sun again," she replied, after a pause.

"Not much chance of that, I'm afraid."

"Pity." Her eyes found his again. "What about you?"

"I . . ." There were lots of things he could say, but he settled for the thought that had pressed to the front of his mind. "I wish I could see Flea again. Just to . . ." He shrugged, huffed out a breath. "Say sorry, I suppose. And tell her what her friendship means to me."

"What does it mean?"

"Everything." That had been a realization he'd come to, at some point in the night—far too late, as with everything else. His childhood had been a lonely one, and Amicia and Jaques had been his only friends—or lover, in the former's case—at the Academy. He'd not seen or heard from either of them since he was expelled. And while he'd met many people on the road ever since—some he might have even called companions—none of them had been a friend to him the way Flea was. None of them had given so much and asked for so little in return. *And what little she did ask for, I didn't give her.* He felt a cold fist close round his heart. *Too late now.*

"She already knows," Ashra replied, as if sensing his regret.

"Do you think so?" he replied, hating the fragile hope in his voice, but wanting to believe it so badly.

"I know so."

Lukan wanted to ask how she could be so sure, but the approaching echo of footsteps silenced him. There was no time. Not for that, not for anything.

"Three people," Ashra murmured. Her brow creased. "No, four."

Maybe it's Lady Marni and her entourage, Lukan thought, a last desperate hope ghosting through him. *Or maybe Razin has managed to pull some strings after all.*

"Hobnailed boots," Ashra added, her eyebrows angled as if to say *stop lying to yourself.*

She was proven right as four Sparks appeared, led by the same dour guardsman who'd accompanied Misko the night before.

"Time," the man grunted as he unlocked the cell door.

"What for?" Lukan replied, forcing a lightness he didn't feel. "Breakfast?"

"Execution."

"Hands behind your backs," one of the other Sparks called.

"Was that too many words for him?" Lukan asked, nodding at the dour guardsman. The second Spark gave an unpleasant smile.

"Out," the first said, pushing the door open.

"I'm fine where I am, thanks." Lukan glanced at Ashra, hoping to see a gleam in her eye, something that might suggest she had a plan to enact a daring escape. But the thief merely returned his gaze and shrugged.

"Let's just get this over with," she said, rising from her bed.

"No," he replied, stepping close and lowering his voice to a whisper. "I'm not going meekly to the noose." He forced a smile. "Passion before reason, remember? Or in this case, death or glory. Probably death, but . . ." He turned and leaped at the doorway, and managed to slip past the dour guardsman.

"Stop!" the man bellowed.

Lukan twisted away from another guard's lunge and sent a

third stumbling with an elbow to her face. Elated at the prospect of an unlikely escape, he hurled himself at the final guard—a bear of a man—only to bounce off his barrel chest. He swung a desperate punch against the guard's jaw, but he might as well have been striking stone. The man grinned, his gaze flicking over Lukan's shoulder.

Lukan spun just in time to see the dour guardsman's fist filling his vision.

Darkness followed.

Light caresses on his skin, like lips brushing his cheek.

A pressure round his waist; strong arms holding him up.

A memory stealing into his mind: standing on a windowsill, his mother's arms round him as he watched lightning flash across the sky, stray raindrops falling against his face. A sense of safety and belonging, of childlike wonder.

A hard slap to his right cheek.

Lukan jolted, eyes snapping open.

A man's face: the dour guardsman leering at him.

A groan escaped his lips as reality asserted itself.

Instead of the overgrown gardens of his family's estate, he saw a small courtyard, surrounded by stone walls and dark windows. A downward glance revealed not his mother's hands round his waist, but large, calloused hands under his armpits—a man's hands. And as he looked up, the dawn's sleet striking his face, it wasn't lightning that he saw, but a noose.

Shit.

"You're back," a voice said. "Just in time."

Lukan looked over to see Ashra standing beside him, arms tied behind her back, another noose already looped round her neck.

"I like a fashionable late entrance," he replied, tongue feeling thick and heavy in his mouth. He winced at an ache in his jaw, remembered the dour Spark's fist filling his vision. He tried to raise a hand only to realize his own hands were also tied. "Hey," he said over his shoulder, to whoever was supporting him. "Let go. I can stand."

The hands under his arms were withdrawn. Lukan's knees trembled but held. *Weak as a lamb before the butcher's block.* Fear squirmed in his belly, but he took a breath and forced it down. It felt important not to be afraid. Movement drew his gaze to a far corner of the yard. A door had opened and more guards were filing through. His heart sank when he saw who followed them. *Oh, seven hells . . .*

General Razin's face was grim as he approached the gallows. The general was in full uniform, the gold tassels of his epaulettes bringing a touch of color and grandeur that the occasion scarcely deserved. Flea trailed behind him. Even in the grey light of the dawn Lukan could see her red-rimmed eyes, the tracks of tears down her cheeks. *They weren't allowed to visit and say goodbye,* Lukan thought, his anger rising, *but they're allowed to watch us hang.*

Flea cried out as she saw them. She ran toward the gallows, only to find her way blocked by a couple of Sparks. "Lukan!" she called, her expression one of anguish. "Ashra!"

"You shouldn't be here," Lukan called back, his heart lurching. "You don't need to see this."

"I want to," the girl replied, lashing out as one of the Sparks tried to usher her away. "I *need* to."

"I tried to get her stay behind," Razin said with a grimace of apology, as he placed a hand on the girl's shoulder, "but . . ." He shrugged.

"She wouldn't listen," Lukan said, smiling weakly. "What a surprise."

"I'm sorry," the girl called out, fresh tears welling in her eyes. "This is all my fault. If I hadn't got distracted, none of this would have happened."

"Hush, *majin*," Ashra said, her voice soothing. "Remember our lessons."

"Emotions make for poor allies," the girl replied, furiously wiping her eyes.

"Flea, listen to me," Lukan replied firmly. "Look at me. You are *not* to blame, all right? This is on me. Not you. Don't ever think otherwise."

"But I left you!" Flea replied, looking utterly bereft. "I should have stayed. I should have—"

"It doesn't matter," Lukan interrupted, feeling a surge of desperation. He needed her to understand. "The fault is mine, you understand? *Mine*."

"I don't want you to go!" the girl cried, dissolving into tears. She tried to run forward, only for Razin to pull her back and hold her close.

"Goodbye, kid," Lukan called, his voice almost cracking. He could feel tears pricking at the corners of his own eyes. "Without you I'd be dead already. Find happiness. Live your best life."

"Go well, *majin*," Ashra said, calm as ever. "Be brave."

"You can't go," Flea gasped, her knees buckling. She would have fallen if Razin hadn't held her up. "Please . . ."

"Enough," the dour guardsman barked from where he stood at the edge of the platform. He pointed at Lukan. Smiled. "Him first."

"Lady's blood," Lukan replied, feigning shock. "You *can* string more than one word together." He could only hope the morning had more surprises up its sleeve. *Some chance.*

Another Spark approached, a sackcloth in her hands. "Would you like a hood to spare your dignity?"

"That's a very kind offer, given how hard I elbowed you in the face." Lukan flashed her a smile that was more like a cornered animal baring its teeth. "But you can take it and shove it up your arse."

"Any last words?" the woman asked, unperturbed.

"I've said them already." Lukan winked at Flea, doing his best to ignore the growing tremble in his right knee, and the fear squeezing his heart. As the guard moved away, he locked eyes with Ashra. He tried to think of something to say, but came up short and settled for a nod instead. The thief nodded back.

It would have to be enough.

"Face forward," a man said from behind him, as the same hands that previously held him up now placed the noose over his head. Lukan swallowed as he felt the weight of it, the rope rasping against his skin. He took a deep breath and held it as he tried to stop himself from shaking. He couldn't bring himself to look at Flea, couldn't bear to see the anguish carved into her young face, so instead he looked to the sky and watched a flock of birds flapping across its iron-grey expanse. *Any moment now*, he thought, his heart pounding as he waited for the trapdoor beneath his feet to drop.

He closed his eyes.

Wished he could close his ears to Flea's desperate sobs.

"Lady's blood, just get on with it," he croaked, for the girl's sake more than his own.

The moment stretched.

Raised voices sounded, growing louder as they approached. Lukan opened his eyes and saw movement in the far corner of the yard—figures striding through the door. Men in some sort of livery, moving with purpose. A fleeting hope rose inside him. Had Marni decided to show after all?

It didn't matter.

It was too late.

Lukan gasped as the trapdoor collapsed beneath him. He kicked helplessly as he dangled from the rope, a crushing pressure round his neck. His eyes felt like they might pop out of his head. Blackness rushed in.

The last thing he glimpsed—through his own tears—was a blur of red.

15

THE LADY IN RED

Red.

That was all Lukan saw when he opened his eyes. A scarlet haze, pooled around him. *Blood*, he thought, jolting in panic. It was several heartbeats before he realized he was in fact swathed in scarlet, silken sheets. *I'm in a bed*, he realized. *But whose?* Slowly he pushed himself on to his elbows, a faint smile on his lips as he waited for memories of the night before to return—a night, it seemed, that had ended very well indeed. His smile became a frown as no recollection was forthcoming. Working his tongue around his dry mouth, Lukan glanced at his surroundings.

Everything in the spacious room—the rugs on the floor, the tapestries on the walls, even the walls themselves—was red, or scarlet, or crimson, or whatever other shades of red there were. Carmine? Who the hells knew. Even the furniture—a dresser, a table and chairs—were carved from what he guessed was bloodwood, an expensive material from the Southern Queendoms. The only sound was the crackle and pop of a fire burning in a hearth. He put a hand to his head, trying to remember what had happened the night before, but no memory surfaced.

Lukan's gaze fell upon a goblet studded with garnets, standing on a bedside table. He reached for it, expecting it to contain red wine, but all it held was water. He pressed it to his lips, gulped thirstily at the cool liquid within . . . and groaned as pain clamped round his throat. Water spilled from his lips, soaking the bedsheets. *What in the hells* . . . He tried swallowing again. The same pain, as if he was trying to swallow a hundred tiny blades. Gingerly he reached up and touched his throat, wincing at how tender it felt. He felt some sort of rash across his throat. A line. *As if I'd been . . .*

His jaw dropped as the memories flooded back: the steely dawn sky, the dour guardsman's face, Flea's tears, Ashra's stoicism, the coarseness of the noose round his neck. The jolt as the trapdoor collapsed beneath his feet.

The blur of red before the darkness took him.

"She came," he murmured, then laughed, only to stop as the pain in his throat returned. "Lady's blood, she actually *came*." His elation faded as he thought of Ashra standing alongside him on the gallows. Had she also been saved? Or had Marni left her to her fate? His insides clenched at the thought that maybe he'd survived when Ashra had died. He glanced around, but there was no sign of the thief. *She's alive*, he told himself. He wanted it so badly to be true.

Lukan pulled back the covers and realized he was naked. Fortunately, a red silken gown had been folded across the back of a chair. He rose and pulled it on, the silk whispering against his skin, and approached a tall mirror. *Seven hells, I look like a gigolo from some Parvan bawdyhouse*, he thought, frowning at his lank blond hair and stubble that had long since passed the fashionable stage. *Albeit not one anybody in their right mind would want to spend the night with*. His frown deepened as he stared at the greyness around his eyes, and he winced when he pulled back the gown's high collar to fully reveal the ugly bruise that circled his neck. He gently pressed a finger to the red, inflamed skin, and hissed softly at the immediate pain. *Still, I'll take being alive and looking like shit over being dead*.

He swayed, suddenly feeling light-headed. It was too warm in the room, the air too close. His gaze fell upon a set of doors leading to a balcony, and he pushed them open. A cold breeze seized him as he stepped outside, a welcome reprieve from the bedroom's heat. Korslakov lay before him, surrounded by the towering peaks of the Wolfclaw Mountains. He leaned against the stone balustrade and stared at the city, his eyes drawn to the purple flame atop the alchemists' tower, bright against the gathering dusk. He must have slept most of the day, assuming it was even still the day of his execution. He smiled at that. *Failed execution, more like. Better luck next time, Baranov.*

Lukan stepped back inside and looked around for his clothes. His eyes found an oil painting on one wall instead. He stepped closer, his curiosity piqued. The canvas depicted a cliff face with a doorway built into the stone. The surrounding arch was black as pitch, but the door itself was a deep crimson. The artist had given it a metallic sheen, as if it was catching the light. It was only when Lukan saw the small people standing before the door that he realized how massive the structure was.

"You're awake."

He turned to find a red-haired woman watching him from the bedroom door.

"And alive," he replied, his voice hoarse. "Thanks to you."

"Yes," Lady Marni said, smiling faintly, as if that fact amused her. "You are."

"And I'm deeply grateful."

"I should think so."

"Might I ask . . ." Lukan paused, almost afraid to voice the question. But he had to know. "There was a woman with me on the gallows. Ashra. Is she . . ."

"Alive?" Marni gave him a sly look as she let the moment stretch. "She is."

Lukan barely concealed his relief. "That's . . . good to know. Thank you."

"You can keep your thanks. I was content to let her hang, but then a little girl demanded I save her as well. She even had the nerve to threaten me with a crossbow when I refused, the little brat. Still, I must confess I liked her spirit. And when she told me that Ashra was a master thief, I thought it couldn't hurt to have such a person in my debt." She smiled. "Just as you are."

Lukan didn't like the weight she placed on those words, nor the coldness of her smile. But his trepidation was outweighed by his relief at knowing Ashra still lived. That was enough for now.

As for Lady Marni Volkova, she was just as striking as Lukan remembered. More so, even. She wore an extravagant crimson dress, the sleeves of which were slashed with silver, and the same ruby-studded tiara as when they'd played the pyramid game, which accentuated her fine, sharp features. She wore the same teasing smile too, and her red eyes—presumably altered by some sort of alchemical tonic—shone with amusement.

It took Lukan a moment to realize why.

Shit, he thought, realizing his gown had fallen open to reveal his nakedness. He hastily wrapped it round himself. "My apologies . . ."

"Save your blushes," Marni replied, as she sauntered into the room with the confidence of someone born to wealth. "Nothing I've not seen before." She joined him before the painting. "Besides," she purred, glancing at him sidelong, "I very much like *what* I saw."

Lukan supposed that was just as well, since she could easily send him back to the gallows if she didn't. And until he learned what she wanted from him—and there would be something—he figured it was best to keep her happy any way he could. Even if that meant standing around with nothing but a silken gown to protect his modesty.

"Simply wondrous," Lady Marni murmured.

"I like to think so."

"I'm talking about the painting." Her lips curled in amusement. "I commissioned Castravano to paint it when he was in Korslakov the summer before last. The Frostfire Council threw a fit of course, Father among them. Builder forbid we let a foreigner set eyes on the Crimson Door." She gave a slight shrug. "But their outrage only made it sweeter."

"I'm sorry," Lukan replied, struggling to catch up. "Your father— you mean Lord Volkov? I'm afraid I don't recall his name . . ."

"Fyodor," Marni replied, mouth twisting as if the word tasted sour. "He's away in Seldarine on business, or at least that's what he told me. I suspect he's spending time with the lover he thinks I don't know about. And he has the nerve to tell *me* how to conduct myself . . ." Marni paused, the heat that had entered her voice retreating. "Regardless," she continued, "it's lucky for you. If Father had been home, you'd still be hanging from that rope."

"Then I'm glad Lord Volkov's absent."

"Yes," Marni replied, her expression thoughtful. "So am I." She gestured at the painting. "Have you heard of the Crimson Door?"

"I don't believe . . ." Lukan paused as the name rang a distant bell in his mind, and he realized his father had once spoken of it. He studied the painting more closely. The black stone of the door's arch reminded him of the Ebon Hand. "It's Phaeron," he said, recalling what little he knew. "And it's never been opened."

"Correct," Marni replied, a hint of approval in her voice. "No one has ever managed to unlock it. But that never stopped the speculation as to what lies beyond."

"And what do you think that is?"

"Power, of course," she replied, her red gaze intensifying as she stared at the painting. "Knowledge. Divinity." The was a touch of awe in the way she said the last word.

Of course, Lukan thought, remembering the tattoo he'd seen on Marni's wrist, and the exchange he'd had with Juro as he recovered from playing the pyramid. *She belongs to a Phaeron cult—what are they called? The Scarlet Throne. That was it.* The Scrivener's man, Juro, had claimed the cult worshipped the Phaeron as gods. That was why Marni had played the pyramid game, risking pain just to be close to a Phaeron artifact. He'd seen that sort of obsession before, in his father. The thought he now owed his life to another Phaeron obsessive wasn't a pleasant one. *Still, it's better than the alternative.*

"If I may," he said, "I don't believe you plucked me from the gallows just to show me a picture."

"You're right." Marni glanced at him, a coy smile returning to her lips. "I didn't."

"In which case I find myself wondering *why* you did so."

"Perhaps I enjoyed your company so much when we played the pyramid that I wanted to experience it again."

"That's what I assumed, but I didn't want to seem presumptuous."

"Ah, there's the quick wit I recall." Marni gave him an appraising look, ruby lips pursed. "But do you still have the courage you
showed when playing the pyramid? That same sense of daring?
The same desire to beat the odds?"

Lukan recalled the huge gamble he took in the great hall of
the Grand Duke's palace, the cold probing of the Wolf's mind as
it touched his own. *One hardly strikes a deal with the Faceless
without such qualities.* Not that he could tell Marni that. "I do,"
he replied.

"I'm glad to hear it. Given the trouble I went to—and how
furious Father will be when he finds out—it would have been disappointing to know it was all for nothing."

"You would ask something of me."

"Yes. I have a task for you."

"A task," Lukan repeated, not liking the sound of those words.
If this exchange was playing out within the pages of a cheap
bodice-ripper—the kind his friend Jaques used to read and glee-
fully recite passages from—then Marni would inform him his task
was to ravish her every nightfall for the next thirty days. And Lukan, for his part, would have done so willingly: Marni was just as
beautiful as he remembered, and just as alluring. To his dismay,
he found himself hardening at the thought, and willed the notion
from his mind. This was real life, not a novel.

There would be a serious price.

There always was.

"What would you have me do?"

Amusement danced in Marni's scarlet eyes, as if she knew his
thoughts. She tilted her head, smiling that tantalizing smile of hers.
"What would you do for the woman who saved your life, hmm?
And who still holds it in her hands?"

"Almost anything," he admitted.

"*Almost?*"

"I won't kill for you."

Marni gasped with feigned outrage. "Not even to save your
own skin?"

"No. I won't." Lukan was surprised by his own conviction. But he'd not forgotten the promise he'd made to himself: that if he somehow cheated death, he would try to be better. Well, somehow he had survived. Now he had to make good on that promise. He'd been given a second chance, and, if this new chapter of his life began with him taking someone else's, then perhaps it was better it didn't begin at all.

"Why all the frowning?" Marni asked. "Fear not, Lukan Gardova. I won't ask you to commit murder. After all, the woman I want you to find is already dead."

"Already dead?" he echoed, masking his relief. "What do you want with a corpse?"

"We'll talk business later. I prefer to put pleasure first. The Inventors' Parade is in three days, and it's been too long since I've attended with a handsome man on my arm."

"I've rather had my fill of parades."

Marni gave him a curious look. "Ah," she said, as realization dawned. "You mean the bloodbath at the Grand Procession."

"Were you there?"

"No, though I wish I had been. It sounded *so* dramatic." She smirked, as if the murder of the Grand Duke and his two sons was amusing, and not one of the most horrifying things Lukan had ever seen. "Fear not," she continued, "the only things that die at the Inventors' Parade are the careers of inventors who don't gain the patronage they seek. Besides, it's a parade in name only. We shall sit and drink wine and eat candied nuts, while a succession of blackthumbs demonstrate their latest inventions to us." She shrugged. "In truth it can often be dull, but there's always a chance someone's coat might catch fire."

"Has that happened before?"

"Yes. More than once."

"Well, better a coat than an arm," Lukan replied, thinking back to the pyramid game.

"So you'll join me, then?"

He knew it wasn't really a question. "I will."

"Excellent." Marni leaned toward him, close enough for him to smell her perfume—the scent of red roses. *Of course.* Her lips parted, and Lukan thought she was going to kiss him. For a moment he wanted her to. But then she tilted her head, her lips brushing his ear, and murmured, "Lord Baranov will be there." Her eyes glinted with amusement. "Perhaps you'd like to have a word with him."

I'd like a lot more than a word, Lukan thought, as Marni spun away from him in a swirl of silk. He wondered how much Ashra had told her. *Not much, I'll wager.*

"This task," he called after her, his voice little more than a rasp. "Once it's done, will that make us even?"

Marni turned and regarded him from the doorway. "Will it clear your debt to me, you mean?"

"If that's how you want to phrase it."

"So desperate to be free of me already, Lukan Gardova?"

"That's not what I meant," he lied.

"Complete the task I set for you, and I'll consider your debt settled." She gave a light shrug. "If you're still alive."

"What do you mean, if I'm still—"

"My butler will return your clothes and see you out," Marni interrupted, her red gaze intensifying. "A carriage will come for you in three days, at the twelfth bell." She smiled coyly. "Dress smartly."

With those words, she was gone.

An hour later, Lukan stood before Razin's front door. Strange to think that just a few days ago he had stood here, questioning his choices, whereas now he knew there was nowhere else he'd rather be. *And no one else I'd rather be with.* He knocked three times, causing an instant round of barking from Ivan, and smiled as he heard Razin's voice approaching the door. "Behave yourself! Ivan! For the love of . . ."

The door opened, light spilling out. Ivan followed, tail wagging.

"Hey there, boy," Lukan murmured, ruffling the dog's great head as it stared up at him, eyes bright and tongue lolling. "General," he said by way of greeting, turning to Razin and offering his hand—only to be nearly knocked off his feet as Flea hurled herself at him, hugging him so tightly he could barely breathe.

"I'm all right, kid," he said, hugging her back. An act that might once have felt awkward. No longer.

"I thought you were going to die," the girl said, pulling away.

"I nearly did."

"I'm sorry, if I hadn't got distracted—"

"Hey, enough of that." He sank to his haunches, so their faces were level. "I already told you: none of this was your fault. Anyway, what's done is done. Let's both just try to do better, all right?"

"All right." Flea's face brightened. "Come and see Ashra!" She spun and disappeared back into the house, Ivan barking as he raced after her.

"General," Lukan repeated, standing and offering his hand again.

"Lukan," the man replied, shaking firmly. "Welcome back."

"Thanks. You have no idea how glad I am to be . . ." He waved a hand as if to say *having to deal with all this again.*

"I'm sorry I couldn't get you out," Razin said, his brow knitting. "Called in every damned favor I had left. All for nothing."

"You did what you could," Lukan replied, slapping the man's shoulder. "And I'm deeply grateful."

"Hmm, well." The general stood aside and gestured for Lukan to enter. "One thing I *can* offer you is a drink."

"That," Lukan said as he stepped through the door, "is the greatest favor of all."

Ashra was standing by the fireside as Lukan entered the living room, as if she was still trying to dispel the cold of the cell. The wary look she gave him banished his hope that their shared neardeath experience might have closed the distance between them. *Still some work to do there, it seems.* But now wasn't the time.

"Glad you're still breathing," he said to her, with a nod.

"You too," she replied. "Seems Lady Marni came through for you after all."

"She came for both of us."

"Yes." Ashra's smile faded. "She did."

Lukan didn't miss the note of wariness in her voice, which hinted at an unspoken concern. He didn't need to ask what about. He felt it too: the weight of their debt to Lady Marni, and a trepidation about what it might involve. *The woman I want you to find is already dead*, she'd said. What in the hells did that mean? Perhaps Ashra knew more, but that conversation could wait for later. This evening was for celebration, not for worrying about whatever came next. Still, he felt he needed to at least acknowledge their predicament.

"It was the only way," he said.

Ashra nodded. "I know."

"What about your ring? Did you get it back?"

"I did."

"And the sketch of the Rook?"

"That too. Along with everything else the Sparks took."

Razin appeared and thrust goblets into their hands—wine for Lukan, water for Ashra. Flea and Timur joined them, the former with a small glass of wine that Lukan was prepared to overlook, and the latter with a polite nod of greeting, which he returned.

"To friends returned to us," the general said, wine sloshing as he raised his glass. "And to justice being served."

Justice most certainly hadn't been served, Lukan mused. Not with Zelenko dead and his murderer, Lord Baranov, a free man. But he kept those thoughts to himself. Besides, the first half of the toast was the important part. He raised his glass with the others, noting Flea's grin and Ashra's faint smile. A sense of contentment—something he'd not felt for so long—stole over him, accompanied by an unfamiliar feeling of belonging. Whatever Lady Marni had in store for them, he'd face it with Ashra and Flea at his side. For now, that was enough.

16

THE INVENTORS' PARADE

The League of Inventors was headquartered in a grand building in one corner of the Square of Sacred Memories, where Lukan had met Razin for the second time. And it was, he noted, about as far from the forges of Emberfall as could be. In fairness, he supposed the quill-pushers couldn't be expected to work to the relentless sound of hammers battering iron, but he couldn't shake a suspicion that the headquarters' location owed more to its superiors' desire to profit from the industry without setting foot anywhere near a furnace. It was a feeling that only intensified as he and Marni approached the League's pillared entrance.

"Ah, Lady Marni! A delight to see you." The speaker was a man in his late fifties, swathed in fur and purple velvet. His symbol of office—a golden chain of interlinked cogs—gleamed as he bowed. "Radiant, as always," he added.

Lukan had to agree. Marni looked eye-catching in a velvet dress—scarlet, of course—with rubies stitched into its high collar. Rubies also studded her tiara, which held back her red hair and accentuated her high cheekbones. She was sleek and sharp, elegant yet cold. *Like a snowflake dipped in blood*, he thought.

"A pleasure, Grand Artificer," Marni replied, her flat tone belying her words.

"And you, sir?" the man chirped, blinking at Lukan through his half-moon spectacles. "I don't believe I've had the pleasure . . ."

"Lord Gardova, of Parva," Lukan replied, offering his hand.

"Well met, my lord! I am Grand Artificer Vilkas." The man's grip was weak, and Lukan wondered if he had ever held a hammer in his life. "Enjoy the parade," Vilkas added, his eyes already peering over Lukan's shoulder. "Ah, Lady Viramov! Always a delight . . ."

"Take my arm," Marni commanded.

Lukan obliged and allowed her to drag him through the doorway. He caught only the briefest glimpse of the League's grand entrance hall—gleaming marble, polished wood, purple carpets—before Marni hauled him into a large chamber illuminated by the glow of alchemical globes. Glass display cases lined the room, showcasing various contraptions and inventions, all of which were a mystery to Lukan. But there was nothing unfamiliar about the gathering of aristos who stood at the center of the chamber with their feigned smiles and guarded glances. This was a scene he'd encountered many times, and before his banishment from the Academy he'd have been in the thick of it, dropping jests and veiled insults with aplomb. As he watched the gossiping aristos, he felt a flicker of yearning for the life he'd once had, tempered by a sense of relief that he'd left it behind. He envied these nobles as much as he resented them. The realization left him in an uncertain, liminal space. He felt like an outcast, who didn't fully belong in one world or the other.

"Look at them," Marni said, disdain in her voice. "Like children at a pantomime. Excitable and easily impressed by smoke and mirrors. Not realizing all they're seeing is a fiction. A shadow."

"A shadow of what?"

"True power." A light seemed to shine in Marni's eyes.

"What do you mean?" Lukan asked, though he already knew. He'd seen the same look on his father's face many times.

"You played the pyramid with me," Marni continued, glancing at him. "You saw its genius. Its majesty. Its *divinity*."

"I wouldn't say watching a centipede burst out of my arm felt particularly divine."

"No?" Marni seemed almost surprised. "Then you didn't realize what a gift you'd been given. You didn't just see a glimpse of Phaeron ingenuity; you *felt* it."

"I seem to recall you weren't so keen to feel it yourself. I was told you resigned from the game after I blacked out."

"The pyramid is a mere curio. I seek far more than to experience a glimpse or a brief sensation. I desire to hold artifacts that contain the Phaeron's true power, their essence. I want to touch the divine. To see the faces of gods." Marni's lip curled as she watched the gossiping aristos. "My peers think all this"—she gestured at the room and its various exhibits—"represents the height of invention and technological prowess. They don't realize these are mere trinkets. That human intellect is but a candleflame compared to the Phaeron's blinding sun."

"Then why are we here?" Lukan asked. "Why bother with all this?"

"Because even trinkets have value—a lot of value, if you back the right one. That's the real reason everyone's here. They talk about technological prowess, but really it's about coin. It always has been."

"I've seen your home. You don't strike me as needing more money."

"We don't. My family is the richest in Korslakov." Marni's tone was almost indifferent. "But I have interests that are . . . expensive. Interests my parents are unwilling to fund."

"Like the Scarlet Throne," Lukan guessed. Marni's surprised glance told him he was right. He would have liked to ask her more about the secretive cult she belonged to, but now wasn't the right time—not least because of the young woman who was approaching them.

"Lady Marni," she said, slightly breathlessly. "Good afternoon. I hope I'm not intruding." She dropped into a curtsey.

"Of course not," Marni replied, the edge to her tone indicating otherwise. "Ludmilla, isn't it?"

The woman beamed as she straightened. "It is, Lady Marni." There was a friskiness to her manner, the excitable energy of a freshly minted aristo enjoying their first high society event. *No doubt it'll wear off quickly enough*, Lukan thought. But for now Ludmilla was bright-eyed and, like most young aristos, looking to bathe in the glow of their more illustrious peers in the hope some of their shine might wear off on them.

"This is Lord Gardova of Parva," Marni said, gesturing to Lukan.

"Your lordship," Ludmilla said, performing another curtsey, her blue eyes flitting to him and away again before he could even reply. "Lady Marni, I wondered if I might be so bold as to beg a favor—"

"Didn't you become engaged recently?" Marni cut in, tapping her lips in feigned thoughtfulness. "To Lord Saburov's youngest son?"

"I did." Ludmilla flashed a gold ring set with an indecently large emerald. "It's a Consigni signature piece. Danton told me I deserved the best."

"And quite right he is too. Though . . ." Marni pursed her lips as she made a show of studying the ring. "I'm afraid the cut of that emerald looks a touch rough for a true Consigni . . ."

So it begins, Lukan thought, as Ludmilla's blue eyes widened in dismay. He'd seen such exchanges a hundred times: the barbed comments, the feigned benevolence, the constant probing for an edge or advantage. It was a game he'd once played himself in the ballrooms and smoking parlors of Parva, until he'd realized that playing rummijake with scoundrels in Parva's backstreet gambling dens was far more enjoyable. Even if it did carry the potential of a knife in the ribs. Looking back, perhaps that's why he preferred it. There was more honesty in a few inches of steel than an aristocrat's smile.

As Ludmilla fought back tears while Marni casually dismantled her, Lukan plucked a glass of wine from the tray of a passing server and held it to his nose. *Parvan Red*, he realized with delight. *Perhaps this afternoon holds some promise after all.*

"Was that really necessary?" he asked a moment later, as Ludmilla—having lost her battle with her tears, which now spilled down her powdered cheeks—fled into the depths of the room.

"I was doing her a favor," Marni replied, with a shrug of indifference. "Better to know your betrothed is a liar before you . . ." She trailed off, her face darkening. "Oh, really?" she breathed.

Lukan followed her stare to see a man striding toward them. *Lord Volkov*, he realized instantly. *Marni's father.* He didn't need her to confirm the man's identity; it was clear in the way the other aristos nodded in deference, and in how his features mirrored those of his daughter, with a high brow, prominent cheekbones and a blade of a nose you could cut yourself on.

"Father," Marni said, as the man stopped before them.

"Daughter," Volkov replied, without warmth or affection. "I wasn't expecting you back so soon."

"My business in Seldarine concluded promptly. Which is just as well, since I hear that you've plucked a murderer from a prison cell, on the strength of our good name." His steely grey eyes flicked over Lukan. "And this, I assume, is the killer himself."

"No murderer, my lord," Lukan replied, unable to let the comment go unchallenged, despite his better judgment. "I merely had the misfortune to be there when the Sparks arrived." He offered his hand. "Lord Lukan Gardova, of Parva. The pleasure is mine."

"Yes, it is," Volkov agreed, making no move to accept the handshake. "You may be a lord in whatever Heartlands backwater you crawled from, but here in Korslakov your name means nothing." He leaned in close. "Hear me well, Gardova," he said in a low voice that was smooth and cold as ice. "I don't know what use my daughter thinks she has for you, but, if you do anything to sully my family's name, I'll ensure you've got another noose round your neck before nightfall." Lord Volkov glanced at his daughter. "A word."

Marni opened her mouth, as if to object, but her father was already striding away. She settled for glaring at his back. "I won't be long," she said, stepping away.

"Take as long as you like," Lukan replied, meaning every word. Sipping his wine and studying the exhibits was a far more enticing prospect than having to endure more aristocratic games. He glanced around the room, but saw no sign of Lord Baranov. *Perhaps that's for the best.* He wasn't sure he'd be able to maintain decorum if confronted with the man, and the last thing he needed was to make a scene—particularly now that Lord Volkov had marked his card. He took a sip of wine and watched as the two Volkovs performed the age-old trick of having a furious public row while retaining forced smiles.

"There's no love lost there," a voice said.

Lukan turned to find a well-dressed man of roughly his own age standing behind him, leaning heavily on a jeweled cane, his dark eyes on the arguing pair. "Rumor holds that Lord Volkov wanted a son for his heir," the man continued, smiling wryly. "Fyodor's old-fashioned like that. That's why his relationship with Lady Marni has always been strained. Marni's involvement with the Scarlet Throne has only made matters worse. The Scarlet Throne is—"

"A cult that holds the Phaeron as gods," Lukan cut in. "So I've heard."

The man bowed his head. "My apologies for assuming your ignorance. And for not properly introducing myself." He extended a hand. "Lord Shiro Arima."

"Lord Lukan Gardova," Lukan replied, accepting the handshake.

"A pleasure." Arima's smile became pained. "And now it seems I must take my leave . . ."

Lukan turned to find Marni approaching, her expression of icy indifference not masking the disdain in her scarlet gaze.

"Shiro," she said coolly. "What a delight."

Lord Arima inclined his head, accepting the insult with good grace. "Wonderful to see you, Lady Marni," he lied, with the ease of the practiced aristocrat. "Forgive my intrusion, but I didn't want to leave your guest on his own."

"How thoughtful of you. But Lord Gardova's a grown man, so I'm sure he'd have survived."

"Of course." Arima dipped his head. "I will take my leave."

"Yes. You do that."

As the man departed, leaning heavily on his cane, Marni looked at Lukan, accusation in her eyes. "What did he want with you?"

"I didn't have a chance to find out. We'd barely exchanged pleasantries. Why?"

Marni didn't reply, merely stared after Arima with thinned lips. "Don't talk to him again," she said eventually.

"Why not?"

"Because I say so." Lukan felt a spark of irritation as Marni turned her scarlet gaze to him. "And because he's got ideas above his station. His family always has." She smirked. "Fortunately, Shiro's the last of them. There have been rumors about his virility for years."

"How fascinating," Lukan replied.

"That sounded dangerously like sarcasm."

"That's because it was." Lukan knew such insolence was unwise, but felt a need to push back against Marni's causal malice. "How was your chat with Daddy? He didn't seem too happy."

The glare Marni gave him made it clear he hadn't overstepped so much as taken a giant leap over an invisible line. As it was, he was saved quite literally by the bell.

"My esteemed lords and ladies!" Master Vilkas was calling, shaking a silver bell in one hand. "I regret to inform you that due to a minor malfunction . . ." He trailed off as shouting came through the door behind him, followed by a loud hiss and the sound of metal striking stone. Vilkas winced as he eased the door shut. "Forgive me, my lords and ladies, but due to this minor setback we must delay the parade by half an hour."

A murmur of annoyance rolled through the room.

"More wine for our esteemed guests!" Vilkas called, gesturing frantically at a couple of nearby servers, before he ducked back through the door.

"Don't mind if I do," Lukan murmured, only for Marni to grip his arm.

"You've had enough."

"I've had one glass."

"You'll need your wits about you if you're to confront your nemesis." Marni's coy smile returned. "Oh, and look. There he is."

Lukan followed her stare to where a large group of aristos stood in conversation. His pulse quickened as he saw Lord Baranov among them, standing still and silent as the others in the group talked animatedly.

"Why don't we go and say hello, hmm?" Marni slipped her arm through his. "Come."

It was only then that Lukan realized that *this* was why Marni had brought him here: to humiliate Baranov by parading Lukan in front of him. It was a classic example of aristocratic one-upmanship, and he felt a fool for not realizing it before. As much as he wanted to have words with Baranov, this didn't feel like the time or place.

"No," he replied. "let's not."

"No?" Marni raised a thin eyebrow. "I'm calling the shots here, Lukan. Or did you forget your debt to me? Come."

Lukan had no choice but to follow.

The circle of aristos fell silent as they joined the gathering, Marni's presence alone enough to still tongues. A few—lesser names looking to ingratiate themselves, Lukan assumed—murmured greetings and made obeisances, all of which Marni ignored. The others offered curt nods or forced smiles or—in Baranov's case—nothing at all. Lukan thought he would be staring daggers at her for saving him from the gallows, but the man barely seemed to notice her at all. Instead, his penetrating gaze was on Lukan, a line creasing his brow.

Not pleased to see me, are you? he thought, holding the man's stare.

"Are you quite all right, Grigor?" Marni asked, feigning concern as she pushed the metaphorical knife a little deeper. "You seem on edge."

"I'm perfectly well," Baranov replied stiffly.

Marni smiled, though Lukan sensed her disappointment with Baranov's muted reaction. "Well," she said, twirling a finger in the air as the silence grew awkward. "Don't neglect your important conversation on my account, my lords."

"Oh, it was nothing," a young man replied, affecting boredom as he swirled the wine in his glass. "Just Dragomir pretending he knows what that bad business in Saphrona will do to the silver trade."

"I *do* know," another man retorted, his broad face reddening. "I told you; my uncle has contacts."

The first man rolled his eyes.

"Speaking of Saphrona," Marni said, clearly sensing another opportunity, "Lord Gardova and I were there recently. I left the day before the Grand Duke's assassination, but Lord Gardova saw the whole sorry business. Isn't that right, Lukan?"

"It is," Lukan replied, forcing a smile as he felt a dozen pairs of eyes on him, including Baranov's. He hadn't told Marni of his role in Marquetta's downfall—that would attract the sort of attention he didn't need—but he had admitted to being at the bloodbath that had unfolded in the shadow of the Lady's House. Now he wished he'd denied being there at all.

"I say, Lord Pavlova . . ." an older man said, only to pause as a woman of similar age whispered in his ear. "*Gardova?*" he said, frowning. "That's what I said!" He turned back to Lukan. "Is it true the Zar-Ghosan ambassador murdered the Grand Duke?"

"And his two sons," Lukan replied. "Except that . . . actually, never mind."

"I heard sorcery was involved," someone else chimed in.

"I think that's likely," Lukan replied. *Just not the kind you're thinking of.*

"But I thought she killed the duke with some sort of Phaeron spear," another noble said.

"Builder's balls, who cares what killed him?" Dragomir exclaimed. "The old man was in his seventies anyway."

"Yes, positively *ancient*," said a dry voice, belonging to an older woman who Lukan hadn't noticed—not least because she stood barely five feet tall. "No doubt the Grand Duke was little more than a skeleton," the woman continued, before taking a drag on the cigarillo she held in a gloved hand. "I daresay," she finished, exhaling smoke from her nostrils, "that the poor man burst into dust as soon as the spear skewered him." She turned to Lukan. "Is that what happened, Lord Gardova?"

"Not exactly," he replied.

"No. I thought not." She gave Dragomir a cold look, and Lukan found himself warming to her immediately.

Dragomir's blowhard act withered in the face of her glare. "I meant no disrespect, Lady Wretzky," he said tightly.

"None taken, my dear boy." The old lady tapped ash into a little silver dish she held in her other hand. "But perhaps you could do me a favor."

"Of course."

"Shut the hells up." Dragomir reddened but remained silent. "Now," Lady Wretzky continued, turning to Lukan, "Please do share your story with us, Lord Gardova. I'm sure we're all keen to know which of the whispers we've heard about the Grand Duke's death might be true."

"I have no wish to know," Baranov declared, giving Lukan a final stare before breaking away from the circle, leaving a confused silence in his wake. *They don't know*, he realized, as some of the aristos exchanged surprised looks. He'd assumed Marni would have subtly spread the word that she'd engineered his release to thwart Baranov, to add to his humiliation. Such was the nature of aristocratic games. But the way these nobles whispered to each other behind cupped hands suggested they were in the dark. Only Lady Wretzky seemed unsurprised as she watched Lord Baranov disappear into the depths of the room.

"I apologize, Lord Gardova," she said, "for my fellow archon's lack of decorum."

"Not at all," Lukan replied.

"Now," Lady Wretzky continued, eyeing him over the glowing end of her cigarillo, "I'm most interested in hearing your story of this debacle in Saphrona, if you're willing to share it."

Lukan forced a smile. "It would be my pleasure."

"Well, that was a disappointment," Marni said, as they finally took their seats.

"It's the truth," Lukan replied. It wasn't, as it happened; he'd told the tale of the Grand Duke's assassination while leaving out certain key elements. Such as the fact that it was carried out by the Faceless, for example. That would only provoke more questions, not to mention ridicule. Embarrassing Marni in front of her peers seemed like a certain way to end up back on the gallows.

"I'm not talking about your story," Marni replied, pouting. "I'm talking about Baranov's reaction to your presence. He seemed . . ." She paused, considering.

"Confused?" Lukan offered.

"Yes. Maybe even annoyed. But he was a long way from the anger I expected to see." She gave Lukan a searching look. "You *have* been honest with me, haven't you? Because if you haven't . . ."

"I have," Lukan said firmly. And he had been. He'd seen little choice but to tell Marni all about his suspicions relating to Baranov's involvement with the Rook, including the letters they found, only to find out that Ashra had already done so. The thief had been more forthcoming than he'd expected. Perhaps because, as tight as the leash was that Marni had round his neck, the one Ashra wore was tighter still.

"Well," Marni replied, examining her fingernails—red, of course. "The Iron Dame enjoyed your story, at least. And it's never a bad thing to be in Lady Wretzky's good books."

"The Iron Dame?" Lukan echoed, spying the small woman as she took a seat on the opposite side of the hall, another cigarillo dangling from her lips. "How did she earn that name?"

"By outliving three husbands, two children and a grandchild," Marni replied, a grudging respect in her voice. "Not to mention smoking fifty of those filthy things a day."

Iron Dame indeed, Lukan thought. The old lady had seemed particularly interested in his tale, come to think of it. And she was staring at him now, he realized, her wrinkled brow knitted in thought, the cherry of her cigarillo glowing. Feeling strangely uneasy, he looked away, taking in the grandness of the hall. Tiers of seating, carved from white winterwood, rose up on two sides of the room, granting spectators a good view of the marbled floor below. Oil paintings of inventors and machinists hung from the paneled walls above, while higher still a huge clock hung from the vaulted ceiling, its innards exposed as if it had partially exploded. Lukan watched the cogs and gears and pistons moving, slowly turning the great hands on its face. He had the feeling this was going to be a long afternoon.

"My esteemed lords and ladies," Grand Artificer Vilkas called as he strode out into the center of the floor. "My apologies again for the delay to proceedings, and my deepest thanks for your patience—"

"Get on with it!" someone called—Dragomir, Lukan realized, looking in the direction of the guffaws that followed. The young aristo was sitting in the front row on the opposite side of the hall—the perfect place from which to hurl insults, Lukan surmised—surrounded by a little group of sycophants. Dragomir's smirk suggested he'd already shaken off the dressing-down he'd received earlier at the hands of the Iron Dame.

"It's my pleasure," Vilkas continued, ignoring the jibe, "to welcome you to the one hundredth and twenty-fourth Inventors' Parade! As always, we have some remarkable inventions to share with you. All our inventors seek your patronage, and I hope that you see fit to extend your generosity to them—all in the name of progress, of course."

Of course, Lukan thought wryly. *I wonder what size cut Vilkas takes from each agreement.*

"Now, without further ado," the Grand Artificer continued, throwing up a hand, "I'm delighted to introduce the first of our exhibits, a semi-automated printing press—"

"Boring!" one of Dragomir's flunkies trilled, causing more laughter.

"—designed by Master Willem Kovács," Vilkas finished. His smile looked increasingly strained as he left the floor. A rumble filled the hall as a large machine emerged from a set of double doors, rolling in on a wheeled platform. Half a dozen red-faced attendants pushed the contraption into the center of the floor, followed by a tall, bespectacled man who wrung his hands nervously.

"Good afternoon," the man said haltingly. "I, um . . ." He hesitated, seemingly overawed by his audience, some of whom already seemed to be losing patience. "I'm here to, ah, demonstrate my new printing press," he managed, his voice barely more than a mumble. "It differs from the standard press in that—"

"Speak up or shut up!" Dragomir yelled.

More laughter, though Lukan noticed a few glares being thrown the young aristo's way.

Kovács glanced at Vilkas, who nodded encouragingly.

"The refinements I've made mean that my press can print a thousand pages a day, instead of mere hundreds," Kovács continued, gesturing at his machine. "As I will now demonstrate."

A hush fell over the room as the inventor began to pull various levers, while two aproned assistants fed sheets of parchment into one side of the machine, as if they were feeding some sort of mechanical creature. The machine hissed and whirred and then suddenly those same sheets emerged from its other side, with neat lines of black text printed clearly on them. As the process continued, Lukan noted various aristos leaning forward with interest, one or two exchanging murmured comments. Master Kovács wore the look of a man who had walked into a lion's den and, to his surprise, hadn't been dismembered and devoured.

A high-pitched mechanical squeal was the first sign that all was not well. The sound of tearing parchment was the second. Kovács's smile slipped from his face as a loud rattling noise filled the hall. He leaped forward and desperately reached for a lever.

Too late.

With a strangely human groan, the machine shuddered and vomited sheets of parchment in every direction.

Many of the aristos roared with laughter.

Not so Lukan, who felt only pity for the inventor, who stood frozen, his face white as he watched his hopes of patronage disappear in a flurry of chewed-up pages. He slunk from the hall with jeers ringing to the rafters.

The three inventors who followed Master Kovács managed to avoid such a humiliating fate, yet also failed to arouse any interest with their inventions. The first two—a peculiar device called a microscope, and another that could apparently predict the weather—were both met with bafflement, while the third—a new take on the piston pump, whatever the hells that was, attracted outright scorn.

"Piston pump?" Dragomir yelled. "More like *pissed-on* pump!"

As the demoralized inventor departed to the sounds of laughter, Lukan belatedly realized that the Inventors' Parade had a dual purpose. For the inventors, it was a chance to showcase their inventions in the hope of securing patronage. For the aristocracy, it was mostly a chance to laugh and sneer and demean the very men and women who were the city's industrial lifeblood, and who toiled in the footsteps of those who had forged Korslakov's reputation.

He felt anger quicken inside him.

The artificers he'd seen so far that morning worked themselves to the bone, no doubt dealing with failure after failure as they strove for progress. By contrast, the only adversity that most of the gathered nobles had to face was the threat of running out of their favorite wine.

As Lukan glanced at the sneering faces around him, he felt nothing but contempt. No, that wasn't true: he felt shame as well. Shame that he was one of them. It was an unjust world where the honest and hard-working were in thrall to the greedy and indolent. But perhaps he could change that, in his own small way. When he finally returned to his estate in Parva, he could do right by the farmers and laborers who worked his land and lived under his jurisdiction. He could restore the Gardova family name. Make it a byword for decency and prosperity, not scandal.

"Lukan." Lady Marni's voice, edged with impatience, cut through his thoughts. He glanced up to find the hall alive with activity as the aristos made their way toward the doors.

"Is it finished?" he asked, perhaps a little too hopefully.

"No," Marni replied, her fine brows slashing into a frown. "This is a break for refreshments, as Vilkas *just* said."

"Right." Lukan stood, the prospect of another glass of wine making the thought of witnessing more scorn and cruelty just about bearable.

"You were deep in thought," Marni said, as they made their way to the doors.

"I was just reflecting on what we've seen this morning," he replied. *Or what I've seen, at least.*

"Amusing, don't you think?" Marni smirked. "The parade never fails to entertain."

Lukan didn't reply.

His fear that the second part of the parade would be another exercise in scorn and ridicule—perhaps even worse, given the alcohol that had been imbibed during the interval—was quickly allayed after the restart. The first invention to be rolled into the hall was a triple-barrelled cannon, which silenced the watching aristos for the first time that afternoon, and sparked an immediate bidding war the moment the inventor finished his speech. *Of course it would be a weapon that gets them excited*, Lukan thought, his disgust returning. *Why invest in a printing press when you can blow your money on a killing machine?*

"Daddy's keen," he whispered, as Marni's own father made his pitch to the increasingly flustered inventor.

Marni's lips thinned at his choice of words. "Of course he is. Our family name is synonymous with military innovation. Many of Korslakov's greatest victories against the clans were won with Volkov technology. It's how we earned our reputation. And our fortune."

"Easier than fighting in the wars yourselves," Lukan replied, daring to let a little scorn bleed into his voice. "Leave that for the poor folk, eh?"

Marni gave him an icy look. "That sounds dangerously like criticism."

"I'm just saying . . . shouldn't progress be measured, and reputations earned, through inventions that, you know, don't murder people?"

"Don't be a fool," Marni replied.

The parade and afternoon slowly ground on. Many of the inventions on show served military purposes, and, while none caused as much excitement as the cannon, nor did they earn the scorn and ridicule shown to the likes of the printing press and piston pump. Lukan increasingly found himself staring at the deconstructed clock high above, willing the hands on it to move faster.

After what seemed an eternity, the parade reached its conclusion.

"My esteemed lords and ladies," Vilkas called out, spreading his hands, "we have just one more invention to show you." He glanced at his scroll of paper. "Please welcome Master Hulio Arcardi, who is here to demonstrate his . . ." The man frowned. "Entrapment circle." He stuffed the scroll under one arm and clapped enthusiastically, but few of the aristos followed suit. Perhaps it was fatigue settling in, but Lukan suspected something else entirely, and was proven right when an old man sitting near him muttered, "Another bloody Talassian." For some reason the gathered aristocrats had treated the one previous Talassian inventor with particular scorn, and the various sneers they wore now suggested this man would get much the same treatment.

Not that the inventor himself seemed to care.

The man was a similar age to Lukan, somewhere in his late twenties, with the dark hair and olive skin of a native-born Talassian, and the attitude to match. Most of the inventors who had graced the floor had scuttled in with their heads bowed, but Hulio Arcardi strode into the hall with his chin raised. The silence that greeted him might've unnerved most of his peers, but Arcardi stood tall in the face of it, daring to stare back at the aristos with a disdain that matched their own. Lukan recalled another Talassian, Madame Delastro, who had looked at him in much the same way. He could only hope Arcardi didn't share Delastro's murderous nature.

The Talassian's invention, which was being wheeled in behind him, didn't *look* particularly threatening. A dark metal disc, about three yards in diameter, lay flat on the wheeled platform, with three pedestals standing at points around it. Roughly cut, greenish crystals were affixed to the top of each pedestal with copper wire, which then trailed down and connected to the central disc. It looked unlike any of the other inventions, and its purpose was unclear. Perhaps that was why most of the aristos stayed in their seats. Or perhaps it was the force of Arcardi's gaze that kept them there, as the inventor prowled before them.

"Golems always do what we tell them," he said suddenly, his strong voice rising all the way up to the high ceiling. "Correct? They are incapable of disobeying us." He nodded at Master Vilkas, who gestured toward the doors. A clanking sound filled the hall as a construct entered the room. Lukan's gaze followed the golem as it walked to where Arcardi stood. They were a familiar sight to him now, yet he still found himself intrigued by them in much the same way Flea was. "You," Arcardi said, turning to the golem. "Stand in the center of that metal disc." He gestured at his invention. The construct obliged, the wheeled platform creaking as it clambered on. "Raise your right arm," the inventor commanded. The golem did so. Arcardi then pulled a lever on the side of one pedestal. A hum filled the air, and the three crystals suddenly glowed with a faint green light. "Lower your arm," Arcardi ordered.

The golem didn't move.

"Lower your arm," he repeated.

Still the construct remained motionless. Whispers broke out as aristos exchanged bemused glances.

"Step out of the circle," Arcardi ordered.

The golem stood exactly as it was.

"Step out of the circle and hit me in the face."

That brought a gasp or two from the audience, but elicited no response at all from the construct.

Arcardi pulled the lever again; the strange humming sound faded, as did the greenish glow from the three crystals.

The golem seemed to shudder, as if it had been released from an invisible hold. *Just like the Zar-Ghosan ambassador after the Faceless relinquished their control*, Lukan thought, leaning forward. He watched as the construct stepped out of the circle and down from the platform. It strode toward Arcardi with intent and raised a huge metal fist.

"Stop," the inventor said.

The golem obeyed.

"Lower your hand."

The construct did so.

Arcardi nodded in apparent satisfaction. "I call it an entrap-ment circle," he said to the watching aristos, before launching into an explanation that flew almost entirely over Lukan's head; something about charged lodestones and magnetism and copper conductors. None of it made much sense to him, but the final ef-fect was clear enough. "It traps anything made of metal, so that it cannot move," Arcardi was saying. "A golem. A soldier in a suit of armor. Once held, the subject cannot break free." He reached into a sack and pulled out a metal breastplate. "Who would like to try?"

Silence.

"I will," a voice said.

Murmurs and rustling as everyone craned their necks to see who had spoken. To Lukan's surprise, it was Lord Arima, who had risen from his place in the front row and was hobbling toward Arcardi.

"How will *you* prove it works, Arima?" Dragomir shouted, his cronies sneering alongside him. "You couldn't fight your way out of a courtesan's embrace."

Laughter.

"Would you like to try instead?" Arcardi asked coolly.

The laughter faltered. Dragomir looked momentarily lost for words, blinking as if he couldn't believe the inventor had dared speak to him. His face darkened as sniggers sounded around him. He surged to his feet. "When you speak to me, you will address me as *my lord*, or I'll—"

"Shut your trap, Dragomir, there's a good boy," Lady Wretzky interrupted, tapping ash onto her silver dish. "No one needs to hear your voice." *Iron Dame indeed*, Lukan thought.

Dragomir turned and glared at the old lady, but, as he had be-fore, he did as he was told.

Arcardi, meanwhile, appeared oblivious to the exchange as he helped Lord Arima into several pieces of armor. "There," he said, as the final vambrace was strapped to the aristo's arm. "Now, please stand in the circle." Lord Arima moved slowly toward the disc, his cane tapping on the polished floor. One of the attendants helped him onto the platform.

"Raise your right arm," the Talassian said, once he was in position.

Lord Arima obliged, though his grimace suggested it wasn't easy with the armor weighing him down.

Arcardi pulled the lever, and the hum returned. The stones glowed green.

"Lower your arm."

Lord Arima's face contorted with apparent effort, but he remained still, his arm raised.

"Walk off the disc," Arcardi called.

The man remained where he was. Sweat gleamed on his face.

Arcardi pulled the lever again. The hum vanished, the glow disappeared, and Lord Arima dropped to his knees, panting heavily.

"The entrapment circle," the Talassian inventor said, offering a small bow to the watching nobles, and receiving a smattering of applause in return.

"Wonderful!" Vilkas said, clapping enthusiastically. "Just wonderful! An invention quite unlike any other! And just *imagine* the implications of such powerful technology. Why, you could . . . you could . . ." He swallowed. "Well, I'm sure there's limitless possibilities." He looked around hopefully. "Now, who might be interested in offering patronage to Master Arcardi?"

"I will," Arima called, waving from the center of the disc, where he'd regained his feet. "I will extend Master Arcardi fifty gold ducats to develop his invention further." He studied one of the green crystals. "Actually, make that one hundred."

A murmur of surprise swept across the hall.

"You fool, Arima," Dragomir sneered, apparently still seething at his earlier dressing-down. "A king's ransom for this worthless trinket? You've taken leave of your senses."

Mutterings of agreement greeted his outburst, and Lukan wasn't surprised. A hundred ducats was likely several years' wages for a common laborer. But then Master Arcardi was far more than that, and clearly Arima had seen something in his invention that his peers had not. The lord had ignored the jibes thrown his way and was already deep in conversation with Arcardi. The few other inventors who had received aristocratic patronage had all bowed and scraped before their indifferent new masters, but Arcardi was responding to Arima's interest with nothing more than a raised eyebrow.

"Do I hear any counter-offers?" a beaming Vilkas asked the room. When only silence greeted his question, he swept an arm toward the door. "In that case, my esteemed lords and ladies, that concludes the one hundred and twenty-fourth Inventors' Parade! Please join us in the rear courtyard for food and refreshments."

Lukan's stomach growled in approval, but he didn't share its enthusiasm. As hungry as he was—and as fine as the wines were here—he'd had his share of Lady Marni and the rest of Korslakov's elite for one day.

"Well, this has been a most enjoyable afternoon," he lied, rising to his feet, "but I must be away. I've some personal matters to attend to."

Lady Marni thrust out an elbow. "Take my arm."

"With respect," Lukan replied, choosing both his words and tone carefully, "I feel I've held up my side of the bargain." When Marni's eyes narrowed, he added, "For today, at least."

"What's that sound?" Marni replied, tilting her head and pursing her red lips. "It sounds like . . . a rope, swinging in a breeze."

Lukan swallowed his sigh and took her arm.

17

ARISTOCRATIC GAMES

Dusk was falling as they stepped out into the rear courtyard, where a dozen alchemical globes kept the deepening gloom at bay, and a peculiar device provided some atmosphere by playing a jaunty tune. Lukan's stomach rumbled again as he caught the scent of roasting meat, and his mouth watered as he caught sight of an entire hog roasting on a spit above a fire pit. As befitted the League of Inventors, the spit was being turned by some sort of mechanical contraption. Unlike several of the inventions Lukan had seen that afternoon, this one seemed to be operating smoothly, though an attendant stood close by just in case. *Can't have the machine suddenly deciding to launch a roast hog at the cream of the Korslakov society*, Lukan thought. *More's the pity.* He watched as the attendant pulled a lever to stop the spit, then began carving off slices of meat.

"Shall I fetch us some food?" he asked hopefully.

"No," Marni replied, her red eyes scanning the various groups of nobles.

"Fine, I'll just fetch some for myself."

"You will not." She fixed him with her gaze. "I won't have you eating with your hands like a commoner and embarrassing me by getting grease all over your chin." She lifted two glasses of wine from a passing waiter and handed one to Lukan. "Follow me."

Lukan had little choice but to obey, the glass of Parvan Red in his hand a small consolation set against the prospect of an evening spent with Marni and a group of her peers—a group, he noted, that contained Lord Baranov. Somehow, he felt that wasn't a co-incidence. Lukan noted two other familiar faces as they joined the circle: Lord Arima, who gave him a subtle nod in greeting, and Lady Wretzky, who was smoking yet another cigarillo. Lord Baranov made a point of ignoring them.

The aristo who was currently the center of the group's attention didn't notice them arriving at all; he was too busy showing off a crossbow, cradling it as if it was a newborn. ". . . my artisan recommended oak for the body, but I insisted on winterwood," he was purring. "He also advised me against adding the emeralds, but I told him there's no point having a deadly weapon if it doesn't look the part."

"Quite," another man said acidly. "Only, those gems look rather like green garnets to me . . ."

"What? No, they're emeralds. My artisan sourced them himself."

"Isn't your artisan Talassian?"

"Well, yes, but—"

"Never trust a Talassian."

Murmurs of agreement sounded around the group.

"Its range is unmatched by any other crossbow," the aristo blurted, sensing he was losing his audience and whatever respect he'd hoped to gain. "This beauty can hit a target at two hundred yards."

"Really?" said a woman, with the smirk of someone who'd just sensed an opportunity to humiliate a rival. "Perhaps you could demonstrate, Pavel."

"What?" The aristo's eyes widened as he realized the trap he'd walked into. "I, well . . . another time, perhaps." He forced a laugh. "It's rather dark now, after all."

"Nonsense," another lord said. "Try and hit one of those ravens over there." He pointed to a couple of the birds perched on a ledge high above them.

The crossbowman squinted against the gloom. "Those are rooks, not ravens," he replied petulantly, a weak riposte by any standards. "Rooks are smaller."

"Oh, don't be such a bore, Pavel," the lady said, pursing her lips. "Anyway, if you shoot one of them down, we'll find out, won't we? Whether it's a raven or rook."

Words formed on Lukan's tongue—words he knew he shouldn't say. But he was tired and irritable and couldn't quite help himself. *Besides*, he thought, *all the best social gatherings need a bit of scandal.* "Why don't you ask Lord Baranov," he said, affecting nonchalance. "He knows a thing or two about rooks."

Sharp intakes of breath around the circle. A couple of gasps. A variety of did-he-actually-just-say-that expressions. Lukan expected Marni to offer up a half-hearted apology on his behalf, but she wore a smile that suggested the evening had finally borne the fruit she'd been hoping for. *She wanted something like this to happen.* He thought Lady Wretzky might intervene instead, as she had during Radomir's boorish outbursts, but the Iron Dame merely studied him over the glowing cherry of her cigarillo. Lord Arima, too, watched with veiled interest.

The moment stretched.

Baranov's face might as well have been carved from granite, such was his unyielding expression, which gave no hint as to his emotions. Not so his eyes, which burned with anger, and left Lukan in no doubt that he'd pushed the man to the brink. And perhaps that was where he should have left him—or even drawn him back with an apology, some weak patter about how he was merely jesting. But he couldn't bring himself to do it. Because Baranov had tried to have him and Ashra killed. He was a liar and murderer. And in that moment—as Lukan held the man's furious gaze—he only wanted to twist the knife.

"What do you think, Lord Baranov?" Lukan asked casually, gesturing at the birds above them. "Ravens or rooks?"

"I think," Baranov replied in his deep voice, "that you've insulted me one too many times, Lord Gardova." Such was the weight of his voice, and the anger contained in each word, that the lord and lady standing on either side of him stepped away. "First, you accost me in the gardens," he continued, "and make untrue accusations in the presence of my daughter. Now you're doing the same in the presence of my peers. So, I will repeat what I already told you, to put an end to this obsession of yours. I know nothing about the Rook."

"No?" Lukan fired back. "Then why did you have Viktor Zelenko murdered? Why did you frame me and my friends for the crime? Why did you interfere to ensure we didn't even receive a fair trial?"

"You've lost your mind," Baranov said, feigning confusion as he turned to his peers. "I don't have the faintest idea what this madman is talking about."

"On the contrary," Lukan told the group, glancing at the circle of shocked faces, "Lord Baranov knows *everything*. I have letters. Diagrams relating to the construction of the Rook. Because the Rook is a construct. And Baranov *paid* for it."

A stunned silence fell, broken only by the chatter and laughter from other groups of aristos, who remained blissfully unaware that the scandal of the season was unfolding nearby.

"Letter?" Baranov repeated, affecting bafflement. "What letter?"

"The one you kept in your son's bedroom," Lukan replied, wishing now that he'd brought the letter with him. He knew he was playing a dangerous game, but also knew he was in too deep to back out now.

Anger shone in Baranov's eyes. "My son? *You* were in my son's bedroom?"

"Well, I wasn't there myself," Lukan replied, sensing the metaphorical ground shifting beneath him. "But—"

"How dare you." Baranov's voice was quiet but shook with his fury. "How *dare* you."

Lukan was aware of other heads turning in their direction, of a lull falling across the wider gathering. He was also aware that he'd fanned the flames of a fire that was now threatening to rage out of control. "Perhaps," he said, lowering his voice, "we should settle this matter in private."

"We can settle it right now," Baranov snapped, his impassive facade gone as he shrugged off his coat. "And we'll settle it with blood—yours." He looked around the courtyard, which had now fallen entirely silent, save for the musical machine that was now playing an awkwardly upbeat tune. "Let it be known that Lord Gardova has called my reputation into disrepute." His dark eyes, still bright with fury, found Lukan's gaze. "And I challenge him to a duel."

Excited whispers spread through the gathering, but Lukan barely heard them. He was lost in a memory of another time and place.

"Do you accept?" Baranov asked.

Lukan remembered how Giorgio Castori had asked that same question. His condescending tone. The sneer on his lips. He recalled his own response. *Can I finish my wine first?* He felt a strange thrill as they formed on his tongue once more, as if they hadn't wreaked enough havoc the first time round. He felt lightheaded as his mind raced, already running the angles. *Baranov's taller than me, so he'll have a longer reach ... He looks stronger too, but I'll wager I'm faster ... I'm younger too, so he's more likely to tire first ... How good is he with a blade though? That's the question ...*

"Do you accept?" Baranov repeated.

The moment crystalised: suddenly Lukan was aware of Baranov's barely contained fury, and the nervous energy of the crowd. But most of all he became aware of the direction of his own thoughts, and the dangerous current that drove them. That same dark current that seven years ago had borne Giorgio to his death, and Lukan to a vicious cycle of anguish and despair. That had driven him apart from his father, away from Amicia and his home, away from the entire course his life was meant to take.

The rush of blood he'd felt just a moment ago faded. *Seven years of shadows and regret*, he thought, feeling a crushing bitterness. *Seven years, and it seems I've learned nothing at all.*

"Lord Gardova," Baranov asked yet again, a sharp edge to his tone. "Do you accept my challenge?"

"I'll be your second," Lady Marni whispered in his ear, her

breathless excitement suggesting this was what she'd hoped for all along: to not just taunt Baranov, but to see him humiliated in front of their peers. Lukan felt a fool for only now realizing the extent of her scheming. The fact that Marni clearly expected him to best Baranov was little consolation. As she whispered something else in his ear, Lukan caught sight of her father, Lord Volkov, whose murderous expression made it clear he didn't share his daughter's excitement. As their eyes met, Lukan recalled the man's warning: *if you do anything to sully my family's name, I'll ensure you've got another noose round your neck before nightfall.*

Lukan closed his eyes, sensing two paths before him.

Only one could be chosen.

"Builder's blood," Baranov swore. "Lord Gardova, do you *accept*?"

Lukan wanted to. Despite the ruin his previous duel had wrought upon his life, despite the fact that *this* duel could see him dead—at Lord Volkov's hand, if not Baranov's—he wanted to draw steel so very badly. To punish Baranov for his lies and treachery. Just one word was all it would take. One simple word.

Lukan took a deep breath, locked eyes with Baranov.

"No," he replied.

It pained him to say it. Shamed him, almost. It felt like defeat. Submission. But he hadn't forgotten the promise he'd made to himself on the morning of his execution: that, if he somehow survived the day, he would do better.

This was where it started.

A murmur that was equal parts disappointment and disapproval passed through the gathering. "Coward," someone muttered—Dragomir, perhaps. The same word Amicia had spoken to him as Giorgio lay dying. Lukan almost smiled at the irony. *At least this time I'm a coward for doing the right thing.*

"All bark and no bite," Baranov said scornfully. "Do you, then, take back your baseless allegations?"

Lukan bristled, but knew he had no choice. "I do," he replied grudgingly.

"Then I consider this matter concluded." Baranov's gaze flicked to Marni. "I suggest," he said coldly, "you keep your pet on a tighter leash. Perhaps leave him chained up in your outhouse, where he belongs." The man shot a final glare at Lukan, before departing, the crowd parting to let him through. With the drama seemingly over—and the scandal of the season failing to come to fruition—the aristos drifted back to their conversations.

"How disappointing," Marni murmured as her peers melted away. "I was hoping for a demonstration of what my generosity had bought me."

"You just got one," Lukan replied.

"I expected to see the boldness you showed when we played the pyramid, not timidity and weakness. Now I'm wondering whether I should have left you to hang from that rope after all."

Weakness? Lukan thought, smiling wryly. It had taken every ounce of strength he had to turn down Baranov's challenge.

"What's so funny?" Marni asked, her red eyes narrowing.

"Nothing," he replied. "You've no need to worry. I'll repay the favor."

"Debt," Marni corrected.

"Call it what you want."

"I will. And you'd better repay it, otherwise—"

"Gallows. Rope. I know."

"Good." Marni's gaze swept the courtyard. "Enough frivolity for one night, I think," she said, her lips thinning. "Come. My carriage awaits."

Lukan breathed a sigh of relief, feeling the weight of countless stares on his back as they departed.

"Why did you not accept Grigor's challenge?" Marni asked, as her carriage bore them through the wide avenues of the Mantle. Her eyes were blood red in the light of the alchemical globe, and Lukan fancied, if her voice possessed a color in that moment, it would have been the same.

"You heard what your father told me about not sullying your family name," he replied, lightly. "I didn't fancy calling his bluff."

"Don't pretend this is about my father. Besides, you wouldn't have sullied our family's name if you'd won the duel. Quite the opposite. So, why did you refuse the challenge?"

"Because . . ." Lukan looked out of the window, watching the darkened estates pass by—walls and gates and flashes of purple fire.

"*Because*?" Marni echoed, her voice sharp enough to peel an apple.

"Because I fought a duel before," Lukan replied, finally meeting her bloody gaze. "It was the worst mistake I ever made. I have no wish to make the same mistake again."

"You don't think you would have beaten *Grigor*? The man's twice your age!"

"It's not about winning. I won the last time, and lost everything."

"Oh, don't be so dramatic. It would only have been to first blood. Were you afraid?"

"No."

"Then what stayed your hand?"

"Fear of a path I don't want to tread."

"Don't mistake the reason I plucked you from the gallows," Marni said icily, glancing out the window. "It wasn't out of charity. I saved your life because I remembered your wit and courage. Because I thought that you could be useful to me." Her red gaze snapped back to him, pinning him to the velvet cushions. "Now I'm starting to wonder if you're really up to the task I would demand of you."

"I'm wondering the same thing," Lukan retorted, "because you've *still* not bloody told me what it actually is."

"That's better," Marni said, a flicker of a smile thawing her features. "I knew that fire was in there somewhere. You'll need plenty of that where you'll be going."

"And where's that?"

"I'll explain tomorrow. Be at my townhouse, at the tenth bell of the morning. Unless . . ." She tilted her head, red eyes glinting. "Perhaps you'd like to join me for dinner? You could even stay the night . . ." She ran a red tongue across ruby lips. "Make up for disappointing me earlier."

Lukan hated the thrill that surged through him, hated how much he wanted to say yes. Despite Marni's controlling nature, and her petty vindictiveness, he couldn't deny her beauty. Already his mind was rushing to justify this course of action—that it made sense to keep her happy, that he deserved a little pleasure after everything he'd been through. Just a few days ago he'd have agreed without a second thought. But that was before he'd stared his own death in the face. Before he'd judged his own life and character, and found them both wanting.

"I think . . ." He paused, the words sticking in his throat, as if his own voice was trying to betray him. "I think it's best if I return to my friends."

Marni's eyes seemed to turn a deeper shade of red. "I could *make* you, you know."

"I know."

She stared at him for a long moment. "Fine," she said eventually, sitting back and studying her red nails with feigned indifference. "My townhouse at the tenth bell. Don't be late."

They passed the rest of the journey in silence.

18

Some Sort of Monster

"Stop pacing."

Those were the first words Ashra had spoken since they'd arrived at the Volkovs' family home. Previously, she'd let her expression do the talking: a narrowing of her eyes at the extravagance of the townhouse, followed by a curl of her lip that only grew more pronounced as they were ushered through its plush interior. By the time the silent butler deposited them in Marni's personal solar, Ashra's expression could've drawn blood at a hundred paces. *Perhaps that's why the butler departed so quickly*, Lukan mused.

"You know I do this when I'm nervous," he replied, turning to face the thief, who remained standing in a corner of the room, as if distrustful of the fancy furnishings.

"Why are you nervous?"

"Why am I . . . isn't it obvious?" He started pacing again. "We're about to find out what task Marni's got planned for us, and all I can promise you is that it won't be good." He paused, feigned a thoughtful expression. "Did I miss anything out—oh, and, if we refuse, we'll find ourselves back on the gallows." He threw a hand at the thief. "Why are you *not* nervous?"

"Because it's pointless worrying about something that hasn't happened," Flea piped up, from where she was lounging across a chair, one leg up on the armrest.

"Well said, *majin*," Ashra replied.

"And when it *does* happen?" Lukan asked.

"Then we'll deal with it." Ashra shrugged. "Whatever it is."

"Well, we'll find that out soon enough," Lukan muttered, glancing at the gilded clock on the mantlepiece. *Nearly the eleventh bell. Marni's almost an hour late.* He huffed out a breath. "She's keeping us waiting on purpose," he said.

"I know," Ashra replied. "I'm starting to understand these games you aristos play. Words as weapons. Influence as currency."

"Sounds stupid," Flea put in.

"You're not wrong," Lukan admitted. "But Marni's influence is the only thing keeping us alive at the moment, so best keep your opinions to yourself."

Muffled footsteps sounded beyond the door. Lukan glanced at Flea and gestured for her to sit properly. The girl scowled as she adjusted her position, knocking a cushion to the floor just as the door to the solar creaked open.

"Lady Marni," the butler announced, before withdrawing. The woman herself strolled through, resplendent in a flowing scarlet dress, assorted garnets and rubies and red diamonds gleaming at her fingers and throat. "So kind of you to wait," Marni purred, her red eyes flitting across them. "But if you'd taken me up on my offer last night, Lukan, you wouldn't have had to wait at all, would you?"

Lukan ignored the glances that came his way.

"Ah, you brought your little friend." Marni's eyes flicked from Flea to the fallen cushion. "What a delight. How sharp is your tongue today, hmm?"

"Sharp enough," Flea shot back. "And my name's Flea."

"Indeed. A fitting name it is, too."

Flea opened her mouth to reply, only to fall silent as Lukan furiously made a slicing gesture across his own neck. Instead she glared as Marni settled onto one of the sofas, but the aristo's gaze had already moved elsewhere.

"Do sit," Marni said, waving a jeweled hand at the sofa opposite.

Lukan obliged, though Ashra only did likewise after Lukan shot her a *please do as she says* look. Even then, the thief sat as lightly as she could.

"So," Lady Marni said, clasping her hands, a knowing smile on her lips that made Lukan uncomfortable. "What do you know of Ashgrave?"

"Ashgrave," Lukan echoed, already fearing the direction the discussion was moving in. "That's not the conversation opener I was hoping for."

"Oh? And what *were* you hoping for?"

"You announcing that, in a fit of sudden generosity, you've decided to dispense with the debt we owe you." Lukan shrugged. "Admittedly that would be at the more optimistic end of the spectrum. At the other end, I don't know . . . 'Would you like some coffee and a cinnamon pastry before we get started' would have been perfectly acceptable."

"There was a sickness," Ashra said pointedly, straight to business as always. "Nearly twenty years ago. It spread quickly. They had to burn bodies on pyres."

"And the authorities panicked," Lukan said, recalling the story that Grabulli had told them on their voyage from Saphrona. "They barricaded the streets and walled off the entire district to stop the spread of the disease. Thousands of people were trapped inside and condemned to death. The place has been abandoned ever since." He shrugged. "That's what we were told, anyway."

"Grabulli said it was haunted," Flea piped up. "He said no one goes there now because it's full of monsters."

"Grabulli's a braggart and a liar," Lukan replied dismissively. "He was just telling tales . . ." He fell silent at the look of amusement on Marni's face. "Lady's mercy," he muttered, "don't tell me he was telling the truth."

"He was," Marni replied.

"So it *is* haunted?" Flea asked, eyes wide with excitement. "By ghosts?"

"Not ghosts. Something far worse."

"Like what?" Ashra asked.

Marni met the thief's gaze and held it for a few moments, as if to remind her who was in control. "We'll get to that," she said eventually.

"If you're going to ask us to go into Ashgrave," Ashra replied, unfazed, "then we need to know what we're up against."

"*Ask* you?" Marni replied. "I'm not *asking* anything. You owe me a debt."

"One we haven't forgotten," Lukan interjected, as the two women stared at each other. "The last time I was here you mentioned a corpse you wanted us to find. I'm assuming it's somewhere in Ashgrave?"

"It is." Marni turned her attention to him. "Though I imagine she's a skeleton now. The poor woman's been there for some time."

"Then how are we supposed to find her? If thousands of people died there, the place will be full of skeletons."

"I know where this woman was staying when the madness unfolded. There's good reason to believe she's still there. And that she still has the object I seek."

"Which is?"

"A scroll that contains an alchemical formula."

"A formula? What for?"

"That's none of your concern. All you need to do is retrieve it for me."

"So you're asking us to find one skeleton among thousands, in a part of the city that's haunted by something you've declined to explain." Lukan rubbed his jaw. "You're not exactly selling it to me."

"I don't need to sell it."

"No, of course not. The debt, and all that." He sighed and gestured between himself and Ashra. "Why us? Aside from the fact that we owe you."

"Because despite the weakness you showed yesterday," Marni replied, "I still remember the qualities you showed when we played the pyramid. Bravery in the face of danger. Determination to beat the odds. Qualities few truly have. The same qualities this task requires."

"I didn't play the pyramid," Ashra pointed out.

"No," Marni replied, lips pursing. "But you snuck in and out of Grigor's townhouse without being caught. Besides, the Sparks showed me the tools they confiscated from you. Lockpicks and all manner of curios. The tools of a professional thief. I can't think of anyone more suited to my task." She gave a light shrug. "Besides, I have no one left to ask."

"We're not the first," Lukan prompted, the realization striking him like a punch to his gut. "You've sent others into Ashgrave."

"Yes."

"They're dead."

"Yes."

Wonderful, he thought, a sense of dread stealing over him. *Still, there's one positive side to all this.* "So, if we retrieve this scroll for you," he ventured, "that'll settle our debt?"

"It will."

"And if we refuse . . ."

"It's back to the gallows with you."

Lukan searched for a trace of humor in Marni's red eyes, in her voice, but there was none. *She's deadly serious.* He turned to Ashra. The thief's face was impassive as always, but she met his gaze and shrugged as if to say *what choice do we have?* "Fine," he said, turning back to Marni. "We'll do it."

"But you need to tell us everything," Ashra cut in, fearlessly holding Marni's gaze. "Every detail, no matter how small. We need to know exactly what happened all those years ago. What caused the plague. How we get into Ashgrave and how we get out. Where this skeleton is and how we'll recognize it."

"And the monsters," Flea piped up. "We need to know about them."

"Yes." Ashra's expression hardened. "Them most of all."

Lukan expected Marni to react poorly to such demands, so was surprised when she merely nodded. "Very well," she replied, with a smile that immediately put him on edge. "But it's better I show you." She picked up a silver bell and shook it, the high-pitched chimes carrying across the room. A servant appeared in the doorway and bowed. "Bring the woman," Marni commanded. The servant bowed again and disappeared.

"It's hard to find survivors," Marni continued. "Few made it past the barricades. But some did."

The servant reappeared, escorting a woman into the room. The latter walked with her head bowed, shoulders stooped. Age had left its mark on her, hollowing out her cheeks and carving lines across her skin. She was shown to a chaise, which she perched on, clasping her gnarled hands, her plain, patched-up dress incongruous against the red velvet. The woman kept her gaze lowered but stole a quick glance at them, in the manner of a frightened animal, and as their eyes briefly met Lukan saw a glimmer of youth in her blue eyes. *She's not as old as she looks*, he realized.

"That will be all," Marni said to the servant, who bowed and departed. "Now," she said, turning her attention to the newcomer, who shrank beneath Marni's red gaze. "Nika—it *was* Nika, wasn't it?"

"Yes." The woman's voice was barely above a whisper.

"Yes, *my lady*," Marni corrected, as she picked up a hinged case of polished wood from a nearby table. "Now, I want you to show my guests here exactly what you showed me. Can you do that?"

"Yes, my lady."

"Excellent." Marni opened the case, revealing what looked like two silver circlets, nestled among folds of silk. Both bore dark gems set in their centers. Gently Marni picked one up and offered it to Nika. "You know what to do."

The woman took the circlet with trembling hands and placed it on her head.

"Now," Marni said, glancing between Lukan and Ashra. "Who would like to go first?"

"To do what?" Lukan asked.

"To see Nika's memories of the plague." Marni smiled as Lukan and Ashra exchanged glances. "These are Phaeron artifacts," she continued, running a finger along the curved edge of the circlet in her hands. "They allow us to experience each other's memories as if they were our own. As if we had lived those experiences ourselves." Reverence shone in her red eyes. "Incredible, don't you think? These are the only pair we've ever found."

"*We* being this cult you belong to?" Lukan asked. "The Scarlet Throne?"

"Cult? The Scarlet Throne is no cult. Not that it's any of your concern." Marni held out the circlet. "Who will go first?"

"I will," Flea said, reaching out.

"Not you."

The girl huffed and flicked her little finger.

"Let me," Lukan said quickly, before Marni could notice the insult. He reached out and took the circlet, noting the bluish sheen of the metal alloy, and the sleek, flawless craftsmanship that characterized all Phaeron-made objects. "So how does this work?" he asked, feeling a flicker of anxiety as he placed the object on his head. His previous experiences with Phaeron artifacts hadn't exactly left him desperate for more.

"You'll see," Marni replied. "Nika, start at the beginning. Leave nothing out."

"Yes, my lady." Nika closed her eyes. A moment later her circlet's gem flared with a turquoise light.

Just like Ashra's rings, Lukan thought, wondering if his own gem was shining in response. He inhaled sharply as he felt a sudden sensation, almost like a weight, inside his head. *Is that Nika's mind joining with mine?* He was immediately reminded of when the Wolf had done the same, but this felt different somehow. *Like a connection, rather than an invasion.* His gasped, his heart racing, as the room around him, and everyone in it, faded to black. Suddenly he was falling, as if in a dream; he tried to cry out, but couldn't find his voice. There was nothing but darkness, all around him.

And then:

A woman lying tangled in bedsheets, her eyes wide and vacant, black veins—tendrils—spreading across her body like ink beneath waxlike skin. Lukan reached out with a hand—not his hand, but a child's—to touch the woman, only for a man to haul him away. The man placed hands on his—her?—shoulders and said something that carried a hint of reassurance—it'll be all right, we'll be all right—but his eyes were brimming with tears and a black tendril was already working its way across his cheek—

A cobbled street covered in piles of burning bodies, funeral pyres, black smoke rising and blocking out the sun. Men and women with rags tied around their faces dragging bodies—some of them very small—and throwing them onto the corpse mounds. Parents watching children burn. Children watching parents burn. Screaming, Lukan was screaming—

Men in uniforms the colors of fire—Sparks—shouting and waving swords. Lukan tried to dart round one of them but the man was quick; a powerful arm wrapped round his shoulders and threw him to the cobbles. Pain flashed in his side. The man loomed over him, a figure of authority, yet his eyes were wide with panic. Spittle flew from his mouth as he shouted something. Get back. Other sparks stood nearby, a line of them across the street, guarding the golems that worked behind them. Lukan squinted through the press of bodies and the smoke of a nearby fire. A wall. The golems were building a wall—

Night. No moon, but the light of the fires bathed the streets in a hellish glow. It wasn't just the bodies that burned now. Screams carried on the wind. Crying. Laughter—frenzied, hysterical. Hunger clawed at Lukan's belly as he crept down the street, keeping to the shadows. He almost tripped over a body—a man, his skull shattered, hair matted with blood. Another scream—closer, this time— drew his attention: a woman fleeing across the street, pursued by a man. They disappeared into an alley. The screaming stopped. Hunger roiled in Lukan's belly again, so strongly he almost collapsed—

Shivering, but not from the cold. He could barely breathe for the fear that gripped him. Maybe that was for the best; if he didn't breathe, the thing wouldn't hear him. Even from inside the wardrobe where he hid, Lukan could hear the monster moving around downstairs. He hoped Artem was all right. If he wasn't . . . A soft moan escaped his lips as he heard the stairs creaking. It was coming. It was going to find him. The window, he thought desperately. It was his only hope. He slipped out of the cupboard, crept across the bedroom and reached for the latch—only to whirl in panic at the sound of a hiss behind him. The monster stood just beyond the bedroom door, swathed in shadow. Slowly it stepped forward, its clawed feet clicking on the floor. Lukan turned back to the window and struggled with the latch. It seemed frozen in place. He screamed as he heard the monster behind him, closed his eyes as he waited for its talons to tear into him, its forked tongue to flicker over his face. A cry split the air, followed by a thump as something hit the floor. Lukan dared a look—and saw Artem straddling the monster's back, the creature thrashing beneath him. Go, the blacksmith's apprentice shouted, his eyes wide with terror. Run.

Lukan ran.

The memory blurred, as if being stretched at the seams, and once again he felt the sensation of falling—

He jolted, eyes snapping open, his breathing quick and ragged. The first eyes he found were Flea's, which were wide with concern.

"Are you all right?" she asked.

"Fine," he replied, his voice barely above a whisper.

The same couldn't be said for Nika. The woman sat with her face buried in her hands, shoulders heaving as she sobbed, the circlet askew on her brow. *She was just a child*, Lukan thought, feeling a deep swell of pity. *How many times has she been forced to relive these memories?*

"Compose yourself," Marni told Nika, her lips a thin line of disapproval. "Think of the coin I promised you." Her words had the desired effect; Nika lowered her hands and tried to sit up straight, blinking away her tears. "That's better." Marni looked at Ashra. "Your turn."

"No," Lukan replied, removing the circlet from his brow. "We've seen enough. I don't want her"—he nodded at Nika—"to have to relive that again just for our sake."

"I thought you wanted to know everything," Marni said, her voice edged with displeasure. She looked at Ashra. "Don't you want to see what awaits you?"

"It was like a scene from the hells," Lukan said, before the thief could reply. "Fire. Death. Misery. Hunger. And then I"—he paused, then gestured at Nika—"*she*, was chased by something that I can't even begin to describe. Some sort of monster." He looked at Marni, who remained silent, her red gaze holding his. "What was that thing?" he asked. "Are there more of them?"

"No one knows," she replied, with a nonchalant shrug. "Because no one ever comes back."

"We'll come back," Flea said, sticking her chin out.

Lukan wished he shared the girl's confidence. He turned to Ashra and held out the circlet. "See for yourself, if you really want, but . . ."

Ashra eyed the circlet, her gaze flicking to Nika. The silent plea in the woman's eyes was unmistakable. "I'll take your word for it," the thief replied.

Nika sagged with relief as Lukan offered the circlet back to Marni. *The anguish it must cause her*, Lukan thought, glancing at the woman. *The pain she must feel, having to relive these memories over and over again.*

"As you wish," Marni replied, her tone indifferent. She leaned over and plucked Nika's circlet from her brow. "You can go," she said, with a dismissive flick of her fingers. "But since your memories were only required once, I will only pay you half the amount we agreed."

Nika's eyes widened, her mouth opening in protest, but she knew better than to voice her objections. Instead she nodded meekly, eyes downcast.

Lady's mercy. In trying to save her from her own anguish, all Lukan had managed to do was make her coin purse lighter. *And by the looks of it, she needs every coin she can get. Must have been hard, losing everything at such a young age. Having to rebuild your entire life.* He noticed Nika's hands then, her fingers red as if the skin had been scourged over and over again. *A laundress*, he thought. *Hours spent stooped over a tub, scrubbing at some fancy prick's clothes until her fingers are raw . . .*

"Pay her the full amount," he said.

Marni gave him a venomous look. "How strange," she said, with feigned surprise. "I could have sworn you just gave me an order." Her eyes narrowed. "The woman who holds your life in her hands."

"Not an order," he replied, raising a hand. "Merely a request."

"You're in no position to demand things of me."

"Did Nika cry like that when she showed you her memories?"

he asked, careful to keep his tone even. Marni's silence told him that she had. "You've seen what it costs her," he continued. "How much it pains her. Please pay her the full amount. It's the least she deserves after what she's been through."

"Such insolence." Marni's lips were a thin red line. "Perhaps I should just send you back to the gallows."

"Do that and you won't get your scroll," Ashra replied, rising from her seat. "You've already admitted your other attempts have failed. We are your only chance."

"I can find others," Marni replied icily. "You're not nearly as indispensable as you think."

"Ashra's the best thief in the Old Empire," Lukan said evenly, aware of the tightrope they were walking. "Flea is one of the best shots with a crossbow I've ever seen—"

"*One* of the best?" the girl interrupted, scowling at him.

"And I . . ." He paused, uncertain of what to say. How could he even begin to describe himself?

The moment stretched.

"You're an idiot," Flea offered. "But very brave."

"Agreed," Ashra said, a flicker of amusement in her eyes as she caught Lukan's gaze.

Lukan grinned and turned back to Marni. "What they said. We can get this scroll for you. But not if we're hanging from the gallows. Your choice."

Marni remained silent, but the anger in her eyes was unmistakable. For a moment Lukan wondered if they'd pushed it too far. But then Marni sighed, and gestured dismissively, as if bored of the entire exchange. "Very well," she said. "Nika shall have her money. I care not."

"Thank you, my lady," Nika whispered, clasping her hands.

"Get out," Marni replied.

As Nika rose, her eyes passed over Lukan and Ashra, and she gave them a grateful nod that caused Marni's jaw to clench. She waited until the woman had gone before speaking again.

"Let us be clear," she said, the ice in her voice a counterpoint to the fire in her eyes, "that, if you talk to me like that again, I *will* send you back to the gallows. Compassion is a weakness, and weakness isn't something you can afford in Ashgrave."

"Speaking of which," Lukan said, relieved to return to the matter at hand, "how do we get into the district? Are the walls they built still standing?"

"Of course they are. And they're all guarded, as entry into Ashgrave is forbidden. So one of my men will row you across the Kolva. The river is also watched, but one of the captains has proven amenable to a bribe. He and his patrol will look the other way. Their shift starts at midnight and ends at the sixth bell the following morning, so you have six hours to get in and out. My man will wait for you to row you back."

"And if we're not back in time?"

"You'll find my man gone and yourselves stranded." Marni smiled coldly. "So best not linger."

"Best not," Lukan agreed, sharing a look with Ashra. *If we get desperate, we can always use the Rings of Last Resort.* But that would mean leaving Flea at Razin's, and, judging by the glare the girl was now giving him, that wasn't something she would readily accept.

"When do we go?" he asked, turning back to Marni.

"Tomorrow night. My man will be waiting for you at the pier behind the Sacred Suckling Pigs tavern."

"And this woman? The dead one, I mean. Where will we find her?"

"She was staying at an inn called the Joyous Brewer of a Thousand Barrels, near the heart of the district. I have a map with the inn's location marked on it."

"How do you know she's still there?" Lukan asked, recalling the chaos of Nika's memories. "If she tried to flee, her body could be anywhere—she could have ended up on one of those pyres, for all you know."

"Don't presume to question what I know," Marni replied sharply, her piercing red eyes holding Lukan's own. "I have strong reason to believe you will find her at the inn."

"Fine," Lukan conceded, certain he wasn't being told everything. "But if others were sheltering there too, there could be dozens of skeletons. A hundred, even. How will we know which is hers?"

"Because she'll be the only one holding a scroll with an alchemical formula written on it." Marni shook her head in mock pity. "Honestly, Lukan, sometimes I wonder if there's anything going on in that pretty head of yours."

"All I'm saying," Lukan replied tightly, "is that it could take time to search through whatever bodies are there—time we can ill afford. And it's going to be dark, and there's . . ." He trailed off, remembering the monster from Nika's memory. "*Things* out there. The faster we find this woman, the more likely it is that her scroll ends up in your hands." *And the better chance we have of getting out alive.*

Marni's silence suggested her acceptance that he had a point. "The woman you're looking for was an alchemist," she said eventually, her tone cautious, as if choosing her words carefully. "It's likely she was wearing the uniform of the Tower."

"Blue and purple robes," Lukan mused.

"Likely no more than rags now," Ashra replied.

He shrugged. "It's something."

"When you return," Marni said, "there will be a carriage waiting for you. My man will tell you its location. You are to head there as soon as you're off that boat. I don't want any dawdling." She leaned closer, her gaze intense. "And do not show the formula to anyone, you understand? Not to the boatman. Not to the carriage driver. No one."

"Understood."

"Good. I suggest you be about your preparations," Marni continued. "Study the map I'll give you. Buy whatever equipment you might need. I will cover the cost, but do *not* test my patience with frivolous purchases." She rose from her sofa. "You disappointed me yesterday, Lukan. Do not do so again."

With those words, she disappeared in a swirl of silk.

19

ROOM FOR IMPROVEMENT

"What did the monster look like?"

Lukan took a sip of his wine and stared into the fire, pretending he hadn't heard Ashra's question. Hoping that she might not ask again. *Fat chance of that.* The thief had been angling for this conversation ever since they'd left Marni's townhouse, the question shadowed in her eyes even if it never found its way to her lips. Her reluctance to broach the topic in front of Flea had given Lukan a stay of execution, as had the couple of hours they'd spent in Emberfall, where they'd poked around the various artificers' stalls and workshops in the shadow of the alchemists' tower. Lukan had purchased a sleek new sword (which he was determined not to lose), while Flea disappeared and returned a while later with a wide grin and a quiver of crossbow bolts.

Once they were back at Razin's, though, there was no avoiding the question.

"Lukan," Ashra prompted. "What did you see?"

"Chaos," he replied. "Madness. A nightmare."

"You know what I mean. At the end. You said—"

"I know what I said." He pictured it again, that image he'd spent all afternoon trying not to think of: the shadow beyond the door, skulking into the light. That face. Those eyes. "I'm not sure what I saw," he said truthfully, forcing the image away by focusing on the flames. "Only that it wasn't human. It stood like a person. Moved like one. But it wasn't. It was something else. Something . . . I don't know. Look, maybe Nika's memory was wrong. Perhaps I didn't see what she really saw, but what she *thinks* she saw."

"Do you believe that?"

Lukan recalled the fear in Nika's eyes. Her tears. "No," he admitted. "But if we're lucky, we'll never find out. Let's just hope we can get in, find this formula and get out again before whatever's lurking in that place realizes we're there."

"And by *we* you mean . . ."

"You and me."

"You mean to leave Flea behind?" Ashra didn't say *again* but Lukan could hear the accusation in her voice.

"I don't want to," he said. "Look, you're right about Flea: I don't need to protect her, and it's not my place to make her decisions for her. If she wants to come with us, I'd accept that—hells, I'd be glad of it. Lady knows we could use her sharp eyes and that crossbow of hers. But we also need to be able to use your rings if things get messy, and we can't summon that portal if Flea's with us. She needs to stay behind."

"Not if I give the second ring to Razin."

"Razin?" Lukan repeated, surprised. He imagined Razin snoring in front of the fireplace as Ashra's ring pulsed desperately on a side table.

"And Timur," Ashra replied, as if sensing his thoughts.

"You'd trust them with it? With your secret?"

"I'd rather not. But I think we need Flea with us."

"We don't need to tell them what your rings do," Lukan suggested, keeping his voice low. "Only what to do if the one they have starts glowing."

"Exactly."

"Though they'll figure it out once a bloody portal appears."

"True. But it'll be too late for Razin to pawn it by then."

"Lady's blood, was that a *joke*?" Lukan asked. He thought he saw a smile ghost across Ashra's face. Maybe it was just a trick of the firelight. "Fine," he said, swilling the wine in his glass. "So, Flea comes with us, then. If she wants."

"I do."

Lukan turned to find Flea sitting on a chair behind him. "Seven shadows," he muttered, "how long have you been there?"

The girl shrugged. "Long enough."

Lukan looked at Ashra. "And you knew she was there?"

"Of course," the thief replied.

"Great." He drained the rest of his wine and set his glass on the mantlepiece. "I'd say you two were thick as thieves, but that would be stating the obvious."

"Did you mean it?" Flea demanded. "When you said you'd be glad if I came with you?"

"Yes," he said truthfully. "But if you preferred to stay behind—"

"I'm coming." Flea turned and left the room, calling for Ivan as she went. The wolfhound bounded after her, tail wagging.

"Guess that's settled then," Lukan said to Ashra. "You ought to speak to Razin and Timur about the rings."

A sharp rap at the front door echoed down the hallway. Ivan started barking in response. "Gods damn it, Ivan," Razin shouted as he stomped through the house. "Get back! I said get *back* . . ."

Lukan heard a squeal of hinges as Razin opened the front door. He couldn't make out the exchange that followed, but he thought he heard surprise in the general's voice. The hinges squealed again as the door closed and two pairs of footsteps echoed down the hallway, heading toward the living room.

"Looks like we have a guest," Lukan murmured.

"Marni?" Ashra questioned.

"No. She would make us go to her if she wanted to talk."

The living room door opened and Razin entered. "Lord Arima to see you," he said, giving them a meaningful look. The young lord entered the room, wrapped in a sable cloak trimmed with white fur.

"Good evening, Lord Gardova," he said, offering Lukan a respectful bow. "I do hope I'm not intruding."

"Not at all," Lukan replied, masking his surprise.

"I'll have Timur take your cloak," Razin said, turning for the door.

"No need, General," Arima replied. "I won't be staying long.

A quick word with your guests is all I require, and then I'll be on my way."

"As you wish," Razin replied.

Arima cleared his throat. "In private, General. If you don't mind."

Razin's face creased into a frown, and for a moment Lukan thought he was going to object, but the general's respect for authority won out over any disgruntlement he felt at being ordered out of his own living room. "Of course," he said gruffly, backing out of the room and closing the door with a little more force than necessary. Arima showed no concern at the general's annoyance.

"You must be Ashra," he said, offering her a bow. "A pleasure, my lady."

"I'm no lady."

"No, I suppose not," Arima said, with a knowing smile. "You're a thief. And a very good one at that, given how easily you slipped in and out of Lord Baranov's estate."

Ashra glanced at Lukan, a question in her eyes: *how does he know?*

"Speaking of which," Arima continued, turning to Lukan, "do you happen to have that drawing you mentioned yesterday, Lord Gardova? The one of the Rook? I would very much like to see it." There was no mocking edge to Arima's voice, no satisfaction at a card being played—his interest, as far as Lukan could tell, was genuine.

Even so, Lukan thought, catching Ashra's subtle head-shake, *best to tread carefully. Until we know what he wants, at least.* "With respect, Lord Arima, I wonder if we might discuss the business that brings you here."

"Of course." The man adjusted his weight, leaning heavily on his cane.

"Would you care to sit?"

"No, thank you. As I told the general, I won't keep you long." He glanced between them, a conspiratorial smile on his lips. "I'm here because I have a proposal for you."

"We're not for hire," Ashra replied. "Just as well you didn't bother to sit."

Arima laughed. "And yet," he said, unruffled by Ashra's lack of decorum, "you're working for Lady Marni."

"Not out of choice," Lukan offered. "We owe her a debt." He gave Arima a knowing smile of his own. "But I'll wager you already knew that."

"I did," the man confessed, with a slight dip of his head. "Just as I know that tomorrow night you'll be venturing into a part of the city where you *really* shouldn't be going, to search for a skeleton with a scroll." He wetted his lips. "A scroll with a certain alchemical formula on it."

"How do you know all this?" Ashra asked.

"Because he's an aristocrat," Lukan said. "And if there's one thing aristocrats love as much as wealth, it's power. And power often comes from knowing your rivals' secrets—am I right, Lord Arima?"

"An astute observation, Lord Gardova."

"If you two are done blowing kisses at each other," Ashra said sharply, "let's cut to the bone." She eyed Arima. "What is your proposal?"

"He wants the scroll," Lukan offered.

"Obviously," Ashra replied, not taking her eyes off the aristocrat. "What I want to know is what he's offering us in return."

"Information," Arima replied.

"About what?"

"The Rook," Lukan murmured, reading the knowing gleam in the aristocrat's eyes. He felt a flicker of excitement but forced it down. *Mustn't look too eager.* "What do you know of it?" he asked, affecting casualness.

"Me?" Arima shook his head. "Nothing. But you seem to think that Lord Baranov knows a great deal." He smiled and placed a hand on his chest. "And I can make him talk."

"How?"

"Let's just say I have . . . leverage on Lord Baranov."

"He owes you money," Lukan guessed.

Arima waved the statement away. "The details don't matter. All you need to know is that, if Baranov knows anything about the Rook, I can force him to reveal his secrets." He raised a finger. "But only if you bring this scroll to me, instead of Lady Marni."

"An interesting proposition," Lukan replied evenly, scarcely able to believe his luck. He'd been starting to doubt he'd ever get his key back. Now, this fool's errand that Marni was sending them on might just give him the chance he needed. "There's just one issue," he continued, his enthusiasm fading.

"Marni will send you straight back to the gallows."

"Worse, I imagine. She was very clear that we weren't to show the scroll to anyone. If she learns we've given it to one of her peers . . ." Lukan trailed off, not wanting to consider what manner of death Marni might devise for them. "Could you protect us?"

"From Marni?" Arima's expression was pained. "No. Few can challenge the power of the Volkovs."

"There has to be a way," Lukan murmured, his mind racing through the implications.

"Forget it, Lukan," Ashra urged. "Baranov's information is useless to us if we're hanging from a rope."

"Come now," Arima replied, seeming almost nervous with the direction the conversation was heading. "I'm sure there's a solution to be found to this minor inconvenience."

"Inconvenience?" Ashra echoed, her eyes narrowing. "You're asking us to risk our lives. But what do you care, as long as you get what you want?" She curled her lip. "You're just like any other aristo. Happy to sacrifice the lives of others to get what you want."

"You know nothing of me!" Arima snapped, eyes bright with anger as he stepped toward Ashra. The thief didn't move, didn't so much as blink. "You know nothing," he repeated, though he seemed suddenly chastened. "I—I'm sorry," he mumbled. "I didn't mean to lose my temper."

"No harm done, Lord Arima," Lukan said quickly. "And perhaps you're right that there is a way around this. A way to turn what Marni asks of us to our advantage."

"She'll see us dead," Ashra replied.

"Not necessarily," Lukan replied, the faint stirrings of an idea forming in his mind. He almost didn't want to probe them, lest they broke apart.

"What does that mean?"

Lukan gave her a look that said *I'll explain later.* "This scroll," he said, finding Arima's gaze once more. "Marni told us there's an alchemical formula on it, but not what the formula actually is." He paused meaningfully. "Will you?"

"No," Arima replied, with a rueful shake of his head. "I'm afraid that must remain a secret—for now, at least. But I can tell you *why* I want it."

"Go on."

"Lord Gardova, you were at the Inventors' Parade yesterday. Tell me, what was your impression of the regard that my peers feel for me? Did you feel they hold me in high esteem?"

"Not exactly," Lukan admitted, recalling the sneers directed at Arima when he'd expressed interest in the entrapment circle. "I'd say there's room for improvement."

"Room for improvement," Arima repeated, with a humorless smile. "Yes, that about sums it up." His expression darkened. "Ten generations," he continued, a sudden bitterness in his voice. "That's how long my family has been in Korslakov. We've helped the city prosper. Even shed our blood for it—one of my ancestors died in a war against the clans. But because of this"—he gestured at his face, the unmistakable bronze skin that revealed his eastern ancestry—"we've never been fully accepted. We've always been outsiders, always regarded as somehow lesser than everyone else. I aim to change that. To finally earn the respect that my family has been owed for so long. To prove that we belong here."

"And the formula will help you do that?" Lukan asked. "How?"

"You'll see." Arima smiled. "Everyone will see. All you need to do is give the scroll to me."

"So, this is about power," Ashra said scornfully. "You'd have us risk our lives just so you can earn some respect."

"Builder's blood, were you not listening to me?" Arima took a breath, trying to compose himself. "I apologize again," he said, his voice even once more. "I'm not an unreasonable man, no matter what you might think. I understand the risks I'm asking you to take. Give me the formula and I will provide you with a letter. When you present it to Baranov, he will have no choice but to reveal what he knows about the Rook. On top of that, I'll do whatever I can to help you retrieve your key. How does that sound?"

"Tempting," Lukan admitted, doing his best to ignore the fierce glare Ashra was giving him. "But all I can promise"—he glanced at the thief, as if to say *I hear you*—"is that we'll consider your proposal."

"I understand," Arima said, bowing his head. "That's all I ask. When the time comes, I hope you'll realize that I can offer you much more than Lady Marni." He bowed to them both in turn. "Now, I've taken up enough of your time. I'll see myself out."

With those words, he made for the door, unheeding—or perhaps not—of the daggers that Ashra was glaring at his back.

"You have a plan," she said, once the man was gone. Her tone was almost accusing. "What is it?"

"It's not a plan. Not yet." Lukan bit his lip. "More like a faint idea."

"Whatever it is," the thief said, "we need to be sharp." She glanced back at the door as Ivan started barking in the hallway beyond. "I don't trust him."

"Do you trust Marni?"

"No."

"So, who do you trust when you can't trust anyone?"

"Yourself."

"Exactly." Lukan smiled. "So, let's do that and see where it takes us."

20

ASHGRAVE

The boat was waiting for them where Marni had promised.

Ashra saw it first, her enhanced eyesight revealing the shape of the boat, barely visible against the blackness of the water, and the hunched shape of the man who sat within. The noise of the tavern—shouting, laughter, the strains of a fiddle and the low thump of a drum—accompanied the three of them as they stole down its flank to the jetty at its rear. Ashra wasn't one for taverns, or for drinking, but in that moment both seemed preferable to the task that the night held in store for them. As they took the stone steps down to the pier, Ashra looked across the river toward Ashgrave, but a fog had settled over the water, and not even she could see through it. Perhaps that was for the best.

"Damned fog," Lukan muttered, for no obvious reason other than to have something to say. He'd talked all the way to the tavern, spinning a series of jokes and anecdotes, but Ashra could sense the nerves that lurked beneath his words. Flea's fear, by contrast, manifested in her silence. Ashra wondered if the girl was having second thoughts about accompanying them. She didn't blame her if she was. She wondered too if her own fear was evident to the others, for she could feel it within herself, a dead weight that sat in her stomach, its claws occasionally scratching at her insides. *The third rule of thievery*, she reminded herself. *Never give fear a share of the spoils.*

The wooden planks of the jetty creaked beneath their feet as they approached the boat and the hooded shape within it. "You Marni's man?" Lukan asked in a low voice.

"I am," the man replied, his voice a soft rasp. "Get in."

"Nice night for it," Lukan quipped as he stepped into the boat. The man made no reply. Flea and Ashra followed, the boat rocking slightly with their weight as they settled. Ashra could hear the girl's staccato breathing, could feel her body trembling. "You okay?" she murmured.

"Just cold," the girl whispered back.

"Me too." Even wrapped in a cloak, and wearing gloves, Ashra could still feel the chill pressing against her, an insidious presence that always seemed to be probing, searching for a way in. What she'd give to feel the warmth of Saphrona's sun on her skin, even for just a moment. She winced. That had been a mistake. Thoughts of her home city birthed thoughts of Alphonse. Was he still safe? Had he evaded the Twice-Crowned King's grasp? She pushed the thoughts away. *The eighth rule of thievery*, she reminded herself. *Distraction invites disaster.* If they were going to survive the night, let alone succeed in their task, she had to be fully focused. To lose concentration for a moment could prove fatal.

The boatman tossed a mooring rope aside and took up the oars, not bothering to ask if they were ready. What would be the point? He knew where they were going, and that no one could ever be ready for such an undertaking. The sounds and lights of the tavern faded as the boat moved across the river, and soon the mist surrounded them on all sides. As she glanced at the hooded boatman—and as she listened to the silence, broken only by the creaking of the oars and the splashing of water—Ashra was reminded of the Zar-Ghosan myth of Zarmenos, the boatman who rowed souls across the Black River to the afterlife. She snorted softly at that. If only they were headed somewhere so glorious with nothing but eternal bliss before them. But Lukan had told her what he'd seen in Nika's memories, the chaos and panic and fear he'd felt, and it was clear that where they were heading had far more in common with the hells than with a sunlit paradise.

After a while a light appeared in the darkness—a lantern hanging at the prow of another boat, which slowly emerged from mist, looming over their own. Cowled figures leaned over the rails, pointing crossbows at them.

"Identify yourselves," a voice demanded.

"We're on Lady Marni's business," the boatman called over his shoulder.

Perhaps the guards wouldn't permit them to pass. Marni couldn't punish them if her own efforts at securing their passage had failed, could she? Ashra hated her own weakness at the thought, but clung to the faint hope all the same.

"Proceed," barked the voice, and the guards lowered their weapons.

Ashra's fear gripped her again but she gritted her teeth and forced it down, annoyed at herself for her momentary lack of courage. Avoiding a problem only gave it more time to sharpen its claws. Better to face it and get it done. The sooner they retrieved this scroll, the sooner they'd be free of Marni's control—but only if Lukan agreed to give it to her. Arima's appearance the night before had complicated matters. Ashra didn't trust the man; he knew far too much about them and their debt to Marni. Lukan, of course, had been seduced by Arima's promise that he could get Baranov to reveal his secrets. He wouldn't be drawn on whatever plan he was kicking around, but the thought of going behind Marni's back had Ashra on edge. When the time came—*if* it came—she would insist they give the scroll to Marni to clear their debt. They would find another way to recover Lukan's key. How exactly, she wasn't sure. Right now, their priority was finding the scroll and escaping with their lives. Nothing else mattered.

Tall shapes loomed out of the mist: three-story buildings, their first glimpse of Ashgrave. The structures seemed to huddle together, as if cowed by the horrors they'd witnessed, but as Ashra looked closer she saw little sign of the chaos that had engulfed the district—the glass in the windows was intact, and the stonework appeared unblemished. Other shapes revealed themselves on the riverbank—barrels, crates, a winch for unloading cargo. All dusted in snow, but otherwise looking as if they'd only been abandoned moments ago, rather than decades. It only made Ashra feel more uneasy. She couldn't shake the feeling that, as she looked at the buildings, their dark windows stared back, *seeing* her. She took a steadying breath. Just nerves, she told herself. Breathe. Focus. Stay in control.

"We're here," Lukan whispered unnecessarily, as they drew alongside a stone pier. "You remember the plan?"

Of course she remembered. They'd argued over it countless times. Ashra was to scout ahead and locate the inn where the alchemist's body was supposed to be. If all seemed clear, she would return to the boat and then the three of them would head to the inn to search for the scroll together. That final detail was the one she'd fought against—who knew what might change in the time it took for her to double back and for them to return? Far better that she go on alone—get in, find the scroll and get out again. She could do it far more quickly on her own, and would cause less disturbance. She'd be back at the boat in no time. But Lukan wouldn't hear of it. "You're not going in there alone," he'd told her, standing firm in the face of her objections. While she knew his stance came from a place of concern—whatever he'd seen in Nika's memories had shaken him, and he didn't want her to face it on her own— she knew it was a mistake. She'd always worked alone. That was how she'd forged the myth of Lady Midnight. She'd done so again when she broke into Baranov's townhouse. What made this task any different?

"Ashra," Lukan whispered again. "Do you remember?"

"I remember," she replied curtly, as she rose to her feet. "Let's get this over with."

"Good luck," Flea said, the first words she'd spoken in some time. She reached out and gripped Ashra's hand. Ashra smiled at her in the gloom.

"Thanks, *majin*. I'll be back before you know it."

"If you see anything," Lukan continued, "anything at all—"

"I'll scream and bring it right back here." Ashra shot him a reproving look he likely couldn't see. "Relax. I know what I'm doing." She turned and stepped out of the boat, not waiting to hear his reply as her hands roved over her belt and crossbody strap. It was a familiar habit, to make sure her tools were all present and correct, but the action didn't bring the reassurance it normally did.

Ashra inhaled a lungful of the cold air. Let it out.

And started forward.

As she stole along the pier and ascended the steps carved into the side of the wharf, Ashra recalled the route she was to take, picturing the faded lines of Marni's map. Fifty yards west, turn north at the crossroads, first left heading west again for another hundred yards, then north again . . .

Ashra froze as she reached the top of the steps. Her heart lurched, breath suddenly frozen in her throat.

Bones.

Half-buried by the thin layer of snow, they lay scattered across the wharf in their hundreds, some still forming partial skeletons. Skulls lay among them, black eye sockets staring at her. As Ashra stood motionless, something General Razin had said last night at dinner came back to her: "Many people tried to escape across the river, but the Sparks were waiting in boats. Shot the lot of them right there on the wharf. Terrible business."

As her gaze moved over the skulls and bones, Ashra realized some were smaller than others.

"Everything all right?" Lukan called in a hoarse whisper.

Ashra raised a hand in acknowledgment, not trusting her own voice. Taking a slow breath, she studied the thoroughfare before her, which she assumed to be the Avenue of the Seven Silver Saints—the main route into Ashgrave. She glanced around for a street sign, but—while the mist wasn't as thick as it had been on the river—she still couldn't see more than fifteen yards in front of her. She'd be heading into an unfamiliar place mostly blind. The only consolation was that anyone—or anything—lurking in the mist would have the same problem. She hoped.

Enough introspection.

Ashra picked her way across the wharf, taking care not to step on any of the bones, and started down the avenue. This had been a prosperous part of the city, Razin had told them, and the wide street and tall, timber-framed houses supported his claim. Even though they were half-swathed in mist Ashra could sense the grandeur that still lingered in their stonework and wrought-iron railings. All the stranger that it was here the plague broke out, and not in the cramped, filthy warrens of the Cinders. What had really happened? She pushed the thought away. Speculation would only slow her down, take the edge off her awareness. She needed to be fully alert.

Especially with the mist the way it was. It concealed the street before her, and, when she glanced over her shoulder, she could no longer see the river. Silence reigned, and her own breaths seemed far too loud in the quiet. The snow was much thinner here, she realized, as if even the weather preferred to avoid this place. Still, at least it wouldn't hinder her progress.

She froze.

A noise: skittering claw across stone.

Ashra's heart raced as she turned a full circle, watching, listening, hand on the stiletto at her left hip.

Just a rat, most likely. Yet the sound had possessed a certain weight.

She stood silently, staring into the mist, but the noise didn't come again.

Had she imagined it? She shook the thought away. Better to focus on the knowns than the unknowns, and what she knew was that further down this street was the crossing that would take her one step closer to the inn. She pressed on, moving with newfound urgency, unable to shake the sense that something was watching her leave.

A short while later Ashra reached the crossroads. Marni's map might have been old, but it was accurate. She felt a spark of hope as she turned onto the Street of Fallen Stars. Not far now. Her progress had been swifter than she'd anticipated. Yet her pace slowed as she noted the blackened houses that had been gutted by fire, and the Xs that had been slashed across their doors in white paint.

And the pyre. What was left of it.

A wide circle of blackened cobbles was visible beneath the thin crust of snow. Shards of bones lay within it. This, then, was where they burned the bodies. Her fragile sense of hope flickered out as she stared at the charred bones. Some bore teeth marks, as if they'd been gnawed.

A noise sounded behind her: metal scraping across stone.

Ashra whirled, eyes scanning the mist. Nothing moved. She counted thirty heartbeats, but the sound didn't come again.

She steeled herself and walked on.

The large square still retained some of its former grandeur.

Twenty years ago, it would have been the heart of the district. The weathered signs that hung outside the grand buildings signified a bank, a notary's office, a lawyer's chamber, a merchants' guild. People would have come here to meet and do business, or sit and watch the world go by on one of the stone benches arranged around a great fountain.

No more.

Ashra's gaze swept over an abandoned carriage, an upturned wagon, splintered boxes and collapsed barrels and a handcart still loaded with cargo, its tarpaulin twitching in the breeze. And another pile of charred bones, one of the biggest she'd seen. All were echoes of the madness that had engulfed the district. It was strange to think that the rest of Korslakov had moved on, whereas here time stood still, the horror of the past preserved in silence and stone and snow.

Ashra's gaze flicked again to the inn on the square's far side. A sign hung above the door, carved in the shape of a beer keg. She couldn't make out the words painted on it, but knew what they would say: *The Joyous Brewer of a Thousand Barrels*. There was nothing joyous about the place now, not with its smashed windows and the white X painted on its front door. Still, its sight offered Ashra a scrap of comfort. If luck was on their side, this was where they'd find the dead alchemist and her scroll. Their ticket to freedom—if Ashra had anything to say about it.

And it was so close.

Reluctantly she turned away. She had to retrace her steps now, head back to the boat and inform the others the way was clear. That was what they'd agreed. But now she found herself hesitating. Why waste all that time doubling back and then returning, when she could just enter the inn herself? What threat might have emerged by the time they returned? Better to seize the moment. She could be in and out in no time. There was no reason to put the others at risk. Lukan would sulk about it, but what did it matter if they had what they needed?

All of these thoughts were true, but there was another that lurked behind them. An admission that she wanted to go in alone to prove to herself that she could do it. Her successful infiltration of Baranov's townhouse had offered temporary reprieve, but her doubts had gradually crept back. This was the perfect chance to banish them. To prove she was still the master thief she thought she was.

She *needed* this.

Ashra turned back to the square, her decision made. She watched and waited. Nothing moved. Nothing broke the silence. She felt a stab of trepidation, a fleeting feeling of guilt. Swallowed both down. Took a deep breath. And then she darted forward, crossing the square as silently as possible. The inn's front door stood ajar.

Ashra eased it open, the hinges screeching as if in remembered anguish. Nothing but blackness beyond, a darkness not even her eyesight could fully penetrate. She pulled her glowglass from beneath her collar to aid her search. Hesitated at the itch on the back of her neck. At the sense of being watched.

Ashra whirled and scanned the square.

Nothing. No—wait.

A figure stood in the corner of the square where she'd just been standing, though *stood* wasn't the right word; instead the figure stooped, as if it was hunched over. A heartbeat later it was gone, swallowed by the mist. Ashra took a slow breath to master her racing heart, not daring to look away, not daring to even blink as she stared at the shadows where the figure had been.

It didn't reappear.

Had she imagined it, the moonlight and mist and shadows conspiring to create the illusion of a person? Perhaps. But she was sure she hadn't imagined those unseen eyes watching her.

No matter. Chances were that it was just a scavenger or an opportunist, looking for something just as she was. Yet as she turned back to the door, Lukan's earlier words slipped to the front of her mind. *It wasn't human. Moved like one, but it wasn't. It was something else.*

Ashra dismissed the thought. If someone—or some*thing*—was stalking her, she had a few tricks of her own.

She slipped into the darkness beyond the doorway. Her glowglass pushed back the gloom, illuminating a hallway. A counter stood to one side, an open doorway behind it revealing a small room lined with hooks. Someone would have once stood there, welcoming guests and taking their coats and cloaks. The only thing that greeted Ashra was the smell of damp and decay that hung in the air, thick and cloying. Something crunched underfoot as she stepped forward—shattered glass, spread across the floor. If someone was following her, at least she'd have some warning of their entry. Would it be enough? Perhaps not.

She opened a pouch on her belt and withdrew a handful of tiny paper sachets—snapbangs, she called them. Each one contained a powder that emitted a loud *crack* when force was applied. Ashra usually threw them to distract a guard's attention, but they made the same noise when stepped on. She knelt down and carefully arranged them among the shattered glass. There. If she *was* being followed, she'd know soon enough.

Onward. She'd wasted too much time already.

Another doorway further down led to a large room, a fire-place dominating one side. The inn's common room, she guessed. Once.

Now it was a tomb.

Dozens of skeletons lay on beds cobbled together from flour sacks. Victims of the plague whose bodies never made it to the pyres. Ashra took a tentative step into the room. The damp musk of rot was thick in her nostrils, and the air was heavy, as if it remembered the misery of what had happened here. She turned slowly, eyeing the haphazard rows of skeletons, the darkness roiling beyond the light of her glowglass as if furious at her intrusion. She felt like a trespasser. She supposed she was. This was no place for the living.

An object caught her eye, glinting in the light: a bronze statue of the Builder, lying face down on the floor, as if someone had hurled it against the boards. Ashra could imagine their rage, their desperation, as they demanded of their god: how could this happen? She'd asked the same question herself, every time she'd seen an injustice in the Splinters, which was most days. How could these things happen? Why didn't the gods do anything? She never got an answer, not from the Lady of the Seven Shadows, nor from her mother's Zar-Ghosan gods. Such silence—indifference—was why she prayed to no deity.

Better to put your faith in yourself.

Ashra ghosted through the room, checking each skeleton as she went, doing her best to shield her light from the windows. She looked for any signs of the alchemists' distinctive uniform, that purple tunic with blue sleeves and silver stitching, but saw only rags of brown and grey. As for a scroll case, none of the skeletons bore any personal effects at all—not even rings, which had likely been stolen by opportunists whose minds turned to profit even in the midst of death. She'd seen that happen many times in the Splinters as well.

Ashra left the room, glad to be away from the suffocating air and the sightless eyes. Her exploration of the rest of the inn's

ground floor uncovered a kitchen, pantry and cellar. She found old
pots over cold ashes. Crates of produce, now black and despoiled.
Enough barrels and bottles of wine to bring a tear to Lukan's eye.
But no dead alchemist. No scroll case.

Upstairs it was, then.

Ashra found the winding staircase at the back of the inn. A
trolley nestled in the nook at its base, stacked with trays, plates
and silver cutlery—strange that no one had pilfered the latter. She
took the stairs slowly, out of habit, but quickly realized that such
noises wouldn't trouble the dead. She quickened her pace. The
inn's upper floor comprised a large room intended for multiple
occupants. As she pressed forward, her light revealed beds, chests
and wardrobes. Skeletons, too. Just three this time, lying on two
beds that had been pushed together. They were swathed in rags
that had once been blankets, as if they'd been huddling together to
keep warm. Ashra doubted any of these three were her alchemist,
but looked anyway.

She wished she hadn't.

The skeleton in the middle was that of an adult. The two others
were smaller. A parent—or guardian—and two children, huddling
together as the world collapsed into chaos around them. Ashra
moved deeper into the room, her light revealing something painted
on one wall with wild, sweeping strokes, in the same white paint
that marked so many of the doors she'd seen.

the Builder has abandoned us
    why?

Beneath the second word, someone had scratched *bastard* into
the plaster with a knife. The final letter had a long tail, as if the
carver had put all their fury into it and slashed the wall with their
blade. A final act of defiance against an uncaring god, understandable but foolish. Better to channel such anger into escaping the
darkness, rather than raging against the dying of the light. Still,
that was easy for Ashra to say. If she'd been here, surrounded by

the dead and dying, abandoned—*sacrificed*—by Korslakov's ruling council, no doubt she would have felt differently.

Ashra moved away, a sense of despair stealing over her as she approached the far side of the room, the darkness grudgingly receding before her to reveal nothing but empty beds and the occasional discarded personal artifact: a razor, a cloak, a belt, a pair of gloves. All abandoned as their owners fled, or disregarded as their bodies were hauled to the pyres.

The alchemist wasn't here.

No. She had to be. Otherwise—

Wait.

Ashra's heart quickened as her light revealed a corridor at the far end of the room, lined with two doors on either side. Private rooms for those with a desire for privacy and the coin to pay for it.

Could an alchemist of the Tower be such a customer? She hoped so.

The first door yielded easily to her touch, revealing a well-appointed room that felt oddly out of step with the chaos that had engulfed the rest of the inn: the bed was neatly made, the floor was covered in dust but uncluttered, the dresser was free of personal items. The room must have been empty at the time the plague broke out. Ashra backed out and tried the opposite door. This room was also empty, though the unmade bed spoke to the former occupant's hasty departure, as did the handful of coins left on the dresser. She noticed a faded pamphlet on the window sill. She picked it up and brushed the dust off, revealing the crudely drawn image of a man holding up his fists, with BAREKNUCKLE BOXING AT TALLARD'S HOTHOUSE printed below. While it was possible the alchemist had an interest in organized violence, Ashra's gut told her someone else had been staying here when the chaos unfolded.

The third room also bore signs of a panicked exit, with a half-packed case lying open on the bed. She picked through the clothes that spilled from it, little more than rags now. Nothing that pointed to their owner being an alchemist—no purple and blue tunic, or apron covered in burns, or whatever they wore when they were working on their craft. She swore softly and faced the final door.

Last chance.

If the alchemist wasn't here, then she wasn't at the inn as Marni believed.

Ashra tried the door handle.

Locked.

For some reason that felt like a good thing. No one leaving in a hurry would bother locking the door behind them. But someone looking to escape the chaos may well lock themselves *in*. Ashra considered the lock, which looked simple enough, and set to work. The lock only resisted for twenty heartbeats. She stowed her tools and eased the door open, its hinges creaking. Her light illuminated a floor covered in scattered papers, all bearing flowing script and undecipherable diagrams. Promising. She stepped into the room, her eyes taking in the dresser, which bore a number of conical glass flasks and a variety of implements she couldn't name. Definitely the possessions of an alchemist, though she kept her eyes averted from the bed in the room's far corner, not daring to hope.

She took a slow breath.

Looked at the corner.

An empty bed, covered in various papers.

Damn. The alchemist must have fled, but had the presence of mind to lock her room before she left. Perhaps she believed she'd be returning to it once the panic was over. The fact that her room remained locked suggested she'd either died in the chaos that had engulfed the district, or had escaped and never returned. Regardless, she wasn't here. Why had Marni been so sure she would be?

Ashra turned back toward the doorway. Froze. Stared at the corner behind the door.

The skeleton stared back, its skull grinning.

Ashra stepped closer, her heart quickening as she noted the purple and blue tunic it wore, its silver stitching gleaming in the light, still bright even after all these years.

"Found you," she murmured.

For some reason the alchemist had wedged herself into this corner of the room between the door and the wardrobe. Why hadn't
she just fled with everyone else? Perhaps she was already ill with
the plague, but then why hadn't she retreated to her bed? Ashra
dismissed the question. It was the sort of pointless detail Lukan
would concern himself with. The woman was dead. All that mattered was whether she still had the scroll.

The tubular case she held suggested she did.

Ashra crouched before her and reached out, gently easing the
case from her skeletal hands. It took some effort, as if the skeleton was reluctant to give up its prize, but eventually it came free.
The embossed motif had faded with time, but was still unmistakable: a tower with a flame at its summit. She twisted off the top
of the tube.

Moment of truth.

Ashra tilted the tube toward her and breathed a sigh of relief. A
scroll of parchment nestled inside. Gently she fished it out with her
fingers and unrolled it. The parchment's upper right corner had
somehow been burned at the edges, but otherwise the document
had weathered the intervening decades well, and the alchemical
symbols that had been etched on it in black ink were clear and
bold. Ashra had no idea what they meant. Not in scientific terms,
anyway. But the scroll's value was another matter.

Ashra replaced the parchment in the tube and replaced the lid.
She hesitated as she noticed something else.

A piece of paper nestling in the breast pocket of the alchemist's
tunic.

She slid it free and unfolded it. Shaky, cursive writing filled both
sides. Her instinct was to slip it into her pocket—she'd been gone
too long already—but she paused as the letter's opening words
caught her attention.

I am to blame. That, dear reader, is my firm conviction.
And my final conviction, because I—Safiya Kalimara, Al-
chemist of the Third Rank—am not long for this world.

Given all that has transpired in the past few days, I can only count that as a blessing.

Ashra stood and glanced at the doorway. She should go. Lukan would surely be growing concerned at her continued absence. The last thing she wanted was him and Flea risking their own safety by coming in search of her.

And yet . . .

Her gaze flicked back to the skeleton. All that remained of the alchemist, who, for reasons unknown, had ended up in this room as the world around her descended into chaos. Reasons that might be revealed if she read a little further. Besides, the letter likely held answers about the formula and Safiya's fate. For some reason Ashra felt the need to read them in the alchemist's presence. What was left of it. Perhaps it was because Safiya had died alone, or because she'd borne a name of the Southern Queendoms, like Ashra herself. Regardless, it seemed important to hear her story now, in this place where she'd lived her final moments. Even if it went against all of Ashra's instincts. It wouldn't take long.

Ashra sat down on the bed and started reading.

21

THE KINGS OF ASH AND RUIN

Where to begin. At the start, I suppose.

I arrived at this inn nearly six months ago. I needed lodgings after being dismissed from the Tower (I won't go into detail about my dismissal, but suffice to say I fell victim to Tower politics.) I lacked the coin to rent a place of my own, and shared lodgings would inhibit my ongoing experiments. Fortunately, I heard of an inn that was looking to add some alchemical flair to its drinks (spirits that are aflame and smelling of black powder are apparently fashionable). That's what brought me to the Joyous Brewer. In return for my alchemical assistance, I was given a private room at a discount. Not only that, but I was permitted to continue my experiments in my room—so long as I always kept the window open.

I passed several productive months in this fashion, assisting the brewmaster when required, and devoting the rest of my time to my research. Initially I struggled with the noise—the damned songs!—but eventually adapted. I even found myself humming along at times while pondering my equations.

Then everything changed.

I cracked the formula.

Even now, writing those words, I can scarcely believe them. To think I discovered the secret to unlocking the Crimson Door, when so many failed before me. Hubris has been the downfall of many an alchemist, or so the Tower tells its initiates at their robing ceremony, but I'd be lying if I didn't feel great pride.

It was the greatest moment of my life.

And the biggest mistake I ever made.

I didn't realize it at the time, of course. All I could think about was the acclaim I would receive, the respect I would win. The Tower would have no choice but to readmit me to its ranks—how could it not? My achievement was the greatest alchemical triumph since the creation of the first construct. My name would be immortalized on the Wall of Revelations. The very thought made me feel giddy. But first, I had to decide which of the families I would sell the formula to. In a sense it didn't matter; all of them would pay handsomely, not that wealth held much importance to me. No amount of money in the world can fix the condition that affects my lungs, which leaves me gasping for air after climbing the inn's stairs. Yet it didn't feel like a decision to be taken lightly. After all, we know nothing of what lies beyond the Crimson Door. Riches? Perhaps. Phaeron artifacts? Likely. Power? Certainly. And power in the wrong hands leads to dark places.

In the end I decided to approach Lord Baranov. A young man to be putting such faith in, perhaps, but I've heard that he's already ruffling feathers in the Frostfire Circle by championing various reforms. I was told he's an intelligent man with strong principles, which makes him a rare beast among those of noble blood.

The young lord responded to my letter immediately. Of course he did! Korslakov's aristocracy have been obsessed with unlocking the Crimson Door for centuries. He visited me here at the Brewer, as I requested—my condition would make a trip to the Mantle far too strenuous. I expected Baranov to arrive with the usual crowd of attendants, but the young nobleman arrived alone. I must say I was impressed with him. He was courteous, with a keen mind and a ready laugh. But more importantly, he understands that he has a moral responsibility to Korslakov and its citizens. A duty of care to them. As we spoke, he treated me as an equal, and by the end of our conversation I knew I could trust him. Whatever lay beyond the Crimson Door, I felt it would be safe in his hands.

We made an agreement. I would create the substance that would unlock the Door, a process that would take me two days. Lord Baranov would then return with a letter of credit for an amount of money that I feel indecent writing down. We would exchange the two and that would conclude our business. His only stipulation was that I agree to two of his household guards standing vigil outside my room, for he knew, perhaps even more keenly than I, the value of what he stood to gain—or lose, if one of the other lords discovered our secret deal. Before he left he promised he'd return in two days.

I never saw him again.

Thus we arrive at the end of what I know for fact. What follows is speculation.

I don't know what caused the plague. Larson, one of the kitchen boys, was the first to fall ill. I heard he was found slumped over a barrel in the cellar, his skin waxy and his breathing shallow. Then he started coughing up blood. A local physician was called, and by the time the man arrived at the Brewer he had more than one patient. The cook who found Larson was showing similar symptoms, as were others at the inn.

Baranov's guards told me to stay in my room and keep the door closed. Over the course of the afternoon, I heard muffled voices through the walls and floorboards, and occasional footsteps on the stairs, always quick, as if people were departing in a hurry. I heard shouts and cries from outside—a man kept yelling that no one was to enter the inn. I cursed the fact that my only window looked toward the building next door. Even if I stood on a stool and leaned out, I could see only a sliver of the square.

Silence fell as darkness descended. I called out to my guards but received no answer. I spent that first night in a state of agitation, prowling around my room like a caged animal. At some point I slept.

When I awoke with the dawn, I realized I couldn't bear another day of confinement. I needed to know what was happening. Mastering my fear, I unlocked my door and stepped out into the corridor. My guards had left—dead, or fled, I had no clue. The inn was silent, but I caught movement in the corner of my eye and turned to the bay window to my right.

People were in the square.

I watched them carry bodies out of buildings and lay them on the ground. Watched as people bared their grief. I saw one man sobbing over the body of a child, only to throw up blood over his daughter's corpse. Within moments he was lying dead beside her. Even with the window closed I felt I could smell the death in the air. Soon the dead in the square outnumbered the living. Those that still lived stumbled around as if in a daze, or frantically piled their belongings onto carts.

It was then that a boy raced through the square, crying at the top of his voice, "They've walled up the western gate! There's barricades in every street! They're not letting anyone out! There's constructs everywhere . . ."

Panic.

The living abandoned the dead, abandoned their carts and wagons and sacks of belongings, and fled. Briefly I wondered if I should flee too, but merely walking down the stairs is enough to leave me heaving for breath. Besides, this plague was making short work of haler people than me. I would be easy prey for it. So I decided to stay put and take my chances. Perhaps the boy was mistaken.

I knocked on the doors to the other private bedrooms, but no one answered. The communal bedroom was empty, and no one replied when I called down the stairs. I considered going down—a slow, laborious task given my condition—but feared the plague that might be festering down there. So I spent the rest of the day at the bay window, trying to quell my growing nerves.

As dusk drew in, darkness fell across the empty square. At times I thought I could hear distant screams, but otherwise all was quiet. As was the inn. Every so often I would return to the

stairs and call out, but no one ever answered. Occasionally I'd
see someone run through the square, dodging between the bodies. I'd opened one of the smaller upper windows, so I called to
those who came near, but they merely glanced up at me and kept
running. I longed to know what was happening, even though
it was obvious. The plague had swept like wildfire through the
district and it seemed the rest of the city had abandoned us. I
began to feel a great despair, not at the realization that I was
surely to die, but at the knowledge that the greatest achievement
of my life—and of the pursuit of alchemy itself—would go unrec-
ognized. Arrogant, perhaps, to think such a thing. But that was
where my thoughts went as the darkness returned.

There were more screams that second night, but somehow I
slept.

I awoke to a blood-red sun behind a haze of smoke. My first
instinct was to panic—I thought the district was on fire. Then
I realized it was not buildings that were burning, but bodies. A
great pyre of corpses burned in the middle of the square. Even
with the bay window closed I could smell the stench of burning
flesh. Every so often, a dozen figures in makeshift masks would
appear with a wagon full of corpses and toss them unceremoni-
ously onto the pyre before disappearing again.

I saw the first looters a while later. Half a dozen of them
broke into a jeweler's shop in the corner of the square. They
swaggered away afterward, pearl necklaces clutched in their
hands. Perhaps they thought they could bribe the guards at the
barricades, or they still believed a future existed for them where
such valuables would prove useful. The masked figures heaping
the bodies on the pyres already knew there was no escape. Their
minds had turned to survival, to trying to burn the plague away.

At some point in the afternoon, I could no longer ignore my
desperate thirst and hunger (I had drunk the last of the water
from my washbasin and consumed the nuts and fruit I kept in
my room), so I tore a strip from a bedsheet, wrapped it round my
face and ventured downstairs to retrieve what supplies I could.

There was precious little left in the pantry. I made several trips over the course of several hours, my pace painfully slow, carrying as many pots of water and sacks of vegetables upstairs as I could. When I slumped, exhausted, into my seat by the window, I saw the masked figures still working in the square, throwing ever more corpses on the pyre. There were fewer of them now, and so it took them longer to unload their wagon. When they returned later that evening, for the final time, only three were left to handle the bodies.

That night the screams were closer than before. Not carrying from the edges of the district, where the barricades supposedly were, but from all around. The night sky glowed orange—not from the corpse pyres, but from buildings set aflame. Just two days before, this place had been a prosperous district of Korslakov. Now it was a maelstrom of horror and death.

The masked figures did not return the next day.

A pall of smoke hung over the square, the funeral pyre nothing but smoldering ashes. I only saw five people that day. The first two were a woman and a girl, rags covering their faces and fear in their movements. Two looters passed through later, strutting as if they fancied themselves the kings of ash and ruin. The last was a boy, who appeared as night was descending. He ran as if pursued, only to trip over a corpse and fall to the ground. As he picked himself up, he must have seen the glow of my candle by the window, for he glanced up at me. Our eyes met. He raised his hand and waved. I waved back, my heart swelling as my loneliness and despair briefly melted at the warmth of human connection. Then he bolted, running into the gloom, and I was alone once again.

That kind boy was the last person I ever saw.

There were no screams that night. Perhaps there were no voices left to give them.

I spent the days that followed lost in thought. I thought of my childhood in Zar-Ghosa. The warmth of the sun, the weariness of my mother, the cruelty of my father. I recalled discovering my

love of chemistry, and my talent for it, which led to me crossing
the Scepter Sea in search of my destiny. I remembered former
loves—their faces, their voices. But wherever my thoughts went,
they always circled back to the same question.

What caused this plague?

The timing of the outbreak—so soon after I made my agreement
with Lord Baranov—was suspicious. Had one of his rivals learned
of our deal and taken extreme steps to prevent it? It seemed possible, but why condemn the entire district to death? And how did
they even manage it? This plague is deadlier than any disease
I've ever seen. I've tried to convince myself there's another explanation. That even the aristocrats of Korslakov, obsessed as they
are with being the first to unlock the Crimson Door, are not so
cruel as to commit such an atrocity. I tell myself it was mere co-
incidence that the plague broke out now. That nothing more than
simple chance had stolen all those lives, as it will soon steal mine.
And not just my life, but my life's work. My crowning glory. My
legacy. Snatched away by the whims of fate.

Lies, all lies.

Power corrupts. The mere thought of it drives people to madness.

Someone deliberately started this plague, and its purpose was
to stop Lord Baranov obtaining my alchemical solution. I'm sure
of it.

Which means I am to blame. If I never discovered this formula, none of this would have happened. Hundreds, perhaps
thousands of people would still be alive.

But they're gone. Soon I'll join them. There's a certain justice
in that.

My final hour draws near. I have no food or water left, and
I don't have the strength to search for more. It is almost a relief
to know this will soon be over. The more my strength fades, the
more my mind plays tricks on me. I've not seen a living soul in
days, but I still hear screams every night. In my exhausted state,
they sound animalistic. Inhuman. Yesterday, as dusk was falling,

I saw a figure crossing the square. My elation at seeing another survivor after so long quickly faded as I noted their strange, erratic movements. Instinct made me snuff out my candle. As they came closer, I realized they were naked, their skin too pale and their limbs too long and emaciated. They froze, their head suddenly snapping upward, moving from side to side as if tasting the air. It was then I saw the jaundiced eyes and the extended jaw, lined with teeth. I closed my eyes, fear bursting in my chest, recalling all the folktales from my homeland about undead revenants that stalk battlefields and graveyards.

Ghūls.

Ashra lowered the letter as a memory stole into her mind: her mother scolding her for bad behavior. Behave yourself, Ashra Seramis, she'd said, lest I lock you out at night for the ghūls! Ashra felt the familiar ache, indulged it for a moment, forced it back down. She turned back to the letter.

When I opened my eyes again, the figure was gone. And now I wonder if it was ever there at all, or whether my traitor mind is taunting me with nightmarish visions of half-remembered monsters from childhood stories.

Today I tried to burn the formula. I don't know why—a final act of defiance, perhaps. A final hope of redemption. I held it to the fire, watched as the flames licked at my life's work, tasting its edges. And then I pulled it back, because even now, despite all that's happened, all I am responsible for, I can't bear to do it. I have too much pride. And it sickens me.

I beg you, dear stranger, to do what I could not. Burn the formula. Perhaps then my soul will know peace. Whether or not I deserve it, I leave to Llalu, in her golden grace, to decide.

Safiya Kalimara

Alchemist of the Third Rank

22

NOT LOOKING FOR TROUBLE

Ashra lowered the letter, her heart breaking for a woman whom she'd never met and yet somehow felt she knew intimately. What a way to die. Trapped in a room as chaos and death spread around you. Alone with your memories and regrets and failures. And guilt, most of all.

"None of this was your fault," Ashra whispered to the skeleton. She knew how it felt to believe you were responsible for something terrible. She had felt that way for years after her father was murdered in front of her eyes, despite her mother's insistence that she was not to blame. That, if she hadn't been settled on his lap, if he hadn't been so concerned for her safety, he would have been able to defend himself against the masked assassins that broke into their house. No wonder Safiya had tried to burn the formula. Ashra slid the scroll from its case again, pressed a finger to the blackened edges. How she wished she could follow the alchemist's plea and feed the scroll to the flames. Give her soul the release it yearned for.

But she couldn't.

"I'm sorry," she murmured, sliding the scroll back into its case and tucking it beneath her belt. "But I need this. Forgive me."

Ashra rose from the bed and knelt before the skeleton, placing a finger against the skull's forehead. Gently she traced a circle and crossed it with a horizontal line, marking the symbol of life, death and rebirth, which she'd seen administered to the dead as part of Zar-Ghosan funerary rites. "Go with grace," she whispered.

Advice she could do with taking herself, though speed would avail her more. How long had she spent in Safiya's company? Too long. Lukan and Flea would surely be thinking about following her, if they hadn't already.

Ashra stood and gave the room a final glance—a thief's old habit, checking for anything she might have missed. Satisfied, she returned to the corridor, pausing to look out of the same bay window that Safiya once gazed through. She looked to the corner where she thought she'd seen the figure. Nothing moved in the darkness, but the word Safiya had used echoed in her mind.

Ghūl.

Was there something out there? Some undead revenant prowling the night? No. Her mind was playing tricks on her, just as Safiya's had done. But perhaps she'd take a different route back to the boat.

Just in case.

Ashra retraced her steps to the communal bedroom.

And froze.

A figure stood in the doorway on the far side, blocking her way to the stairs.

She drew a breath and her stiletto at the same time, and released the former after a long moment. The blade she kept in her hand.

The figure remained still.

"Who are you?" she asked.

No response.

"I got what I came for," Ashra continued. "Now I'll be on my way."

Still the figure didn't move. Didn't speak. Just stood in the doorway. Watching. Ashra felt the weight of its unseen gaze, but not nearly as much as the weight of its silence. Its stillness. She swallowed and tightened the grip on her blade. It was just a person. A scavenger. A survivor who had somehow carved out an existence in this awful place. She had nothing to fear.

So why was there a tremor in her hand?

"I'm not looking for trouble," Ashra said firmly.

The figure stepped into the room. Its movements were quick and erratic; it took several short steps and then paused, its head tilting with a jerky motion as it regarded her. Sizing her up. As if deciding whether she was a threat.

Or prey.

It scuttled forward again with quick, short steps that possessed a feral quality. Now the figure stood no more than five yards away, just beyond the light of her glowglass. Close enough that she could hear its hoarse, ragged breaths, as if air was being drawn into shriveled lungs. A couple more steps, another tilt of the head. The breathing was louder now, a rasping growl. A death rattle.

"That's close enough," Ashra warned. She slowly moved her free hand toward her belt.

The figure stepped into the light.

Ashra felt numb as she stared at the long, emaciated limbs that ended in talons. The sharp, angular panes of its cadaverous skull. Green eyes that gleamed with a sickly light. A distended lower jaw that split in two, revealing a maw lined with dozens of needle-like teeth.

Terror twisted inside her.

Safiya had not been mistaken.

"Get back," Ashra said, forcing the words past the horror that gripped her.

The ghūl hissed, its head snapping one way and then the other, its plague eyes never leaving her.

"Last chance," she said, her free hand working to unclasp a small glass sphere from her belt.

The creature raised an arm, revealing a hand with knife-like talons. It hissed again, jaws flaring wide.

Then it leaped.

Ashra twisted to one side and hurled her flashbomb. She closed her eyes just before light bloomed beyond her eyelids, bright as Saphrona's noonday sun. A screech tore the air. As darkness returned, she opened her eyes to see the ghūl blindly slashing at the air with its talons. Ashra raced for the stairs.

The creature screeched again as she reached the door to the landing.

She turned just as the ghūl grasped her shoulders, a hiss escaping her lips as its talons sliced into her flesh. How in the hells had it recovered so quickly?

No time to think. Only to act.

Ashra rammed her stiletto into the creature's belly. The ghūl shrieked in her face, its breath reeking of the grave. She responded by driving her blade into it again. Then a third time. With her fourth stab, the creature's grip on her loosened enough for her to twist away. She raised her stiletto, blood roaring in her ears and trickling down her arms, but the ghūl made no move to attack.

Instead, it remained still, talons twitching. Then it raised one hand to its jaws. A tongue flicked out, licking her blood from its talon.

As if mocking her.

Ashra backed away until she felt the banister press against her back. She glanced at the stairs. Instinct screamed at her to run. Reason whispered that it would be pointless. But what was the alternative? She'd inflicted wounds that would have left the toughest back-alley bruiser dead on the floor, but the ghūl had barely flinched.

And yet.

Blood—black in the light of her glowglass—seeped from the gashes in the creature's belly. Ashra felt a flicker of hope. If the ghūl could bleed, then surely it could die. She adjusted her feet, ignoring the creature's rattling breath and twitching talons. *Intent is always in the eyes*, Alphonse had once told her. She met the ghūls jaundiced gaze. Stared back at the sickly green irises where no trace of humanity lingered. She didn't dare blink.

The moment stretched.

Ashra dove to the right as the ghūl leaped, its talons slashing the air where she'd been standing. The wooden banister splintered as the creature slammed into it and fell over the side, disappearing into the darkness of the stairwell. A metallic cacophony rose up from below as it landed on the trolley stacked with silver trays.

Ashra hurtled down the stairs, stiletto raised and teeth bared. Ready to end it.

There was no need.

The ghūl lay across the shattered trolley, its neck twisted at an impossible angle. Ashra watched intently, not daring to believe her luck. Eventually she sagged against the wall in relief. Pain flared in her shoulder where the creature's talons had pierced her flesh. The wounds would need cleaning and binding.

She had to get back to the boat.

Ashra stepped around the ghūls prone body and made for the front door. She paused to snatch up the snapbangs from the floor. Strange that the creature had evaded them. She peered outside. Were there more ghūls out there? She couldn't see any. With luck it would stay that way.

As Ashra slipped through the doorway, a distant screech pierced the silence. A chill passed through her as several others answered. The cacophony fell silent, but somehow the quiet that followed was worse.

The hunt was on.

Ashra started running.

23

NOTHING BUT BONES

She's been gone too long, Lukan thought.

"Ashra should be back by now," Flea said, as if reading his mind.

"Yes," he sighed. "She should."

"Do you think something's happened?"

"What I think," he replied wryly, "is that our thieving friend has gone rogue." He paused. Was it possible to go rogue when you were already a rogue to begin with?

"You think she's looking for the alchemist on her own?" Flea asked. Even in the darkness, he could see the girl's expression harden. "She was meant to come back to get us. She promised."

"She did," Lukan agreed. "But people break promises. Even Ashra, it seems."

"And Matteo," the girl said, her head dropping a little. "My brother promised he'd come back. But he didn't."

"I remember."

"I won't ever break a promise," Flea said defiantly. "Not ever."

"Then you're a better person than most."

They passed the next few moments in silence, lost in their own thoughts. Which, as it happened, were both the same.

"But what if something *has* happened to her?" Flea asked.

"I'm sure she's fine," Lukan replied, without conviction. He thought again of the monster he saw in Nika's memories. If Ashra had run into that thing . . .

"But what if she's not? What if she's I n trouble?"

"Then she better be handy with her stiletto." The lightness of his tone belied the dread curling inside him, at the grudging realization of what he had to do. He'd ignored it for as long as he could, but he couldn't any longer. Not when each passing moment might place Ashra in greater danger. *Damn it all.* The boat pitched beneath him as he rose to his feet. "Come on. We won't find out what's happened to Ashra by sitting here."

"Lady Marni told me to wait 'til the sixth hour," the boatman grunted as they disembarked. "But I'm not waiting a moment longer."

"If we're not back by the sixth hour," Lukan replied, adjusting his cloak round his shoulders, "then I expect we'll have greater concerns than losing our ride home." He glanced at Flea. "Ready?" When the girl nodded, he turned and started up the stone steps. *Damn, it's cold.* He'd declined the woolen jodhpurs that Razin had offered him, put off by the suspicious stains they bore, but now found himself regretting his decision.

But not nearly as much as he regretted having to leave the safety of the boat.

Flea bumped into him as he froze at the top of the steps.

"Argh," the girl muttered, giving him a shove, "what are you . . ." She trailed off as she saw what he'd seen.

"They're just bones," she said after a long pause. "We saw more in the catacombs."

"We did," Lukan agreed, the thought bringing scant comfort. "Let's just hope there's no sorcerous wolf this time." *Then again, I'd rather face another glowing wolf than the monster in Nika's memories. Better the devil you know.* "Hold this," he added, handing Flea a wooden torch. Its head was wrapped in cloth and soaked in pitch. The girl obliged, holding it still as Lukan struck flint and steel. Flames sprang into life, pushing back the gloom.

But only a little.

Lukan took the torch back and stared at the avenue that stretched away into darkness. He waited a moment, hoping to see Ashra emerge from the mist.

Nothing stirred.

"Right," he said reluctantly. "I suppose we ought to—"

A distant screech broke the silence. Several others rose in response. By the time they fell silent, Lukan's heart was racing.

"Was that the monsters?" Flea asked, an unfamiliar note of uncertainty in her voice.

"I don't know." *I bloody hope not.* He glanced at the girl. "Look—perhaps you ought to stay here. If I'm not back in—"

"Don't be stupid," she interrupted. "I'm coming too."

"Fine," he said, secretly relieved. "Then let's go."

Ashra was no stranger to running for her life.

Perfumed merchants, surly constables, enraged guards—all had chased her many times, but she'd never been caught. She was too quick, too sharp, with more to lose than they had to gain. Such desperate flights had grown fewer in number as she'd grown older and more experienced, but, on the rare occasion she was required to make a quick exit, she always escaped the hunters on her tail. The one exception—which still pained her when she thought of it—was when she'd been brought to heel by the Twice-Crowned King's enforcers. Even then, she'd evaded their grasp for some time before they finally cornered her.

But all those hunters had shared a common trait.

They were human.

And what hunted her now was not.

Where humans might grow tired, or bored, or distracted, Ashra guessed the creatures stalking her would chase her until she dropped. And then they'd be on her like starving dogs, sharp talons rending her flesh, fangs bright with blood—

Ashra whirled, expecting to see one of the creatures lunging out of the mist, braced to feel its fetid breath against her face.

Nothing.

She stood still for a moment, alone in the mist, her breath rasping in her chest. Enough, she told herself. There was no need to imagine monsters when the real ones were on her tail.

Another screech tore the silence of the night.

Close, far too close.

Other calls answered the first. Ashra turned, ignoring her pounding heart as she tried to pinpoint their locations.

Damn it. They'd circled around her. Again. Every time she thought she'd evaded them they flanked her, driving her further and further away from the river. As if they knew that was her destination. She didn't even know where she was now. Couldn't tell north from south, save for when the mists and looming buildings deigned to give her a glimpse of the moon. Panic gripped her once more, and again she forced it down, knowing its claws were just as deadly as those of the creatures behind her.

Focus.

Breathe.

Move.

Ashra set off, running through the mist and into another street that looked much like the others. The howls sounded again as she ran, and she tried to forge a course that moved away from them while still bringing her round back toward the river. Not that she was even sure where that was. She reached a crossroads and veered left, instinct telling her the water lay in that direction. If she was right, she could follow the river back to the boat. If it was still there. Even if it was, what if Lukan and Flea had already left in search of her? There were far too many *ifs* in the equation. She cast the thought aside. Speculation only slowed you down. Find the river— that was all that mattered.

Easier said than done.

In Saphrona, Ashra knew almost every street, every alley, every ratway from the Splinters to the Silks. Whenever flight had been the only option, she always knew where to turn, which direction would lead her to safety. She was always several steps ahead of her pursuers, both physically and mentally.

Not so here. Not in this unfamiliar city of snow and stone. Here it was as if she'd been scoured by the biting cold and strangling mist, her knowledge and expertise bled from her. She was vulnerable and she knew it; the doubts and insecurities she'd managed to keep at bay were now like hooks in her flesh, tearing at her skin, slowing her down, making her doubt her every move. All she had left was her instinct, which remained sharp as ever, and the iron-hard resolve that had kept her going all those years.

They would be enough. They had to be.

She didn't see the ghūl until she nearly ran into it.

The creature stood in the middle of the street with its back to her, claws twitching. Even from several yards away Ashra could hear its breath rattling in its throat. Somehow it didn't seem to have heard her. She took a step back. Another. The ghūl tensed, its head snapping to one side. Ashra froze. Her eyes flicked to her left, where the darkness of an alley beckoned invitingly. It wasn't far. A few steps at most. If she could just reach it—

The creature whipped round.

Ashra drew her stiletto, but knew it was futile. She'd got lucky with her earlier kill. These creatures were faster than her. Stronger. She couldn't hope to defeat another. A strange calm settled over her. There was strength in accepting your fate. Embracing it.

"Come on then," she hissed.

She braced herself, expecting the ghūl to accept her invitation. But it remained still. Then it flung back its head and screeched, its entire body tensing. Ashra knew an opening when she saw one. Without thinking she hurled her stiletto, and the creature's cry turned to a gurgle as several inches of steel punctured its throat. Ashra threw herself at the ghūl and knocked it to the ground. Talons slashed at her, tearing at her clothes. Fire erupted across her right cheek as a claw sliced her face, but she ignored it as she pulled her stiletto from the creature's throat.

When backed into a corner, always go for the eyes.

Ashra gritted her teeth and drove the blade into the ghūls right eye. It thrashed beneath her, its screeching breaths hot against her face, but she didn't stop. She stabbed it again. Again, again, again. Only when the creature slackened beneath her did she pull her blade free and rise to her feet. She staggered, suddenly dizzy, but kept her balance. She put a tentative hand to her cheek. Her fingers came away bloodied.

No matter.

To bleed was to be alive. But she wouldn't be for long, not if she remained standing there. Ashra started running as another screech sounded somewhere before her. She skidded to a halt as others sounded on every side.

She was surrounded.

Hesitation was a thief's deadliest enemy, yet it seized her now and hopelessness followed in its wake. To think that she'd killed two of these damned creatures and yet they would still take her. Anger sparked defiance, which snapped hesitation's chains.

She wasn't going to die today.

Ashra started forward, eyes scanning the street. She tried the doors of several townhouses, but they were locked, their windows shuttered. She cursed and the screeches rose in volume, as if her pursuers sensed her desperation. All she could do now was find a place to make a stand. As she looked around, the mist shifted, revealing a large shape further down the street.

A carriage.

As she ran toward it, she could make out the elegant words painted on its side: *Blackfire Banking House*. Similar carriages were operated by the Three Moons Counting House back in Saphrona, like the one they'd stolen the Sandino Blade from. They tended to be sturdily built, with reinforced doors and windows, to guard against trouble. A quick glance told her the carriage was in good shape, despite the twenty years it had stood abandoned in the street. Its door hung open invitingly, tempting her with a promise of safety. But it was nothing more than an illusion. A temporary reprieve. If she locked herself inside, she knew the carriage would become her tomb.

Reluctantly, she stepped away. There had to be another option.

The ghūl emerging from the mist ahead suggested otherwise.

As soon as the creature saw her, it broke into a run, and closed the distance between them in a few heartbeats. Ashra leaped into the carriage and pulled the door closed just as the ghūl slammed against it. She drew the double bolt and pressed herself into a corner, as far as she could get from the door. With any luck the small window contained some sort of alchemically strengthened glass and wouldn't crack beneath the creature's attacks. The ghūls talons squealed across the glass as it hammered at the door, but the carriage held firm.

Screeches pierced the night.

Ashra gripped the cushioned seats, the carriage rocking beneath multiple blows as more ghūls joined the assault. She huddled inside, hating how powerless she felt. Her Rings of Last Resort were useless here; the portal would manifest outside the carriage. Yet there was *always* a way out, and she could see one now in the point of her stiletto. A chance to end things on her own terms. To control the manner of her death.

No, she decided, hating her own weakness.

It was never over until it was over.

Eventually the assault ceased. Ashra peered out of the small window, feeling a fragile hope that maybe the ghūls had given up.

She recoiled as one of the creatures pressed its nightmarish face to the glass, its green eyes peering inside, mouth widening in what might have been a smile.

Screeches slashed the night.

The assault began again.

"Flea." Lukan swore under his breath and quickened his pace, raising his voice as loud as he dared. "*Flea.*"

"What?" the girl whispered back, glancing over her shoulder.

"You're getting too far ahead. Stay close to me."

"Why, you afraid?"

Lukan chose to remain silent over admitting that, yes, actually, he was very bloody afraid, and that Flea would be too if she'd seen Nika's memories for herself. "Just stay in the light," he replied, his voice too loud in the quiet. Words didn't belong here, not in these desolate streets. Words were for the living, and these silent avenues and empty houses belonged to the dead. Lukan was no stranger to setting foot where he didn't belong, but never had he felt as unwelcome as he did now. The mist swirled around him like a living thing, as if aware of his presence.

Or maybe it was just his imagination.

He'd certainly been imagining plenty of things since they'd set off into the mist: movements beyond the torchlight, the scraping of talons on stone. The gleam of eyes in the darkness. But all just tricks of the mind. Or so he told himself.

The screeches were a different matter.

They came again now, a distant rising chorus, somewhere to the west.

"This way," Flea said, darting forward, Lukan's earlier words already forgotten. With a curse he ran after her, wielding his burning torch in his left hand and sword in his right, heart racing as he eyed the darkness for any sign of danger. But there was nothing but thin snow and bones, gnawed and charred and plague-brittle. So many at times that every step he took had to be made carefully so as to avoid rolling an ankle. "Flea," he hissed again, reluctant to raise his voice. "I told you to stay in the—"

Something lunged out of the darkness to his right.

Lukan saw pale, sinuous limbs, caught a glimpse of talons and teeth, and then the figure slammed into him, knocking the sword from his hand. He heard the steel clang as the blade struck the cobbles, quickly followed by the back of his head as his attacker bore him to the ground. Lights exploded behind his eyes as the breath was punched from his lungs. He felt a weight on top of him and thrashed in response. Somehow he'd kept hold of the burning torch, and his clumsy attempt at shoving it in his attacker's face was met with a hiss of foul breath and a brief release of the weight on his chest. Lukan gasped as the torch was struck from his hand. He found himself looking up at green eyes set above a nose that was nothing more than a slit, and a fanged mouth that was a vertical slash.

Two pale hands thrust down and clamped round his throat, talons digging into his skin as they squeezed. Darkness swept in at the edges of his vision until all he could see were those green eyes. He gritted his teeth and lashed out, again and again, trying to drive his fists into those twin pools of poisonous light, but the monster's grip was unrelenting. A deep, distant panic rose inside him. *Can't die like this*, he thought desperately as the darkness closed in, the two eyes like diseased suns that were about to burn out.

Suddenly the creature jolted. Its grip on Lukan's neck slackened as it fell forward, its hideous face brushing his own. Gasping, Lukan shoved the creature aside and squirmed out from under its weight. Two crossbow bolts stuck out of the back of its skull.

"Three times," Flea said as she stepped into the light and lowered her crossbow. "I should start charging you." Her grin faltered as she saw the monster properly for the first time. "What *is* that?" she asked, stepping closer.

"I've no idea," Lukan replied, his heart still racing. *And I've no wish to know.*

"Looks like you first thing in the morning," Flea said, though the tightness in her voice revealed her underlying nerves. She grimaced and covered her nose. "Urgh, it stinks. Also like—"

"Me first thing in the morning," Lukan cut in, "yes, I get it. If only your jokes were as good as your shooting." He picked up his torch and studied the creature. Flea was right; it stank of the grave. Yet gaunt as it was, its pale, lithe body showed no signs of decomposition. He glanced at its face, at the fangs and the vertical, teeth-lined slash of its mouth. What in the hells was this thing? He reached to pull the two crossbow bolts free, only to pause as a glint caught his eye—a gleam of gold on the monster's left hand. His eyes widened.

A wedding ring.

"Lady's blood," he breathed.

"What is it?"

"Our friend here was once married." He pointed at the hand.

Flea stared at the ring. "You mean . . ."

"This thing was once human."

"Did the plague do this?" the girl asked, gesturing at the creature's nightmarish face. "Did it turn him into a monster?"

"I don't know."

A distant screech sounded. Several more joined it to create a chilling cacophony.

"There's more of them," Flea said, not able to mask her fear this time.

"Sounds like it." Lukan pulled the bolts free and offered them to the girl. "And I have a feeling that where we find them—"

"We'll find Ashra."

Lukan nodded. "You all right?"

"Me? You're the one who was jumped by a monster."

"I'll take that as a yes." Lukan retrieved his sword. "Let's go. And this time, stay close to me."

Flea didn't argue.

The window was breaking.

Ashra watched as cracks spiderwebbed across the glass. For a long time it had resisted the ghūls' attacks, giving her hope that she might live to see the dawn. Would the ghūls leave when the sun rose? She could only hope so. And hope the glass held until then.

For a while it seemed it might.

Then one of the creatures had fetched an iron railing and thrust the pointed tip against the glass. The first few blows merely bounced off. But then the ghūl had reversed the railing and slammed its flat base into the window. Several savage blows left a small crack in the glass. Ashra knew then she was doomed.

Now it was a matter of moments before they broke through.

The creatures knew it too. Their screeches took on a triumphant note as they sensed victory. Ashra glanced around again, seeking some sort of salvation among the plush upholstery of the carriage, but there was nothing. Some carriages had a trapdoor to enable its occupants to escape through the floor, but not this one. Clearly that had been an expense too far for the Blackfire Bank. Bloody coin-counters. They loved making money, but spending it? Not so much. Muttering a curse, Ashra grabbed the one object available to her: a velvet cushion.

The base of the railing struck the window again. A single shard of glass flew inward, landing on the seat across from her. One more strike would surely do it. Fear and defiance warred in Ashra as she sat and waited for the moment to come, clutching the cushion like a noblewoman preserving her modesty. But there was nothing modest about her. She was the best damned thief that ever prowled the streets of Saphrona. Dying at the hands of these ghūls wouldn't change that. She only hoped Lukan and Flea didn't risk their own lives by coming to look for her.

Another shard of glass fell from the window. Ashra took a deep breath and thought of Saphrona. Of home. The blue skies, the sun flashing off the bronze domes, the sound of bells ringing across the red rooftops, of Alphonse and his jokes.

The window shattered.

Glass flew.

Ashra's cushion protected her from the shards. As she peered round it, she saw a pale, sinuous arm reaching through—but not for her.

It was reaching for the door bolts.

She snatched up her stiletto and stabbed at the arm, her steel puncturing the pallid flesh. The ghūl hissed and withdrew its limb. Its fanged face glowered at her through the window. Intelligence gleamed in its green eyes. How had it known to unlock the door? She had no time to consider the answer before the next assault came. Not an arm this time, but the railing. And not the flat base, but the sharpened tip.

As the railing flashed toward her, she used the cushion to knock it aside. She managed to deflect the next attack too, and the third, but the fourth time the tip tore the cushion open. Feathers fluttered as the ghūl drew back, preparing for a final strike.

Ashra tossed the ruined cushion aside and gritted her teeth, heart pounding as she raised her hands. If she could just grab the shaft, somehow wrest it away from her attacker—

Wait.

She tilted her head, listening.

Were those . . . footsteps?

Surely not. She must be imagining them.

The snap of a crossbow string told her she wasn't.

With a hiss, the ghūl at the window turned away and leaped down from the carriage step. Ashra took the chance to peer through the window. Relief, edged with guilt, washed over her at the sight of Flea raising her crossbow for another shot. Lukan stood behind her, a torch in one hand and sword in the other. Three ghūls faced them, talons twitching as they sized up this new threat. One of them had already taken a crossbow bolt to a shoulder.

Ashra fought the urge to cry out, not wanting to distract Flea and Lukan. They were in enough danger as it was. But Flea must have seen her shadow in the gloom, for the girl's eyes snapped to the carriage window. "Ashra!" she called out, her gaze swinging away from the ghūl with the iron railing.

A mistake.

The ghūl lunged, thrusting the tip toward Flea's chest. The girl managed to twist aside, only to slip and fall to the ground. The creature loomed over her, drawing back for a killing thrust. Ashra's heart sank like a stone as Flea struggled to rise, her eyes wide with horror. She wasn't going to make it. Time slowed, the moment coalescing round the railing's tip as it hovered with deadly promise.

"No," Ashra breathed.

The ghūl thrust.

And then Lukan was there, teeth bared as he deflected the railing with his sword. He leaned away from the lunging talons of another ghūl and sliced the monster across the back as it surged past. The ghūl bearing the railing was preparing for another attack, but this time Flea was ready. As the monster loomed over her, the girl calmly shot a bolt right between its eyes. The ghūl's head snapped back and it staggered before falling to the ground. Flea wasted no time revelling in victory; her fingers were already searching the quiver at her hip for another bolt.

"Ashra?" Lukan called, brandishing his burning torch at one of the ghūls. "We could really use a hand here." While his words were flippant, his tone was not, nor was there anything cocky about the way he held his sword. Flea had told Ashra of Lukan's duel with

Amethyst in Saphrona's cemetery, but the only times Ashra had seen Lukan fight were in the sparring sessions he'd had with the sailors of the *Sunfish*. There he'd fought with a half-smile and a certain performative indolence, but she saw nothing of that now as he dodged another attack and delivered a sharp riposte that almost skewered his opponent. He was grim-faced and economical in his movements, imbued with the same sense of purpose he'd shown when standing before Marquetta and the Faceless—almost a different man entirely to the one she usually saw.

Ashra pulled back the bolts and shouldered the door open.

Lukan could look after himself.

Flea, by contrast, was backing away as she worked to reload her crossbow. The ghūl facing her had been distracted by Lukan, but now it hissed and raised its claws as it closed in. Flea wasn't going to have her crossbow loaded in time. The look on her face suggested she knew it.

"Hey," Ashra called, drawing a throwing knife from her belt.

The ghūl didn't turn.

"Have it your way." Ashra hurled the blade, which struck the creature between the shoulder blades. The ghūl staggered, hissing in fury as it spun round.

Ashra raised her stiletto. She knew she had one chance.

The ghūl stalked toward her, only to shudder and stumble. For a moment it stood still, talons twitching. Then it collapsed to the ground, one of Flea's crossbow bolts protruding from the back of its skull. The girl grinned at her. Ashra turned to aid Lukan, only to find there was no need. The final ghūl was on its knees before him, one taloned hand to the ground, black blood seeping from its legs where Lukan's blade had hamstrung it. The ghūl hissed and swiped at Lukan with its free hand, but he was out of reach. Ashra expected a witty jibe from him, now that the battle was won, but his expression was grim as he raised his blade. With one powerful stroke he decapitated the creature.

Black blood sprayed.

Flea was racing toward her before the ghūl's head hit the snow.

Ashra was almost knocked from her feet as the girl leaped at her, hugging her fiercely. "You're bleeding," Flea said as she pulled away, concern in her eyes. "Are you all right?"

"I'm fine, *majin*. It's just a cut."

Lukan's greeting wasn't nearly as warm.

"We had a plan," he said as he approached, sword still drawn. Even with the fight over, he hadn't lost his grim aspect; if anything, it had only intensified.

Ashra forced herself to meet his gaze, an unfamiliar sense of shame stealing over her.

"I know I made a mistake," she replied. The words tasted like ash on her tongue. "And I'm sorry."

"I damn well hope so. What in the hells were you thinking? You were meant to—"

"Oh, shut *up*," Flea snapped, breaking away from Ashra and giving Lukan a glare of disgust. "Ashra's alive. That's all that matters." She glanced back at the thief with concern. "You *are* okay, right?"

"I'm fine," Ashra replied. "Thanks to you." She met Lukan's gaze again. "Both of you."

"You put yourself in danger," Lukan replied, unwilling to let it go. "You put *us* in danger." He gestured at the dead ghūl with the railing. "That thing almost speared Flea like a pig."

"Lukan's just annoyed because I saved his life," Flea said, grinning at Ashra. "Again."

"I'm annoyed," Lukan replied heatedly, "because we had a *plan*, and—*oof*."

The scroll case struck him on the chin, Ashra having thrown it with more force than necessary.

"The hells was that for?" he demanded, rubbing at his face. His scowl wavered as he glanced down at the scroll case at his feet. "Wait . . . is that what I think it is?"

"Take a look," Ashra replied coolly.

Lukan sheathed his sword and picked up the scroll case. "Flea, hold this," he said, handing her the burning torch. The girl pulled a face but did as he asked. Lukan opened the case and carefully slid out the parchment within. He unrolled it slowly, his smile widening as he scanned the formula inscribed on the scroll. "You found the tavern, then?" he asked. "And the alchemist?"

"I did," she replied. "Her skeleton was in her bedroom at the inn."

"Pity she wasn't still alive," Lukan murmured, frowning at the scroll. "She could have told you what the hells this formula means."

"She did."

Lukan glanced at her. "What do you mean?"

A distant screech split the air before Ashra could reply. Her fear returned as more followed.

"Shit," Lukan spat, glancing around at the darkness. "Of *course* there's more of them." He shoved the scroll back in the case and slipped it into a coat pocket. "We need to go."

"This way," Ashra said, starting forward. "I think this leads back toward the river."

"Forget the river," Lukan replied, drawing his sword and snatching the torch back from Flea. "Use your rings. Summon a portal."

Ashra hesitated. "I'm not sure that's a good idea."

"And I'm not running all the way back to the river to find the boatman's already gone. The old man looked ready to fill his britches, and that was before the screeching began. Let's take the easy way out." He frowned, as if remembering the consequence of using the rings. "Easier, anyway."

"But if he's still there," Ashra countered, "Marni will wonder how we made it back across the river."

"Let her wonder. As soon as she has the formula, she won't care."

"So you *do* think we should give it to her instead of Arima?"

"I didn't say that." Lukan gave her one of his infuriating smiles. "I'll explain as soon as we've finished shivering in Razin's living room."

Despite the suggestion that Lukan might be coming round to her way of thinking, Ashra still found herself unwilling to use her Rings of Last Resort. She'd always been careful to conceal their power. But Marni could demand the secret from her, if she chose. Worse, if she realized that Ashra's rings were Phaeron artifacts—which she surely would—she would try to seize them for herself. Ashra couldn't let that happen. Using the rings now was too big a gamble.

The screeches drew closer.

But not as big as the risk they currently faced.

Ashra swore under her breath, her decision made. She thumbed the ring on her left hand, rubbing its surface in a circular motion. A symbol flared with turquoise light, flashing three times.

Then it faded.

Ashra stared at the ring in disbelief. She rubbed the ring a second time; again the symbol glowed and faded.

"What's wrong?" Lukan asked, sensing her agitation. "Don't you dare tell me that . . ."

"It's not working," Ashra replied, trying a third time and getting the same result. "It's not bonding to the other ring." She looked up and met his gaze. "Razin and Timur haven't activated it."

"But . . . you told them what to do, right?"

"Of course I did."

"Then why isn't—"

"I don't know," Ashra retorted, struggling to keep her cool. She imagined her other ring glowing on a side table while Razin snoozed in his chair. But why had Timur not noticed it?

"Lady's blood," Lukan swore, pointing his sword at Flea. "This is exactly why we needed you to stay behind."

"If I'd stayed behind," the girl fired back, "that monster would still be chewing on your face."

"Enough," Ashra snapped, causing both to look at her. She took a breath, reached for calm. Found it. "We've only got one option," she continued, her voice even, "and unless we take it now we won't even have that."

"We run," Lukan said grimly.

"We run," Ashra agreed.

"And hope the boatman's still there," Flea added.

More screeches cut through the night.

They ran.

24

There's Always a Way Out

Ashra led them down side streets and across wide avenues, driven by an instinct that the river lay somewhere ahead. But each turn revealed only another row of darkened townhouses, another pile of blackened bones. Another false hope.

"Look!" Flea cried, her eyes sharp as ever.

There it was: the silvered glimmer of water.

"Finally," Lukan gasped. "Let's just hope our friend is still . . ." He trailed off as several figures swept out of the gloom to block their way, green eyes gleaming. "Shit."

"Let's double back," Ashra said, spinning on her heel. She took one step and froze as a screech sounded from the darkness before her.

"We're trapped," Flea said, her voice tight with fear.

"Not yet," Ashra replied, darting toward an alley between two houses. "Follow me." Flea sprang after her. Lukan cursed further behind. "Watch your feet," Ashra called over her shoulder as she picked her way between rotting crates and gnawed bones, her eyes searching for the end of the passage. With any luck they'd find themselves in a parallel street and would be able to veer back toward the river. But luck, as her fifth rule of thievery went, was a fickle lover that could turn on you in an instant.

As it did now.

"Damn it," Ashra whispered as she skidded to a halt and Flea almost collided with her. Far from depositing them in another street, the alley had led them to what had once been a storage yard, judging by the old barrels and piles of mouldering firewood that were stacked in the corners.

"Keep going!" Lukan panted as he reached them. "They're right behind . . ." He fell silent as he turned in a circle, his torch throwing shadows across the stone walls around them.

A dead end.

"Fantastic," he muttered, turning to face the way they'd come. "Best get your crossbow ready, kid."

"No," Flea replied, defiance overcoming her fear. "There's always a way out."

"That's right, *majin*," Ashra replied, but her hope was dwindling with every passing moment as she eyed the sheer walls. Those to their left and right were the sides of houses, their windows all shuttered. But the wall directly before them rose twenty feet to a higher, adjacent street. She could see more buildings looming above her—and a dark space between them. An alley.

A way out, perhaps.

Ashra uncoiled her grappling hook and squinted against the gloom, seeking something at the top of the wall that she might be able to catch. All she saw was darkness. She threw the grapple anyway, watched as its metal prongs sailed over the top of the wall and out of sight. She heard them skittering against stone somewhere in the alley above. Then the grapple tumbled back down.

"Try again!" Flea urged, and Ashra's heart broke a little at the desperation in the girl's voice. She gathered her grapple, spun it in her hand and hurled it up a second time. Again it fell.

"I'm sorry, *majin*," Ashra said, tossing the hook aside and drawing her stiletto. "There's no way out. Not this time."

"No," the girl replied, shaking her head defiantly. "There has to be."

A screech echoed down the alley.

"They're coming," Lukan said, his voice dull, as if he'd already accepted his fate. "Flea, get behind me."

"No."

"Lady's blood, now's not the time to argue."

"Can't shoot them if I'm staring at your arse, can I?" the girl yelled, raising her crossbow.

"I guess not," Lukan replied, a hint of amusement in his tone. He turned to Ashra. "I don't suppose that ring of yours has decided to start working?"

Ashra rubbed at her ring again. The turquoise symbol glowed and faded.

"Pity," Lukan murmured. He looked around the yard and huffed out a breath. "What a place to die."

"No one's going to die," Flea insisted, pointing her crossbow at the darkness of the alley. "I won't allow it."

"Shit," Lukan said, raising his sword. "Here they come."

The ghūls prowled into the yard, staying just beyond the glow of Lukan's torchlight. Five, six, seven of them, all gleaming green eyes and twitching talons.

Too many.

"I'll try and draw them away," Lukan murmured. "If you see an opening, run for it."

"No," Flea hissed back, "we're not leaving you."

"Yes, you are. I can at least die happy if I know for once you did as I asked."

"You're not dying!" the girl insisted. "No one is!"

One of the ghūl lunged toward them. Lukan twisted away from its sharp claws and delivered a slashing riposte that carved a line across its right flank. The creature snarled and backed away.

"First blood!" he called in mock triumph. "Under conventional duelling terms, that makes me the winner. What say we just call it a day and leave it there, gentlemen?"

The ghūls regarded him, breath rattling in their throats.

"No? Fine. Who's next, then?" He glanced at Flea and Ashra, his grim expression belying his flippant words. "Wait for the opening," he whispered. Another ghūl darted forward, only to stumble as Flea's bolt took it in the left leg. Lukan seized the opportunity, thrusting his sword through the creature's neck. Dark blood gushed as he pulled his blade free and sent the ghūl staggering backward with a kick to its chest. "Come on!" Lukan shouted, his sword flashing in the torchlight as he waved it at the creatures.

"It's me you want." He moved to his left, clearly hoping to lure enough ghūls away to create an opening. One took the bait, but the rest remained at the mouth of the alley.

"Hey!" Ashra yelled, moving toward the opposite side of the yard. "Over here." Three ghūls stepped toward her, leaving just two in the center. Few enough that Flea might be able to evade them. That was all that mattered now.

"Get ready," she told the girl.

"I'm not leaving you," Flea retorted.

"Do as Ashra says," Lukan put in, waving his torch at a ghūl who got too close. The creature hissed and drew back.

"No!" the girl snapped. She held her crossbow steady even though her eyes gleamed with tears. "Passion before reason."

Ashra's heart broke in that moment and guilt stormed into the breach. This was her fault. If only she'd not given in to her pride, not felt the need to prove herself.

She tensed as something thudded to the ground behind her. Ashra turned to find a rope dangling from the top of the wall, its end coiled on the ground. Flea was staring at it as well, her eyes round as saucers. Ashra glanced upward, but couldn't see whoever had thrown it down.

"Go!" she urged the girl, and for once Flea didn't argue. She fired her second loaded bolt at the closest ghūl, then hooked her crossbow over her belt and ran for the rope.

"Lukan!" Ashra called as the girl started shimmying upward, nimble as a dockside rat. Lukan stole a glance at her, then frowned when he saw the rope. Hope kindled in his eyes.

"You go," he shouted back, moving toward the center of the yard. "I'll hold them off."

It was a death sentence. They both knew it. Ashra hesitated, feeling a fresh rush of guilt. She shouldn't abandon Lukan to his fate.

"Bloody go!" Lukan shouted, slashing at a ghūl who had ventured too close.

Ashra sheathed her stiletto and darted toward the rope. A ghūl made to follow her, but Lukan leaped in front of it, swinging his burning torch and driving it back. She scrambled up the rope as the creatures closed around Lukan. He swung his torch back and forth, keeping them at bay, but there were too many. One of them leaped from the crowd, talons raking Lukan's shoulder. With a curse, he shoved his torch in its face. The creature screeched and retreated.

"Lukan," Ashra called from halfway up the wall, "take the rope!"

"No time," he yelled back, not taking his eyes off the ghūls.

Ashra cursed, knowing he spoke the truth. The instant he turned his back on them they'd tear him to pieces before he'd got one foot off the ground. But Flea was right. There *was* always a way out. With her free hand she reached inside a pouch at her belt, groping for the snapbangs she'd retrieved from the inn's floor. There were half a dozen at best.

They'd have to do.

Ashra twisted round and looked down. "Run for the rope on a count of three," she called.

"The hells are you talking about?" Lukan yelled back.

"Three," she shouted, not wasting time to explain. "Two. One . . . Now!"

As Lukan sheathed his sword and turned for the rope, Ashra hurled the snapbangs as far as she could. The sachets landed among the ghūls, emitting sharp *crack*s as they struck the ground. The noise wasn't nearly as loud as she would have liked, but it was enough. For a brief moment the creatures were distracted. Lukan added to their confusion by hurling his torch into their midst. Then he leaped for the rope and started hauling himself up.

"Keep climbing!" Ashra yelled at Flea, who clung to the rope not far above her, eyes wide as she watched Lukan's efforts. The girl obliged, scurrying up the rope as fast as she could. Ashra followed, resisting the urge to look down, focusing instead on keeping her feet flat on the wall as she placed one hand above the other.

A cry from below dragged her attention back down.

She swore as she saw Lukan dangling from the rope, kicking desperately at a ghūl who had hold of his right foot. "Let go, you filthy piece of—"

"Lukan!" Flea cried, panic in her voice. "Ashra, do something!"

But there was nothing to be done. Not this time. She was out of snapbangs, had already used the one flashbomb she had, and none of the other tools she carried offered a solution. She drew her stiletto in desperation, but with Lukan twisting and kicking she couldn't get a clear angle for a throw. Somehow he kicked himself free, and for a moment it looked like he might haul himself above the grasping claws. Then another ghūl seized him, dragging him back down as others crowded round.

"No!" Flea cried, her eyes widening in horror. "Ashra, *do* something—"

Suddenly the rope jerked, the movement stealing the words from the girl's throat. Ashra gripped more tightly, her shoulder grinding painfully against the wall as the rope moved upward. Whoever had thrown it down was now pulling them to the top of the wall. But how? Who could possibly have the strength to pull all three of them up? No, *five* of them: two ghūls were clinging on to Lukan as their rescuer slowly hauled them upward. "Mangy bastard," Lukan spat as he slipped a dagger from his belt. "Let *go*." One of the ghūls snarled as he thrust the blade into its arm where it was wrapped round his thigh. Lukan stabbed again and the creature released its grip, tumbling back down into the pack below. He kicked frantically at the other ghoul, but the creature hissed and held on to his right foot. "Get your filthy hands off me." The creature bared its fangs in response.

And then it fell, taking Lukan's boot with it.

Ashra winced as her shoulder scraped the wall again. With the two ghouls no longer clinging to Lukan, they were moving upward more quickly, their rescuer showing no signs of tiring. Flea was already scrabbling over the top of the wall, and a moment later Ashra joined her, gritting her teeth as she hauled herself up.

"You all right?" she asked Flea, but the girl didn't seem to hear. Instead she was staring at the large figure that stood before them.

Ashra pulled her glowglass from beneath her collar and held it up, the weak light reflecting off the curves of their rescuer's metal body.

"A golem," Flea breathed.

The construct didn't acknowledge them in any way as it continued hauling on the rope.

"Of course," Ashra murmured, recalling the scraping metal sound she'd heard earlier in the mist. Had it been following them this entire time?

"Lady's blood," Lukan groaned as he appeared over the edge of the wall. He grimaced as his sword caught on the stone. "Give me a hand, would you?"

Together Flea and Ashra pulled him up. He flopped onto his back, an arm across his face as a sigh escaped his lips.

"Are you okay?" Flea asked, crouching beside him.

"No," Lukan replied, struggling to sit up. "Those bastards stole my boot." He pointed to his stockinged foot and wiggled his toes.

"Better than your life," Ashra pointed out.

"It was a good boot," he replied sourly. "I'll be lucky not to get frostbite."

"He's fine," Flea declared, rolling her eyes.

"I am," he agreed grudgingly, "thanks to Ashra's little trick." His eyes found hers and he gave her a grateful nod. "And to our friend here," he continued, easing Flea out of the way so he could see their rescuer. His eyes widened. "A golem? What in the hells is that doing here?"

Screeches rose from below.

Ashra peered over the edge of the wall. "They're leaving," she said, as the pale shapes below flitted back into the darkness of the alley. "They'll be coming for us. We need to move."

"No," Lukan replied, wincing as he found his feet. "We need to *hide*."

"Hide?"

"We can't outrun them. They're too quick and there's too many of them."

"We'll miss our ride back."

"It doesn't matter. We're not going to reach the boat at this rate anyway. Better to hole up somewhere and wait for daylight. Keep trying your ring in the meantime."

"But where should we go?" Flea asked.

Metal creaked as the golem raised its right arm, its steel fingers curling in a beckoning gesture.

"Look!" Flea said, grinning. "It wants us to follow!"

"Absolutely not," Lukan said, as the golem turned and ambled away. "We don't know where it'll take us."

"You have a better idea?" the girl demanded.

"I guess not." He grimaced and doubled over, clutching his leg.

"What's the matter?" Flea asked, anxiety replacing her disdain as she moved to his side.

Lukan raised one hand, which was smeared with blood. "One of those bastards sank its fangs into me," he muttered, wincing in obvious pain. "Not sure I can even walk, let alone run."

"No," Flea said, suddenly fearful. "You have to."

"I can barely stand, kid. My damned leg feels like it's on fire." He slipped the scroll case from his coat pocket and offered it to Ashra. "Take it. Go on without me."

"No!" Flea insisted, pushing the case back against his chest. "You'll be all right. You just need a rest."

"There's no time," Lukan replied, gently pushing her hand away. "Those damned things will be here soon." He held out the scroll case again. "Best make sure you're not here when they arrive."

Ashra hesitated, feeling a denial forming on her tongue but knowing it was false. Lukan was right. They had to move. With or without him. Reluctantly she reached out and took the case.

"No!" Flea shouted again, desperation shining in her eyes. "We can't leave him."

Clanking metal announced the golem's return. The construct sank to one knee before Lukan, its arms outstretched.

"Look!" Flea exclaimed. "It wants to carry you!"

"What?" Lukan shook his head. "No. No, absolutely not—"

"You want to stay here and die?" Ashra replied, giving him a shove toward the golem. "Hurry up."

Lukan cursed again but didn't argue, and instead hobbled toward the golem. He hesitated as he stepped between the construct's arms. "How am I meant to . . ." The golem answered his unasked question by sweeping him up with surprising gentleness.

"You look like a baby," Flea said, with a grin. "A big, stupid baby."

Lukan's response was lost beneath the grinding of metal as the golem turned and stomped away into the gloom.

"Let's go," Ashra said, taking off after the construct. She could hear Flea's quiet laughter as she followed behind.

The golem moved with surprising speed, and Ashra had to work hard to match its long strides, glancing over her shoulder every few moments to check Flea was still behind her. The ghūls certainly were, their screeches echoing through the darkened streets. Drawing ever closer.

"They're gaining on us," she called, though the construct made no response. Could it even understand her? She knew golems were only meant to be able to understand simple commands, but this construct had already shown signs of greater intelligence. It had responded to the problem of Lukan's injury by providing a solution. How was that even possible? Golems were unthinking machines with no free will. Or so they'd been told. She cast the question aside. Perhaps they would get answers later.

If they lived long enough.

Eventually the golem turned into a narrow street and led them round the side of a townhouse to a pair of wide doors. Ashra had lost all sense of direction. The construct set Lukan down and she moved to steady him as he wobbled on his feet. Screeches sounded close behind them as the golem pushed one of the doors open, before turning to them and beckoning them to follow.

"I don't like this," Ashra murmured, staring at the darkness within.

"Would you prefer to be torn to shreds?" Lukan asked, without humor.

The screeches sounded again. Closer.

"They're coming!" Flea exclaimed, pushing past them. "We need to get inside."

"She's right," Lukan muttered as the girl slipped through the doors. "For once."

"I heard that," Flea called back from the darkness.

The golem beckoned again. Ashra thought she sensed urgency in its gesture.

Lukan hobbled through the doors. Ashra reluctantly followed him into the darkness. The golem stepped inside and pushed the door closed. Metal rasped as something—a bar, she assumed—was drawn across the doors. They stood in the darkness as the sound of the ghūls drew closer. A moment later they were in the street outside; Ashra could hear their talons clicking on the stones, the rattling in their throats. A hand found hers in the darkness. Flea's. The girl squeezed and she squeezed back.

A ghūl snarled, just beyond the doors.

Ashra's heart raced, her mind racing with it. Could the ghūls sense them? Had they picked up their scent? If so, would the door hold? If not, was there another way out? She glanced around and squinted at the darkness, not daring to use her glowglass. But even her eyesight couldn't penetrate the inky blackness. There was nothing to do but wait. And hope.

Ashra flinched at a distant screech. Claws skittered on stone as the ghūls beyond the doors retreated. The hunt was moving on. Ashra released the breath she'd been holding. No one said a word. There was no need to tempt fate. Even Flea remained quiet, still gripping Ashra's hand. Together they waited in the darkness. Eventually she heard the grinding of metal on stone. The golem was moving deeper into the room, its heavy footsteps loud in the silence. A moment later, a faint light appeared, growing steadily brighter. Not the flickering, warm light of a flame, but the steady, cold glow of an alchemical globe. The light spilled from what must have been an alcove at the far end of the room; she could see neither globe nor golem, but for the first time she was able to get a sense of the space they were in. There was a door in the far wall, and the walls were lined with dozens of wine racks, some still containing dusty bottles.

"We're in a cellar," Lukan murmured, taking a step toward the light.

"Don't go getting any ideas," Ashra warned him. "Last thing we need is you drinking yourself senseless."

"Pity," he replied, "I'll bet some of these bottles have aged wonderfully."

Together they approached the light, Flea slipping her hand from Ashra's. The sight that greeted them as they stepped round the corner of the alcove left them speechless.

"Wow," Flea breathed eventually.

"What the hells is this?" Lukan whispered.

"I've no idea," Ashra replied.

25

HORROR UPON HORROR

Ashra blinked, as if that might dispel the illusion, but the scene remained the same as before. The wine racks that had once lined the
alcove had been removed, and in their place a red velvet divan had
been pushed up against one side. Posters and playbills for theatrical performances, burlesque shows and bawdyhouses covered the
cracked plaster of the walls, while books were piled on the floor. One
rested on the divan, and Ashra read the faded gold letters printed on
its cover: A HISTORY OF THE ALCHEMISTS OF KORSLAKOV, VOLUME
TWO. Other objects cluttered the space: a wooden sword, an ornate
clock edged in gold gilding, a music box with its lid open to reveal a
tiny metal dancer in mid-pirouette. Artifacts from another time and
place. She watched as the construct picked up another alchemical
globe and tapped it gently, a rosy light glowing from within. It repeated the process with two more globes, their soft green and blue
light mixing with the others to create an ambience that helped put
Ashra at ease. That made the alcove feel safe.

It was only then she realized.

This palace was a sanctuary. Had the golem made it? Surely
not. They were unthinking machines with no minds of their own.
Yet this construct's hand in their rescue had made her doubt that
wisdom. Now she doubted it even more.

"It's a den!" Flea said, eyes wide with wonder. She weaved
through the piles of books and sat down on the divan, where she
snatched up the music box and peered at it. "How does this work?"

"Flea," Lukan said, a note of warning in his voice.

The girl flicked her little finger at him as she fiddled with the box.
Ashra barely noticed the exchange. Instead, she studied the golem,

noting the scratches and dents on its metal carapace. The small spots of rust. It looked old; nothing like the gleaming constructs they'd seen around the city. She stared at the old blankets wrapped round its feet—presumably to dampen the sound of its heavy footsteps—and wondered why it had followed her. Why it had saved them. Did it do so on its own whim? Or was someone commanding it?

"Thanks for your help," she told the golem. "And for leading us to your . . ."

She paused, noting Lukan's bemused expression. "What?"

"Nothing," he said mildly, raising his hands. "It's just . . . do you really think it understands you?"

"I'm not sure." Ashra turned her gaze back to the construct, met the amber glow of its eyes. "Do you?" she asked it. "Can you understand what I'm saying?"

The construct regarded her silently.

"Seems not," Lukan said. "It's like Grabulli said: they only understand simple commands."

"Simple commands like saving us from a pack of ghūls?"

"A pack of what?"

"Ghūls. Monsters from Zar-Ghosan folklore. That's what Safiya called them." At Lukan's blank expression, she added, "The alchemist. She saw one from her window."

"How do you know that?"

"I'll explain later. My point is that saving us from the ghūls was hardly a simple command."

"Fine." Lukan shrugged. "Maybe they can understand more complex orders."

"Maybe it wasn't an order."

Lukan frowned at that. "Of course it was an order. Someone must have ordered this thing to save us—probably the same person who made this." He gestured at the sanctuary. "These constructs don't have free will. They don't even have what you might call a mind. They can't think."

"It carried you when you couldn't walk," Flea said from the divan. "We didn't ask it to."

Lukan had no answer.

Ashra turned to the construct again. Stared into its glowing eyes. "Do you understand me?" she asked.

"This is ridiculous," Lukan muttered, only to flinch as the golem suddenly turned and reached down, its metal arm hunting around between piles of books. Then it straightened and held up something in its hand: a stick of charcoal. The construct stepped out of the alcove, and, with a slow, deliberate hand, started drawing on the floor. Her eyes widened as she saw what was taking shape. Not a picture, but a word.

Yes

"I'll be damned," Lukan murmured, disbelief in his voice.

"What does it say?" Flea asked excitedly, knocking over a pile of books as she rushed to join them.

"It says yes," Ashra replied. "This construct can understand us." She held out a hand to the golem. "May I?"

The golem offered her the charcoal stick.

Ashra took it, crouched down and scrawled another word alongside the golem's effort.

No

"That says no," Lukan told Flea.

"I guessed that," the girl replied, elbowing him.

"There," Ashra said as she stood. "Now we might get some answers." She turned back to the golem. Where to start? "Are we safe here?" she asked, gesturing to the surrounding cellar. "Point to your answer."

The golem stepped toward the two words and placed a foot on *yes*. It turned to Ashra, as if inviting another question.

"How is it you can understand us?" Lukan asked.

"Really?" Ashra replied, shooting him a withering look. "How's it meant to answer that with yes or no?"

"My turn," Flea said, before Lukan could reply. She chewed her lip as she studied the golem.

"Sometime this year would be nice," Lukan muttered.

"I'm thinking."

"Oh, is that what that grinding noise is? I thought it was the cogs in the music box."

"Can you punch Lukan so hard he pukes?" the girl asked the golem.

The construct moved its foot to *yes*.

Then it turned and stepped toward Lukan, who backed away, a startled look on his face.

"Wait," Flea said, waving her hands. "I didn't mean it! *Stop!*"

The golem raised a huge, metal fist.

"Shit," Lukan swore as he tripped over a wine crate. He stumbled and fell to one knee, and before he could rise the golem was looming over him, metal arm pulled back. Ready to deliver a punch that would do far worse than make him throw up.

"Stop," Ashra demanded, grabbing the golem's arm, as Flea continued waving frantically. She might as well have tried to hold back the tide; she felt the golem's powerful arm shoot forward despite her hold on it.

"No!" Flea cried.

Lukan raised an arm, teeth gritted as the construct's fist descended in a blur of steel.

The fist stopped a hair's breadth from his face.

Then the golem uncurled its fingers and squeezed Lukan's nose.

"What in the hells . . ." Lukan stared at the construct in disbelief. He reached up and touched his nose, as if to make sure it was still there.

"It was a joke," Ashra said, the realization striking her as Flea started laughing. "Wasn't it?"

The golem returned to the scrawled words and placed its foot beneath *yes*.

"Hilarious," Lukan muttered as he found his feet. "Do we have the alchemists to thank for your wonderful sense of humor?"

Metal scraped against stone as the construct moved its foot.

No.

"Right," Lukan said sarcastically. "Born with it then, were you?"

Another scrape of metal.

Yes.

"Should've taken our chances with the ghūls," Lukan said, glancing at Ashra, before looking toward the door at the back of the cellar. "We still don't know if someone's commanding this construct."

Ashra barely heard him. Her mind was racing as she stared at the golem. Surely what she was thinking wasn't possible. Was it?

"Are you like us?" she asked.

"Lady's blood," Lukan swore, "you cannot be serious."

Ashra ignored him. "Are you human?" she asked the golem.

The golem moved its foot.

No.

"Well, good to have cleared that up," Lukan muttered.

"*Were* you once a person?" Flea asked.

A scrape of metal.

Yes.

Silence stretched as they stared at the construct.

"This is ridiculous," Lukan said eventually, with notably less conviction this time. "How in the hells could this thing"—he waved an arm at the construct—"have been a person?"

"It makes sense," Ashra countered. "It explains how it can understand us. Why it saved us from the ghūls." She gestured at the alcove. "Why it's created a home."

"Oh, come on," Lukan scoffed. "You really think Sir Clanks-a-lot here actually reads these books?"

The golem moved its foot again.

Yes.

"Right," Lukan muttered, shaking his head. "Of course you do. My mistake."

"Is your body inside there?" Flea asked, tapping the construct with the tip of the wooden sword that had somehow made its way into her hand.

No.

"But your mind is?" Ashra said.

Yes.

"How?" Lukan asked, curiosity overcoming his disbelief.

Flea sighed and rolled her eyes.

"My mistake," Lukan said, waving his own question away. "Let me phrase it differently. Um . . ." He frowned. "No, hold on . . ."

The golem evidently grew tired of waiting, for it reached out to Ashra. It took her a moment to realize what it wanted. She placed the charcoal stick in its huge palm. They all watched as the golem leaned down and scrawled another word on the floor.

SOUL

Flea frowned at the letters. "What does it say?" she asked.

Ashra couldn't find her voice. She half-expected Lukan to reply with a joke to tease the girl, but he didn't even seem to have heard the question; instead he remained silent, staring at the crude letters. "That's impossible," he said eventually, his voice barely above a whisper. "Souls don't even . . ."

"Exist?" Ashra prompted. "I thought the Veiled Lady's entire purpose was to absolve your sins so your eternal soul could reach paradise."

"So they say, but . . ."

"You didn't believe it."

"No. I thought it was a scam. The oldest in the book, designed to part the gullible from their coin. I thought once you died it was just . . ."

"Darkness."

"Right. But now . . ." Lukan trailed off, his expression that of a man who had just felt the entire world come loose from its moorings. "Even if this was true," he continued, trying to find a foothold in this strange new landscape, "how is it possible to trap a person's soul inside a golem?"

"You have an artifact that can store memories," Ashra replied, looking at him. "Why should this be impossible?"

Lukan had no answer for that.

"This is amazing," Flea said, her eyes bright with excitement. She strode up to the golem. "Did the alchemists do this?" she asked.

Yes.

"Were you already dead?"

No.

"So . . . did they kill you?"

Yes.

"And then they put your soul in the golem?"

Yes.

"Hold on," Lukan said, raising a hand. "You're saying the alchemists *murdered* you, and then placed your soul in that body?"

Yes.

"Lady's blood," he murmured, meeting Ashra's gaze. She saw the same shock she felt mirrored in his eyes.

"Are the others the same?" she asked the golem. "The other constructs, I mean. Were they all once people?"

Yes.

"And the alchemists murdered them and trapped their souls in metal bodies?"

Yes.

A moment of silence as they all considered that.

"This is . . ." Lukan trailed off, as if struggling to find the words. For once. "Horrific," he said eventually.

"It's worse than that," Ashra replied. She felt sickened. "It's evil."

"Have you been here a long time?" Flea asked, subdued now. Tentative, almost. Most unlike her.

Yes.

"Since the plague?"

Yes.

"Did you help to build the barricade?"

Yes.

"But you got left behind?"

Yes.

"And you've been here ever since?"

Yes.

"All by yourself?" Flea's voice was hushed.

Yes.

"Except for the ghūls," Lukan said, without humor. "They're human, aren't they? Or were."

Yes.

"Wait," Ashra said, reeling at this latest revelation. Horror upon horror. "Why would you think that?"

"One of the ghūls that attacked us was wearing a wedding ring," Lukan replied. For once he didn't try to make a jest.

Ashra thought back to those panicked moments in the carriage, when one of the creatures had reached through the window, talons searching for the door's bolts. She'd wondered how it knew to unlock the door. Now she knew.

"Did the plague do this to them?" Lukan asked the golem. "Did it somehow turn these people into monsters?"

Yes.

"But not all of them," Ashra put in, thinking of Safiya's descriptions of bodies burning on the pyres. "Were only some victims changed in this way?"

Yes.

"Do you know why?"

No.

"Are they infectious?" Lukan asked, sudden trepidation in his voice. Ashra glanced at him and saw that he was staring at his bleeding leg. "Do they still carry the plague?"

The golem was still for a long moment. Then it moved its foot halfway between *yes* and *no*.

"You don't know," Lukan observed, his expression grim. "Wonderful. Do you know what started the plague?"

No.

"Why did you help us? Did someone command you to?

No.

"You just wanted to help," Ashra prompted.

Yes.

"Thank you."

"Yes," Lukan said, with no trace of sarcasm. "Thanks for your help." He frowned, as if he still couldn't believe he was talking to the soul of a dead person. Ashra didn't blame him. She could hardly believe it herself.

"This door," Lukan continued, pointing to the door in the back wall. "Does it lead upstairs?"

Yes.

"And is the house safe?"

Yes.

"Where are you going?" Ashra asked, as Lukan opened the door. Its hinges creaked from disuse.

"Need to think." His brow creased; the look he got when something was on his mind.

"About what?"

"A theory that just occurred to me, thanks to our friend here." He grimaced and glanced at his leg again. "And I need to try and clean this damned wound. I don't fancy turning into a ghūl."

Ashra studied his injury. "We don't know that will happen."

"We don't know it won't. Besides, even a normal infection would be bad news. I've already lost a boot. I'm not losing my damned leg as well." He stepped through the doorway. Stairs rose into darkness beyond. "I'll poke around the kitchen," he said over his shoulder. "See if I can find some vinegar or something."

Metal scraped on stone as the golem picked up an alchemical globe and crossed the floor to give it to Lukan.

"Oh," he said, accepting the globe. "Thanks."

With those words he disappeared through the doorway.

"Were you a boy?" Flea asked the golem, as the stairs creaked beneath Lukan's footsteps.

The construct returned to the chalked words.

Yes.

"I knew it! How old were—no, wait . . ." The girl chewed her lip. "Were you older than twenty when they killed you?"

"Perhaps," Ashra said pointedly, "we should give it a rest. Give our friend here a chance to breathe."

"He doesn't need to breathe," the girl replied, looking at the golem. "Do you?"

No.

"You know what I meant," Ashra said.

"Do you mind me asking questions?" Flea pressed.

No.

She glanced at Ashra, triumphant. "See?" The girl turned back to the construct. "Are you happy we're here? Do you like the company?"

Yes.

"Have you been lonely here on your own?"

Yes.

"I know how that feels," Flea said, a shadow stealing over her face. "I was left on my own for a long time too. Well, not as long as you, but it felt like *ages.* That was when my brother Matteo left me." She shrugged. "I don't know where he went. Did you have any brothers or sisters?"

No.

"What was your name? Can you write it on the floor?"

"Don't," Ashra told the golem firmly, before turning to Flea. "That's enough."

The girl sighed in exasperation. "Why?"

"Because . . ." How to even explain? She could see the bond Flea was already forging with the golem, the speed at which the girl was accepting the construct as a friend. And the closer Flea grew to the construct—or the soul within it—the harder it would be for her to say goodbye. The more it would hurt her to leave. That was the nature of closeness; it made you vulnerable. Ashra had told herself that to be alone, to be self-reliant, was to be strong. Yet it also brought loneliness. It was this, she guessed, that caused Flea to make fast friends with anyone she took a liking to. The disappearance of her brother had left her with a void that she always sought to fill.

"Ashra," the girl pressed, eyes narrowed. "What is it?"

"Nothing," she said, shaking her head. "It's just that when Lukan gets back we'll need to be on our way."

"I thought we were staying here until dawn?"

"Not if I can help it."

Flea sighed. "Okay. But I'll keep asking questions until Lukan gets back." She turned back to the golem. "How old are you? More than twenty?"

Yes.

Ashra sat silently as the girl continued to interrogate the construct. If the soul trapped inside that metal body was happy to answer Flea's questions, who was she to insist otherwise? She shook her head at the strangeness of it all. The horror. She couldn't imagine how it must feel to have your consciousness trapped in a metal body against your will. Worse, to be abandoned in a place such as this. On your own for eternity. No wonder the golem was happy to have company.

Flea glanced up as Ashra moved to the door. "I'm going to check on Lukan," she said, before the girl's question left her lips. She found the golem's amber gaze. "Can you look after her for a while?"

The construct moved its foot to *yes.*

"I don't need looking after," Flea grumbled.

"I won't be long."

Ashra slipped through the doorway and up the stairs, feeling her way in the gloom. She found Lukan in an upstairs bedroom, muttering under his breath as he tied a rag round his leg. He glanced up as she entered.

"How is it?" she asked.

"It's seen better days."

"Haven't we all."

He snorted at that. "I found some old vinegar in the kitchen.

Stung like a bastard but hopefully it'll stop any infection." His expression turned thoughtful. "What the hells do you think they are?"

"The ghūls? I don't know."

"You said that alchemist saw one."

"She mentioned it in a letter I found on her body. She thought it was her imagination."

"If only." Lukan winced as he tightened the rags round his leg. "Did she write about anything else? Did she have any theories about the plague?"

"She believed it had been started deliberately."

"How? By who?"

"She didn't know. But she believed it was to prevent her giving her formula to Lord Baranov."

"Baranov?" Lukan looked up sharply. "What's he got to do with this?"

"Safiya had agreed to sell the formula to him. She guessed one of his rivals wanted to sabotage the deal."

"By unleashing a plague upon an entire district? Seems a bit extreme. What's this formula do, anyway?"

"It unlocks some sort of door. I don't recall the name." Ashra slipped the letter from her pocket and scanned the writing. "Safiya called it—"

"The Crimson Door," Lukan interrupted.

"That's right." She frowned at him. "How did you know?"

"Marni told me about it. It's a Phaeron door, set into the side of a mountain."

"Where does it lead?"

"That's the whole point—it's never been opened." He nodded to himself, realization dawning in his eyes. "That's why Marni's so desperate to get her hands on the formula. She's obsessed with the Phaeron. No wonder she wouldn't tell us what it was for. She wants to open the door and claim what's inside."

"And Lord Arima wants to do the same," Ashra said, following the logic, "to improve his family's reputation. To win the respect he thinks he's been denied."

"And we get to decide which one of them gets to realize their ambition," Lukan replied, with a wry smile. "If we get out of here, of course." His eyes found Ashra's, suddenly intent. "But you didn't come and find me to talk about that."

"No. I didn't." She paused, unsure of how to proceed. She'd never been that good with words. Hadn't had much need for them since her father's death and her mother's accident. Since the joy was stolen from her life. "I'm sorry," she said eventually. "I shouldn't have gone on alone. I should have stuck to the plan."

"Apology accepted." Lukan hissed softly as he stood, gingerly testing his leg.

"Just like that?" Ashra replied, surprised.

"I can shout at you again if you like, but I'm not sure I've really got the energy."

"But . . ." Ashra took a breath, tried to find the thread of her thoughts. "I put you and Flea in danger." She gestured at his bandaged leg. "You got hurt."

"And lost my boot." He lifted his other foot. "Fortunately, I found another. Bit tight, but it'll do."

"It's my fault we ended up here," Ashra continued. "Trapped."

"Yes. It is. You messed up." Lukan shrugged. "We all do. It happens. You're not infallible." He managed a half-grin. "If anything, it makes you more human. That golem downstairs is more outgoing than you."

Ashra felt a flicker of irritation. Not at the jibe, but at Lukan's usual reliance on humor. "I need you to take this seriously."

"I am." His expression became earnest once more. "And I'm telling you it's fine. But do me a favor? Trust in us. Me and Flea. I wasn't lying when I told you we have your back. You don't have to do everything on your own. Let us help you."

Ashra nodded. "I'll try." She turned toward the door. "I ought to get back."

"There's one more thing."

She knew straight away what was coming. Knew it had been coming for a while. She turned back to face him. "Go on."

"That conversation we had in the cell."

Ashra wished she could forget that awful night. She'd lost her cool in a way she hadn't in years. And as much as it had been justified, she regretted the loss of control. Promised herself it wouldn't happen again. "I'm not sorry for what I said to you. About . . ."

"How I'm reckless and only care about myself?" Another half-smile. "Nor should you be. You were right. But it's what you didn't say that I'm interested in. Because I'll wager it's the same thing that has pushed its way between us. Can you feel that gap growing? Because I can. And I'd like it to stop. For Flea's benefit, as much as my own."

Ashra lowered her gaze. Felt the old grief shift deep inside her, where she'd buried it. Where it had remained until recently. "I . . ." She paused, hating how hesitant she sounded. She never felt so vulnerable as when revealing her emotions to someone. Which was why she so rarely did it. "I lost my father the same way you did. To assassins. Except I was there. I saw it happen." Memories flashed in her mind: the masked men bursting through the door, the gleaming knives, the blood on her father's lips. "I saw *everything*."

"I know. Flea told me."

"I never found out who killed him. Or why." She took a slow breath, trying to smother the old fire that was rising inside her. "Not that I didn't try. But I never found the answers." She gritted her teeth. "And it killed me. It still does. To know that my father's killers may still be out there . . ."

"I know how you feel. I feel the same."

"Do you?"

Lukan frowned. "Of course I do."

"Then why do you make bad choices? Why do you waste the opportunities you've been given?" She had to fight to keep her voice even. "You've been gifted the one thing I've always longed for. A chance to get answers. That key offered you an opportunity to win justice. Vengeance. And you threw it away for the sake of a good time. Your actions are an insult to those of us who will never have the same chance."

Lukan stared at her, seemingly at a loss for words. For once.

Eventually he simply nodded. "I hear you. And I won't disrespect you again." He stepped toward her and held out his hand, palm upward. A mark of respect among the Kindred. Ashra met his gaze, but saw no trace of his usual humor. She reached out and placed her own hand on top of his.

Lukan smiled. "Now we can head back. Together."

They went via the kitchen, where Ashra used the vinegar to clean the cut on her cheek. She applied it as well to where the ghūl's talons had punctured her shoulder. The wound wasn't nearly as bad as she'd feared. Small mercies. With Lukan's help she bound it with cheesecloth, which would do until they got back to Razin's. She expected him to make a joke about her being in a partial state of undress, but for once he stayed quiet as he tied the cloth around her shoulder.

Flea was still chattering away to the golem when they returned, telling him all about the street gang she'd run with when she was growing up in Saphrona. She was so engrossed in her tale that she barely even noticed them return. As Ashra sat back down on the divan, Lukan perused the few bottles left in the cellar's wine racks. He pulled one free and blew dust from the label. "Tantallon Blush," he muttered, pulling a face as he slammed it back into the rack. "Lady's blood. Some people have no taste."

"Ashra," Flea said in a low voice, as Lukan moved further away, "what will happen to Clank?"

"Clank?" she whispered back.

The girl tapped the golem with the edge of her wooden sword, resulting in a dull metallic sound. "Clank. See?"

"What about him?"

"We can't just leave him here. We should take him with us."

"We can't. We've no way of getting him across the river. He'd sink the boat."

"Maybe your ring is working now," Flea said hopefully.

Ashra rubbed her ring. The girl sagged in dejection as the glyph on its surface flickered and faded. "Sorry, *majin*," she murmured, her even tone masking the concern that gnawed at her. Why had Razin and Timur not activated her other ring? Something was badly wrong. She knew it.

"Sorry Clank," Flea said, despondent. "You have to stay here."

"That's more like it," Lukan said from a corner of the cellar. He strode back to them, a triumphant smile on his face and a bottle in his hand. "Parvan Red, '23 vintage. Looters must have missed it." He frowned and looked at the golem. "You, ah, don't mind, do you?"

The construct moved its foot to *no*.

Lukan patted the golem on its metal shoulder. "Much appreciated."

"We should go," Ashra said, rising from the divan.

"Now?" Lukan replied, slipping the bottle into a coat pocket. "I thought the plan was to wait for dawn. Razin and Timur are bound to activate your ring eventually."

"We can't rely on that. We need to take the boat. And we should go now, before the ghūls return."

"But we don't know the way. And if the ghūls find us bumbling around in the dark . . ." He shrugged, not needing to elaborate. They all knew they wouldn't be escaping a second time.

"Clank," Ashra said, turning to the golem. "Our boat is moored at the wharf near the Avenue of the Seven Silver Saints. Is that far from here?"

The construct moved its foot.

No.

"Can you take us there?"

Yes.

Ashra caught Lukan's gaze and raised a questioning eyebrow.

"Fine," he conceded. "Let's get moving, then."

"Flea," Ashra said, turning her gaze to the girl. "Are you ready?"

"I guess so," she mumbled, eyes downcast.

The golem strode to the doors and slid back the bolts. Slowly it pushed them open and looked out. Then it turned and beckoned to them.

"Here we go," Lukan murmured, drawing his sword. "Once more into the breach." He followed the golem out the door, still limping slightly from his wound.

"Stay close," Ashra whispered to Flea. The girl nodded glumly. Together they stepped into the cold dark.

THE SENSIBLE COURSE
OF ACTION

Ashra eyed the darkened doorways as they ran. The windows. The alleys. The roofs. She didn't allow herself a moment of respite. It would have been easy to lower her guard in the presence of the golem, such was the obvious strength of the construct, but their enemy was quick and cunning and numerous. It would only take one to slip past the construct and open someone's throat with a wicked talon.

So, she kept watch, her eyes never resting. Clank moved quickly, its feet muffled by the blankets tied round them. They made swift progress through the darkened streets. Lukan's breathing was ragged as he ran, his gritted teeth suggesting that, while his bandaged leg was holding up, it came at a cost. He'd stumbled not long after they'd left the golem's sanctuary, but Ashra's suggestion that he might like to let the construct carry him was met with a stony silence, so she let it be. Perhaps it was for the best. If they were attacked, they needed everyone ready to fight.

Not that there'd been any sign of their hunters. And, save for one distant screech, no sound either. She could only hope it stayed that way until they reached the boat. Time lost all meaning as they ran, along with any sense of direction, but the golem seemed to know where it was heading. Ashra had expected it to make straight for the river, where they could follow its curve back toward the boat, but instead the construct led them through the heart of Ashgrave. There was logic in that: if they were ambushed, there would be a way out. Not so if they found themselves trapped with the river at their backs.

"I think we're close," Lukan gasped, the first words anyone had spoken since they'd left Clank's sanctuary.

Ashra was doubtful; Lukan's grasp of the city's geography up to this point had been almost nonexistent. But as they turned onto another wide boulevard, she realized he was right: this was the Avenue of the Seven Silver Saints. A few moments later the mist parted, revealing the dark expanse of river ahead of them. Their boat was close.

Assuming it was still there.

"Hold up," Lukan gasped. "Hey! Clunk."

"It's Clank," Flea replied in a hoarse whisper.

"Clank, then," he wheezed, taking a moment to catch his breath as the golem turned toward him. "All right, I've got a plan."

"We already have a plan," Ashra said, not liking where this was going. "We're getting in the boat."

"I don't mean that. I'm talking about what we do with the formula. There's no time to explain now—"

"Here it comes," Flea sighed.

Lukan frowned at her. "Here what comes?"

"The bit where you say we just have to trust you."

"Right, well . . ." Lukan shrugged. "You just need to trust me. It's a good plan. I'll explain everything once we're back on the right side of the river. For now, I need you"—he pointed at Flea—"to do something for me. And it's not keeping your mouth closed, for once. Quite the opposite, in fact."

"Will you get to the point?" Ashra urged, glancing at the darkness around them. The ghūls were out there somewhere. "We have to get away from here."

"I need you to pretend to be ill," Lukan told Flea. "I'm going to carry you—"

Carry me?" the girl said, with clear disgust. "No way."

"I'm going to carry you to the boat," Lukan repeated firmly, "and you're going to pretend to be ill. Coughing, moaning, that sort of thing."

"Why?"

"Remember what Lady Marni said?" Lukan asked, glancing at Ashra. "She wants us to report to her as soon as we return. But if my plan is going to work, we need to buy ourselves some time. Pretending that Flea is ill and needs a physician will give us the time we need."

"To do what?" Ashra asked.

"I'll explain as soon as we're safely back at Razin's." Lukan crouched before Flea and spread his arms. "Let's go."

"Wait." The girl approached the golem and hugged the construct's right leg. "Goodbye, Clank," she said. "I wish you could come with us, but you'll sink the boat." The golem responded by gently placing a hand on her back.

"Thanks for your help," Lukan said, slapping the construct's shoulder. "We wouldn't have made it without you. And I'm . . ." He paused, gestured awkwardly. "Sorry about what happened to you."

The golem held out its hand.

Lukan only hesitated for a moment before clasping it. Then he turned back to Flea and spread his arms. "Ready?"

The girl sighed but hopped into his embrace.

"Damn, you're heavy," Lukan grunted as he took a shaky step forward.

"Am not."

"You are. Damn it, will you stop wriggling . . ."

"Goodbye, Clank," Ashra whispered, placing a hand on the golem's right arm. "Thanks for saving us. Take care of yourself." The golem dipped its head in response, amber eyes glowing.

As Ashra strode after the others, her gaze fell upon the skulls and bones that littered the ground. She knew her own bones should have joined them. Perhaps she would have deserved it. She'd broken her companions' trust. Yet they'd come for her all the same. They'd risked their lives to save hers. She felt shame at knowing that, but also something else. A warmth, as if a flame had ignited deep inside her.

Perhaps she was a shadow of the thief she'd been. Maybe this cold, dark city had stolen some of her confidence, blunted her edge. But Lukan was right: she could rely on them. She was stronger with her companions at her side than she was alone.

That knowledge more than made up for whatever she'd lost.

"Wait," Flea said, as they neared the water's edge.

Lukan stopped. "What is it?"

The girl strained to see over his shoulder and then waved. Ashra glanced back to see Clank raise a hand in response. Then the construct turned and trudged away into the gloom. The mist closed behind it.

"Bye, Clank," Flea whispered.

"Ready for the moment of truth?" Lukan asked. "Because"—he grimaced, and shifted Flea in his arms—"I know I am."

"Ready," Ashra replied.

Together they approached the river and peered down at the dark water.

The boat was still there.

So was the boatman, huddled at the stern. He jumped as they appeared above him, almost losing one oar to the dark waters. "Get back!" he spluttered, eyes wide, "I . . ." He fell silent and gaped at them. "It's *you*," he managed eventually.

"Were you expecting someone else?" Lukan inquired.

"No . . . I mean—I heard . . ." He swallowed. "Noises."

"Oh, that's just the ghūls that were hunting us," Lukan replied, as he started down the steps to the jetty. "Don't worry, we gave them the slip." The boatman stared at him. "For now," Lukan added, as he stepped carefully into the boat. "So best ready the oars." Ashra followed, the boat tilting beneath her.

"What's wrong with her?" the boatman asked, looking suspiciously at Flea, who was limp in Lukan's arms.

"She's unwell," Lukan replied, with a convincing tone of concern. "Some sort of ill humor. She needs a physician."

"Muuuuuuuuuuuuuh," Flea moaned. Ashra noted the subtle shake Lukan gave her as if to say *don't overdo it*.

"Plague," the man whispered, his eyes widening as he made the sign of the Builder.

"It's just a passing sickness," Lukan replied, as he set Flea down by the prow. "Some lingering malaise in the air. She'll be fine."

"No," the boatman said, his voice panicked. "You need to leave her. She's infected. She'll kill us all."

"Don't be a fool. We're not abandoning her."

"Then get off my boat. I'm not taking the risk."

"Fine," Lukan said, with a shrug. "But if we're getting off, then so is Lady Marni's prize." He slid the scroll case from his pocket. "How do you think our mutual friend will feel when she learns it slipped through her fingers because you were spooked by a sick girl?"

The boatman scowled. "Fine," he grunted. "Sit yourselves down and let's be off." He threw a dirty look at Flea. "And keep her away from me."

"Muuuuuuuh," the girl moaned in response.

The journey back across the river proved uneventful.

The guards on the patrol boat huddled around their brazier, standing with the listless posture of men who knew they would soon be relieved, and whose thoughts had already turned toward warm beds. They barely even glanced up as the rowing boat slipped past them.

Aside from Flea's occasional moans—fewer now, after Lukan had given her a sharp poke in warning—the creaking of the oars, and splashing of water, they passed the journey in silence. Lukan wore a distant expression the entire time, the kind he usually had when he was deep in thought. No doubt he was working over the plan he'd mentioned earlier. Ashra didn't know why they couldn't just give the formula to Marni and be done with it. With one stroke they could clear their debt and return to the task of hunting down the Rook. It was a simple course of action that made sense. But nothing was ever simple when Lukan was involved. He leaned toward her now, as if sensing her thoughts.

"Don't worry," he whispered.

"Who says I'm worrying?" she replied.

"Aren't you?"

"I just want you to remember what's at stake."

He sat back with a sigh. "As if I could forget."

"Nearly there," the boatman whispered hoarsely.

A moment later the tall chimneys of the Sacred Suckling Pigs tavern emerged from the mist. The boatman sighed with relief, the act of a man who hadn't necessarily expected to see them again. Ashra didn't blame him. They were all lucky to be coming back. The boatman stopped rowing and let the boat drift alongside the small jetty they'd set out from the previous evening.

It felt like a lifetime ago.

"I'm told there's a carriage waiting for you," the boatman said, throwing a loop of rope over a wooden post. "You're to report to Lady Marni right away."

"We're aware of our obligations," Lukan replied. "And under different circumstances we'd be happy to oblige. However, we have more pressing matters to attend to. Our friend here needs a physician."

The boatman glanced at Flea, who responded with a loud moan and a shiver of suppressed laughter. "Lady Marni won't like that," he muttered, as he pulled the boat flush with the jetty. "She wants to see you immediately."

"Well, in that case, perhaps you'd do us the favor of watching over our friend here while we pay the Lady Marni a visit." Lukan gestured at Flea, who faked a coughing fit in response. "We shouldn't be gone long."

The boatman shrank back and raised a hand as if to ward off the girl's illness. "I'm only passing on the Lady's orders. Whether you obey them or not isn't my problem. I've done my part."

"Yes, and you've done it wonderfully. Superb rowing, expert mooring and saintlike patience. Though, if I may be so bold, I'd say your conversational skills could improve." Lukan rose to his feet. "Still, I'd heartily recommend you to anyone looking to risk their lives against the horrors of Ashgrave." He turned to Flea, feigning concern. "Can you walk?" Leaning in close, he whispered, "Because I'm not bloody carrying you again."

With a final, theatrical moan that caused the boatman to again protect himself with the sign of the Builder, Flea allowed Lukan to escort her off the boat. Ashra followed behind. She waited until they were halfway down the side of the silent inn, and well beyond the boatman's hearing. Then she asked the question that was on her mind.

"So, what's your plan? And why is it better than just giving Marni the formula?"

"I'll explain when we're back at Razin's," he replied over his shoulder.

"No, you won't. You'll have a drink or three and then tell the general a more dramatic version of the night we've just survived."

"I'm not sure there's any need to make it more dramatic."

"Tell me now. This is my debt as much as yours."

Lukan huffed out a breath but turned to face her. "Fine. What I intend to do is . . ." He caught himself. "What I think *we* should do is give the formula to Lady Marni, like you said."

Ashra eyed him suspiciously. "That's your plan? The one we already had? No. What's the catch?"

"We give it to Lord Arima as well."

"A copy," Ashra ventured, quickly grasping Lukan's true plan. "Two birds. One stone."

"Exactly," he replied. "Our debt to Marni will be fulfilled, and Arima will make Baranov reveal what he knows of the Rook. We can clear our debt *and* get my key back."

"And when they find out that we've double-crossed them?"

"We'll have already left Korslakov."

"And if we haven't?"

"Well . . . I expect we'll be in a little trouble."

"A little?"

"A lot then."

"I don't like it. I think we should play this straight. Give the formula to Marni."

"That will just leave us back where we started."

"With our debt paid," Ashra calmly pointed out. "And with

Marni off our backs, we can work on finding the Rook and getting your key back."

"But Lord Baranov is our only lead."

"We'll find another."

"How?"

Ashra had no answer for that.

"I know I'm asking a lot," Lukan said, "and Lady knows the last thing I want to do is land you in more danger. And—no, listen—if you refuse then I'll respect that. I will. But you remember what we spoke about earlier, back in Clank's house? Well, this is my chance. Please just consider that."

Ashra had no answer for that either. Fortunately, Flea came to her rescue.

"Can we go home now?" the girl asked, hugging herself. "I can't feel my feet."

"Yes," Ashra replied, "let's go." She caught Lukan's eye again. "We'll talk again later."

She only hoped she had an answer by then.

The job's not over 'til it's over.

Ashra's sixteenth rule of thievery. She always had it firmly in mind while making her escape. Complacency had ended the careers—and lives, in some cases—of many thieves she'd known. A job wasn't over until she was back in one of her boltholes, safe and secure. Until then, she stayed vigilant and kept her guard up.

But not tonight.

She was distracted by Lukan's request, which played over in her mind. Torn between insisting they take the safe option and indulging him by agreeing to take their chances. As they crept through the empty streets of Hearthside, she didn't pay attention to the darkness beyond the street lights. Didn't listen to the sounds of the night. Didn't remind herself the job wasn't over until it was over.

If she had, she might have glimpsed the masked figures. Might have heard the rustle of their cloaks, or the soft crunch of snow beneath their boots.

But she didn't.

By the time she saw them, it was already too late. Like a murder of crows, they swept from the shadows—four, five, six of them—and closed around Lukan, Flea and Ashra like a fist. A deadly fist, at that: all of the figures wielded small crossbows similar to Flea's own, midnight black like their clothes and the masks that hid the lower parts of their faces.

"Oh, of course," Lukan muttered, throwing up his hands and looking to the heavens. "Of *course* something like this happens."

Flea's only response was to raise her own crossbow.

"Don't," Ashra murmured, gently pushing it down. "They don't mean us harm."

"But they're pointing crossbows at us," the girl pointed out.

"Ashra's right," Lukan said wearily. "If they wanted us dead, we'd be so already."

"Quite right," a woman's voice replied, in sharply accented Korslakovan. The speaker stepped from the shadows, the ring of masked figures parting to make space for her. "What happens next is up to you."

"If it's coin you're after, then you're out of luck. We're just travelers, new to the city. We have nothing of value."

"I rather think you do."

Lukan frowned, as if he recognized the speaker's voice and was trying to place it. "I don't know what you mean," he replied cautiously, then jumped as a crossbow bolt struck the cobbles near his feet.

"The formula," the speaker said, her tone brisk. "Did you find it?"

"Are you Lord Arima's people?" Lukan replied. "Because there's really no need to—"

"Answer the question."

Lukan lowered his gaze, his jaw tightening. Ashra guessed he was weighing up whether to reveal the scroll case in his coat pocket. She didn't see any point in lying.

Neither did he.

"Yes," he replied wearily. "We did."

"Pity. It would have been better if you hadn't."

"Better for who?"

"You." The woman gestured at the city around them. "Everyone."

"I don't understand."

"No, you don't." The speaker took a step closer. "I must say, I didn't think you'd succeed where so many others had failed. The *striga* of Ashgrave are not known for their hospitality."

"You mean the ghūls? We've faced worse."

"Yes, I know. I've heard of your exploits in Saphrona, Lukan Gardova. Your infiltration of the Ebon Hand. Your escape from the Twice-Crowned King's cell. The deal you struck with the Faceless. Impressive, I must say."

"Who are you? How do you know about me?"

"I know about all of you. Ashra Seramis—or should I say Lady Midnight? And Flea, the sharp-tongued street rat."

"I've got a bolt here sharper than my tongue," the girl fired back, raising her crossbow once more. Again, Ashra pushed it down.

"Enough talk. Give me the scroll."

"No," Lukan retorted. "Not until you tell us who you are."

The woman paused, as if considering the question. "I am the leader of a faction that does not wish to see this formula fall into the wrong hands," she said eventually. "That is all you need to know."

"And whose hands are the wrong ones?"

"Anyone's but mine."

"If you know so much about us, then you'll know what's at stake if we don't give this scroll to Marni. She'll send us back to the gallows."

"Not if you leave the city immediately."

"We can't . . . *I* can't. I have business here I need to see through."

"That's not my concern. Hand the scroll over. I won't ask again."

Lukan tensed. For a moment Ashra thought he might do something foolish, but instead he pulled the scroll case from his coat pocket. "Have it your way," he said, tossing it to the woman.

She caught the case, removed the lid and peered inside. She pulled off one glove with her teeth and withdrew the scroll. "Have you made a copy of this formula?" she asked, as she unrolled the parchment and studied it.

"When would we have done that? Before being chased by fanged monsters, or afterward?"

"Answer the question."

"No, of course not."

"Have you memorized this formula?"

"No."

"Lucky for you," the woman replied. She slid the scroll back into its case. "If you had, I would have to kill you." She tucked the case under one arm and pulled her glove back on. "I suggest you leave the city at first light. Lady Marni is not the forgiving sort." With those words, she disappeared into the shadows. The six figures followed, leaving the three of them alone in the street. A distant bell began to toll, marking the start of a new day. The last they'd see, if Marni had her way.

"Come on," Lukan whispered, "we've not got much time."

"Time for what?" Flea asked.

"Time," Ashra said pointedly, "to get back to Razin's and say our goodbyes before getting out of here. Right, Lukan?"

"Actually—"

"Because that's the sensible course of action."

"Do you think I'm a sensible person?"

"No."

"Well, there's your answer."

"If we move quickly, we can be out of the city within an hour. By the time Marni realizes what we've done, we'll be long gone."

"You go if you want. I'm not leaving without my key."

"Then you'll be hanging from the gallows by noon."

"No, I won't." Lukan smiled. "Not when I've got what she wants."

"What do you mean? Surely you didn't memorize the formula?"

"I didn't need to." Lukan started walking. "I'll explain when we're back at Razin's. Then you can decide if you want to stay and see this through."

"Whatever scheme he's conjured up," Ashra whispered to Flea, "we don't have to agree to it. We can say no. You understand?"

"Yes," the girl replied. "But we will agree to it, won't we?"

Ashra took a deep breath. "We'll see."

27

GRISELKA OF
THE BLACK QUILLS

"By Brandur's frozen balls!" Razin exclaimed, as he opened his front door and saw the three of them standing on his doorstep. "You're alive! All of you!"

"With no thanks to you," Ashra replied curtly, her concern for the fate of her ring finding purchase in her words. "Why didn't you activate my ring? We almost died back there."

"Can we at least get inside?" Lukan urged, glancing over his shoulder as if an unseen spy lurked in the shrubbery. "We can discuss this later."

"We'll discuss it now," Ashra insisted, not taking her eyes from Razin. "Well? What happened?"

"Yes, well, you see . . ." Razin tugged at his mustache. "There was a . . . complication."

"A complication," Ashra echoed, not liking the way the general winced as she repeated his words back at him.

"It's all in hand," he replied hurriedly. "There's no need to worry."

"If you've lost my ring, I swear I'll—"

"No! No, nothing like that. I know exactly where your ring is." Razin beckoned them to enter. "Come in and I'll explain everything."

He stood aside as they filed past. Ashra waited for him to close the door.

"Where's my ring?" she asked, as soon as he'd slid the bolt.

The general turned slowly, his expression sheepish. "It's . . . in Ivan."

They all turned to the hound, who regarded them with a lolling tongue and wagging tail.

"It's *what*?" Ashra demanded.

"Are you saying," Lukan asked with a grin, "that Ivan swallowed Ashra's ring?"

"It was an accident!"

Lukan's laughter echoed through the hallway as Ashra pinched the bridge of her nose and wondered if she was hallucinating. Perhaps some sort of lingering vapors in Ashgrave had addled her senses. She hissed out a breath. If only.

"I will explain everything," Razin assured her, clasping his hands.

"Damn right you will," she shot back.

"You have nothing to fear, I assure you. Ivan has a military sense of regularity when it comes to his bowel movements, and—"

"On second thoughts," Ashra interrupted, raising a hand, "I really don't need to know."

"You'll have your ring back by noon, I promise. That's when Ivan tends to . . . well, you know."

"Just make sure it's clean."

"Of course!"

"*Spotless.*"

"I'll see to it myself."

"I'd rather you let Timur handle it."

"I'm sure he'll be honored." Razin sagged in momentary relief, as if he'd expected this particular conversation to end with Ashra's stiletto in his belly. "And if there's anything else I can do for you," he continued, offering her a little bow, "you only have to ask."

"As it happens, there is," Lukan replied, his demeanor turning serious. "I need a scribe—someone who's fast, does good work and can be trusted. And I need them now."

"Now?"

"Yes."

"You mean . . . right at this moment?"

"That's usually what *now* means, General," Lukan replied tightly. "Please," he continued, pressing his palms together. "Just fetch a scribe. It's urgent. Agree to pay them whatever they want." Seeing the concern in the man's eyes, he added, "Lady's blood, *I'll* pay."

"Let me speak to Timur," Razin said, striding away down the hall. "He'll know someone."

"And tell the scribe to bring the oldest parchment they can find!" Lukan called after him.

"I think it's time you explained your plan," Ashra said, once Razin was out of earshot.

"Not until I've got a glass in my hand." Lukan pulled the bottle of Parvan Red from his pocket and strode toward the living room.

"Really?" Ashra replied as she followed. "Marni will soon be out for our blood and all you can think about is drink?"

"Marni holding our lives in the palm of her hand is precisely why I need a drink. And if it helps me forget what we saw in the Plague District, then so much the better."

Ashra had no response for that. The horrors of the night were still fresh in her own mind. She kept seeing the ghūls, their gleaming eyes and twitching talons. Their awful faces at the carriage window. The glass giving way.

"Will it?" she asked. The question passed her lips before she could stop it.

"Help me forget?" Lukan replied, glancing at her as he filled a glass with dark scarlet liquid. "No. But it'll take the edge off. For a while, at least." He frowned at her. "Do you want some?"

Yes. She did. But she couldn't.

"If ever you've earned a glass of wine," Lukan said, sensing her reluctance, "it's tonight."

"My father drank a lot," she replied, saying the words out loud to steel herself against the temptation that gripped her. "In the days before he died, I mean. He'd never been a big drinker. A glass of wine here or there. But in the weeks before he died, I noticed he was drinking more. Something was bothering him, but he never said what it was. He'd been drinking the night he was murdered. He was already a few glasses in when the assassins came. I always thought that if he'd been sober . . ." She trailed off, the memory of that dreadful night surfacing yet again. A leviathan rising from the black depths of her mind. "My mother sought comfort in the bottle after my father's death. She tried to hide it from me, but I could often smell the wine on her breath." Ashra paused, scarcely able to believe what she was saying. She'd not spoken of this to anyone, not even Alphonse. Even now, as the words passed her lips, it felt like it was someone else speaking. In a way, perhaps it was. A voice that she'd deemed too vulnerable, now taking its chance to be heard. Even now, her instinct was to force it back down to where she'd buried it all those years ago. But she resisted. Perhaps it was time for this part of her to finally speak.

"My mother had been drinking on the day of her accident. She'd been a dancer, so she was small. Thin. It didn't take much to have an effect." Ashra took a breath, struggling to keep her voice even. "I still wonder if she hadn't had a glass of wine that afternoon whether she'd have seen that cart. Whether she'd have moved quicker to avoid it."

Flea approached her and wrapped her arms round Ashra's waist. She didn't say anything. There was no need.

"That's why you don't drink?" Lukan asked after a moment. "Because of what happened to your parents?"

"That's why," Ashra replied, hugging Flea back. "And it's why I won't have a drink now."

"Understandable," Lukan said, looking thoughtfully at his wine glass. "I wish I had a sliver of your strength." He smiled ruefully. "But I don't."

Razin appeared in the doorway. "Fate smiles on us, my friends," he announced, rubbing his hands together. "Timur knows a scribe who owes him a favor, and he'll go and fetch her immediately. He's pulling on his boots as we speak." His eyes moved to the glass in Lukan's hands. "Starting early, eh?"

"It's late for me, General."

"I suppose it is. Pour one for me, would you?"

Ivan entered the room, tail wagging, and padded over to Flea, who began fussing over him. Ashra stared at the dog's belly. Somewhere in there was her ring, a thought so ridiculous she could scarcely believe it. Was Razin lying, buying time before he had to admit what had really happened? No. He was telling the truth. Allowing his dog to swallow her ring seemed in keeping with his air of organized chaos.

"So did you find it?" the general was asking now, sniffing the wine in his glass. "This scroll?"

"We did," Lukan replied, with a wince. "And then it was stolen from us."

"Stolen?" Razin's bushy eyebrows rose in indignation. "By who? Not that damned Rook again?"

"No. By a woman. She was hooded and cloaked, as were the lackeys she had with her." A line formed between Lukan's brows. "Her voice was muffled by her mask, but there was something familiar about it. And she knew a lot about us and our mission." He shrugged. "She demanded the scroll, and, given we had half a dozen crossbows pointing at us, we weren't in a position to refuse."

"Damn," Razin said, tugging at one end of his mustache. "So, neither Lady Marni nor Lord Arima will get what they want."

"On the contrary," Lukan replied, "if Timur's scribe is up to the job, they're both going to get what they want." At the general's baffled expression, he added, "We're going to forge two copies of the formula."

"But how?" Flea asked, still fussing over Ivan. "You said you've not memorized the formula."

"I haven't. I can't remember it at all." He reached into a pocket and withdrew a small black object that was ovoid in shape. "Fortunately, I don't need to."

"You've saved your memories of it," Ashra said, recognizing the artifact the Faceless had given Lukan back in Saphrona. The same object the Wolf had placed its own memories in, which had helped them convince the Saphronan Inquisition of Marquetta's guilt.

"I did," Lukan replied, with a satisfied smile. He pressed a finger to the object. A prism of golden light rose from its surface, sparkling motes dancing within. "It occurred to me a while ago," he continued, "that, if the Wolf could place its memories into this artifact, then perhaps I could as well. And to my surprise . . ." The golden motes within the light formed into the image of a huge worm rising from a hole, its teeth-lined maw gaping wide. "I found I could."

"That's Gargantua!" Flea exclaimed, her eyes bright with excitement. "And Lady Jelassi!" Razin's eyes threatened to pop from their sockets as the worm reared over a woman who stood with her chin raised defiantly, despite being chained to a pillar. "We thought Gargantua was going to eat her," Flea continued, "but then she turned and—hey!" She glared at Lukan as he removed his thumb from the object, causing the glowing light, and the images within, to vanish. "It was just getting to the good part. Gargantua was about to eat that other man."

"I think that poor fellow has suffered enough without having his death preserved for our entertainment," Lukan replied.

"You did it when we were at Clank's house," Ashra said, thinking back over the night's events. "When you went upstairs."

"I did."

"Hold on, who's Clank?" Razin inquired.

"Clank's a golem," Flea replied. "He used to be a man but the alchemists turned him into a construct. He was left behind when they walled off the Plague District. He saved us from the ghūls."

"A man?" Razin echoed, utterly baffled. "And they made him into a construct? What in the hells are you talking about?"

"That's how constructs are made, General," Lukan replied, his expression turning grave. "Your celebrated alchemists murder people and somehow trap their souls in metal bodies."

The general snorted a laugh, and glanced around as if waiting for everyone to join in. When all he received was silence, he shook his head. "No, that's ridiculous. It's preposterous."

"It's true!" Flea shouted, suddenly indignant. "The alchemists murdered Clank and put his soul in a golem's body and he's been stuck in Ashgrave for years and years on his own."

"But—but," the general spluttered. "But *how*?"

"We don't know," Lukan said, "but it's the truth. Why do you think golems can understand spoken commands? Little wonder your alchemists never reveal their secrets." He pressed his finger to the black object again. The prism of golden light returned, this time showing a scroll of parchment with a single line of formula written across the top. "While Flea was pestering Clank for his life story, I memorized the formula, one line at a time." The image flickered, this time showing a different line. Then another. And another.

"Clever," Ashra admitted.

Lukan shrugged and pocketed the artifact. "I have my moments."

"So, we have Timur's scribe make two copies. What then?"

"Arima knew about our mission, so he must have spies in Marni's household. We'll have to give him the formula first. Once I've got the letter he promised, we'll then give Marni the other copy. She won't know Arima already has it. So, she'll consider our debt paid."

"Arima will learn that we double-crossed him."

"It doesn't matter. By then I'll have already given Baranov the letter, and he'll have spilled his secrets about the Rook."

"What if Arima retaliates?"

"We'll worry about that when the time comes."

"And Marni? What if she learns we betrayed her?"

"Hopefully we'll have left Korslakov by then."

"And if we haven't?"

Lukan sighed, ran a hand through his hair. "I admit there's a lot of risk. And I know it's not just my decision. We all have to agree to it." He took a swallow of wine, as if to steel himself. "So," he said, glancing at the pair of them. "Are you in?"

"I'm in," Flea said immediately.

"Ashra?"

Her instinct was to refuse. To insist they play it straight: give Marni the formula, and figure out another way to get the key. But that route might not lead them to the key. And now, seeing the hope in Lukan's eyes, she realized how much he needed this. She had criticized him for wasting the opportunities given to him. Who was she to deny him this chance now?

"All right," she said. "I'm in."

Another half-hour passed before Timur returned.

Ashra expected the scribe he brought with him to be a quiet, bookish sort. Bespectacled, with a squint from staring at scrolls all day. So she was surprised at the large, red-faced woman who strode into the room behind the small man.

"Lukan, your scribe has arrived!" Razin announced as he followed them in.

"I'm nobody's scribe," the woman replied brusquely. "Not at this time of the morning, and not when I haven't been given an inkling of what is required of me." She unclasped her cloak and flung it at Razin, who barely managed to catch it. "Especially," she continued, "when I'm yet to see a single copper."

"You'll be paid well for this service," Lukan replied, stepping forward and offering his hand. "My name is—"

"I don't care," the woman interrupted, placing her leather satchel on the table. "And you're damned right I'll be well paid for this. I've got a handsome young buck warming my bed, and now it seems I'm going to spend the morning scratching ink for you instead. So, the coin better be worth it, and it better be in my hands the very moment we're done."

"This is Griselka," Timur offered, almost apologetically. "She's the Major General of the Black Quills, the army's scribing division."

"The Black Quills?" Lukan said, with the wry curl of his lips that suggested a quip was coming.

"That's right," Griselka replied, sliding a black-feathered quill from her satchel. "And if there's a joke about the quill being mightier than the sword worming its way toward this conversation, I suggest you let it die on your tongue."

Lukan closed his mouth, but Ashra swore she could hear the grinding of his teeth. Few things seemed to bother him as much as a good joke gone to waste.

"Timur, some fresh coffee if you please," Griselka said, placing a pot of ink on the table. The man nodded and left the room. "Razin?"

"Yes?" the general asked, still struggling to fold the scribe's cloak.

"Get out," Griselka replied. "The last thing I need is you bumbling around while I'm trying to work."

Ashra expected Razin to puff up like an indignant peacock, but instead the old man nodded and backed out of the room, looking almost relieved. It seemed that Madam Griselka was not a woman to be argued with. Ashra liked her already.

"Right, you," the woman said to Lukan as she slid a roll of parchment from her satchel. "Tell me what needs doing, and don't use a single word more than is necessary."

"How good are you at scribing from memory?" Lukan asked.

"Scribing *what* from memory?"

"Alchemical formulas."

"I don't know any," Griselka replied, regarding him as if he was stupid. "I'm a scribe, not an alchemist."

"I'm not talking about *your* memory," Lukan said, smiling at his private joke. He pressed his thumb to the black artifact, releasing its prism of golden light. "I'm talking about mine."

28

TOO EARLY FOR METAPHORS

Two hours later Lukan was standing in a reception room in Lord Arima's townhouse, holding a steaming cup of black coffee. It was a special blend, apparently, imported all the way from the young lord's ancestral homeland on the far side of the Mourning Sea. Or so Arima's fussy steward informed him. Lukan couldn't give a shit. It was scaldingly hot, blacker than sin, and right now the only thing keeping him standing upright. Exhaustion from the night's adventures had finally caught up with him, which was why he didn't dare sit down; he was convinced that just a moment's respite would see him fall asleep. The last thing he needed was to wake up in a gutter somewhere, with the formula—Arima's copy, at least—no longer in his possession. Not that he really suspected the man was capable of such an act, but it was better to be safe than sorry. Especially when the aristocracy was concerned.

Instead he wandered about, sipping his coffee and studying the room's furnishings. Lord Arima might have been Korslakov-born, and determined to make his mark on his native city, but he'd decorated his reception room with reminders of his family's roots. Beautiful porcelain vases—which Lukan took care not to step too close to—bore detailed depictions of fantastical beasts, while silken tapestries of red and gold depicted figures in elaborate armor engaging in battle. Other hangings revealed exquisitely stitched landscapes, bordered by symbols that Lukan couldn't begin to decipher.

But it was the bronze artifact on a raised plinth that drew his attention. Rectangular in shape, it was the size of a large book and had the appearance of a tablet, yet there was a perfect sphere of what looked like amber set at its center. Lukan was reminded of pieces of amber he'd seen at the Academy, which had insects trapped inside them. He couldn't see anything in this one. Verdigris tarnished much of the tablet's bronze surface, particularly the concentric designs that spiraled around the amber sphere, suggesting the object had spent considerable time exposed to water. While its past—not to mention purpose—was a mystery, Lukan had no doubt as to the object's origin. "Phaeron," he murmured, tracing a finger along one of the curving lines, verdigris flaking off underneath his fingernail. "But what the hells is it?"

"A question I've often asked myself."

He turned to find Lord Arima standing behind him, a faint smile on his lips. Lukan hadn't even heard him approach. It seemed the long night and lack of sleep was starting to take its toll. *Best watch my step.* "My apologies, my lord," he replied, offering the man a deeper bow than decorum demanded. "I didn't mean to pry."

"Nonsense," Arima replied, waving his apology away. "Never apologize for curiosity, Lord Gardova."

"Lukan, please."

"As you wish." Arima turned his attention to the tablet. "Magnificent, isn't it? A thousand years under the sea, and its craftsmanship only shines brighter."

"Under the sea?" Lukan echoed, curious despite his fatigue.

"Of course." Arima gestured at the object with a flourish. "You are looking at one of the nine fabled tablets of Shizuna."

"Shizuna," Lukan repeated. In his exhausted state, it took him a moment to place the name. "That's the sunken Phaeron ruin, isn't it? The one at the bottom of the Mourning Sea?"

"No ruin, my friend," Arima replied, with the faintest creasing of surprise round his eyes, "but an entire Phaeron city, still as impressive as the day she was lost beneath the waves." His lips pursed in a wistful smile. "Tradition holds that the mournful wind that gives the sea its name is weeping for all the souls who have died in the wars that have blighted my homeland. But I like to think perhaps it laments the loss of Shizuna to the waves, and the untold knowledge it took with it."

"How does anyone even get down there?"

"Shizuna isn't that far below the surface. Divers who can hold their breath for long periods of time are able to explore freely. But it's a dangerous business."

"If I've learned one thing," Lukan said, with a wan smile, "it's that danger and the Phaeron seem to go hand in hand."

"Oh, it's not the Phaeron city that's the problem. It's more the black sharks that inhabit the ruins. Lots of fish for them to hunt, you see." Arima shrugged. "And sometimes they happen to snare larger prey."

"I know someone who survived an encounter with a black shark," Lukan said, recalling Grabulli's boast. "He had teeth marks all along his arm."

"With respect, Lukan, if your friend had encountered a black shark, he wouldn't have an arm to show you."

Another lie, then. Lukan smiled inwardly. *You bastard, Grabulli.*

"So what is it?" he asked, gesturing to the tablet.

"No one knows. The nine tablets all possess an amber sphere, like this one, but the designs etched on their surfaces are different. As to what it *is*? It's knowledge, Lukan. Knowledge that was lost and will never be recovered. Given what happened to the Phaeron, perhaps that's for the best. Perhaps it's not meant for us. And yet . . ." Arima clenched a fist, his gaze suddenly distant. "Sometimes, we have to seek it anyway, like . . ." He raised a hand, fingers moving as if grasping for the air. "Forgive me, I'm not used to such stimulating conversation so early in the morning. I'm certain there's a metaphor there, somewhere."

Lukan was fairly sure the metaphor was somewhere up Arima's arse, but he certainly wasn't going to go in search of it.

"Speaking of lost knowledge," he said, pulling the scroll case from his coat pocket, "perhaps we could get to business?"

"You found it, then?" Arima asked. His tone was casual, almost disinterested, but Lukan caught the gleam in his eye. *A gleam of what, though?* he wondered. *Excitement at getting his hands on the formula? Or the anticipation of me walking into his trap?* He knew there was a chance—if Arima's spies had been waiting for their return—that the man knew the original formula had been stolen. Which would leave Lukan on very thin ice, and raise all manner of awkward questions.

"See for yourself," he replied, unclasping the lid of the case— not the original one, but another suitably weathered case Griselka had provided. His concern faded as Arima reached out. There was an eagerness to the man's fingers as they slipped inside and withdrew the parchment, and an intensity to his gaze as he read the lines of script. *He doesn't know*, Lukan realized, breathing a silent sigh of relief. *He thinks this is the real deal.*

"Remarkable," Arima murmured, as he stared at the lines of script. "To think this formula was just lying there for twenty years, waiting to be found."

"Mmm," Lukan agreed. In actual fact, the parchment had spent barely half an hour on Razin's kitchen table, as Griselka scribed the formula onto it, using a watered-down ink at Lukan's request. When combined with the parchment's poor quality—which Griselka had described as "One rung above an arse rag"—the overall effect made the document look decades old. Or so Lukan hoped. He wasn't entirely sure. He'd been surrounded by old documents at the Academy of Parva, but had never actually bothered studying any of them, and so he had little idea how convincing this forgery truly was. Arima, on the other hand, seemed exactly the type to spend hours staring at dusty papers. And he was certainly staring now, his lips moving as he silently read the script, his eyes widening. "Oh, by the Builder," he suddenly said, shaking his head. "You must think me a fool."

Shit, Lukan thought. *He's not buying it.* "My lord," he put in, raising a hand, "I can assure you that—"

"A fool!" Arima repeated, louder this time, but instead of anger there was a beatific smile on his face. "Of *course* it would be this simple! All those nights, all those *years*, spent brewing all manner of liquids . . ." He shook his head again, a breathless laugh escaping his lips.

Lukan could only stare at him in confusion.

"My apologies," Arima said, recovering himself. "I . . . this is a lot to take in. Not that you have the faintest idea to what I'm referring, of course."

"Of course," Lukan agreed quickly.

"I'm deeply grateful to you for bringing me this," Arima continued as he rolled up the parchment and slid it back inside the case. "Know that you will always carry my favor."

"Yes, about that . . ."

"You want your letter. I haven't forgotten." Arima reached into a pocket and withdrew a folded piece of paper, sealed with purple wax and stamped with an insignia Lukan took to be his family crest. "This," he added, holding the paper up, "will have Lord Baranov spilling his secrets about the Rook faster than . . ." He winced, shook his head. "As I said—"

"Too early for metaphors," Lukan offered.

"Or similes." He lowered his hand, Lukan's eyes tracking the letter all the way. "However, it's not too early for a good story. And you, I'm sure, have a fascinating one to tell. I imagine your time in Ashgrave was . . . eventful."

"You imagine correctly," Lukan replied, wincing at a twinge in his leg. Timur had cleaned his wound with some foul-smelling alchemical tonic and bound it as tight as a miser's purse. Despite the odd flicker of pain, it was already feeling stronger. "But with all respect," he continued, "I have urgent business I need to attend to." *At least that's not a lie.* "But I can give you a short account of the night we spent there."

"Yes?"

"It was a nightmare." Lukan held out his hand. "The letter, if you please."

A flicker of disappointment passed across Arima's face. "As you wish," he said, holding out his hand. "However, I must ask you not to read these words. The matter between Baranov and myself is deeply personal. Besides, if the seal is broken, Lord Baranov will question its authenticity. And I am in no mood to have to convince him otherwise."

"Understood," Lukan replied, as he took the letter. "And if it doesn't work?"

"It will. Baranov is no fool." Arima smiled, and there was a touch of the wolf about it. "Fear not, Lukan. He will talk. I should warn you, though, he won't be pleased."

"An angry opponent is more likely to make a mistake."

"Quite so." Arima tilted his head. "Which philosopher said that?"

Lukan smiled, imagining Ashra's scorn at being labeled as such. "Good day, my lord."

A quarter-hour later he stood in front of Lord Baranov's front door, Arima's letter in one hand, the hammer-shaped door knocker in the other. *Got to make this quick*, he thought, as he rapped three times on the door. The longer he took to report to Marni, the more suspicious she would get. And if one of her servants happened to see him standing at Baranov's front door . . . He swore under his breath and knocked again. "Come on," he muttered, shifting impatiently, his breath clouding in the air. It had dawned bitterly cold, a bruised sky hanging ominously over the city. Somehow it didn't feel like a good omen.

Finally, the door creaked open.

A man's face peered round it, heavy-lidded eyes scrutinizing Lukan from behind a pair of spectacles. "Yes?" he inquired, lips pursing as if he didn't like what he saw. "May I help you?"

"You may," Lukan replied with his best smile, which didn't thaw the fellow's frosty facade. "Please could you inform your master that Lord Gardova is here to see him."

Lukan might as well have slapped the man, given how he

recoiled. Suddenly the door was closing, the opening shrinking to a tiny sliver.

Lukan stuck one boot in the gap, wincing as the door crushed his foot.

"I asked politely," he said, his tone resigned. "But we can do this the hard way if you prefer."

"Remove your foot at once!" the butler demanded. "Or I'll call the guards."

"You mean the guards who already let me through?" Lukan asked, gesturing at the two liveried men who stood smoking by the front gate. "Go ahead."

The butler's expression hardened. "What do you want?"

"I told you. Tell your master I'm here to see him."

"Well, he has no desire to see you."

"I'm sure he also has no desire to incur Lord Arima's wrath."

That gave the man pause. Briefly, at least.

"Lord Baranov isn't home," he said, with a sniff. "Now if you don't mind—"

"This letter," Lukan said, raising the envelope, "is from Lord Arima. And it's very much in your master's interests that he reads it. Now."

The butler's eyes flicked to the folded paper and back to Lukan. "Very well," he said primly, taking the letter with a white-gloved hand. "Wait here."

"Gladly," Lukan replied, as the door slammed in his face. He sighed and sagged against the stone doorway, exhaustion stealing over him once more. How he envied Flea and Ashra their warm beds. They'd offered to come with him, but he didn't see how that would help matters. Better that they get some rest. If this all ended up going to shit—and there was a higher chance of that than he'd like—then they would need their wits about them. Right now, with fatigue digging its claws into him, he felt like his wits were round his ankles, ready to trip him up at the slightest opportunity.

Footsteps echoed within. The door creaked open.

"My master will see you," the butler said, his voice cold as ice. "Follow me."

As Lukan followed the man down an austere corridor, he recalled something Ashra had said after her nocturnal trip to this very house. He'd barely paid attention at the time, being more interested in the evidence she'd found. *What had she said?* Something about a sense of despair lingering in the air. Lukan fancied he could feel it now. A presence—or perhaps an absence. There was a coldness to the house, an emptiness, as if Baranov's grief had seeped into the very walls and made the house an extension of his loss. Despite his antipathy toward Baranov, Lukan could sympathize. He was still working through the tangled knot of his own emotions. His father had become a distant figure, whom at times he resented— even despised—yet the strength of his grief often surprised him. Baranov, by contrast, had lost a wife and a son in quick succession. No wonder his house had all the joy of a tomb.

Under different circumstances, Lukan might have felt guilty about the pressure he was exerting on the man. But it was hard to feel sympathy for someone who had framed him for a murder and tried to have him killed. In any case, now wasn't the time for compassion. Lukan wasn't leaving until he had the answers he needed. He just hoped Arima's letter was enough to loosen Baranov's tongue.

The butler led him to a reception room and departed without another word, but not without a final glare. Lukan stood on the threshold, steeling himself as he remembered Arima's words: *he won't be pleased.*

He took a deep breath and stepped through the doorway.

Whereas Lord Arima's reception room had been full of color and a rich sense of history and culture, the space Lukan now found himself in was colorless and imbued with a muted feeling of despair. Someone—not the butler, he guessed—had left some fresh white flowers in a vase, as if to brighten the place, but they only served to heighten the sense of prevailing gloom. It was as if the anguish that had pervaded the very stones of the house had coalesced in this room.

Likely the man standing before the unlit fireplace had something to do with that.

Baranov stood with his back to Lukan, Arima's letter in one hand. His other hand grasped the mantlepiece, his knuckles white. His head was bowed, his shoulders hunched, making him look smaller than he really was. Lukan took a cautious step forward, expecting the man to whirl round, murder in his eyes.

Baranov didn't move.

Lukan took another step. Still the man didn't turn. Yet his large frame seemed to convulse, as if he was physically shaking with rage. Lukan placed his hand on his sword in case the man suddenly turned and sprang at him. The memory of Giorgio Castori performing a similar action flitted through his mind. He recalled the shudder of his own wrist as his sword skewered the boy's neck. The horror in Giorgio's eyes. The brightness of his blood. Lukan blinked the images away. He had no desire for a repeat performance, but you could never be too careful. He took another step forward.

Still Baranov didn't acknowledge his presence.

Lukan made to speak, only to find he didn't know what to say. He'd a couple of witty rejoinders already prepared, depending on the level of hostility he faced, but what he hadn't expected was silence. The quiet was broken only by the man's heavy breathing, as if each breath was measured in fury. Lukan's grip on his sword tightened. He opened his mouth to speak, still unsure of his words, but Baranov beat him to it.

"Why?"

The question—spoken so quietly he almost didn't hear it—caught Lukan off guard. He took a moment to regain his composure.

"You know why," he replied, adopting an even tone. "The Rook took my key. I need it back. You have information about the Rook you won't share. I was left with no choice but to force your hand."

"I told you," the man replied, his voice hoarse, "I don't know anything about the Rook."

"With respect, Lord Baranov, I don't believe you."

Baranov turned then—not quickly, as Lukan had expected, but slowly, almost wearily. And as Lukan met his eyes, he found them not full of fury, but wet with tears. He was so surprised he almost took a step back.

"Why do you insist on tormenting me?" Baranov asked, shaking Arima's letter. "As if losing my wife, my son, was not enough, you now threaten to bring ruin down upon my entire house?" He shook his head. "Why?"

For the second time in quick succession, Lukan was at a loss for words.

"I just want information," he replied, raising a placating hand. This wasn't going the way he'd expected; he'd anticipated anger, not vulnerability. But Baranov's raw anguish had left him flat-footed. *What in the hells was in Arima's letter?* "Just tell me where I can find the Rook and I'll be on my way," he offered. "You'll never see me again. And whatever threats Arima has made in that letter won't come to pass."

"I already told you," Baranov replied, crushing the letter in his fist, "I don't *know*." He punctuated his last word by hurling the scrunched paper to the floor. Then he turned and walked to an armchair, where he sat with a great sigh and buried his head in his hands, shoulders heaving with silent sobs.

I should go. There was something unsettling about seeing Baranov like this. It felt indecent. Callous, even. And the fact that Lukan was responsible only made it worse. He took a step toward the door, instinct demanding he leave Baranov to his misery. *But where does that leave me? Without answers. And without a damned clue as to what to do next.* He paused, grinding his teeth. There was nothing to do but finish what he started. Baranov knew *something*. He had to.

"If you don't know anything," Lukan replied, pulling a folded paper from his coat pocket, "then why did we find a sketch of the Rook in your son's bedroom?" He held out the drawing.

Baranov took the paper and stared at it, then turned it over and read the note on the other side. His dark eyebrows lowered. "This is the so-called evidence you mentioned at the Inventors' Parade?" he asked, his voice hollow.

"It is."

"I've never seen this before."

"Then why was it in your son's bedroom?"

"Why were *you* in there?" Baranov demanded. He surged to his feet, his face dark with barely contained fury. "How dare you defile my son's memory in such a way!"

"It wasn't actually me that was in there—"

"I care not who sullied my son's bedchamber! I'll see you hanged for this."

"You already tried," Lukan said, unable to stop a hint of scorn slipping into his voice. "Didn't quite work out, though, did it?"

"What in the hells are you talking about?"

"Don't play the fool," Lukan said, his patience cracking. "When you realized your sketch had been stolen, you feared the thief would seek out Zelenko, and would learn the truth of your connection to the Rook. So, you had Zelenko murdered to stop him from talking. Did you also plan for the thief"—Lukan gestured at himself—"to be arrested and charged for the murder? Or was that just happy coincidence?"

Baranov just stared at him.

"Regardless," Lukan continued, "you used your influence to ensure that I—and my friend—didn't even get a trial. You arranged for us to go straight to the gallows, just to protect your own sordid secret."

"Secret?" Baranov echoed, with a frown. "What secret?"

"That the Rook—this same thief that's been terrorizing half the city—is a golem." Lukan jabbed a finger. "A golem that Zelenko created at your request."

"You've lost your mind," Baranov retorted, shaking his head. "I've never seen this sketch before."

"Then I'll ask you again: why was it in your son's bedroom?"

"I don't know."

"Who is Izolde?"

"I don't know!" Baranov thundered, surging to his feet. He tore the sketch apart and hurled the pieces into the air. "To the hells with your damned evidence," he snarled, taking a step toward Lukan. "And to the hells with your lies. I won't listen to such nonsense. Now get out of my house."

"Not until I have the information I need," Lukan replied.

"I told you, damn it," Baranov barked, spittle flying from his lips, "I don't know anything about the Rook, or your bloody key, or this sketch, or . . ." He flailed an arm. "Anything about any of this." He paused, his chest heaving as he glanced at the letter again. Glowered and let it fall to the floor. "If Lord Arima's spite falls upon me, then so be it. As the Builder is my witness, I know *nothing*."

Lady's blood, Lukan thought, a sinking feeling in his gut. Not once had he actually considered that Baranov's pleas of ignorance might be genuine. *There's got to be something I've missed.* His mind raced, seeking the one detail that would unravel the man's deception.

"Father?" a voice said from the doorway.

Lukan turned to see Galina standing in the doorway, hands clasped before her.

"Daughter." Baranov's anger cooled as the young woman stepped into the room.

"Miss Baranova," Lukan said, offering her a bow. "A pleasure to see you again. You are well, I hope?"

Galina didn't look well. Not at all. Quite the contrary, in fact: she looked pale, anxious, her eyes darting from her father, to Lukan, to the torn pieces of paper on the floor.

"Galina?" her father asked, brows knitting in concern. "Is something the matter?"

"I heard your voices," his daughter replied. "I heard you arguing about the Rook." She glanced between them and wrung her
hands, uncertainty writ large across her face.

Uncertainty . . . and something else, Lukan realized. "Miss Baranova?" he prompted. "Are you well?"

"Yes. I just . . ." She took a deep breath and closed her eyes. "I
just can't do this any more."

"Do what?" her father asked.

"My father is telling the truth," Galina said, her eyes flicking
open and finding Lukan's gaze. "He knows nothing about the
Rook." She swallowed. "But I do."

"Galina, please," Baranov said, his voice thick with concern.
"What are you saying? You are not yourself."

"No, I'm not," his daughter agreed, with a pained smile. "I haven't been for months. Not since Gavril died."

"Nor me," Baranov said gently. Gone was his fury. Now, only
concern shone in his eyes. But there was still an edge in his voice
as he turned and spoke to Lukan. "Lord Gardova, my daughter is
distressed. She's still deep in her grief over her brother's death, and
your presence has upset her. You must leave."

"No," Galina said firmly, locking eyes with her father. "Lord
Gardova needs to hear my story. And so do you."

29

AN ACT OF LOVE

"What story?" Baranov asked in bewilderment.

"The story of my guilt." The young woman lowered her eyes. "And my shame."

"Galina . . ." Baranov fell silent as his daughter raised a hand for silence.

"Please," she said, "let me speak." She took a slow breath, visibly steeled herself. "When Mother died, a piece of me died with her. And when Gavril fell ill . . ." She shook her head. "I couldn't bear the thought of losing him as well. Then Izolde told me that maybe I didn't have to."

"Izolde?" Lukan prompted, feeling a rush of hope.

"My lover." She gave a wan smile. "She's training to be an alchemist at the Tower." She looked at her father, but Baranov remained silent, his gaze distant.

"'My dearest G,'" Lukan said, as realization dawned. "That letter we found in your brother's room was addressed to you, not your father."

"You mean the letter you stole. No, don't apologize." Galina waved away the response forming on Lukan's lips. "It's my fault it came to this." She was silent for a long moment. "One night, after the physicians said Gavril only had a few days left to live, Izolde told me a secret. One that she wasn't meant to know. She told me there was a way to save my brother. Not his physical body, but his mind. His consciousness."

"His soul," Lukan offered.

Galina nodded.

"What in the Builder's name are you talking about?" Baranov asked, glancing between Lukan and his daughter.

"The constructs in this city contain human souls," Lukan replied. "That's how they understand commands."

"Souls?" Baranov's voice was heavy with disbelief. "That's absurd."

"It's true, Father," Galina replied. "Some of the prisoners sent to the camps in the Clanholds never leave the city. They're given to the Tower instead. The alchemists execute them and then place their souls in the golems' bodies."

Baranov stared at his daughter, open-mouthed. "Galina," he managed eventually, "daughter—look at me. You're not well. And I don't know what nonsense this Izolde has put in your head, but—"

"She's telling the truth," Lukan interjected.

"How in the hells would *you* know?" Baranov demanded, rounding on him.

"Ah, well . . ." Lukan smiled ruefully. "That's a long story. Suffice to say I heard it straight from the horse's mouth. Or the golem's mouth. Well, foot, actually."

Both Baranovs stared at him.

"Never mind." He waved away his own words. "Lady Galina, you were saying . . ."

"I didn't believe Izolde at first. I've always accepted that we have souls, because that's what the Builder's scripture says. But the notion that they can be placed in a new body after a person dies . . . it just seemed like something out of a fairy tale. But Izolde insisted it was real. She said the alchemists use a Phaeron artifact to capture the soul at the point of death, and then transfer it into a new receptacle."

"Of course," Lukan said, with a snort. "I should have known the Phaeron would be involved. How does it work?"

"I don't know. I'm not sure Izolde knew either. Somehow the artifact captures the soul, and then the alchemists transfer it to a piece of amber."

"Amber?"

"Yes. Izolde said that souls can't escape it. All golems have a piece of amber in their heads that contains the soul that controls them."

"That's why they all have amber eyes," Lukan said, recalling all the constructs he'd seen. While there were often points of difference between golems, the amber eyes were a constant.

"Yes," Galina replied. "And the glow you see in the amber is the light of the soul inside. That was what swayed me in the end. I realized that not only could I save Gavril, but I'd be able to look into the construct's eyes and actually *see* him. My brother, in his purest form. And we'd be together."

"This is madness," Baranov murmured.

"We waited as Gavril's conditioned worsened," his daughter continued, blinking away a tear. "When the priest started talking about administering the Builder's final blessing, I sent word to Izolde. She brought the artifact to me. Stole it from one of the master alchemists. She risked her career to do so. Perhaps more. She called it an act of love." The shadow of a smile passed her lips. "It's only a little thing. The artifact. I thought it strange how such a small object could hold power over life and death."

"Galina," Baranov said, his voice no more than a whisper. Almost pleading. "What are you saying?"

"I concealed the artifact beneath my dress," she continued, her eyes downcast. "I waited as the priest finished his prayers. As Gavril breathed his last breaths. I remember how fragile they were." She swallowed and was silent for a moment. "And when he breathed his last, I activated the artifact the way Izolde showed me. To capture Gavril's soul as it left his body."

She glanced at her father as he raised a hand to his face.

"You already had a construct's body prepared," Lukan said gently, gesturing to the torn letter on the floor.

"Yes. Izolde saw to that. My brother was always fascinated by the rooks and ravens that perched outside his window, so we had it fashioned in their image."

"By Master Zelenko."

Galina nodded, not meeting his gaze, the unasked question about her involvement in the golem maker's death filling the space between them. *A question for later.* "What happened next?"

"Later that night we took the construct's body to my brother's bedroom and laid it on his bed where his real body had been. I don't know why I wanted to do it there. It just seemed . . ."

"Right," Lukan offered.

"Yes. Izolde then transferred Gavril's soul from the artifact to the amber receptacle, which she then slotted into the construct's head. I just stood and watched, praying it would work. And then I saw the construct's eyes begin to glow, and the body started to twitch. And then it—Gavril—saw me. And he sat up and hugged me, and I cried because I had my brother back."

"Oh, Galina," Baranov murmured, his eyes wet with tears.

"And is he here now?" Lukan asked, glancing at the ceiling. "Is the Rook upstairs in your brother's room?"

"No. Gavril doesn't stay with me. He only visits from time to time."

"When he takes a break from stealing from people."

Galina glanced away. "I'm sorry about your key. Gavril was always up to mischief as a boy. I've told him to stop stealing, but he won't listen." She smiled faintly. "He never did."

"Could you ask him to return my key?"

"I can. I can't promise he will."

"When will he next visit you?"

"I don't know. Sometimes he visits often, other times I don't see him for weeks on end."

"I don't have weeks. I might not even have days. I need my key now."

"I could take you tonight."

"Take me where?"

"To where Gavril's nest is. So to speak."

"And where's that?"

"The Glasshouse."

Lukan thought of the great glass structure in the Gardens of Undying Grace. To think he'd spent days hanging around in that park with the Rook no more than a stone's throw away. He almost smiled at the irony. "Why does he hide there?"

"It was his favorite place to visit. Would you like me to take you?"

"I would," he replied. "It's . . ." He was going to joke that it was the least she could do after trying to have him executed, but thought better of it. There was no sense in antagonizing Galina, not when he was so close to getting his key back. "Most kind," he said instead, inclining his head. "Thank you."

"Meet me there at midnight," the young woman replied. "Come alone."

"I shall. And now I will take my leave."

"Wait." Baranov's voice was dull, as if he'd been hollowed out by his daughter's revelations. "This Zelenko figure. Wasn't he the one who was murdered?"

Galina remained silent, twisting a ring round her finger.

"What have you done?" Baranov asked, his gaze imploring. "Galina, please tell me you didn't . . ."

"I didn't." She took a shuddery breath. "That was Izolde. When I was woken by our guards and told an intruder might be in the house, I immediately remembered our meeting in the park, Lord Gardova." Her gaze met his and flicked away. "I checked Gavril's room as soon as I was able, and found the sketch missing. I know I was foolish to keep it—how damning it might look if it was ever discovered. But on nights when I missed Izolde, I liked to read the letter she wrote on the other side. Her words brought me comfort." She stared at the torn pieces of paper on the floor. "I sent word to her first thing the next morning. I feared not for myself, but for her. That her role in this would be uncovered. She told me not to worry. That she would fix it." Galina shook her head, her lips pressed thin. "She told me later she didn't mean for Zelenko to die. She said the thugs she hired got carried away."

"Did she mean for me and my friends to take the blame?" Lukan asked.

"No." Galina wouldn't meet his gaze. "But when she saw you enter the workshop soon afterward, she saw an opportunity. And . . ." Now she did look at him, regret in her eyes. "She told me that you knew too much. That . . ."

"You couldn't let us live."

"Yes." She wiped away another tear. "So I wrote a letter demanding your immediate execution and forged my father's signature."

"You did *what*?" Baranov breathed.

"I'm sorry," she told Lukan, trying to hold back a sob. "I—I never meant for it to go this far. I wasn't in my right mind. I didn't mean for any of this to happen."

"Neither did I. But if you can get my key back for me, what say we call it even?" Galina smiled at that. "I'll see you at the Glasshouse at midnight." He turned his attention to Baranov, who seemed to have aged twenty years in the past quarter-hour. "My lord," he said, offering him a bow, "I apologize for the act of breaking into your house. And for the accusations I made. I realize now I was mistaken."

"No, Lord Gardova," the man replied, his tone weary. "Your suspicions were well placed." He looked at Galina, and there was a depth of emotion in his glance: anger, shock, grief, all mixed together. He took a deep breath, as if unsure what to think. What to say. "I hope you find your key," he said eventually. "And now, if you please, it seems my daughter and I have much to discuss."

Lukan nodded. "I will see myself out."

30

CAREFUL WORDS

"What time do you call this?" Marni asked, as Lukan was shown into her solar. There was no gleam in her eye, or playful curl to her lip. Only ice in her voice.

"Too bloody early," Lukan replied, "especially when you've been up all night." A risky response, given he was a snap of Marni's fingers away from the gallows, but exhaustion had now properly got its claws into him. He just needed this conversation to be over as quickly—and painlessly—as possible.

"I didn't say you could sit," she replied, as Lukan did just that.

"I can barely stand." He bit back a sigh as Marni's eyes narrowed. "May I sit?"

"No."

"As you wish. Could I at least have some coffee?"

"No." Ruby rings glittered as Marni tapped her fingers on her armrest. "I told you to report as soon as you returned. And yet I'm told you went in search of a physician for that little brat sidekick of yours."

"She's well, thank you for asking."

"It's your own health you should be concerned for. I'll ask again: why didn't you report immediately?"

"You already answered your own question."

"Then let me rephrase it: why did *you* not report immediately, and leave that thief to look after the girl?"

"I was worried," Lukan replied, choosing his words carefully. "Flea had taken ill and was in a bad way. Some sort of ill humor she picked up in Ashgrave. I panicked. All I could think about was finding help." He shrugged. "I wasn't thinking straight."

"Evidently."

"If you'd seen the horrors we saw in that place, then you'd be more forgiving."

"I'd very much like to see them." Marni gestured to the two circlets that rested on a nearby table, the same ones through which Lukan had seen Nika's memories. "If you care to share them."

Lukan shifted uncomfortably. If he agreed to share his own memories, what was to say Marni wouldn't also see what came after—their encounter with the masked figures, Griselka scribing away at Razin's kitchen table? One glimpse of that and his plan would fall apart. "I'd rather not relive those memories," he replied. "In fact, I'd rather forget them entirely."

At least there was no need to lie about that. Fortunately for him, Marni had her eyes on another prize.

"Fortunately for you," she continued, "I'm told you recovered the formula."

"We did."

Marni held out a hand.

Lukan pulled the original scroll case from his coat pocket and handed it over. Marni took it from him and scrutinized it, as he knew she would. It was why he'd kept the alchemist's case for her and given Arima another. He knew she wouldn't miss a detail. So it proved; the woman's red eyes lingered on the faded emboss of the Tower before she opened the case. She paused, eyes closed, as if savoring a personal moment of triumph. Then she slid her red-painted nails inside and withdrew the parchment within. Griselka's second forgery was just as convincing as the first. Yet it was all Lukan could do not to squirm in his seat as Marni studied the script. She didn't mimic Arima's reaction; there was no widening of her eyes, no dropping of her jaw. Instead, she frowned and tapped a finger against her blood-red lips. Lukan tensed, fearing some small detail or imperfection had betrayed him, but relaxed when Marni made a satisfied noise in her throat and slid the scroll back into the case. *She can't read the script*, he realized. *She has no idea what the formula actually means.*

"What a good boy you've been," Marni said, favoring him with the sort of smile a fox might offer a chicken. "Risking your life for me."

"Not like I had a choice."

"Oh, don't be like that," she said, affecting a pout. "We've had such a fun time together, don't you think? Though it could have been even more enjoyable." She tilted her head, a coy smile on her lips. "It still could be, if you like. What better way to conclude our partnership, hmm?"

"It concluded the moment I gave you the formula. My debt to you is paid in full. Ashra's too."

"So keen to slip from my grasp, Lukan?"

Yes. He almost voiced that feeling, but thought better of it. "I have other affairs to see to."

"Ah, yes," Marni replied, affecting boredom. "The matter of your key. How disappointing. You didn't strike me as the sort to put business before pleasure." She made a gesture of dismissal. "Fine. Be on your way then." Her red gaze flicked back to the scroll case. "I have my own business to see to."

31

TO WISH IMPOSSIBLE THINGS

"You're late," Galina said.

"I know," Lukan replied, with a wince of apology as he stepped into the light of her lantern. "I was . . ." *How to even explain it? I was trying to extricate myself from another of General Razin's tales while simultaneously trying to convince a bored girl and a master thief not to follow me out the door.*

He'd failed at the latter. As Galina now noticed.

"I told you to come alone," she said, an accusatory note in her voice as she glanced at Flea and Ashra, who emerged from the darkness behind him. After spending the day sleeping, neither was in the mood for an early night—nor an evening spent listening to Razin's war stories.

"I know," Lukan said again, offering her a helpless shrug. "Sorry."

"No matter," Galina replied, with a pained smile that suggested she wished none of them were there at all. Or perhaps it was her father's presence that perturbed her.

"Lord Baranov," Lukan murmured, giving the man a nod. Baranov made no response; in fact, he barely seemed to register Lukan's presence. Lukan couldn't say he blamed him; no doubt he had other matters on his mind. *Like the fact that his son's soul is trapped in a construct's body.* Lukan couldn't imagine how it would feel to lose a loved one, only to find out they were still alive. *In a manner of speaking, at least.*

"Let's proceed," Galina said, pushing the left gate open. "Follow me."

"I thought these were locked at night," Lukan said as he followed.

"They are. I bribed one of the Sparks to leave them unlocked."

Lukan glanced at Baranov, but, if the revelation unsettled the man, he gave no sign. In any case, Lukan reasoned, it was far from the most shocking thing his daughter had told him that day.

He glanced across the dark expanse of the Gardens of Undying Grace, the winterwood trees still and silent in the night. It was strange to think that his last visit here had resulted in his first confrontation with Baranov, whereas now they were stealing through the darkened grounds together, united by common purpose. Baranov, it seemed, desired to find the Rook just as much as Lukan did. *But to what end?* he wondered, as they neared the great expanse of the Glasshouse. *Does he want to see what his son has become? To hold him one more time?* He only hoped the man would get whatever closure he sought. It was the least he deserved.

As they arrived at the main entrance to the Glasshouse, Galina slipped a heavy iron key from her coat pocket. "Gavril gave it to me," she said, in response to Lukan's inquiring glance. "After he became the Rook." Lukan thought he heard Baranov sigh in response, as his daughter unlocked the door and pushed it open.

A rush of warmth enveloped Lukan as he followed Galina into the Glasshouse, almost stealing the breath from his lungs. The air was heavy and close, thick with the smell of earth. It reminded him of the neglected greenhouse on his family's estate, where he used to hide in his younger years and drink whatever bottle of wine he'd lifted from the cellar. He smiled at the memory.

"This way," Galina said, leading them down a paved walkway. She adjusted her lantern, letting more light spill out to illuminate the strange plants that loomed around them.

"Look at that," Flea whispered, pointing at a spiky plant with purple veins, which stood beside a large bush with leaves that looked like drops of blood. Both were lost to darkness as Galina strode on, her pace brisk, as if she was determined to get the night over with. That suited Lukan just fine.

"Have you visited your brother before?" he asked, as he caught up with her.

"No."

"But you know where we'll find him?"

"I have an idea."

Galina didn't elaborate and Lukan didn't probe further. As big as the Glasshouse was, they were making swift progress through its interior. He'd have his answers soon enough. *And my key, with any luck.* He glanced back and saw that Ashra had removed her coat, while Flea was struggling out of hers.

"If I'd known how warm this place was," the thief said, "I'd have spent all my time in here."

"It's *too* warm," Flea muttered.

Lukan felt sweat trickling down his back, and had to admit the girl was right. The warmth—so welcome at first—was already becoming uncomfortable. He unbuttoned the front of his own coat as he hurried to catch up with Galina. "How is it so hot in here?" he asked, tugging at the collar of his shirt. "Some sort of alchemy?"

"The Glasshouse has its own heating system," Galina replied. "It's powered by steam, though I couldn't say how it works."

By the time she led them through a passage and into another section of the Glasshouse, Lukan had removed his coat altogether. Baranov kept his on, but sweat shone on his brow.

"Not far now," Galina said, her voice barely above a whisper.

Lukan glanced at the shrubs and trees that grew on either side of the path they followed, but he saw no gleam of amber eyes among their leaves and branches. "How do you know the Rook— your brother, I mean—will be here?"

"I don't. He could be picking pockets in Hearthside, for all we know."

Lukan thought Baranov tensed beside him. Perhaps it was just a trick of the light. "And if he is?" he replied.

"Then we'll wait for him to return." Galina glanced at him, a half-smile on her lips. "Unless you'd rather get your beauty sleep."

"I'll wait all night if need be."

Galina's smile faded. "You might have to."

A short while later they reached their destination.

"Look at that!" Flea said, too loudly, earning a warning glance from Galina.

The southwestern corner of the Glasshouse's second chamber was home to a great tree that rose so high its upper branches were lost in the darkness, and Lukan couldn't tell where they ended and the glass ceiling began. What he could see of the tree revealed thick, twisting limbs and long slender leaves shaped like daggers. Even in daylight, he imagined, the upper boughs would be invisible from the ground. *No wonder the Rook picked this for his hideout*, he mused, as Galina motioned for them to stop.

"Stay here," she said, stepping away before Lukan could reply. Baranov made to follow, only to hesitate as his daughter turned and shook her head. "You too, Father," she whispered.

"I would see Gavril," Baranov replied, his words edged with grief. "I would see my boy."

"You will. But I must speak with him first."

Baranov's shoulders slumped but he remained still as Galina made her way to the foot of the tree. She looked up into the darkness of its boughs and called, "Brother? It's your sister, Galina. Come down to me."

Nothing stirred.

Lukan squinted as Galina called out again, and then a third time, but he saw no flash of amber eyes squinting back at him. He swore silently as the woman's voice echoed off the glass walls a fourth time.

"The Rook's not here," Ashra said flatly.

"Seems not," Lukan agreed, not quite managing to keep the bitterness from his voice. "He must be out picking pockets." Baranov looked at him sharply, but he couldn't see the man's expression in the gloom, and he didn't much care if he'd ruffled his feathers. He'd not been lying when he'd told Galina he'd wait all night, but it was one thing to say that and something else entirely to actually do it. Especially with Baranov for company.

If Galina heard their words, she made no reply. Instead, she placed her lantern on the ground, slipped the bag from her shoulders and withdrew a long, thin object from within, which she then pressed to her lips. *A flute*, Lukan realized, as a high note sounded. More followed, gaining clarity and rhythm as Galina seemingly grew in confidence. The melody—sweet but with a touch of melancholy—rose into the humid air of the chamber.

"Gavril's favorite tune," Baranov murmured. "We would sing it to him to get him to sleep." He bowed his head and raised a hand to his face, his shoulders shaking. Lukan looked away, searching the tree's darkened branches for any sign of movement.

Flea, of course, saw it first.

"There!" she whispered, pointing.

"Where?" he asked, squinting harder.

"There!" Flea repeated, jabbing a finger that could have been directed almost anywhere.

"Lady's mercy, can you be more . . ." Lukan trailed off as he saw a branch move. He held his breath and waited. Hope sparked inside him as he saw another twitch of movement. Then another branch rustled further down.

"He's coming," he said, but Baranov was already moving toward the tree. "Wait," Lukan urged, grasping him arm and pulling him back. He expected the man to shrug him off, but Baranov remained still, his breaths shallow and quick. Together they waited as Galina continued to play.

"Look!" Flea exclaimed, but Lukan had already seen it: an amber gleam in the darkness.

He watched, still clasping Baranov's arm, as the Rook appeared on the tree's lower branches, clambering down with the same agility he remembered from their previous encounter. The Rook dropped the final ten feet to the ground, and in that moment—

with the birdlike mask, and cloak stretched between its open arms like wings—the figure looked just like its namesake.

Galina continued to play as the Rook approached her, its movements tentative, as if it was ready to bolt at any moment. *And if it does*, Lukan thought, *we might not get another chance.* He tightened his grip on Baranov, fearing the man might let his emotions get the better of him and ruin everything, but he remained utterly silent, as if the sight of the Rook had stolen the breath from his lungs. Only when the construct stopped a few paces from Galina did the woman finally stop playing and slowly place her flute on the ground.

"Brother," she said, kneeling and spreading her arms.

The Rook took a cautious step, then paused, amber eyes flashing to the figures standing a short distance behind her. Lukan wondered if it recognized its father in the darkness.

"Gavril," Galina murmured, "don't mind them."

The Rook waited a moment longer, then sprang into her arms. As Galina held her brother, Lukan held Baranov as the man sagged, heaving a great sigh that was halfway to a sob. After a long embrace, Galina spoke to the Rook in a voice too low for Lukan to hear. At one point the Rook's amber eyes flicked toward Lukan and seemed to regard him from afar. Eventually Galina turned and beckoned to him. "Lord Gardova, will you join us?"

Lukan released his hold on Baranov, half-expecting the man to fall to his knees, but he remained standing. He shot Ashra a look—*keep an eye on him*—which he wasn't sure she'd seen in the dark, and slowly approached the two figures. The Rook was watching him closely now, and there was something defiant in the way it regarded him.

"Do you remember Lord Gardova?" Galina asked as Lukan joined them.

"I certainly remember you," Lukan said, offering the Rook a smile the little rascal didn't deserve. "You've led me on quite the chase."

"Lord Gardova needs his key back," Galina continued. "Will

you give it to him?" The Rook tilted its head as it stared at Lukan. He couldn't help but feel there was a touch of mischief about the gesture. He opened his mouth to speak—hells, he would beg if he had to—but Galina spoke before the words even formed on his tongue. "Please, Gavril," she urged gently. "Will you do it for me?"

The Rook looked at its sister.

The moment stretched and Lukan felt his own frantic heartbeat drumming in his ears.

Then the Rook nodded.

The construct was gone in a flash, scampering back to the tree and scaling the trunk before Lukan could even draw a relieved breath.

"You're in luck," Galina said, with her half-smile again. "My brother still has your key." Her eyes found his. "I know I have wronged you, Lord Gardova, but will this settle things between us? And . . . between you and my father?"

"It will," Lukan assured her, barely able to believe his good fortune. And still not entirely trusting it. "You'll never see or hear from me again."

Galina merely nodded at that.

They waited in silence for the Rook to return.

A short while later, Lukan saw the branches of the tree shaking once more as the small golem descended. And this time, it had something clutched in its right talon. Lukan finally allowed himself the sigh of relief he'd been holding back as he saw the gleam of garnet and amethyst. *At last.*

"Thank you, Gavril," Galina said, as the Rook held out its hand.

"Yes," Lukan added, as he reached out. "Thank you." He half-expected the Rook to snatch its talon away just as his fingers brushed the key that lay in its palm, and it took all his resolve not to grab at the key himself. But the little golem made no move as he slowly lifted the iron key from its palm. *Finally*, he thought, as his fingers closed round the key and he felt the reassuring weight of it in his hand. The gems glinted in the lantern light, and he noted scratch marks in the metal around them, as if someone had tried to pry them loose. He gave the Rook a knowing smile as he slipped the key into his coat pocket, but the golem wasn't watching him. Instead, its amber gaze was fixed on Baranov, who was slowly approaching.

"Gavril?" the man said, his voice hushed.

The Rook glanced at Galina, who nodded. The little construct took a step forward, head tilted in the manner of its namesake.

"Son? It's me." A tear rolled down Baranov's cheek. "It's your father."

The Rook hesitated a heartbeat longer, then closed the distance between them in a flash and flung its arms round the man, who hugged the construct to him. "My boy," he gasped. "My boy."

Lukan backed away to give Baranov some privacy. Flea and Ashra remained where they were, but he could tell the former was watching the Rook with interest. "What will happen now?" he asked Galina in a low voice. "Now that your father knows the truth about your brother?"

"I don't know." Her expressed became pained. "I suppose Gavril could come home, but it won't be the same, will it? Not really. Because we will get older, but Gavril . . ." She swallowed, thumbed a tear from one eye. "In my grief I wasn't thinking clearly. I missed him so much I was willing to do anything to bring him back. It never occurred to me that it wasn't my decision to make. It wasn't my right to decide his fate." She lowered her gaze. "And I didn't know it would have such awful consequences."

"Don't be too hard on yourself. Grief makes us wish for impossible things."

"Yes. And I wish now that none of this had happened. That Master Zelenko was still alive, and that I could see Izolde's smile again. And hold her. But with all that's happened . . ." Galina closed her eyes, took a long, slow breath. "I can't change the past," she continued, finding Lukan's gaze. "But I can give Gavril back the fate I stole from him. If he wants it."

"Your brother seems more than happy to me."

"True, but it might not always be so. If such a time comes, then I can release him."

"Release him?" Lukan echoed, suddenly curious. "You mean free his soul? How?"

"Izolde told me that, if the amber receptacle is shattered, his soul can escape it. And pass on to . . ." She shrugged. "Whatever comes next."

"Galina," Baranov said, motioning to her. His other arm was still wrapped round the Rook. "Join us."

"I must go," she told Lukan. She gestured to his key. "I hope you find what you're looking for, Lord Gardova."

"You too," he replied, as she stepped away. He watched as she joined her father and brother in an embrace. Then he strode back to where Flea and Ashra waited in the darkness.

"What now?" the thief asked. "Back to Razin's?"

"Yes." He showed them the key. "And first thing in the morning, I've got my own family business to attend to."

32

THE GAME OF SMOKE
AND SHADOWS

It was well past the first bell of the morning as they made their way back to Razin's townhouse, yet the upmarket Hearthside taverns were still busy with revellers. A door opened as they passed, and a couple of giggling youths spilled from it, as if riding the wave of jaunty music that flowed out with them. Lukan glanced inside at the laughing faces etched in candlelight and the scarlet gleam of wine glasses, and felt an urge to step inside and join the revelry, the music and laughter as strong as any siren's call.

But no. Not this time.

"What happens next?" Flea asked later, as they made their way through the quiet avenues of the Mantle. Ashra walked a little way ahead of them, her hood turning left and right as she watched the darkness beyond the street lamps.

"A nightcap for me," Lukan replied. "Bed for you." Not that the girl had ever slept in the bed provided for her, preferring instead to sprawl across Ivan every night. *A flea on a hound*, he thought, smiling to himself. *Who'd have thought.*

"No," the girl replied, "I mean, what happens once we've opened the vault?"

"It depends what's in there."

"Are you sure there's not going to be lots of money inside it?"

"What did I say the last time you asked that?"

"Probably not?"

"Exactly." They turned onto the avenue where Razin's house stood. "Then again," he added, "who knows? I thought my father was an obsessed scholar who rarely left his study, but it turns out that before that he was a plunderer of Phaeron ruins."

"So?"

"So, it stands to reason that my dwindling family fortune might—*might*," he repeated, as the girl looked hopefully at him, "be greater than I thought."

"But probably not."

"Probably not."

They walked a few paces in silence.

"But if there *is* money in there," the girl started.

"Lady's mercy . . ."

"If there *is*," she pressed, as they passed through the gate to Razin's estate, "I deserve half of it. At *least*. Given how many times I've saved your life, and all."

"Done. Perhaps you can use it to pay for a one-way voyage to the Mourning Sea, so I no longer have to answer your endless questions."

"Maybe I will," Flea shot back as they approached the front door. "Maybe I'll hire Grabulli to take me there."

"That old rascal?" Lukan chuckled. "Chances are he'd toss you overboard before you even—"

"Hsst!"

They both fell silent and looked to where Ashra stood near the door, one arm raised in warning.

"The front door," Flea whispered, eyes sharp as always. "It's open."

Lukan swore and drew his sword, as Flea readied her crossbow. He glanced around, expecting to see masked figures emerge from the shadows of the grounds, but nothing stirred. His mind raced as they crept toward Ashra. Had Arima discovered their betrayal and reacted with force? Was Marni awaiting him inside, ready to send him to the gallows? *Better not to go in at all*, he thought. But what if Timur and Razin were being held under duress? "What are the chances," he whispered, "that Razin just forgot to close the front door?"

"Possible," Ashra replied, drawing a stiletto. "But we can't take the risk. Follow me."

The thief slipped through the entrance and Lukan followed, Flea at his back. The hallway was dark, but ruddy firelight spilled through the living room doorway at the far end. A voice came with it, speaking in a low but animated tone. *Razin*, Lukan realized, though he couldn't decipher the general's words. At Ashra's gesture they stole down the hallway.

"GET YOUR FILTHY HANDS OFF ME, YOU COWARDS!"

Lukan heard those words well enough. "Come on!" he breathed, racing to the front.

"Lukan, wait!" Ashra whispered hoarsely.

"No time," he replied, shouldering open the door and raising his sword. "General?" he called, glancing wildly about the living room. He caught sight of the old man sitting in an armchair. His hands were raised, his eyes wide with surprise.

"Lukan!" Razin exclaimed. "You're back! And just in time for the best part of the story."

"Story?" Lukan repeated.

"Indeed! I was telling my esteemed guest here about the trials and tribulations of my fourth campaign."

Lukan met the eyes of the white-haired woman sitting opposite Razin. She held a glass of wine in one wrinkled hand, and a lit cigarillo in the other. *Lady Wretzky*, he realized. *The Iron Dame. What the hells is she doing here?*

"Lukan?" Razin said, eying his drawn sword. "Everything all right?"

"Yes," he replied, looking back at the general. "I mean—I don't know. Is it?"

"Is it what?"

"All right?

"Is what all right?"

"You!"

"Me?"

"Yes!"

A moment of silence followed, broken only by Lady Wretzky taking a drag on her cigarillo and exhaling the smoke through her nose.

"Of course I'm all right!" Razin retorted, staring at him in bafflement. "Why wouldn't I be?"

"The door was wide open! We thought someone might have broken in."

"Hmm." The general tugged at his mustache. "I could have sworn I closed it. Maybe the latch didn't quite catch."

"General Razin was just telling me one of his war stories," Lady Wretzky put in, a knowing glint in her eye. "One of the best ones, he says."

"Indeed," the general huffed, "and I was just getting to the good part where the King of the Crags was shouting—"

"Get your filthy hands off me, you cowards," Lukan put in, recalling the general's earlier words. He sighed and sheathed his sword, feeling like a fool.

"Allow me to introduce Lady Wretzky," Razin said, gesturing to his guest.

"We've met before," Lukan said, offering the woman a bow.

"A pleasure to see you again, Lord Gardova," she replied, inclining her head.

"Likewise, my lady. And apologies for my intrusion. If you'll excuse me, I'll leave you to your conversation."

"On the contrary, Lord Gardova, I'd far rather you joined it." Lady Wretzky's eyes flicked to Flea and Ashra. "And your friends, as well."

Lukan caught Ashra's gaze. Her look of suspicion mirrored his own thoughts. *What does the Iron Dame want with us?* He doubted it was anything good.

"Very well," he said, "but it's a little past Flea's bedtime—"

"Is *not*," the girl retorted.

"—and I'll need a glass of something in my hand. If you'll give me a moment?"

"Of course." Lady Wretzky swallowed the last of her wine, and turned to Razin. "Leopold, might I trouble you for a cup of tea? This wine's got me feeling a little light-headed."

"Oh . . ." The general looked downcast at being denied the climax to his story, but recovered quickly. "Of course," he replied, struggling up from his chair. "I'll be back in a moment."

"Thank you." Lady Wretzky beamed a smile at Flea. "That's quite the crossbow you've got there, young lady. But I do hope you're not going to point it at me all night."

"Oh." Flea lowered her weapon. "Sorry."

Lukan noted that Ashra made no move to sheath her stiletto. Mistrusting as always. Even of an old dame who smoked cigarillos like her life depended on it. He eyed the remnants of Razin's drinks cabinet, which was dwindling by the day. He was more than a little responsible for that. Whether there was coin to be found in his father's vault or not, he ought to buy the general a few new bottles. It was the least he could do. He picked up one of the survivors and tilted it toward the fire to read the label.

Movement flashed in the glass.

Lukan whirled as a hooded figure slipped through the door, crossbow levelled at him. "Shit," he murmured. He dropped the bottle, which shattered on the floor, and retreated back toward the fireplace. "We've got company," he called over his shoulder, drawing his sword. A second figure appeared, then a third. *Too many*, he realized, even as Flea raised her own crossbow, baring her teeth at the intruders. "Don't be rash," he warned her, as thoughts raced in his mind. *Are these Arima's men?* If so, the man's response to Lukan's betrayal was far more aggressive than he'd anticipated. *Or did Marni send them? No, this doesn't seem like her style.* He positioned himself in front of Lady Wretzky. "General!" he called, doubting Razin could hear him from the kitchen on the other side of the house. Or Timur, if he was sleeping upstairs. They were on their own.

Silence descended, broken only by the crackle of the fire. The intruders kept their crossbows raised. They wore dark clothes, with scarves covering their lower faces. *Just like the ones who ambushed us in the street.*

"Drop your weapons," Lady Wretzky said mildly.

"You heard her," Lukan called, trying to seize what initiative he could. Perhaps the presence of aristocracy would give the intruders pause. "Drop those crossbows."

"I was talking to you, Lord Gardova."

Lukan's stomach lurched. *What in the hells* . . . He turned to find Lady Wretzky regarding him. The warmth she'd exuded just moments earlier was gone as if it had never been, replaced by an icy countenance, her mouth a thin line, her eyes holding his with a cold gleam.

"Me?" he replied.

"Yes. You."

"I don't understand."

"You said the same last night."

Lukan's eyes widened in realization, but Ashra spoke first.

"It was you," the thief said. "In the street. *You* took the formula from us."

"I did," Lady Wretzky agreed, without a hint of apology. "And I told you to leave Korslakov. What a pity you didn't listen." Her eyes shone with amusement. "Still, I must shoulder some of the blame. After all, the Scrivener did warn me you were trouble."

"The Scrivener?" Lukan echoed in surprise. He'd barely thought about the master forger since leaving Saphrona. "You *know* her?"

"Of course. Laverne and I go way back." Lady Wretzky smiled. "It was I who first set her on the forger's path. She was reluctant at first—can you imagine? But they were paying her a pittance at the Blackfire Bank and Laverne needed the money. So she agreed to forge a writ for me, and discovered she had a natural talent. The rest is history, as they say."

Laverne. Lukan tried to connect the name to the Scrivener's sharp features, but couldn't make it fit. "That's how you knew about us," he guessed. "About what we did in Saphrona."

"Correct. Laverne sent me a very detailed letter. I believe it arrived on the same ship you did."

"I trust she spoke highly of me?"

"I suppose I should have expected as much from a disgraced aristocrat—not to mention Lady Midnight." She smiled as Ashra tensed. "Yes, my dear, Laverne told me all about you as well. In far more glowing terms, I should add."

"You don't know me," Ashra replied.

"Perhaps not." Wretzky took a final drag from her cigarillo and ground the stub into her dish. "But I do know," she added, exhaling smoke, "that the pair of you have placed the entire city in grave danger."

"Here we are!" General Razin announced, as he stepped into the room with a tray bearing two steaming mugs. "Hot tea. I even found some biscuits . . ." He fell silent as he saw the hooded figures with their crossbows. "Oh . . ."

"Should've made more tea, General," Lukan said.

"It's all right, Leopold," Lady Wretzky said, beckoning the man into the room. "These are my men."

"Forgive me, Olga," Razin replied, remaining in the doorway, "but I can't help noticing that they're pointing crossbows at my guests."

"It's fine, General," Lukan said, "if she wanted us dead, we'd both be pincushions by now." He looked at Lady Wretzky. "Isn't that right? You want something from us. Hence this thrilling conversation we're having."

"Ah, impertinence," the woman said, lips curling in mimicry of a smile. "I believe I now have the full set." She waved a hand at Razin, who was still standing in the doorway. "Come along, Leopold," she said, with a touch of impatience, "you're standing there like a young man on his first visit to a knocking shop. My tea, please." The general reluctantly entered the room. "Thank you," Lady Wretzky said, as she took a mug of tea from the general's tray. Razin then retreated to another armchair, where he sat nursing his own mug, eyes flitting across the silent, hooded figures.

Lukan felt a twinge of guilt at bringing trouble to the man's door. And annoyance at Wretzky for gatecrashing what should have been a celebratory moment. "Now that we're all settled," he said, more than a touch venomously, "perhaps you could do us the courtesy of telling us why the hells you're even here."

Lady Wretzky blew on her tea, entirely unruffled by his bluntness. "What do you know of the Crimson Door, Lord Gardova?"

"Only what Marni told me. That the Phaeron built it into the side of a mountain, and that it's never been opened."

"Quite right. The Crimson Door has a unique lock, not one that any physical key can open. It's believed only a very specific alchemical solution can do that. That's why Korslakov embraced alchemy. For centuries, the ruling class competed to see who could claim the glory of opening the door and seizing whatever was behind it. This led to the founding of the Tower and the order of alchemists. I suppose in that sense we should be grateful. The Game of Smoke and Shadows, as it was called, inadvertently led to many alchemical discoveries."

"The smoke part, I understand," Lukan said. "But why shadows?"

"Because this was a game that involved subterfuge and skulduggery as much as alchemical experiments. The aristocrats of that time were desperate to be the first to open the door, and equally desperate to stop their rivals from doing the same. Friendships became rivalries, and rivalries became feuds. Bribery, blackmail and beatings became commonplace. Nothing was considered off-limits. The prize was too great. Of course, it was the poor alchemists who took the brunt of it."

"Of course," Lukan said, with derision. "It's always someone else who suffers, isn't it? And for what? Sounds like none of the aristos got what they wanted."

"It's thought a few alchemists came close to discovering the formula. Sadly, in each case their research mysteriously disappeared."

"I'll bet it did."

"I refer you to my earlier point about bribery, blackmail and beatings. Though there was also a case of arson, of a laboratory being vandalised, and of an alchemist being lured to a bawdyhouse and murdered. As I said, nothing was off-limits in the Game of Smoke and Shadows." The Iron Dame paused, then added, "But not all of the sabotage was committed by ambitious nobles. The Sentinels were responsible for some of it."

"The Sentinels?" Lukan asked. "No, let me guess: yet another secret society with a pompous name, correct? As if Marni and her Crimson Door nonsense isn't enough."

"The Sentinels were . . ." Wretzky paused. "A covert organization," she continued, placing emphasis on the two words, "who believed the Crimson Door should remain closed. And were prepared to do whatever it took to ensure it did."

"Someone's always got to spoil the fun. Why?"

"Is it not obvious?" Wretzky asked, frowning at him like a teacher at a slow pupil. "No one knows what's behind that door. Only that it's Phaeron, which should be reason enough to leave it well alone. Are you familiar with the tale of the Brimstone Feast?"

Lukan smiled in recognition. "I am." His father had told him the story more than once. "Some governor back in the days of the Amberléne Empire was given a Phaeron artifact as a gift," he said, for Flea and Ashra's benefit. "He tried to show it off at some sort of formal dinner and ended up causing an explosion that destroyed the entire palace and killed over a hundred people. All that was left were blackened skeletons and the stench of brimstone."

"Now you see why the Sentinels believed the Crimson Door should remain shut," Wretzky continued. "Opening it could potentially doom the entire city. So they watched from the shadows. Only interfered when the need was dire. And ensured that the formula was never discovered." She took another sip of her tea. "Eventually the Game of Smoke and Shadows began to wane. Funding alchemical experiments was expensive, after all, and not even the archons have bottomless pockets. Most aristocrats turned their interest toward artifice and mechanical marvels. The Crimson Door became a novelty, half-forgotten. Until an alchemist finally cracked the formula."

"Safiya Kalimara," Ashra said.

"Yes." If Wretzky was surprised to hear the name from the

thief's lips, she masked it well. "Kalimara had been expelled from the Tower, and I understand that none of the master alchemists regarded her highly. So it was a surprise when word spread that she had solved the puzzle that had defeated the brightest of alchemical minds. Even more of a surprise that she offered to sell the formula to Lord Baranov, when others could have offered her much higher sums. Grigor, of course, jumped at the chance to make history. He was a different man back then. So full of vigor."

"But he never got his chance, did he?" Lukan asked. "Thanks to a plague that mysteriously broke out in the very inn Kalimara was staying at."

"As I said, nothing was off-limits in the Game of Smoke and Shadows."

"Even unleashing a plague? A plague that killed hundreds and turned others into monsters? Don't you think that's a *little* extreme?"

"For some people, the ends justify the means."

"People like the Sentinels, perhaps?"

"You'd have to ask them."

"I am. Or am I mistaken in thinking you're their leader?"

"Ah." The Iron Dame's lips curled in faint amusement. "Was it the men in masks that gave it away?"

"Answer the question," Lukan pressed, tiring of all the doublespeak.

"Don't make demands of me, Lord Gardova." Wretzky's voice had turned to ice. "My patience only stretches so far." Then she sighed and stared down at her mug. "The plague was a tragedy. One of the worst this city has ever suffered. But the one silver lining was that the formula was lost, and the Game of Smoke and Shadows was finally over."

"Not much of a silver lining for the plague victims."

"Or for Safiya Kalimara," Ashra said, an accusatory note in her voice. "I read her last words. A brilliant woman who died scared and alone. She deserved better. All those people did."

"Yes. They did. But I'm more concerned about the living." Wretzky's gaze hardened. "And thanks to you three, we're looking at a catastrophe that would make the plague look like a minor inconvenience. With the recovery of the formula, the Game of Smoke and Shadows has resumed."

"We had no choice," Lukan replied. "We owed Marni a debt. She told us to recover the formula or—"

"She'd send you back to the gallows. Yes, I know the terms of your agreement." Her expression curdled. "Of course it would be Marni driving all this. I always thought that girl's obsession with the Phaeron would be the death of her. And I was quite content with that. But not if it threatens the entire city. And now we have Lord Arima to worry about as well. As if one of them having the formula wasn't bad enough. Twenty years ago I could have handled this with little difficulty, but my network and resources aren't what they were." One corner of her mouth creased. "Besides, I'm getting too old for this shit."

Here it comes, Lukan thought wearily. *The entire point of this conversation.* "You want our help."

"I do. And I'm not asking. I'm insisting."

"I thought the Scrivener said I was—what was it—untrustworthy and unreliable."

"Laverne also said that, while you're very good at getting into trouble, you're even better at getting out of it."

"I'm flattered."

"She also said that Ashra is easily the best thief Saphrona has ever seen. Which makes the two of you indispensable to me."

"And if we refuse to help?"

"Do you?"

Lukan fought the urge to reply in the affirmative. This wasn't his decision to make. Instead, he found Flea's gaze, then Ashra's. He saw defiance shining in both. "We didn't know what the formula was when we agreed to search for it," he said, turning back to Wretzky. "Why should we help you when this isn't our fault?"

"Pity," the Iron Dame replied, pursing her lips. "Don't say I didn't give you a chance." She clicked her fingers. Cloth whispered as the hooded figures raised their weapons.

"Threats at the point of a crossbow," Lukan said derisively, glancing at them. "Or four." He found Lady Wretzky's gaze. "Not exactly subtle."

"I suspect you and subtlety are not on speaking terms," the Iron Dame replied, her voice cold. She held out a hand. "Now, give me your key."

"My key?" Lukan felt a surge of panic. "No. Absolutely not."

"I hoped it wouldn't come to this," Wretzky said. "What a pity. But if the moral weight of my request doesn't move you, perhaps a more straightforward threat will." She signaled to the figures behind him. As one, they turned their crossbows away from him.

And pointed them at Flea.

"I told you that you and Ashra were indispensable to me," Wretzky continued, hand still outstretched. "The same isn't true of your little friend here, though Laverne did mention she's a mean shot with that crossbow of hers."

"Damn right!" Flea retorted, raising Nighthawk and pointing her at the old woman.

"Easy, *majin*," Ashra whispered.

"Give me your key, Lord Gardova," the Iron Dame said.

"Don't do it!" Flea yelled. She was standing tall before the crossbows aimed at her—or as tall as her four and a half feet would allow—her face set with determination, eyes blazing, but Lukan caught the slight quiver in her voice.

"Come now, Olga," General Razin said. "Surely there's no need for this—"

"Hush, Leopold, there's a dear." Lady Wretzky beckoned with her outstretched fingers. "Your key, Lord Gardova. Or the girl's life."

Lukan found Ashra's gaze. The thief nodded.

"All right, fine," he said, turning back to the Iron Dame. "We'll help. We'll do whatever you ask."

"I'm glad to hear it. But I'll take your key all the same. Just to ensure your good behavior. Never fear, you'll have it back the moment our business is concluded."

Seven bloody shadows. The thought of losing his key yet again—especially after just getting it back—sickened him. *But what choice do I have?*

"You would really harm a child?" he asked, playing for time. For once Flea didn't correct him on his use of the term.

"I would do anything to keep that formula out of the wrong hands."

"Like unleashing a plague? Was that your work?"

"If it was," Wretzky replied tersely, "you can be certain that one more death shouldn't make any difference to me. Now." She twitched her fingers. "Your key. Don't make me ask again."

Lukan held the old woman's gaze, searching for a glint of uncertainty, but all he saw was ice. Cold. Unyielding. *Would she really shoot Flea?* He wasn't sure. But he certainly wasn't prepared to risk her life to find out. Even if it meant giving up his key.

"Lukan," the girl breathed, as he reached into his pocket. "*Don't.*" She groaned softly as he pressed the key into Lady Wretzky's hand.

"A wise move, Lord Gardova," the Iron Dame said. She slipped it into a pocket and waved at her men to lower their weapons. "Now, to business. Lord Arima and Lady Marni already have their pet alchemists preparing the formula. We need to interfere with their respective alchemical processes in such a way that our meddling remains invisible, yet renders their final concoctions useless. This will require stealth and subtlety."

"As you said," Lukan pointed out, "subtlety and I aren't exactly on speaking terms."

"Then I suggest you learn each other's language quickly. If either Marni or Arima catch the slightest whiff of our meddling, our plan will fail. We need them to both think they've concocted the formula perfectly. When their respective attempts to unlock the Crimson Door fail, they'll assume the formula was flawed all along."

"And Safiya Kalimara will go down in history as a failure," Ashra murmured, her expression dark.

"I'm sure she can live with it."

The thief glowered but made no reply.

"I never thought I'd regret skipping my chemistry lectures at the Academy, but here we are." Lukan shook his head. "I don't have the faintest idea how to alter the formula without it being obvious."

"I've already sought advice," Lady Wretzky replied. "I'm told that the formula is highly complicated, and that just a slight amendment will be enough to render it useless." She reached into a pocket and withdrew a glass vial filled with a dark red powder. "Did you at least attend enough chemistry lessons to know what this is?"

"Ah . . . devil's dust?"

"Correct. There's hope for you yet."

"It was a lucky guess."

"A mere pinch of this will be enough to unbalance the formula," Lady Wretzky continued, offering Lukan the vial. "Leave Lord Arima to me and my agents. You'll need to handle Lady Marni."

"I can get inside her house easily enough," Lukan said, recalling the whisper of Marni's lips against his ear. Letting her drag him to bed would hardly be a chore, he had to admit. Once she was asleep, he'd slip away and seek out her laboratory. A quick sprinkle of devil's dust and it would all be done. Men had done worse to save untold lives.

"Marni's formula isn't being concocted in the Volkov household," Wretzky replied, puncturing his optimism. "I'm afraid her pet alchemist is working on it in his own laboratory, which is rather tricky to access."

"Why? Where is it?"

"At the top of the Tower of Sanctified Flame." She gave a humorless smile. "The alchemist she has charged with the task is none other than Rastan Albrecht, one of the four masters of the Tower."

"Shit."

"I'd say that's an apt term." The Iron Dame set down her mug and opened a silver case, plucking a fresh cigarillo from it. "The formula will take roughly two days to create," she continued, using a nearby candle to light her smoke. "We've already lost one of those days, so you'll need to move quickly. Tomorrow night under cover of darkness may be your best chance to sneak into the Tower and tamper with that formula without Albrecht noticing."

"And how in the hells are we meant to do that?"

"You're a smart boy. And Ashra's an even sharper woman. I'm sure you'll figure it out." Her cigarillo glowed as she took a drag. "The alchemists run a daily tour of their tower," she added, exhaling a cloud of smoke. "You should go along."

"A tour?" Lukan said dubiously. "I thought the alchemists were meant to be secretive."

"They are. The tour only takes in the lower three floors. Even so, you might find it useful." Lady Wretzky rose from her chair, joints creaking. "By the Builder, I'm getting too old for this. My thanks for the tea, Leopold." She shuffled toward the door. "With me, you four," she said to the hooded figures, who lowered their crossbows and made to follow.

"What happens if we fail?" Lukan called after her.

The woman looked over her shoulder. "Then we'll all have much bigger things to worry about."

33

THE TOWER OF
SANCTIFIED FLAME

The last thing Lukan needed after barely any sleep was to under-
take a guided tour of the alchemists' tower (what they allowed the
public to see of it, at any rate), but that was precisely what he found
himself doing. Or *not* doing, since the guide was late, leaving Lukan
and his fellow sightseers to potter about the Tower's ground floor
while they waited. It was a grand setting, admittedly, all polished
tiles and marble pillars and large oil paintings of long-dead alchemists frowning down from the walls.

The other members of the group seemed harmless enough: a
middle-aged couple, a bored-looking father accompanying an excitable child, and a studious young woman who was engrossed in a
book. As they waited for the tour guide to arrive, Lukan's thoughts
turned back to the task at hand: figuring out how they might sneak
into Master Albrecht's private quarters at the top of the Tower, tamper with the solution he was concocting for Lady Marni—without
it being obvious, of course—and escape without being seen.

Hardly a challenge.

He sighed.

Ashra was fond of saying there was always a way out, but the
question now was whether there was a way *in*. As he glanced at the
two golems that stood either side of the marbled staircase, he felt he
already had his answer. They were buffed to a sheen, seemingly ready
to crack the skulls of anyone who dared set foot where they didn't
belong. An emphatic *stay the hells away* forged in steel. Sentries that
didn't sleep, didn't need to leave their post for a trip to the privy or a

quick cigarillo. That couldn't be bribed or reasoned with. And there were likely to be more on the upper floors. He muttered a curse, earning a sharp look from the father of the excitable child. *This is a fool's errand.*

As much as he desired to open his father's vault, he'd come to realize he valued his friends' safety more. And asking them to go up against the Tower's golems was only going to get them killed— himself included. Perhaps it was time to walk away. Accept that this was one bridge he couldn't cross. He'd done his best; no one could say otherwise. The shadow of defeat would haunt him, of course. He'd always feel a failure for not learning the truth of his father's death and delivering the justice he deserved.

But at least he'd be alive. And so would Flea and Ashra.

Perhaps that was what really mattered.

"Good morning, everyone!"

The cheerful voice cut through Lukan's thoughts, and he looked up to see a young man striding across the entrance hall, his white tunic marred by burn marks. "My apologies for being late," he continued, clasping his hands and offering them all a little bow. "There were a couple of fires that needed putting out. Literal ones, I mean." The group's silence didn't diminish the man's enthusiasm. "My name is Felix Gaspard," he added, puffing out his chest slightly, "apprentice of the second rank, and I'm delighted to be your guide for the next hour or so."

He's from Parva, Lukan realized, noting the man's cultured Heartland accent.

"So, how many of us are there?" Felix asked, glancing around as the members of the group shuffled toward him. "Four, five, six . . ."

Lukan thought about making his excuses and leaving, but he'd already paid his five coppers to the clerk at the front desk. Given the fee amounted to nothing less than daylight robbery, he figured he might as well get his money's worth. Besides, there was always a chance a solution might present itself.

"Wonderful!" Felix clapped his hands. "Six guests, one for each of the forbidden substances! Does anyone know what they are?"

Silence.

"Is Deladrian dandelion wine one of them?" Lukan asked. "Because it should be."

Silence.

"Tough crowd," Lukan added, smiling as he caught Felix's amused gaze. "Good luck."

The apprentice's left eyebrow rose in acknowledgment, before he spun on his heel. "If you'll follow me, please." He started toward the staircase, the group shuffling along behind him. "A few house rules before we begin," he continued, hopping onto the first step. "We'll be visiting the first three floors of the Tower this morning, all of which are busy, working environments, so *please* do not touch anything—that includes each other. A couple of guests once had a quick fumble and nearly set themselves on fire, though perhaps not in the way they'd hoped."

"Daddy," the little boy said, "what's a fumble?"

"Moving on," Felix said hurriedly, saving the father's blushes, "please don't touch the golems either." He gestured to the two constructs standing on either side of him. "They can be . . . overzealous in carrying out their duty to protect the Tower."

"Are there many golems here?" Lukan asked casually.

"Oh, plenty," Felix replied with a nod. "They're always carrying supplies up from the cellars and stockrooms belowground, though some have more specialist roles."

"Marvelous."

"Indeed!" Felix didn't seem to catch the sarcasm in Lukan's voice. "One final rule—please don't talk to any of the apprentices or alchemists. Their work is complicated and requires great concentration. The slightest distraction could be disastrous. I've seen the consequences. Trust me, it's no fun picking shards of glass out of your face." He turned and started up the stairs. "Follow me, please—the first floor awaits!"

Felix Gaspard was a natural showman.

Which didn't surprise Lukan, since in his experience everyone in Parva either wanted to be a performer of some sort or knew someone who did. Nonetheless, he found himself drawn in by the man's flamboyant storytelling as they ascended to the first floor. This was apparently the lowest of the Tower's laboratories, where apprentices worked to produce the substances used in the Tower's famous alchemical globes. By the time they arrived at the top of the staircase, Lukan was expecting scrolls of archaic formula to be flying through the air, surrounded by orbs of colored light, such was the manner in which Felix described the laboratory.

Reality disappointed.

Rows of wooden benches bore a variety of glass equipment, some of it filled with chemicals of assorted colors, and all of it watched over by bored-looking apprentices who did their best to ignore the little group as Felix led them on a lap round the circular room. Their guide gestured to several features, such as the pipes on the ceiling that funneled fumes away, and his various anecdotes worked their magic on the rest of the group, particularly the boy, who looked around with wide eyes. Not so Lukan, for whom the bubbling liquids, bored apprentices and whiff of sulfur in the air stirred memories of tedious lessons in the Academy's chemistry labs. The handful he'd bothered attending, at least. Despite Felix's often amusing anecdotes, the tour was rather dull.

Except for one detail.

"What's that?" he asked Felix, pointing at a bronze door set at the base of a round, protruding part of the far wall, which rose all the way to the ceiling.

"A service shaft," Felix replied enthusiastically, as if it was the most exciting thing in the entire room. Which, to Lukan, it actually was. "There's a platform within that's used to move large or heavy objects between floors."

"And it runs the entire length of the Tower?" Lukan queried, trying to sound casual.

"That it does! From the depths of the storerooms to the rarefied heights of the masters' chambers on the top floor."

"And do the alchemists use it for traveling up and down?" Lukan gestured at the staircase. "There *are* a lot of stairs in this place."

"There are," Felix agreed with a good-natured laugh, "but no. The shaft is for goods only. Riding it is strictly forbidden."

"Hmm," Lukan said, a spark of an idea flickering in his mind.

"Anyway, we must press on." Felix stepped away. "Follow me, everyone! The next floor awaits."

The second floor was much the same as the first: benches covered in scorch marks, scattered formulas and all manner of alchemical equipment, though the apprentices looked more engaged than their fellows on the floor below. Felix suggested this was because they'd survived their first year of training—it took seven years to earn an alchemist's robes—and had moved on to more complex work. Not that you could tell; the bubbling liquids and apparatus all looked much the same. Felix launched enthusiastically into an explanation of what apprentices needed to do to earn their robes, and, from what little Lukan heard, it sounded dismal—years of learning formulas and charts and arsing around with alembics—but in truth he wasn't really listening; his mind was still on the bronze door. There was another one on this floor, and he assumed that was the case all the way up to the top where the four masters had their chambers. *Where Master Albrecht is working on Lady Marni's concoction at this very moment.* If only he could just slip away from the group and ride the platform upward. *And then what?* He would still face the challenge of tampering with the formula, and he didn't expect Master Albrecht would simply stand aside and let him do it. He sighed, his flicker of hope fading. Still, the presence of the goods shaft was encouraging, offering a method of reaching the top of the Tower swiftly. *But how to do so undetected?* Perhaps Ashra would have an idea. If she was here, he could have asked her, but the thief was instead ensconced in a tavern frequented by the Tower's servants, eavesdropping on their chatter and hoping to learn something of value. Lukan had originally volunteered for that role, but Ashra had questioned whether his interests lay more in drinking and gambling than information-gathering. Lukan's response—that it was entirely possible to do all three at once—was met with nothing but a raised eyebrow. Still, at least she'd taken Flea with her, which spared him the trouble of keeping an eye on the girl. The last thing he needed was her fiddling with something and causing an explosion that brought half the Tower down.

Lukan was startled out of his thoughts by a loud *bang*, and turned to see a large cloud of smoke rising from one bench, where a red-faced apprentice stared at the smoking ruins of his equipment. A sarcastic cheer rang around the floor as one of the other apprentices strode to a chalkboard and, under a line that read *Days since Arkady blew himself up*, wiped away the five existing tally marks and marked a new one.

"And on that note," Felix said, with a flourish, "it's time to embark on the final stage of our visit. Follow me!"

The third floor of the Tower—and final stop on their tour—was entirely dominated by bookcases stretching from floor to ceiling, housing countless leather-bound books and assorted other curios: with a single glance, Lukan saw a human skull branded with an alchemical symbol, a circle of black marble inscribed with formulae and a brine-filled jar containing something that might have once been alive, but wasn't any more. Or so he hoped.

"Behold," Felix said, sweeping an arm at the bookcases. "The lower library, one of two in the Tower!"

"This is just a shot in the dark," Lukan said, "but would the other library be called the upper library?"

"Indeed it is! Only fully fledged alchemists may visit the upper library, but its lower counterpart is open to all. The two libraries combined represent the greatest collection of alchemically related literature in the Old Empire. Remarkable, don't you think?"

Lukan couldn't help but agree. He'd seen many libraries over the years—smoked in them, had several fumbles in them, and on one unmemorable occasion even *studied* in one—but he had to admit this library, with its dark wood shelves, sliding ladders and desks with small alchemical globes, was particularly impressive. So too was the librarian, who was made entirely of metal. Lukan watched as the golem—which was noticeably smaller than the others he'd seen—worked nearby, carefully replacing books on a shelf. Someone had stuck a piece of parchment to its back with *Ask me about alchemy* scrawled in red ink.

"Feel free to explore," Felix told the group, "but please don't touch anything. Oh, and keep your voices down. This is a working library, after all." He gestured to a woman working at one of the desks, a fully fledged alchemist judging by her blue and purple robes. "I'll be right here if you have any questions."

Lukan waited as the group dispersed, all with varying expressions of disinterest, particularly the boy, whose frown very much suggested he'd rather be downstairs watching apprentices melting their own faces. As soon as they were all out of earshot, he seized his chance.

"I didn't expect the Tower's tour guide to be a Heartlander," he said, stepping closer to Felix. "You're a long way from home."

"So are you," the young man replied, with a faint smile.

"You mean to say my years on the road haven't taken the edge off my Parvan accent? I'd hoped they'd coarsened my vowels and given me a bit of rough charm."

"I'm afraid they could still cut glass."

"Pity." Lukan waited a few heartbeats, then continued, "I'm surprised, given our home city's love of the arts, that you didn't become a thespian. You've certainly got a theatrical flair."

The young man was quiet for a moment, his gaze distant. "I wanted to be an actor," he admitted eventually, "but my father had other ideas."

"I know how that feels."

"He told me he would only pay for my education if I pursued something worthwhile—his words, not mine." Felix sighed. "I almost ran away with an acting troupe, but I lost my nerve. Instead I studied chemistry at the Academy. And then I came here, hoping I'd discover a passion for alchemy, but . . ."

"You've realized you're better at spinning tales in front of an audience."

"Exactly. Everyone knows it, too. That's why I end up doing these tours more than anyone else. Still, it's better than standing at a workbench for hours on end."

"You could still run away and join an acting troupe."

"Maybe I should." Felix managed a wan smile. "What about you—were you at the Academy?"

"I was. I left about seven years ago."

"Seven years?" Felix asked, a spark of interest in his eyes. "Were you there when that duel happened? What was the fellow's name—Luther something-or-other?"

"Lukan," Lukan said, unable to keep the tightness from his voice. "Lukan Gardova. And yes, I was there. I knew Lukan quite well, actually."

"Really? What was he like?"

"Smart. Sharp-witted. And almost indecently good looking."

"Is it true that he stabbed the other duellist in the back?"

"That's what they say, is it?" Lukan asked, a touch sharply. "No, it's not true. It was the other way round."

"He died, didn't he? The other student?"

"Yes. He did."

"I wonder what happened to Gardova after he was expelled."

"If I bump into him, I'll be sure to ask." Lukan glanced around and lowered his voice. "I wanted to ask you something."

"Of course."

"If you were going to break into this tower with the aim of infiltrating one of the masters' chambers, how would you go about it?"

Felix flinched as if he'd been slapped. "Break in?" he whispered, incredulous.

"Let me explain," Lukan said, with a reassuring smile. "I'm a writer—a novelist, actually. I write under the name Bastien Dubois."

"Oh." Felix shook his head. "I'm afraid I've not heard of you . . ."

"No, of course you haven't. My first book was published by a press in Tantalon, and only reached a small audience. But I have high hopes for my next work. It's . . . well, how to put it. Are you familiar with *Between Blade and Boudoir*?"

"You mean that bodice-ripper?"

"Exactly! My new book will be a little like that, only with more swords and fewer swoons. And as part of the climactic act, I was thinking of having the dashing protagonist infiltrate the villain's tower lair. That's why I'm here, actually. To get a sense of, um, place and atmosphere. That sort of thing."

"I see," Felix said, very much not seeing.

"So I'm wondering," Lukan continued, "how my hero might successfully navigate a tower full of golems and arrive at the top. Say we were talking about *this* tower, what would you do?"

"I . . . well." Felix chewed his lip. "I suppose I'd use the goods shaft, since it goes all the way to the top floor."

"That's what I figured. But how to do so without being seen?"

"I guess I'd hide inside a crate of supplies, or something." Felix shrugged. "But that would be impossible."

"Oh?" Lukan queried, his heart sinking. "How so?"

"All goods being transported up the Tower are checked thoroughly. There was a rather embarrassing scenario a while back with a burlesque dancer, and . . . Well, it doesn't matter. Trust me, you wouldn't make it out of the goods yard without being discovered."

"That's . . . unfortunate."

"Not nearly as unfortunate as what would happen once you were caught."

Lukan's heart sank even further. "And that is?"

"Let's just say the last person caught trespassing was marched into a room and never seen again."

I'll bet they were, Lukan thought, recalling what Clank had revealed to them about the alchemists' dark practices.

Felix smiled and clapped him on the shoulder. "Hopefully the hero of your story somehow gets away with it, eh?"

"Yes," Lukan replied, forcing a smile. "Let's hope so."

———

"You told him you were a *writer*?" Ashra asked, one eyebrow raised.

"I did."

"And he *believed* you?"

"He seemed to." Lukan shrugged. "It's not as far-fetched as it sounds. Everyone in Parva wants to be an artist of some sort. Besides, I did flirt briefly with pursuing a literary life . . ."

"*You?*"

"Yes," Lukan replied, slightly chagrined by her surprise. "Me. Though I never really got around to trying it."

"Let me guess," Ashra said dryly. "Drinking and gambling were more fun."

"They were, as it happens. So were the tavern brawls. Anyway . . ." Lukan flicked a dismissive gesture. "The point is that Felix indulged my imaginary ambition of writing a bestselling bodice-ripper and helpfully described the finer points of the Tower's security system."

"Which is?"

"Golems that will pluck the limbs off anyone who's not meant to be there. The damned place is full of them. There's no way anyone's sneaking up nine floors full of constructs without being turned into paste. Not even you."

"So you learned nothing helpful."

"Well, let's see—I learned that this mission is exactly the fool's errand I assumed it would be. I'd say that's helpful." Lukan sighed and ran a hand through his hair. "I was thinking it might be possible to hide inside a crate or something, but Felix told me all deliveries to the Tower are checked thoroughly."

"Not all deliveries," Ashra replied.

"Oh? Did you learn something at the tavern?"

"No. But Flea did." The thief looked at the girl, who was once more using Ivan as a pillow as she stared up at the ceiling. "Do you want to tell him?"

"One of the masters is on a . . ." The girl paused, her mouth trying to form the unfamiliar word. "Sab . . . utical?"

"A sabbatical?" Lukan asked.

"Yeah! We don't know what this is, but—"

"It's when someone takes a period of absence from their duties in order to do something else for a while."

"So something that only rich people can afford to do," Ashra said dryly. "Got it. Go on, Flea."

"This master is away somewhere . . . I think they said she's in the Southern Queendoms? But apparently she's been sending things back to the Tower. Chests of strange ingredients and rocks and stuff." Flea pushed herself up onto one elbow. "Apparently the first one smelled so bad when they opened it, they sent it straight up to her room, and didn't bother to open the ones that came after."

"So, we find a chest," Ashra said. "One large enough for me to fit inside. We make it look like it's been shipped all the way from Zar-Ghosa. Fill it with something nasty that threatens to stink the place out, and . . ." She snapped her fingers.

"You get a free ride to the top of the Tower," Lukan finished.

"What do you think?" Flea asked with a grin.

"It might just work." He knuckled his jaw and grimaced. "But even if it does, you'll still need to sneak into Master Albrecht's room and tamper with his work without him noticing."

"Oh," Flea said nonchalantly, lying back down against Ivan. "We've got a plan for that too."

Lukan met Ashra's gaze. "You do?"

The thief nodded. "Apparently Albrecht worked through the night last night. A golem brought him a fresh mug of tea every couple of hours."

"Tea? He should try coffee."

"Not everyone likes coffee."

"Yes, I'm aware you heathens walk among us. Anyway, how does this help us?"

"If you can stop interrupting," Ashra said, "I can explain."

34

SPECIAL DELIVERY

Ashra and her father used to play a game.

He would bundle her up in a blanket, spin her round a few times to make her dizzy, then carry her to another room in their modest house. Then he'd set her down and whip the blanket from her, and Ashra—with her eyes closed—would guess which room they were in. Regardless of whether she was right, her answer would always be followed by her father's booming laughter.

She clung to that memory now.

If she concentrated hard enough, she could convince herself the stinking sheets that covered her—pilfered from a leather-works by the river—were really her father's blanket. That the reason she could smell lavender was because her mother had brought some back from the Plaza of Silver and Spice, and not because she wore a beaked mask stuffed with it. That it was her father carrying her, and not a golem. That in the end she would find herself in her old bedroom, or their small kitchen with the herbs hanging from the rafters, and not in an unfamiliar storage room.

But no. Reality asserted itself and she was back in the chest that Lady Wretzky had obtained for them: a battered, salt-stained relic that looked like it had endured an arduous voyage from the Southern Queendoms. Cramped space, aching limbs, breath hot against her own face. A needle of panic pricking at her heart. She willed herself to calm, but multiple anxieties circled her mind. What if the key to the chest's lock didn't work? What if she couldn't get out? She'd practiced, of course. Each time she'd successfully unlocked

the chest from the inside and sprung out. But what if something
went wrong? The key she clutched in her hand was old; what if it
snapped in the lock? What if the golem placed her underneath a
shelf where she couldn't raise the lid?

"Calmness is the key to success," she whispered, repeating her
first rule over and over again, comforted by the shape of the words
on her lips. Gradually her mind settled and her heart slowed, until
all she felt was the rocking motion of the chest in the golem's arms
as it unknowingly carried her into the depths of the Tower.

So far, their plan had worked.

The bargemen who Lady Wretzky hired had delivered her just
after the sixth bell of the evening—beyond the curfew for new
deliveries, as an irritable servant of the Tower had pointed out.
"Builder's balls," the man had said, "another one of Master Severin's little presents, is it?" Ashra had held her breath as his shins had
appeared beyond the keyhole. Someone else said something that
she didn't catch, to which the man replied, "Do you want to bloody
open it? You remember how bad the other crates smelled. Let's just
send it up." He moved away. "Hey, tinhead! Get your metal arse
over here and take that chest up to the attic." Ashra had breathed a
sigh of relief as the chest had risen upward, its weight no problem
for the golem who was carrying it.

Now she could hear winches, could sense upward momentum.
They were in the goods shaft, heading up to the attic storeroom at
the Tower's heights, where the rest of Master Severin's deliveries
had been left. All being well, she would soon join them.

Forward movement again. She caught a glimpse of a stairwell.
Darkness replaced the light beyond the keyhole.

Ashra gasped into her mask as the chest dropped, thumping
against the floor. She jolted as it slid forward and stopped.

Stillness.

Silence.

Then the sound of heavy footsteps moving away until they
faded altogether.

That was the first part done. She took a deep breath, her sense of relief tinged with anxiety. Now she had to get out.

Ashra pushed the rags off her face. She couldn't see anything through the glass eyepieces of her mask. All was dark. She traced one hand across the inside of the chest, feeling the keyhole beneath her fingertips. With her other hand she slid the key into the lock.

Blood thumped in her ears.

She turned the key slowly.

The *click* it eventually made was the sweetest sound she'd ever heard.

Ashra held her breath and pushed at the lid.

It didn't move.

Fear knifed her as she pushed again.

The lid creaked open, stubborn hinges finally giving way.

Ashra rose quickly, all thoughts of stealth cast aside in the face of her desire to be free of the chest. She ripped the mask off. Took a breath of musty air. Glanced around the gloomy storeroom for guards. Nothing moved. No one cried out.

She was alone.

Ashra stepped from the chest. Sagged against the nearest wall. Head bowed, hands on her knees.

She stayed like that for some time.

Eventually she looked up, wrinkling her nose at a faint stench in the air. She closed the lid of the chest, thinking it came from her discarded sheets, but the smell remained. She realized then that it was emanating from a few crates nearby. No doubt they were the shipments that Master Séverin had sent back from the Southern Queendoms. The workers she'd overheard in the tavern hadn't been lying; the smell was vile. She wondered what was inside. Briefly thought about taking a look, but decided against it. Some things you didn't need to know.

In any case, it was time to get to work.

Ashra moved through the storeroom, past chests of dusty equipment, barrels of alchemical substances and a variety of half-forgotten objects all left to gather dust in the fading daylight that filtered through the grimy windows. Another source of light caught Ashra's attention: a glow in one corner of the circular room. She crept toward it, and found two staircases. One that ascended to a closed door that she assumed led to the roof. The other staircase curled downward, partly illuminated by a light that shone somewhere on the floor below.

The floor where Master Albrecht likely worked at this very moment.

She crept down the steps and studied the floor below. Another staircase wound downward directly across the marble floor. A corridor stretched away to her right, illuminated by alchemical globes. Four doors were set in the walls, two on either side. Hatches were set in the middle of the doors, with small shelves extending outward. Above each hatch was a bronze plaque. Ashra crept closer, searching for Albrecht's name. She found it on the first door she checked, on the left side of the hallway.

She studied the hatch but saw no way of opening it. Instead she crouched and peered through the keyhole.

A silver-haired man in alchemist's robes stood with his back to her, studying a scroll in his hands. Now and then he glanced up and frowned at the array of alembics and filters and other alchemical equipment assembled on the table before him. Ashra watched as he reached out and made some adjustments, lips moving as he muttered something to himself. Then he sat down in a chair and stifled a yawn.

If only he would fall asleep. Then she could pick the lock and sneak in. Drop a pinch of devil's dust in a funnel and be out again, quick as you like. No need to wait in the cold, gloomy attic until nightfall.

But Albrecht was back on his feet a moment later, tapping a glass vial that bubbled with a green liquid. He wouldn't be resting until his work was done.

Ashra stepped away from the door and crept back up the winding stairs into the storeroom. She had a long time to wait. Hours and hours.

But that was no problem. Patience was a thief's most valuable weapon.

And she'd spent plenty of time honing that blade.

Metal scraped against stone.

Ashra's eyes flicked open. She listened as the sound grew louder, echoing up the staircase from the floor below. Footsteps, slow and steady. But not those of a person.

The time had come.

She rose silently and crept halfway down the stairs. Swathed in shadow, she slipped from her belt a vial with a colorless liquid within. She pulled the cork.

A figure appeared at the top of the lower staircase, metal head and shoulders gleaming in the light of alchemical globes. A golem, as she'd expected. Not one of the larger types like Clank, but a smaller variety, more suited to traversing the staircases of the Tower. The construct carried a silver tray that bore a mug of tea, with a silken napkin folded over its right arm in the manner of a human butler.

Ashra watched as the golem turned into the hallway and approached Albrecht's door. The construct placed the tray on the shelf below the hatch and pulled on a nearby rope. A bell rang on the other side of the door. She waited as the golem retraced its steps toward the staircase. The silken napkin fell from its arm as it walked, but the construct didn't notice. Ashra willed it to move faster. Every moment counted.

Ashra moved as soon as the construct turned its back. She padded silently down the staircase, her eyes not leaving the tray by the hatch. The golem continued its descent, oblivious to her as she crossed the floor behind it. Just a few more heartbeats. That was all she needed.

Ashra was two steps away when the hatch opened.

She leaped forward as a pair of wrinkled hands appeared, fingers reaching for the mug's handle.

She wasn't going to make it.

But then Albrecht's right hand brushed the side of the mug, which must have been hot, for he yelped in pain. As he jerked his hand back, Ashra reached out and tipped the liquid from her vial into the steaming tea. She flattened herself against the door just as the fingers reappeared and found the mug's handle. She breathed a silent sigh of relief as both hand and mug disappeared. The hatch slid shut.

Ashra dropped to one knee and peered through the keyhole, watching as Albrecht returned to his alchemical apparatus. He placed the tray to one side and sat down.

"Come on," she murmured as Albrecht poked and prodded his equipment. She glanced over her shoulder at the other closed doors. She was exposed here; if one of the other masters was working late and happened to leave their room, they'd see her before she could flee back up the staircase. Yet if she retreated to the shadows, she'd have no idea when Albrecht took his first sip of tea. Timing was everything. So she stayed, trying to ignore the itch between her shoulders that felt like a blade against her back.

Through the keyhole, Albrecht was consulting a scroll of parchment—possibly the very copy of the formula Lukan had given to Lady Marni. His tea was still steaming away beside him. Untouched.

"Go on," Ashra breathed, as if her very words could spur him into action. "Drink it." She repeated these words many times over the next quarter-hour, as the master alchemist continued his work, seemingly oblivious to the steaming tea beside him. Had he forgotten about it? She swore under her breath. In her earlier haste, she'd used her entire vial of Shut-Eye. There would be no second chance.

"Come on," she whispered for what felt like the hundredth time. "Drink the damned . . ." The last word lingered on her lips as Albrecht yawned, an action that seemed to remind him of the tea's presence. Ashra felt a rush of relief as the man finally reached for the mug, holding her breath as he raised it to his lips . . .

And drank.

"One," she murmured as the alchemist set the mug back down. "Two. Three . . ." By the time she reached twenty, Albrecht was swaying in his seat. As she counted thirty, his whole body was tilting forward.

Ashra had her lockpicks out before the alchemist's head hit the table.

The lock was a simple one and she had it open quickly. A moment later she was inside, closing the door behind her. She darted toward the prone alchemist, whose breathing was slow and steady.

Perfect.

With luck, Albrecht would assume he'd simply fallen asleep— the result of too much work and too little rest. But he wouldn't stay unconscious for long. If he woke up to find her in his room, he'd reach an entirely different conclusion.

Ashra had to move fast.

She stepped up to the table and studied the array of equipment. It seemed a complex setup: dozens of glass pipes connected a variety of alembics and retorts, heated by a small bronze furnace beside the table. It seemed to have no beginning or end. No matter. She only needed to tamper with a single part of it.

Her eyes fixed on a funnel whose interior retained a powdery yellow residue. Clearly Master Albrecht had used it to add some sort of substance. It would serve Ashra's purpose as well, though she would need to be careful not to leave any trace of her own contribution. She slipped another vial from her belt, pulled the cork and stared at the reddish devil's dust within.

With a glance at Master Albrecht, who was still unconscious, Ashra leaned over the funnel and carefully tapped the entire vial directly into the hole. She listened for a warning sound as she stepped back. Nothing. Nor were there any visible signs that the alchemical process had been affected. How could she be sure it had worked? Then again, she supposed that was the entire point. Her interference was meant to be invisible.

Regardless, it was time to leave.

She returned to the door and opened the hatch. A quick glance through revealed that the hall was empty. Quickly she stepped through, and closed the door silently behind her. A few prods with her picks and she had it locked again.

It was done.

All that remained was to return to the storeroom and use her Ring of Last Resort to summon a portal. A step and a jump and she'd be home. The grasping cold would be a small price to pay, as it always was. She couldn't help the hint of a smile that curled at the corner of her mouth as she reached the staircase and started upward. Lady Marni's plan to unlock the Crimson Door was foiled. If the Iron Dame held to her part of the bargain, Lukan would soon get his key back. He would finally get inside his vault. And then they could leave this damned city and—

Ashra froze as metal scraped behind her.

She whirled, a throwing knife already in hand.

A golem stood near the top of the lower staircase—the same one as before, she guessed. Why the hells had it returned? Her eyes flicked to the napkin that still lay on the marble floor. The damned construct had come back for it. It was so absurd she could have laughed. Instead she cursed herself for not considering the possibility. She willed herself to calm and considered the golem.

It made no move to attack. Had barely moved at all. Instead, it stared back at her. Perhaps only the larger constructs were told to confront intruders. In which case she could just turn and—

The golem sprang forward, taking the steps two at a time.

Shit.

Ashra turned and raced up the staircase to the storeroom. She darted into the warren of abandoned objects and ducked behind a large copper alembic near the center of the room. She held her breath, feeling her own blood thrumming in her ears. The golem might be quicker and stronger, but it was also noisier; she could hear the clanking of its footsteps as it reached the top of the staircase and paused. Ashra caught a glimpse of the construct as it walked between two piles of junk, saw the amber gleam of its eyes as it searched for her. A human soul, looking out from a metal body.

A moment later it had disappeared from view, but she could hear it navigating the room, circling round to her right. Ashra moved left in response, keeping her body low, her route taking her close to the staircase that led up to the Tower's roof, where the famous purple flames burned.

The roof. That could work.

If she could slip away to the Tower's summit, she could summon her portal as the golem hunted for her below. *It's not a plan if it's got an "if" in it,* Alphonse had told her once. Wise words, but she didn't have much choice.

Ashra crept closer to the upper staircase. She paused and listened for the golem's movement, but all was quiet. Where was it? She rose slowly, stealing a glance around the darkened storeroom, but saw no sign of the construct. She couldn't run for the staircase without knowing the golem's position. She carefully ran her hands over the assorted objects around her, and her fingers closed round a metal disc that rested on the corner of a crate. A coin? No, it was too large and heavy.

But it would do.

Ashra rose from her hiding place and hurled the disc toward the far side of the room. The object must have struck a dust sheet, for the sound it made was muffled, but it was enough; immediately she heard the scrape of the golem's feet as it rushed toward the sound. Ashra moved as well, slipping from cover and onto the staircase. As she crept higher, she glanced through the railings and saw a glimmer of amber as the golem searched the far side of the room. She turned her gaze to the door at the top of the staircase, barely visible in the darkness. She'd checked it earlier and knew it was unlocked.

Just a few more steps to go.

Ashra froze as her right foot touched something. Felt panic as she realized the object was moving; she could hear it rolling away from her. Desperately she tried to grab it, whatever it was, but her fingers closed on empty air.

The object rolled off the step and struck the one below with a metallic clunk.

Down again.

And again. Gaining speed. Rising in volume.

Ashra rose and bolted up the final few steps. She could hear the golem's rapid footsteps on the floor below her, heading toward the staircase. Her heart raced as she grasped the door handle and flung it open.

Cold air slapped her face as she stumbled out onto the roof. She plucked the key from the other side of the door and locked it. Tossed the key away. Hopefully that would slow the golem down and buy her enough time to summon her portal. She turned away and took in the sight of the huge bronze bowl that dominated the roof, the famous purple flame burning within, but casting no heat. Walkways curved away on either side, following the circular edge of the Tower's summit and bordered by a waist-high wall.

Ashra ran left, heading clockwise around the great bowl. She heard the golem slam against the door behind her but didn't turn, didn't slow down, just concentrated on running for the far side of the Tower. When she reached it, having put as much distance between herself and the door as possible, Ashra pressed a thumb to her Ring of Last Resort.

The symbol glowed with a turquoise light.

"Come on," she murmured, hoping that Flea was paying attention. That her other ring hadn't become Ivan's dinner for a second time. "Come *on*."

The symbol on her ring glowed gold.

An identical glyph appeared before her, as if an unseen hand was carving the very air with a golden light. She sighed with relief. Flea had activated the ring's twin and made the connection. The glyph flared and dissolved into a mass of sparks, which began to merge together.

"No," Ashra whispered, her relief giving way to dismay.

The portal was forming in the air a couple of yards beyond the roof's surrounding wall.

A drop of two hundred feet yawned before it.

Ashra swore, her insides clenching at the thought of what she was about to do. Every instinct begging her to find an alternative.

There was none.

The door slammed open on the far side of the Tower. Metallic footsteps rang across the rooftop.

Ashra took a step toward the wall. Hesitated as her resolve faltered. She took a deep breath, glanced up at the silver stars above.

Never give fear a share of the spoils.

She brushed snow from the wall and hauled herself onto it. Korslakov sprawled far beneath her in a blur of purple and orange light. Ashra didn't look down. Didn't look behind her as the golem's footsteps grew louder. Instead, she rose slowly, eyes on the glowing portal before her, liquid gold against the black of night.

So near.

So far.

One slip and she'd be done for.

Calmness is the key to success.

Ashra took a deep breath. Searched for her resolve. Found it.

And jumped.

35

AN UNINVITED GUEST

Lukan jumped, spilling wine over himself as a discordant screech sounded behind him. *What in the hells . . .* He turned to find General Razin grinning at him from the doorway, a violin resting beneath his chin. "Found it in the attic," he said, raising the instrument's bow in his other hand. "Haven't played it in years."

"I'd never have known," Lukan replied, wincing as Razin teased another shriek from the instrument.

"Any requests?" The general walked into the room and gave a series of enthusiastic strokes with the bow. The resulting wails sounded to Lukan like a donkey having a heart attack. "I used to know quite a few tunes back in the day," Razin continued. "'The Ballad of Snow and Steel' was always a favorite with the troops." He paused and chewed his lip. "Damn it, how did it go?" Another shriek sounded. "No, that's not it . . ."

"Perhaps, General," Lukan said, raising a hand, "you might tell me more about your experiences in the Clanholds?" Anything was better than listening to the man murdering a violin. Even exaggerated stories Lukan had heard several times already.

"But of course, my boy!" The general set the instrument down and poured himself another brandy. "Days of glory. Did I tell you about how I was first into the breach when we recaptured Longhorn Watch?"

"Only twice," Lukan said, turning back to the flames that danced in the hearth.

"Twice? Pah!" Razin knocked back his drink and began pouring another. "I could tell you that story a hundred times and it still wouldn't do the tale justice." He settled into the chair opposite

Lukan, which creaked under his bulk. "I'll never forget charging toward that breach in the wall. The clansmen fired so many arrows they blotted out the sun, hammering down on our shields like the wrath of their savage gods. But suddenly we were at the breach, and somehow *I* was first inside, and I thought for sure . . ."

But Lukan wasn't listening; instead, he stared into the flames, his wine glass forgotten in his hands as he thought about Ashra. Telling himself she was fine. Worrying that she wasn't. He wished he shared Flea's confidence; the girl sat on the floor, fussing with Ivan, her belief in Ashra's safe return unshakable. Lukan knew he should feel similarly. The thief was more than capable of pulling off this plan they'd thrown together at speed. And yet he couldn't quite shake the shadow of his own doubt.

". . . and they only had bloody *bears*, didn't they?" Razin said, tugging at one end of his mustache. "Two of the damned things! And the closest one charged toward me. It was only then I realized it was bright pink. And . . ." The general leaned forward in his chair. "Do you know what it said as it opened its jaws?"

"What?" Lukan asked absently.

"It bellowed, 'Lukan's not paying attention to my damned story!'" Razin shouted.

"Lady's blood!" Lukan swore, jumping again and spilling the rest of his wine over himself. Razin roared with laughter as Lukan stared at the mess he'd made. "Was that really necessary?" he asked, snatching up the cloth armrest cover and dabbing at his damp shirt.

"Be glad you're not in the army, my boy," the general replied, chuckling as he sat back. "Inattention was punished far more harshly than that."

"I'm sorry, General," Lukan replied, with sincerity.

"Not at all, lad. But you need to learn not to fixate on things you can't change. Ashra will either make it back, or she won't. No amount of worrying on your part will change that."

"Ashra *will* make it back," Flea insisted from the floor, where she now lay with her head resting against Ivan's flank.

"Of course she will," Razin replied. "All the more reason for us to enjoy a tale or two while we wait."

"So the bear wasn't pink, then?" Flea asked, propping herself up on one elbow.

"Of course not!" Razin rumbled a laugh. "I was merely jesting. But it would have helped if they were," he continued, his humor fading. "Bloody things were hard to spot, despite their size. And let me tell you, there's nothing more terrifying than one of those beasts racing toward you." He tugged at his mustache. "Still, every job has its downsides. And better a soldier than a quill-pusher, eh?"

"Hmm," Lukan replied. To his mind, developing a crooked back and a permanent case of eye strain was far preferable to having your limbs torn off by a bear, but he thought it best to keep that to himself.

"You should have golems in the army," Flea said, settling back against Ivan. "I bet Clank would like to fight bears and clansmen." A shadow passed across her face. "He'd like that more than being stuck in Ashgrave with all the ghūls."

"It does seem a waste to have constructs shoveling snow when they could do your fighting for you," Lukan told the general. "I certainly wouldn't want to go up against one."

"Perhaps," Razin admitted, his tone grudging. "But the Frost-fire Council would never agree to it. The costs would be prohibitive. Why pay a fortune for golems when there's no shortage of brave men and women ready to fight for their city?"

"What about gleamers?" Lukan asked, recalling the Constanza twins who forced Gargantua back underground with their sorcerous power. "We've seen them take down far bigger creatures than bears."

"Gleamers?" Razin practically spat the word. "Absolutely not. The Builder taught us that strength lies in iron and innovation, not in squalid sorceries. That's why you won't find any gleamers in Korslakov. Their kind aren't welcome here. We leave that sort of heresy to the clans." He shook his head in disgust. "The stories

I could tell you . . . There was one time—this would have been on my first campaign—when a great mist was rolling down from the mountains, and we thought for sure that-"

"Actually, general," Lukan interjected smoothly, "there's one story I'm very keen to hear."

"Oh?" Razin leaned forward eagerly, one bushy white eyebrow rising. "And what's that?"

"What happened at Cauldron Pass."

The general's face fell and he slumped back in his chair. "Of course," he sighed, his gaze suddenly distant. "It always comes back to that."

"I'm sorry, General," Lukan said quickly, taken aback by the sudden change in the man's demeanor. "I don't mean to pry. Forget I asked."

"No, no," the general replied, waving away Lukan's words as if dismissing an annoying subordinate. "You've told me your story. It's only fair I tell you mine. Fetch the brandy, would you? There's a good fellow." Lukan obliged, and, as Razin held out his glass, there was no trace of the vigor that had animated him just moments ago, only a shadow that seemed to settle beneath his eyes. "Thank you, my boy. This story's best told with a full glass of brandy to . . . to . . ."

"Take the edge off," Lukan suggested, filling the man's glass.

"Quite so." Razin took a sip of his drink, but made no move to begin his tale. Lukan poured himself a fresh glass of wine and then rejoined Razin by the fire. The silence stretched, broken only by the pop and crackle of the burning logs. Lukan was starting to think the general had fallen asleep when he finally spoke.

"My predecessor, General Broska, was a great man. 'Leopold,' he once told me, 'embellish your victories as you wish, but always leave your failures unvarnished, for it is our mistakes, and how we respond to them, that define who we are.'" He took a sip of brandy. "So, I'll leave this one unvarnished."

The graveness of the general's voice caught Lukan off guard, the edge to his tone making it clear this wouldn't be like the other stories he'd told. Lukan suddenly felt like an intruder treading on a part of the man's past that he'd deliberately kept hidden. He shouldn't have asked. But—like unopened bottles—unspoken words and the secrets they held were something he found hard to resist. Still, he should have known better. He liked the old man, and didn't want to cause him any undue pain. "My apologies, General, I didn't mean to pry."

"It was late autumn," Razin continued, ignoring Lukan's words, his gaze distant. "This was my fifth campaign, but only my second as general. We'd had a few days of bad weather, but this day dawned clear and bright. I broke my fast with quail's eggs and bacon." He shook his head. "Funny, the little things you remember. So much of that day is nothing more than a bloody blur in my mind, yet I remember that meal as if I ate it yesterday. This was a week after the Battle of the Black Ice, where we routed the White Wolf's forces. That's what they called him, this man who had somehow united the clans for the first time in decades. I saw him once—a youth, barely a man full grown, but with hair as white as snow. The clansmen thought he was some sort of mythic figure out of their old tales, some ancient hero reborn. Ha! We disabused them of that notion when we crushed them at the Black Ice. A more magnificent victory Korslakov has never seen—and it was my vision, my leadership, that earned us that victory. *Mine*." Razin punctuated the last word by slamming his left fist on the armrest of his chair. Lukan sensed that the general was no longer in the room with him; his mind was elsewhere, he was telling this story to a wider audience—a gallery of faces that Lukan couldn't see.

"We had the clans on the run," Razin continued. "Or so we thought." He took a long swallow from his glass, as if easing the way for the difficult words to come. "They fled into Cauldron Pass, which is the quickest way through the mountains. I knew there was a chance they were luring us into a trap, but our scouts reported that the way was clear. It seemed the White Wolf had fled with his tail between his legs. We expected no resistance." The man sighed heavily and tugged at one end of his mustache. "They hit us when we were halfway through the pass. Came boiling out of the woods on either side. Hundreds of clansmen and women, painted faces snarling. Wolves and bears too. We tried to rally, but it was hopeless. They hit our line right in the center, cut our forces in two. I realized then the White Wolf wasn't the callow youth I'd taken him for. Panic set in and spread like wildfire. I ordered the retreat, but, as we tried to pull back, the rear of our column was still trying to press forward into the pass, unaware of what was happening. Our escape route was blocked by our own troops. What started as a rout became a damned bloodbath. Three thousand soldiers walked into Cauldron Pass that morning. Fewer than five hundred made it out." The general took a deep breath, his left hand gripping his armrest so tightly his knuckles were white. "Not a day goes by that I don't think of that day and those soldiers who lost their lives. That is a weight I will always carry."

The general lapsed into silence, but even the quiet that replaced his words felt charged with emotion, lying heavily across the room. Lukan stared at his wine glass, feeling like he was trespassing on another man's grief. He should have just waited for the moment to pass, for the regret carved into every line of the General's face to soften. But he sensed words still unspoken. And he couldn't quite resist their lure. Unopened bottles, and all that.

"Forgive me," he said gently, "but I'm curious as to the role of General Orlova in all this. That night I came for dinner, you said something before about her scheming . . ." Lukan trailed off as Razin's jaw tightened, his expression darkening even further.

"Orlova," the general growled, draining his brandy as if to wash away the taste of her name. "Better top me up if we're going to talk about *her*." He held his glass out.

"Who was she?" Lukan asked, as he obliged.

"My colonel and second in command." The curl of Razin's lip made it clear what he thought of that. "She was the daughter of minor nobility and joined the army on an officer's commission purchased by her father, who then used what little influence he had to push her up through the ranks. Orlova's ambition did the rest. When my former second died at the Battle of the Black Ice, I had no choice but to promote Orlova to the rank of colonel, which was a role she didn't deserve and certainly wasn't ready for. But tradition and decorum has ever been a noose round our military's neck." Razin scowled at the flames in the hearth. "I thought becoming colonel would sate her ambition, but it only grew worse. She started questioning my orders, and even spread the rumor that the strategy for our victory at the Black Ice was hers, not mine. And then came Cauldron Pass." Razin took a swallow of brandy, as if to steel himself. "Orlova was responsible for our scouting. She claimed her scouts had told her the way was clear, but of course it wasn't. We soon learned that, to our great cost. At the time I assumed that there must have been some mistake, a failure of communication. That it was nothing more than Orlova's lack of experience finally revealing itself."

"And now?"

"Now, I . . ." Razin's fingers tightened around his brandy glass. "Now I wonder. Did she do it on purpose? Did she lead us into Cauldron Pass knowing the enemy was planning an ambush?"

Lukan leaned forward. "You think she was in league with the clans?"

"Brandur's balls, no. Orlova thinks they're nothing more than savages to be crushed underfoot. No, I think she merely sensed an opportunity. To humiliate me so that she could take my place."

"By condemning thousands to their deaths?" Lukan frowned. "That seems far too high a price."

"No price is too high when ambition is concerned. Especially not for the likes of a pampered blueblood like Orlova. What does she care if a thousand soldiers die, so long as she gets what she wants?"

"A tale as old as time," Lukan said, taking a sip of wine and thinking back to Lord Marquetta and his willingness to sacrifice thousands of lives simply to return Saphrona to an imaginary golden age. "Such ambition rarely ends well," he continued, "but it seems that Orlova got exactly what she wanted."

"Indeed." The general's face darkened further. "The disaster at Cauldron Pass left our campaign in ruins. We had no choice but to return to Korslakov with those damned clansmen hounding us every step of the way. I was dragged before a tribunal and interrogated by aristocrats who didn't know one end of a sword from the other. Orlova was summoned too and told them a pack of lies, which they devoured as if they were truffles—what do you expect when her own damned father was bribing them?" Razin knuckled his jaw. "Timur spoke at the inquest and defended me, as did others. That's what soldiering does, boy; it forges bonds that can't be broken—neither on the battlefield nor in the gilded halls of power." The brief flicker of enthusiasm that edged his words flickered out again. "But it did no good. The tribunal decided the bloodbath at Cauldron Pass was my fault. Orlova was promoted to general, while I was relieved of my duties and cast aside, just like that. Stripped of my pension too, hence . . ." He gestured at the room with his glass, oblivious to the brandy that spilled into his lap. "Thrown to the wolves. Thirty years of loyal service— thirty! And this is what I have to show for it. An empty house. And the guilt that gnaws at me."

"Those soldiers' deaths weren't your fault," Lukan said firmly, feeling a rush of sympathy for the old man, along with a need to try to make him realize the truth.

"I was their general," Razin replied wearily. "Their lives were in my hands, and I failed them. The tribunal was right about that, at least, if nothing else." He drained his brandy and held out his glass yet again. Lukan refilled it. "The first couple of years were hard," Razin continued, "but Timur and my dear wife Eva helped me through them. I started to think that perhaps I could let it all go. Try and enjoy what little life I had left in me. Then . . ." Remembered pain flickered across his face. "Eva died. And . . . I lost my mind, I suppose you'd say. She was a barrier, you see? To all the pain and regret and bitterness. She kept it all at bay. But with her gone, it all came back. The guilt. The rage. And I was helpless before it."

"So you decided to raise an army," Lukan said, feeling a growing fury at Orlova for her ambition and what it had driven Razin to do. This man who—rightly or wrongly—had only tried to his duty, and do right by those under his command. And who had ended up paying a terrible price.

"I did," the general agreed, his voice hollow. "I felt I owed it to all those who died. If the Frostfire Council wouldn't listen to reason, then perhaps they'd listen to the sound of an army at their gates. And if they still insisted on burying their heads in the snow, then I'd have stormed the city and deposed them, mark my words. I'd have given my city the leadership it deserves, rather than those inbred fools who cling to power and care nothing for the people who make this city what it is."

"A noble goal," Lukan said, meaning every word. "Even if it's a touch . . ."

"Idiotic?" Razin suggested, smiling weakly as he waved away Lukan's denial. "No, no. You're right. I was being a damned fool."

"You were struggling with your grief," Lukan offered, trying to soften the blow.

"True enough. I know that now." Razin sighed. "Regardless, no one would lend me the money I needed. I thought maybe the counting houses down in Volstav or Seldarine might . . ." He waved his own words away. "That's how I ended up in Saphrona. Those perfumed princes were my last chance. But they had no interest in funding a war at the other end of the continent. I left the city the day after the Grand Duke's murder, and it was only on the voyage home that I realized, with what little reason was left to me, what a bloody fool I'd been." He looked sharply at Lukan, his gaze intense. "You tread a similar path, my boy. And you mustn't let your emotions consume you the way I let mine consume me."

"I need to find out who killed my father," Lukan replied, a touch defensively. "I need to find out what's in his vault. And I need to find whatever justice for him I can."

"You see? It's already got its hooks in you. You *need* this, you *need* that." Razin held up a hand to forestall Lukan's objection. "I understand. Truly. And your cause is an honorable one. All I'm saying is that at some point you'll have to decide whether the cost is worth it."

"I've already risked too much to give up. Hells, that was true before I'd even—"

"Lukan!" Flea said, sitting bolt upright.

"—arrived in Korslakov," Lukan continued. "And with everything that's happened since, I—"

"Lukan!" Flea shouted, scrambling to her feet.

"Bloody hells, *what*?" His annoyance fled as he saw the Ring of Last Resort the girl held between her thumb and forefinger.

It was glowing gold.

"Builder's balls!" Razin whispered, his eyes wide. "Does that mean . . ."

"It's showtime," Lukan confirmed, rising from his seat as Flea rubbed the ring the way Ashra had shown them. A golden glyph formed in the air, bathing the room in golden light. Ivan sprang to his feet and started barking.

"Is everything all right?" Timur asked as he appeared in the doorway. His eyes widened at the sight of the Phaeron sorcery.

"We're about to find out," Lukan replied, as the glyph burst apart, a hundred sparks scattering to form a circle. He'd seen this before, of course, had even jumped through two of these portals, and yet he couldn't help but feel a touch of awe. It was one thing to touch a Phaeron relic, but something else entirely to see the lost civilization's powerful sorcery at work. For a fleeting moment—as the hair rose on his forearms—he could almost feel the presence of those ancient sorcerers. And as the air began to ripple within the shining circle, he understood, if only for a moment, why his father had been so obsessed with them.

"Get ready," he said, snatching up a woolen blanket, which he would throw over Ashra to stave off the portal's biting cold. Flea crouched nearby, crossbow at the ready. Razin was too busy gaping at the shimmering sorcery to arm himself, not that it mattered. Anyone who followed the thief wouldn't be in a fit state to fight.

Ashra surged through the portal without warning, arms flailing, eyes wide. She hit the floor hard, her body already racked by shivers. Ice dusted her clothes. Lukan stepped forward and raised the blanket.

"F-f-fol . . ." Ashra stammered through gritted teeth, as Lukan crouched beside her.

"What was that?" he asked.

"F-followed," the thief bit out. "G-g . . ."

"Relax," he said, tucking the blanket round her as if she was a child. "If anyone comes through, Flea will give them a couple of bolts for their trouble." He glanced up at the shimmering air. "In any case, it doesn't look like—"

Another figure crashed through the portal.

The newcomer collided with Lukan and sent him sprawling backward. He recovered quickly and surged to his feet, only to freeze as he saw the figure properly. Like Ashra, it was coated in otherworldly frost, but its body wasn't racked with shivers. Such a survival mechanism wasn't really required when you couldn't feel the cold to begin with.

Lukan stared at the golem.

The golem stared back.

"Shit," he said.

The room exploded into motion.

Flea fired her crossbow; the first bolt flew true and pinged harmlessly off the construct's shoulder, the second flew wide and punched into the wall.

The golem surged forward.

Lukan hurled himself at the construct, seeking to protect Ashra, who still lay prone on the floor, and struck the construct with his left shoulder. The golem staggered back but quickly recovered, blocking Lukan's follow-up strike and grasping his other arm in a metal fist. Lukan gritted his teeth as the golem squeezed his wrist, and instinctively thrust his knee into the construct's groin. He gasped as pain exploded in his kneecap. Seemed the instincts he'd honed in the barfights of his youth counted for little when his opponent was made of metal. The golem's amber eyes flashed as it shoved him away. Lukan's foot caught Ashra's leg; he stumbled and ended up on his arse, the construct looming menacingly over him, one arm raised to deliver a crushing blow. Lukan scrambled backward, knowing the golem could knock his head clean from his shoulders, but his opponent moved quickly, grasping his shirt with one hand and hauling him up from the floor. Lukan slapped hopelessly at the golem's head, only to stiffen as the construct wrapped its other arm round his throat.

And squeezed.

Darkness closed at the edges of his vision. Blood roared in his ears. Panic knifed through his mind. He saw Flea screaming, Ashra watching with horror, trying to rise, Timur attempting to loosen the golem's grip.

All hopeless.

He felt something shift in his throat, felt a distance stealing over him. Felt his own desire to fight, to survive, flicker in a fell wind that seemed to shiver through him.

Suddenly he was on the floor, gasping for breath, the room pitching around him. He saw bodies moving, heard distant voices shouting. He tried to rise but fell back. He felt a word pass his lips but had no idea what it was. Suddenly his vision settled and he saw the golem grappling with . . .

Lukan blinked.

Ivan?

The hound had the construct's right leg in his jaws. Gone was the docile dog that allowed Flea to use his head as a pillow; this was a fearsome war hound, who could tear enemies limb from limb.

Except when they were made of metal.

Still, Ivan gave it his best shot, shaking his head from side to side, fury glinting in his eyes. Lukan doubted the dog would've even managed to get his jaws round one of the larger golems' legs, but fate had been kind to them in that regard: the construct that had followed Ashra was one of the smaller golems, much like the one he'd seen stacking shelves in the library, and its metal body wasn't as robust.

As the golem tried to shake the dog off, Lukan couldn't help feeling there was an element of uncertainty—a tentativeness—in its movements. Was the golem afraid of the hound? There was a human soul in there, after all. Perhaps the instinctive fear of a snarling dog lingered. Regardless, the golem recovered quickly, raining down punches on Ivan. The hound refused to relinquish his grip.

"Ivan!" Flea yelled, dropping her crossbow as she raced to the dog's aid, only for Lukan to drag her back. "What are you—let go!"

"You'll only get yourself hurt," he said, holding her tight.

"No!" Flea shouted, as the hound whimpered at the impact from a vicious punch. She elbowed Lukan in the chest. "Do something!"

Lukan glanced around, desperately seeking a solution. Ashra had found her feet, but could only look on helplessly. Timur was hovering nearby, his expression stricken, the cleaver all but useless in his hands. And as for Razin . . .

Lukan's eyes widened in surprise.

The general was reaching for his warhammer that hung on one wall. *Surely not*, Lukan thought. *It'll be too heavy for him.* But Razin lifted the weapon with ease and turned toward the fray. "Stand back," the general commanded. As he strode forward, he seemed to grow in stature; the melancholic, shabby figure Lukan had grown used to vanished before his eyes, replaced by a broad-shouldered and bright-eyed man who moved with the vigor of rediscovered purpose. As Ivan yielded to another punch and finally released the golem, Razin bellowed, "Hurt my hound, would you?"

The golem turned.

Razin roared as he swung his hammer.

Metal crunched as the weapon connected with the construct's head, snapping it backward. The golem staggered, as did Razin from the effort of his swing. The general recovered first. Puffing out his cheeks, he stepped toward his foe and—with clear effort—raised his hammer again. "Answer . . . the damned . . . question," he demanded, landing another blow on the golem. This one only caught the construct's shoulder, but it was enough to knock it back against the wall. "Damned machine," Razin wheezed, his face red. "Told them . . . your kind don't . . . belong in the army." He tried to raise his weapon for the final blow, only for his strength to give out. "Gah!" he muttered as he fell backward onto his arse, his warhammer putting a sizeable dent in the wooden floor.

Fortunately, Timur was on hand to finish what the general had started. He snatched up a hefty log from the fireplace, his face set with determination as he advanced on the stricken construct. A quiet and unimposing man he might have been, but there was nothing soft about the blow he delivered to the golem's shoulder, which drove it down to one knee. The construct lashed out, but Timur stepped nimbly back. He struck the golem's shoulder again; a weaker blow this time. The construct responded by lunging and grasping Timur by his waistcoat.

"The head!" Lukan shouted. "Hit its head. If you break the amber inside, the soul will escape!"

The construct stilled. Then it let go of Timur and raised its hands, metal palms outward. A human gesture of peace. Timur raised his log in response.

"Wait," Lukan urged.

The construct knelt on the floor. Then it looked up, amber eyes glowing. And nodded.

"It wants you to do it," Flea said. "It wants to be free."

"Then I'm happy to oblige," Timur replied. He gritted his teeth and swung the log, catching the construct full in the face and knocking it onto its back. He struck a second blow, then another, and kept striking until the construct's head broke apart. The amber within shattered, its glow instantly fading. *Like a life snuffed out*, Lukan thought. *Or a soul that's now free.* Timur tossed the log aside and doubled over, hands on knees, breathing heavily.

No one spoke.

Lukan released Flea, and she ran straight to Ivan and threw her arms round him—probably the last thing the dog wanted, but he stoically accepted it all the same. Lukan pushed himself to his feet. "You all right?" he asked Razin, who still sat on the floor, his warhammer beside him.

"Fine, fine," the man blustered, blowing out his cheeks as he tried to rise. "Nothing to it. Just catching my breath. But, ah, perhaps you could help me up . . ."

Lukan hauled him to his feet and guided him to an armchair. "That was quite the sight," he told the old man.

"Heh!" the general wheezed as he sank into the chair. "I've . . . still got it."

"That you have." Lukan turned to Ashra. "You all right?"

The thief nodded as she pulled the blanket round her shoulders.

"And the mission?" Lukan pressed.

The thief gave a flicker of a smile. "Done."

36

AN UNWANTED INVITATION

"His excellency, Lord Arima, invites you to bear witness as he makes history and reveals the secrets hidden behind the Crimson Door." Lukan looked up from the meticulous script and found Lady Wretzky's gaze. "He sounds confident."

"Of course he is," Lady Wretzky replied, through a cloud of cigarillo smoke. "He has no idea my agents sabotaged his alchemical process."

"I suppose if he did he wouldn't be putting on such a show." Lukan sniffed the invitation. "Hells, it's even perfumed. But why go to all this trouble? Why not test the formula on the door first to make sure it works?"

"Anyone desiring to unlock the door must make the attempt publicly, in front of their peers. That has been the custom for more than a century. During the height of the great game, you'd often have several aristocrats all making an attempt one after the other. Lord Arima won't break with tradition. Besides, he wants his moment of glory."

"Not knowing that instead it'll be his greatest failure." Lukan set the card down, feeling a flicker of sympathy for Lord Arima. "So did the rest of the aristocracy all get this invitation?"

"They did," Wretzky confirmed, taking another drag on her cigarillo. "It's caused quite the stir, so I understand." She exhaled through her nose, one corner of her mouth curling upward. "Especially in the Volkov household."

"I suspect Lady Marni didn't take the news well."

"You suspect correctly. I'm told she's in the market for a new full-length mirror. Not to mention a new footman, since she fired the one who delivered her invitation."

"I expect she's also in the market for something else."

"Oh?"

"A murder. Mine, to be specific."

"I doubt your death alone will satisfy Marni. She'll want your friends dangling from the gallows as well."

"Good to know," Lukan replied dryly, glancing at Flea, who was fussing over Ivan. The hound didn't seem to have any lasting injuries from his battle with the golem, but was enjoying the attention all the same. "You said you can protect us," he continued, turning back to Wretzky.

"I can," the Iron Dame replied, stubbing out her cigarillo. "I will thwart any attempt Marni makes on your lives, via political channels or otherwise."

Lukan could only hope Wretzky's confidence in her own ability wasn't misplaced. "So what happens when Arima's concoction fizzles out with a whimper and the door stays locked?" he asked, turning back to the matter at hand. "Everyone just rolls their eyes and goes home?"

"Lady Marni will then announce her own attempt. Since Lord Arima called the summit, he has the right to go first. But Marni will seize her opportunity when it arrives, only to face the same humiliation when her attempt fails." Wretzky opened her silver case and withdrew a fresh cigarillo. "Unless," she added, reaching for her tinderbox, "it doesn't."

"It'll fail," Ashra replied, from where she was perched on the edge of a chair. "I tipped in the whole vial of devil's dust, just as you instructed."

"Very good," Wretzky replied. "And I've not heard a whisper of any drama at the Tower, so it seems you managed to do so without alerting anyone to your presence." The Iron Dame struck a flame, not noticing the fleeting look Lukan shared with Ashra. They'd decided not to mention the matter of the golem, which would only lead to difficult questions. Fortunately, aside from a fresh dent in the floor from Razin's warhammer, which Wretzky hadn't noticed, there was no evidence of the fight. "So it seems," the woman continued, taking a puff on her fresh cigarillo, "that we can now spend an enjoyable evening watching two aristocrats embarrassing themselves in front of their peers. Once that's done, you can have your key back. And your lives too, I daresay."

"Hold on," Lukan said, raising a hand. "What do you mean, *we*?"

"Surely you want to come and watch the fun?"

"You just told me that Marni wants us all dead. And I don't imagine Arima will be thrilled to see us either."

"Oh, don't worry about them." Wretzky took a long draw from her cigarillo. "Save for some choice words and sharp glares, there's little else they can throw at you on the night. Besides, I want you there. If we've miscalculated, and that door does open, I'll need your help to deal with what comes next. Builder only knows what lies beyond. It might just be a thousand years' worth of dust, for which I'd be very grateful. Or it could be a vault filled with gold— and if it is, you can bet the other nobles won't just stand there watching while Marni fills her pockets. Or . . ." Wretzky drew deeply, her cigarillo glowing red. "It could be something worse. Regardless, I want cool heads around me."

"Well, that rules Lukan out," Flea called over.

"Quite right, my dear," Wretzky said, with a hint of amusement. "But I was referring to Ashra. Though I could use your skills with that crossbow as well, if things get dicey." She locked eyes with Lukan again. "And I suppose I could use your quick wits, Lord Gardova. Even if you are a touch temperamental."

"I prefer the term mercurial," Lukan replied. "And I should warn you that I charge by the hour—in Parvan Red."

"Yes, Laverne mentioned your love of red wine." Wretzky rose from her chair. "I will send a carriage to collect you at noon tomorrow." With those words, she departed, trailing smoke in her wake.

Lukan picked up the invitation again, eyes roving over the golden script. "So much for keeping a low profile," he sighed, tossing it into the fire.

37

THE CRIMSON DOOR

As Lukan climbed into the carriage after Flea, Ashra and an impeccably dressed General Razin, he wondered how many of Korslakov's aristocrats were doing the same. The sun itself had barely bothered to rise, the day dawning grey and bitter, and Lukan felt sure the great and good of Korslakov (or the moneyed and morally compromised, depending how you looked at it) had better things to be doing than bundling up in their furs and braving the cold. Goodness knew he'd rather be sitting in front of a fire with an expensive brandy in hand. *Perhaps*, he thought, *Lord Arima won't get as big an audience for his moment of glory as he'd hoped.*

Now, however, as their carriage passed through Korslakov's northern gate—far less busy than its southern counterpart—Lukan realized he was wrong. Four carriages rattled along the road ahead of them as it wound upward toward the top of the valley. As their own carriage followed a bend in the road, Lukan saw another two behind them. Korslakov's elite, it seemed, were turning out in force to witness Lord Arima's attempt at opening the Crimson Door. *Of course they are*, he thought, chiding himself for thinking otherwise. He'd strayed so far from his own aristocratic roots that he'd half-forgotten the delight his peers took in watching a rival suffering a public humiliation. That was the true attraction of the afternoon, well worth leaving the comforts of your townhouse for. And if the unthinkable happened, and Lord Arima did manage to unlock the door, well, they'd be there to see history made. *And seize a bit of it for themselves.* Lady Wretzky said tradition decreed that whoever unlocked the door could lay sole claim to whatever lay beyond. *Let's see how well that tradition holds up if it reveals a mountain of gold.*

Flea, her nose pressed against the window, was enraptured by the landscape rolling past, and Lukan couldn't blame her. Unlike the sprawl of humanity that had crept beyond Korslakov's southern gate, the northern side of the valley was mostly untouched by civilization. Snow-dusted fir trees dotted the slopes amidst granite outcrops and the sheer cliffs rose high above them on both sides of the valley, gradually narrowing to the mountain pass somewhere high above them where the Frostfort—the gateway to the Clanholds—stood its lonely watch. *The end of the civilized world,* Lukan thought, recalling the words on his father's map that warned of what lay beyond. *The unmapped lands of men that look like beasts and beasts that walk like men.* It wasn't a comforting thought, especially when you were in a carriage rattling toward that very place. General Razin, by contrast, seemed positively elated, gazing out of the window with an awe that rivaled that of the girl sitting beside him.

"Enjoying the ride, General?" Lukan asked.

"I never thought," Razin replied, his voice thick with emotion, "that I'd travel this road again. All those campaigns. So many memories." He tugged at one end of his mustache. "I should have returned that final time as a conquering hero at the head of a glorious host, but instead I arrived as a pariah, leading a bloodstained rabble. All thanks to Orlova and her damned scheming." He closed his eyes and shook his head, as if trying to shake the memories free. But the shame of it all still clung to him like a shadow. "Nothing made me feel more alive than marching northward at the head of an army. The sense of pride, of purpose. It was like nectar." He caught Lukan's gaze. "But you know what was better?"

"What's that?"

"Coming home again." Razin sighed and looked back out the window. "Knowing I'd see my city again. My wife." A smile brushed his lips. "That moment when we passed through the Frostfort and started back down the valley—'Victory mile,' we used to call it—when Korslakov first came into view, a sight for the sorest eyes . . ." He breathed a sigh. "Glorious."

Lukan wasn't sure the sight of the grey, austere city, with its choking plumes of smoke, was quite the vision Razin claimed it to be. Maybe you just had to be there.

"Though our joy was always tinged with sorrow," the general continued, "for those who didn't come home with us. And for those who did, but lost something of themselves in the Clanholds."

"Well," Lukan replied, "let's just hope we all make it home from this little adventure." *Ideally with our limbs and minds intact.*

Their carriage continued steadily upward, following the rising road as it snaked up the valley and toward the mountain pass at its far end, great cliffs slowly closing in on both sides like a granite fist.

"What I'd give for just a quick glimpse of the Frostfort," Razin murmured, peering out of the window, but his hopes were dashed as the carriage veered left and took a smaller road that peeled away from the highway, leading them through a wood of firs, the trees all draped in their winter finery. "Not far now," the general added, as they approached the western cliff that rose high above the valley. "Never thought I'd be attending another one of these ceremonies."

"Have you been to many before?" Lukan asked.

"Only three. The General of Korslakov's military is expected to be present at these events, but the nobility's obsession with opening the door died off not long after I took the role." He chuckled. "Still, I've seen my share of aristocratic disappointment, let me tell you."

"If the general's attendance is required," Lukan said, choosing his words carefully, "then presumably Orlova will be there?"

Razin's expression darkened once more. "She will."

They rode in silence after that.

A short while later the trees thinned and they arrived at a gate-house with crenelated walls that curved away on either side toward the foot of the cliff, forming a rampart. Soldiers clad in black and purple tabards stood idly on the battlements beside large ballistas, watching as Korslakov's aristocracy assembled in the staging ground before the gate. There were more than two dozen carriages, some still in the process of disgorging their passengers, richly bundled up in fur-trimmed hats and cloaks. Servants fussed over their masters and mistresses, while surly-faced guards eyed each other warily. Lukan caught sight of Dragomir, loudly telling a joke to his eager band of sycophants. The young aristo had enjoyed the various humiliations offered by the Inventors' Parade, and was no doubt hoping for more of the same time today, this time at Lord Arima's expense. Lukan's gaze moved on, searching for a telltale flash of red. He didn't see Marni anywhere, but that did nothing to settle his nerves. She'd be here somewhere. Arima too.

Razin opened the door and clambered out, offering his hand to Ashra, who pointedly ignored it as she followed. Lukan grabbed Flea's collar as she made to scramble out, and shoved her back onto the seat.

"Hells was that for?" the girl demanded.

"You're not leaving this carriage," Lukan replied, "until you've told me our three rules for this afternoon. So, go on. What's the first rule we agreed?"

"I keep my hands to myself."

"The second?"

"I keep my mouth shut."

"And the third?"

Flea sighed, rolling her eyes. "I say as little as possible to anyone who does speak to me."

"Especially if it's . . ."

"Lady Marni or Lord Arima."

"Because we're . . ."

"In enough shit as it is without my big mouth making it worse."

"Exactly!" Lukan gave her a mock round of applause. Flea flicked her little finger at him as she scrambled for the door. Again Lukan shoved her back. "What's this?" he asked, gesturing at the girl's coat, which was several sizes too big for her. "This isn't yours."

"It's Timur's," she replied defensively. "He lent it to me."

"Why? Where's your own coat?" Lukan's eyes narrowed as he noticed the empty sleeve flapping at her side. "And where's your right arm?" he demanded. "Left it at home, did you?" The girl shrugged. "Lady's mercy," he continued, lowering his voice, "tell me you didn't bring your damned crossbow."

A twitch at one corner of her mouth. "I didn't bring my crossbow."

"No?" Lukan leaned forward and lifted the bottom of her borrowed coat, its purpose now revealed as his gaze fell on the sleek weapon's head—and two loaded bolts. "It just decided to tag along, did it?"

Flea shrugged. "You told me to say I didn't bring it."

"You know that's not what I meant." Lukan released his hold. Arguing with Flea was pointless. "Just don't shoot yourself in the feet."

"I'll shoot *your* feet if you don't stop sharking."

He stared uncomprehendingly at her.

Ashra leaned through the doorway. "Griping," she clarified.

Lukan looked between the two of them. "I'm not griping."

"You are." The thief glanced at Flea. "Come on." Flea smirked at Lukan as she scrambled down. Lukan swore as he followed, the cold air closing round him like a fist. Together the four of them made their way past the various carriages and joined the procession that was snaking through the gateway. Three soldiers stood beside the gatehouse, two of them leaning on their halberds while their companion—who had clearly drawn the short straw—carried out the crucial task of bowing to each aristocrat who walked past. For Lukan and his entourage, however, he had only a suspicious stare.

"Lord Lukan Gardova," Lukan said, gesturing to himself. "Ashra Seramis—"

"I know who you are," the guard replied brusquely. "Lady Wretzky told me to let you through." He offered Razin a respectful nod. "General. Good to see you."

"Soldier," Razin replied, his chest swelling a little.

The man's gaze moved to Flea, sizing up her bulky coat and loose sleeve. Lukan could almost hear the cogs turning in his head as he considered whether to question them. Caution won out. "What happened to her arm?" he asked Lukan.

"She has a voice," Ashra replied. "Why don't you ask her?"

The soldier's jaw stiffened, and he grudgingly turned his attention to Flea. "What happened to—"

"Fight with a golem," Flea interrupted, her face creasing with a feigned look of regret. "Damned construct gave my arm a pull and it just"—she snapped the fingers of her other hand—"popped out of its socket, quick as you like, and then—"

"That's enough," Lukan interjected with a pained smile, as he grabbed Flea. He propelled her through the gateway before the guardsman could ask any further questions. "That's rule number three broken already," he hissed under his breath as he released the girl with a less-than-gentle shove. "Great start. Just two to go."

"One, actually."

"What?"

Flea grinned and held up a dagger. Lukan blinked in surprise as the girl turned and darted away. She must have slipped it from his belt. He swore under his breath and started after her, but his intended reprimand died on his lips as they emerged into the grounds beyond the gate. Several groups of aristos stood in the lee of the surrounding wall, their conversation and laughter carrying on the breeze as they chatted over steaming cups of mulled wine. Valets hovered close to their masters, while household guards watched with steely eyes.

Some distance away, beyond a path marked by two lines of burning torches, the Crimson Door stood like a gaping wound at the base of the cliff.

The surrounding arch appeared to be made from the same unknown Phaeron material as the Ebon Hand; smooth as glass, black as jet and stronger than stone. The door itself possessed a faint iridescent sheen that almost gave the impression of movement. *Like a waterfall*, Lukan thought. *A waterfall of blood*. He was suddenly gripped by a strange feeling of unease. He'd scarcely given a thought to what might lie behind the door; his involvement with it was simply a means to an end, a necessary step to recovering his key. But now, confronted by this huge door forged from some strange alloy a thousand years ago, he found himself wondering what it guarded. *Nothing good, I'll wager.* He wondered too if his father had stood in this very spot, staring at the door just as he was now. Unlikely, given how that right seemed reserved for Korslakovan aristocracy. Still, the more he learned about his father, the more he doubted whether that would have stopped Conrad Gardova. He felt his grief shift inside him, a faint ripple in a deep pond.

"There it is," Razin said, as he and Ashra joined them. "The source of so much obsession."

"It needs to stay closed," Lukan murmured.

"It will," Ashra said.

"I don't mean just for our benefit."

"You don't even know what's behind it," Flea scoffed.

"I have a feeling . . ." Lukan couldn't even describe it: a grim certainty that had whispered into his mind and now wouldn't leave. "What's beyond that door belongs to the Phaeron. It's not meant for us."

"Correct," a voice said. "It's meant for *me*." Lukan turned to find Lord Arima standing behind him, flanked by two guards. The young lord cut a striking figure in a high-collared black coat bearing serpents in silver brocade. His boots had been polished to a fine sheen. *At least he'll fail in style*, Lukan thought, as he met Arima's steady gaze. To his surprise, there was no animosity in the man's dark eyes. *No doubt there'll be plenty later.*

"Lord Gardova," Arima said, his tone carefully neutral. "I'm surprised to see you here at the moment of my triumph, though somewhat less surprised that you betrayed my trust."

"Lord Arima," Lukan replied, giving a bow that decorum didn't demand. "I'm sure you understand I had no choice if I wanted to avoid a swift return to the gallows."

"I should have guessed you'd give Lady Marni the formula as well." Arima shrugged. "No matter. It was I who called this convocation, so the first chance to open the Crimson Door falls to me." He smiled, buoyed by belief in his own inevitable victory. "Marni will have no choice but to watch with the rest of them as I make history."

"Good luck with that," Flea put in, grinning up at the man.

And that's the second rule broken, Lukan thought, as Arima gave the girl a curious look. *A clean sweep.*

"Indeed," Lukan agreed, forcing a smile as he gave Flea a sidelong glare. "Best of luck with your attempt, Lord Arima."

"I don't need luck," the young lord replied, meeting his gaze once more. "My alchemist has followed the formula to the letter. The Crimson Door *will* yield its secrets to me. Your betrayal of my trust has only served to make my victory all the sweeter." He smiled, eyes glinting with amusement. "Perhaps I should thank you. Lady Marni certainly won't."

With those words, he swept away, his guards following.

"That could have gone worse," Lukan murmured, giving Flea another glare. "No thanks to you. That's all three rules broken already, and we've only just arrived."

"Do I get a prize?" the girl asked, her grin only growing wider.

Lukan aimed a swipe at her, which she easily dodged. "Just bloody behave, will you? It's almost as if you want us to get in trouble."

"I'd say trouble's already found us," Ashra murmured, her gaze fixed over his shoulder.

Lukan turned to find Lady Marni striding toward him, the golden flames stitched into her scarlet coat a fitting match for the fire burning in her eyes. Her valet was scurrying behind her, whispering furiously behind a cupped hand, but Marni paid him no heed. Two Volkov household guards tramped along behind her.

"I had hoped," Lukan murmured to Ashra, "that she might have cooled down a little."

"I'd say not, judging by the daggers she's glaring at you."

"Daggers? She's got an entire bloody armory in her eyes."

"Yeah, well I bet that bitch doesn't have a crossbow under her coat," Flea put in. Lukan and Ashra both looked at her. "What?" she demanded.

As Marni drew closer, stalking like a cat toward her prey, Lukan adopted an apologetic expression and clasped his hands in contrite fashion. There was no sense in making things worse than they already were, though no doubt Flea would do her best. "Not a word," he hissed out of the side of his mouth, though the girl gave no sign she'd heard. *What to say?* he wondered, as Marni drew closer. *"Sorry" doesn't look like it's going to cut it.*

A sudden clamor rang out, causing Marni to stop. Conversation died as all eyes turned to a white-bearded man who was hobbling out before the gathered aristos, ringing a little bell with all the enthusiasm he could muster. *Saved by the bell,* Lukan thought, unable to stop the smile that crept across his face. Marni's eyes narrowed to thin slits in response, though, like everyone else, she turned to face the bellringer. Judging by her valet's relieved expression, Lukan wasn't the only person glad for the timely intervention.

"My lords and ladies," the man said, once the final peal of his bell had echoed across the grounds. "A good afternoon to you all!"

"It won't be for Lord Arima," Dragomir called out, causing laughter among his little cabal of associates and a ripple of amusement among the rest of the gathering. Arima, for his part, remained unmoved.

"Welcome," the white-bearded man continued, "to the seventy-first attempt to open the Crimson Door!" He swept an arm toward the great door—rather unnecessarily, Lukan thought, since it was pretty bloody hard to miss. The speaker paused, as if expecting a rousing cheer, but received only a stony silence from the gathered nobles. Unperturbed, he pressed on. "It has been nearly twenty years since the last attempt to open the door. No doubt some of you were here that day, whereas others"—he glanced in the direction of Dragomir—"were still in swaddling clothes."

That joke earned him a ripple of laughter as Dragomir bristled.

"Now we are gathered to see Lord Arima attempt to unlock the door and reveal its secrets," the speaker continued. "Truth be told, I didn't expect to live to see another attempt to open the door—"

"You might not if you keep on wittering!" Dragomir shouted, still riled by the earlier jibe. Emboldened by the guffaws of his friends, the young aristo grinned and continued, "In fact, you might say that—"

"Shut your fool mouth, Dragomir," another man interrupted,

backed by murmurs of agreement from his own circle of friends. "Show some respect."

"Respect?" Dragomir snapped, his face flushed red as he stepped toward his opponent. "I'll show respect to those who deserve it!"

The other man shouted a response that Lukan didn't hear, and suddenly the two retinues had collided in a storm of shouting, finger-pointing and literal saber-rattling. The rest of the gathering looked on with expressions that ranged from amusement to disinterest.

"How tiresome." Lukan turned to find Lady Wretzky at his side, her cigarillo glowing as she took a drag. "But sadly," she continued, exhaling smoke from her nostrils, "it seems no gathering these days is complete without a display of idiocy."

"I know Dragomir," Lukan said, as the two men were dragged apart by their guards. "Who's the other man?"

"Lord Zolta. A nobody. Heir to a minor house, like Dragomir." Her cigarillo glowed again. "Hence all the impotent male rage."

"As I was saying," the white-haired man continued, now that the bellowed insults had given way to aristocratic pouting, "it's been twenty years since the last attempt on the door . . ."

"Who's he?" Lukan whispered as the man droned on.

"Lord Moroz," Wretzky replied. "The Warden of the Crimson Door. An honorary title that he holds only because no one else wants it. It mostly involves presiding over attempts to open the door."

"He's not a busy man, then."

"Not exactly."

". . . but now," Lord Moroz continued, "Lord Arima will make a new attempt to unlock the Crimson Door." He paused, as if again expecting a round of applause, only to be met with silence. It seemed the gathered nobles would much prefer the door to remain closed. "Will the door finally yield the secrets it has kept for a thousand years," Lord Moroz continued, "or will it cling to them still? Let us find out. Lord Arima, the moment is yours."

"Thank you, Lord Moroz," Arima replied, smiling as he stepped forward with the easy confidence of a man who believed fate was on his side. "My family arrived in Korslakov over a century ago,"

he said, turning to face the gathering. "My grandfather died fighting the Clans—a fact some of you seem to forget. My father was
a great investor in the League of Inventors. We have given both
blood and gold to our adopted city, and yet it has never been
enough, has it?" Angry muttering broke out among the crowd,
but Arima merely raised his voice and continued, "I know what
you think of me! Scion of a house that you've never accepted,
merely tolerated. To you, the Arimas have been a novelty at best, a
blemish at worst. You have never shown us the respect we deserve,
blinded as you are by your own ignorance and prejudice."

The murmuring swelled, punctuated by a few jeers.

"That ends today!" Arima shouted in response. "I will unlock
the Crimson Door and lay claim to its secrets, and then all of
you"—he swept an arm at the crowd—"will finally show my family the respect we deserve!"

"You deserve nothing!" Dragomir screeched in response, face
flushed red, and the man he'd just been arguing with shouted his
agreement. A ripple passed through the crowd as several hot-
blooded aristos stepped forward, expressions dark, hands on
swords that they'd probably never drawn outside a practice square.

"As I said," Lady Wretzky murmured, "impotent rage."

"Silence!" Lord Moroz demanded, and furiously rang his bell
until an uneasy quiet descended. "You were saying, Lord Arima,"
he said pointedly, his tone suggesting that it might be better if the
young lord didn't say anything at all. In any case, Arima had said
his piece, for he gestured to his valet, who immediately strode forward, carrying a large glass tube on a velvet cushion as if it were a
holy relic. Whispers broke out as he handed it to his master.

"The problem with being small-minded and stuck in your
ways," Arima said, holding the tube aloft, "is that it blinds you to
reason. To appreciating ideas outside your narrow vision of the
world. As I will now demonstrate, by solving the problem that has
confounded your families for generations."

"It seems your syringe is empty, Arima," Dragomir shouted, a
note of glee in his voice. "Just like your balls, if the rumors are true!"

A twitch of his mouth was Arima's only reaction to the jibe, but Lukan sensed the insult had found its mark. He felt a surge of anger then, at Dragomir for his needless cruelty, but also at himself for the ridicule Arima was about to suffer. The man would be humiliated in front of his peers, and Lukan knew just how deeply that would cut him. *And I'm partly to blame.*

"On the contrary, *Lord* Dragomir," Arima replied calmly, making a point of using the other man's honorific, "this syringe is far from empty." He smiled, his gaze passing over the assembly. "Do you understand now? Do you see?"

A hush fell over the gathered aristos, punctuated by one or two murmurs of surprise.

"For the last century," Arima continued, "you and your alchemists have been trying to discover the liquid that would unlock the Crimson Door." He smiled, enjoying his moment of revelation. "But the key, my friends, is not a liquid at all. It's a gas." He held the syringe aloft like it was a trophy. "And I now hold it in my hands."

Arima held the crowd in his hands too; the gathered aristos had fallen silent, stunned by the prospect of one of their peers—and such a lesser one at that—achieving the sort of fame and status they could only dream about. *Except he won't,* Lukan thought. *In the end, Dragomir and his fellow cretins will have the last laugh.*

Lord Arima, of course, was blissfully unaware of the downfall that awaited him, as he lowered the syringe. "Bear witness," he said, turning away from them. "The Crimson Door will yield to me." He started walking, striding purposefully down the avenue of burning torches.

"Lady's blood," Lukan muttered, wishing he could avert the embarrassment Arima was about to suffer. But all he could do was watch as the man approached his doom.

"It's for the best, Lord Gardova," Lady Wretzky murmured, exhaling a cloud of smoke. "What is one man's ambition against the safety and well-being of an entire city?"

"It's not about ambition," Lukan said bitterly. "He just wants respect for his family. Is that so much to ask?"

The Iron Dame had no answer.

Lukan wondered if he should run after Arima and tell him that his formula had been compromised. Whether he should try to save him from the humiliation he was about to inflict on himself. But even if the man believed Lukan's words, forfeiting his attempt would earn him almost as much derision as failing it altogether. Arima's fate was sealed, and all Lukan could do was clench his jaw and watch as he approached the Crimson Door.

The hushed whispers among the gathering quietened as Arima walked to the left side of the door and raised his syringe to a feature Lukan hadn't previously noticed: a glass cylinder, set in the archway.

"I assume that's the alchemical lock?" he asked.

"You assume correctly," Wretzky replied, tapping ash from her cigarillo. "Doesn't look like much from here, does it? But there's a smaller cylinder inside, which contains some manner of sphere. When a liquid is poured into the outer cylinder, the sphere rises in the other. The alchemists believe the trick to opening the door is to get the sphere to rest exactly in the middle of its own cylinder."

"So it's all about mass and density," Lukan said, thinking back to distant chemistry lessons at the academy.

"No." The Iron Dame took another drag on her cigarillo. "It's about ambition and greed. That's what drove all those attempts to find the correct liquid."

"Except it was never a liquid at all."

"Apparently not." Her gaze hardened. "Let us see."

They watched as Arima—presumably done with injecting his gaseous formula—stepped away from the door.

Nothing happened.

Arima peered at the glass cylinder, then glanced down at the syringe in his hands. Lukan could imagine the stirrings of panic in his gut, and felt a rush of sympathy for the man.

Not so the gathered nobles. A murmur swept through the gathering, spiked by someone's gleeful laughter—Dragomir, Lukan guessed, though he couldn't see the culprit. More laughter followed, accompanied by the first jeers.

"Lord Arima!" a voice shouted—definitely Dragomir, this time—"not even the Crimson Door thinks you worthy of . . ."

The aristocrat's voice faltered as a hum filled the air. It was a strange sound, Lukan thought, featuring both a high note that he felt lingered at the very edge of his hearing, and a low note that he fancied he could almost feel in his bones. *Sounds not meant for human ears*, he thought.

"Shit," Wretzky murmured, her expression grave. "That's never happened before."

Gasps sounded as a Phaeron glyph appeared at the center of the door, pulsing with a golden light. Arima dropped his syringe and took a few hurried steps backward. As everyone watched in stunned silence, six smaller symbols appeared around the first, each glowing in turn. While they were incomprehensible to Lukan—and surely to everyone else—the reason for their appearance was clear.

The door was opening.

"I thought you sabotaged it," he whispered, glancing at Wretzky. "You said your agent—"

"I know what I said," Wretzky hissed back. "I was told the mission was a success."

"This would suggest otherwise."

The Iron Dame remained silent.

All seven symbols suddenly pulsed three times in unison. A glowing dot appeared above the topmost glyph and started to move to the left, slowly tracing a line round the symbols, enclosing them within a golden circle. Lukan didn't need to be told what would happen when both ends of the line were joined and the circle was complete. Nor did any of the other onlookers, many of whom now wore fearful expressions. *Are they afraid of Arima's success?* he wondered. *Or afraid about what might lie beyond the door?* The latter, most likely, judging by how many of them were backing away toward the gatehouse.

Lukan's instinct was to back away too, for he knew—just *knew*, somehow, in his bones—that whatever lay behind that huge door was trouble. But he stood his ground, watching with growing dread as the glowing circle reached its halfway point, his fear rising along with the line as it began to curve upward. *Three-quarters*, he thought, the knot of dread working its way up to his throat. *Nearly there.*

The strange humming sound had grown in volume, or at least Lukan felt it had; he could feel it almost like a physical weight in the air, a scream and a sigh all at once, as the circle drew closer and closer to completion . . .

And stopped.

Lukan felt a rush of vertigo, the sense of a precipice looming before him. He felt a hand on his arm, but he couldn't tear his eyes away from the glowing circle, its two ends so close to touching.

But not quite.

And then—to a collective intake of breath from those watching—the glowing line began to retreat, retracing its own path as it curved back down round the symbols. Arima took several steps toward the door, one hand raised imploringly, as if he could somehow force it to submit by his will alone. But all he could do was stand helplessly as the circle retreated until it disappeared altogether, the glyphs flickering and disappearing one by one.

"Thank the Builder," Wretzky murmured, taking a long drag on her cigarillo.

The unnerving humming faded, leaving a stunned silence.

Arima's hand trembled as he lowered it, though from fury at his failure, or fear at the inevitable ridicule, Lukan couldn't say. The man stood there for what seemed a long time, before finally turning and trudging back toward the gathering, head bowed and shoulders slumped.

A few jeers sounded as he returned, led by Dragomir and his cronies, but they seemed half-hearted, and no one else joined in. Not out of sympathy for Arima, Lukan suspected, but because they were still shocked at how close he'd come to succeeding. Perhaps, despite his failure, he'd won a small measure of the respect he so desperately wanted. *Not that it's likely to be much consolation to him.*

"Lord Arima's attempt at opening the door has failed," Lord

Moroz said needlessly, as he tottered out before the gathering once more. "Before I call an end to this conclave, tradition holds that I extend the opportunity to anyone else present. So I ask you all now, do any of you wish to make an attempt to open the door?"

"I do," Lady Marni declared.

A collective gasp passed through the gathering as she stalked forward, coattails swishing around her ankles. Lukan found Lord Volkov in the crowd; the archon's passive expression could have been carved from granite, yet his fury was evident in the dark glare he threw at his daughter as she strode between the burning torches toward the door. Her valet hurried after her, holding a syringe in his hands.

"So begins act two of this performance," Wretzky murmured. "I hope for your sake it has the same outcome."

"You and me both," Lukan replied uneasily. *It's fine*, he told himself, as Marni gestured at her valet to inject the gas. *Ashra sabotaged her formula*. Even so, he felt his heart race as the same events played out again: the familiar hum filling the air, the pulsing symbols, and the golden line tracing a circle round them, enclosing them within its glow.

One-quarter.

Halfway.

Three-quarters.

Lukan held his breath once more as the circle neared completion . . . and released it as the low drone sounded once more, the circle receding just as before.

"As I told you," Ashra said, "I got the job done."

"Seems you did," the Iron Dame agreed, her lined face a mask of relief.

"Yes, Ashra!" Flea said, grinning up at the thief and holding out her right hand. A smile played at one corner of Ashra's mouth as she and the girl performed an intricate dance with their fingers, the meaning of which was lost on Lukan, not least because he was watching Marni's body language and wondering if Wretzky would have to make good on her promise to protect him there and then.

But Marni remained where she was, exchanging words with her valet.

"What's this?" Lukan muttered as the man came hurrying back toward the gathering.

"Lady Marni requests the second syringe," the valet called as soon as he was within earshot, gesturing impatiently to the other members of her retinue.

"A moment, please," Lord Moroz exclaimed, raising a hand. "What is happening here?"

"My lady intends to make another attempt," the valet replied as another of Marni's servants scurried forward, a second syringe in his hands.

"To what end?" Lord Moroz asked, above a flurry of murmurs. "Her formula has already failed."

"This is from a second batch," the valet said as he took the syringe. "My lady feared foul play, and so had another dose mixed in secret."

"Builder preserve us," Wretzky murmured.

"A second batch?" Lukan asked, exchanging a look with Ashra, whose dark expression mirrored his own feelings. "You didn't know about this?"

"Do you think I'd have ignored it if I did?" the Iron Dame hissed back. "I had no idea." She grimaced and dropped her cigarillo, crushing it beneath a boot. "Seems Lady Marni is smarter than I gave her credit for."

"You don't say." Lukan watched helplessly as the valet scurried back to his mistress, the syringe of unimpaired formula in his hands. "I want my key back, you understand? We did what you asked of us. The fact that there's a second bloody batch of the formula isn't our fault."

"If that door opens," Wretzky replied, "you may have far bigger concerns than the fate of your key. We all might."

"Then let's hope it stays closed." Lukan's throat was dry as he watched Marni's valet inject the receptacle with the contents of the second syringe.

"If we're lucky," Wretzky said, "whoever made this second batch made a mistake. Or perhaps the formula itself is wrong."

"It's not," Ashra replied.

"How do you know?"

"I was there," the thief said, her gaze distant. "I saw her. Safiya Kalimara, the alchemist who discovered the formula. I read her letter. Saw a glimpse of her brilliance." She met the Iron Dame's gaze. "Her formula is correct."

"Lady's blood," Lukan swore, as the hum sounded once more. "Here we go again."

For the third time the glyphs appeared, followed by the glowing circle, once more surrounding the symbols as it curled down, round and up again, closer and closer to its apex. *Surely it'll stop*, Lukan thought, as the end of the line closed the distance. *It has to.*

But it didn't.

The line kept moving, and this time it went the full distance, completing the circle.

Nothing happened.

It didn't work, Lukan thought, a spark of hope in his chest. *It didn't bloody—*

The hum intensified; not the low note that he felt in his bones, but the high keening that was almost uncomfortable to hear. Then it cut off, leaving a pregnant silence.

And with a terrible slowness, the door began to open.

38

THIS PLACE WILL
BECOME YOUR TOMB

Darkness.

That was all Lukan could see beyond the Crimson Door as it finally revealed its secrets, rising so smoothly it might have been just yesterday that it last opened. Despite his trepidation, he felt a dislocated sense of awe at the ingenuity of the Phaeron's engineering, still working flawlessly after a thousand years. *More's the pity.* If the gears or cogs had simply rusted away, it would have saved them a lot of trouble. But the Phaeron's work always had immortality in mind, as his father used to say, so it was no surprise that the door's workings had survived the passage of time.

The darkness beyond expanded as the door rose higher.

It was high enough now for Lady Marni to pass through, but she remained still, as did everyone else. No more than thirty heartbeats had passed before the door disappeared into the stone above, leaving a gaping slab of blackness in its wake, as if the mountain had opened its jaws.

The high-pitched hum faded.

Silence.

And then chaos, as the strange lull that had fallen across the gathered nobles lifted, and everyone found their voice all at once. A ripple passed through the assembly as the aristos started forward, their guards and flunkeys scurrying after them, all thoughts of tradition and decorum trampled beneath the booted feet of their collective greed. Some of the younger ones—Dragomir among them—were charging forward, their retinues bellowing at each other. Steel glinted as someone drew a sword. Lukan glanced at Lady Wretzky, expecting her to somehow tame the madness that had afflicted her fellows, but the Iron Dame merely stood there, shaking her head, cigarillo hanging limply from her mouth. For the first time since Lukan had met her, the woman looked every year of her eight decades.

Lord Moroz, by contrast, was waving his little bell furiously and bellowing something at the top of his voice, but his words were lost in the din. A moment later two servants—both slapping ineffectually at each other—collided with him, and all three of them fell to the snow in a tangle of limbs. They weren't the only ones; across the grounds, aristos and their entourages were pushing and shoving and tumbling as they fought to reach the door where Lady Marni stood, seemingly oblivious to the chaos erupting behind her.

"Pathetic," Lukan said scornfully, glancing at Razin. "They're scrabbling like rats in a . . ." He frowned as he realized the general was no longer at his side; instead the man was striding toward a fair-haired woman who wore the purple and black uniform of Korslakov's military, along with a look of growing panic on her sharp features. *General Orlova*, Lukan realized. His first thought was that Razin was taking advantage of the chaos to settle the score with his successor, and it certainly seemed that way, as Razin shouted something at the younger woman. But when Orlova merely blinked at him in surprise, Razin turned toward the ramparts above and made a series of frantic gestures. *What the hells is he doing?* Lukan wondered.

He got his answer a heartbeat later.

A *whump* sounded from atop the wall, and a shadow shot overhead. The ballista bolt slammed into the ground just beyond Dragomir and his cronies, sending a plume of snow into the air.

All movement ceased instantly.

"What in the blazes do you think you're doing?" Razin bellowed, his booming voice echoing across the grounds. "Behave yourselves, damn you!"

"Everyone stay where you are!" Orlova shouted, as if keen not to be shown up by the very man she'd replaced. A detachment of guards followed her as she strode forward. "You will all listen to me and do as I say," she continued, her voice not carrying the same depth of authority as Razin's. "Lady Marni's entourage will enter first, as is her right. I will then follow with my soldiers. The rest of you will then proceed in an orderly fashion, or not at all." She glared at the sullen aristos around her. "If there's *any* further trouble, I won't hesitate to, um . . ." She looked momentarily panicked. "Just behave yourselves!"

"You heard the general," Lord Volkov said, a faint sneer in his voice. "Stand your ground. What lies beyond that door belongs to my family and no one here has claim to it—isn't that right, Lord Moroz?"

"It is, Lord Volkov," the Warden of the Crimson Door replied. He'd regained his feet, but not his earlier enthusiasm. He was hardly the only one.

"Volkov's changed his tune," Lukan muttered to Lady Wretzky, as Marni's father and his entourage swept forward. "A few moments ago he looked ready to strangle his own daughter."

"And now he wants her glory for himself," the Iron Dame replied, lighting a fresh cigarillo. "Greed is a curious thing. A monster that can never be sated."

They watched as the Volkov contingent strode toward the black opening in the mountainside, General Orlova and her soldiers forming up behind them. The rest of the aristos followed in resentful silence. *How they laughed at Arima's failure*, Lukan mused. None of them were laughing now. Instead, they looked grim-faced at the prospect of watching the Volkovs gaining even more power and prestige. What had started as a harmless jaunt to laugh at a peer's failure had turned into something far less amusing. *And it could still get a lot worse*, Lukan thought, *depending on what's waiting in the darkness*.

"Come on then," Lady Wretzky said, cigarillo glowing as she started forward. "Let's see just how much trouble we're in."

"So, about my key," Lukan replied, matching her pace as Flea and Ashra following behind.

"Oh, Builder spare me . . ."

"Marni's first attempt failed," Lukan pressed. "Which means Ashra succeeded."

"Like I told you," the thief added.

"And it's not our fault that Marni was working up another batch of the formula in secret," Lukan continued. "That's entirely . . ." He was going to say *your fault*, but thought better as the Iron Dame glared at him. "All I'm saying," he said, "is that we've done what you asked of us."

"You'll get your damned key," Wretzky said, teeth clenched round her cigarillo, "once this business"—she nodded toward the open door—"is concluded."

Lukan didn't bother to argue.

"This reminds me of being in the Clanholds," General Razin said, wheezing as he caught up with them. "Stout souls pushing into the unknown, bravely setting foot where other civilized feet dare not tread! Nothing better to stir the blood and quicken the heart."

Lukan might have agreed, if it wasn't for the fact that their collective advance had stalled before the doorway because no one had thought to bring any lanterns. Walking into the impenetrable darkness without a flame was clearly a fool's errand, so everyone milled around awkwardly as some of the soldiers ran back to the burning torches and pulled them from the ground. Orlova glared at the aristos gathered behind the Volkov party, her eyes warning them not to even think about stepping out of line. She needn't have bothered. Now that they stood so close to the darkness beyond the doorway, the other nobles had miraculously lost their enthusiasm and seemed content to remain at the rear. Even Dragomir had traded his cockiness for an air of disinterest that didn't mask his unease. Lukan couldn't fault him; he too felt a touch of dread as he stared at the darkness within the mountain. *This place wasn't meant for us.* He felt an urge to back away, to lead Flea and Ashra to the relative safety of the gatehouse and its ballistas. That would be the sensible course of action. *Not that anyone would ever accuse me of having good sense.* But if they left now—and if something happened to Lady Wretzky—he might never see his key again. *What's the worst that can happen?* he wondered, as the Volkov party finally started forward. *What possibly lies ahead, save the dust of a thousand years?*

He knew the answer all too well, having grown up on his father's tales of the Phaeron ruins that littered the Old Empire. The most famous ones were labyrinthine structures that led deep underground, said to be full of traps and dangers that had claimed the lives of hundreds of adventurers over the years. Was this a similar construction? Why would the Phaeron hollow out a mountain in the first place? No doubt his father would have a theory. He always did. As Lukan stepped through the great doorway, he wondered what his father would do if he was there now. Would he willingly walk into the darkness? The Conrad Gardova Lukan had known barely set foot outside his study, but Lady Jelassi had spoken of him as some kind of dashing explorer in his younger days. Lukan no longer felt he knew his father at all.

"Stay close," he whispered to Flea and Ashra, as they followed Orlova and her guards through the great doorway and into the darkness.

No one spoke as they moved deeper into the mountain. Not even Dragomir. The blackness swallowed them entirely, the light from the torches not revealing anything beyond the smooth floor they walked across. Lukan felt a sudden sense of dislocation, as if he might somehow fall into the darkness around them, and he had to look back at the slab of daylight behind them to balance himself. His heartbeat quickened.

"You sharp?" Ashra asked quietly.

Lukan had picked up enough Kindred slang to know what she meant. "I'm fine," he replied. "It's just so bloody dark in here."

As if in response, a bright glow appeared high above—a long, thin strip of golden light that seemed to shine from within the very ceiling. It stretched away into the distance, revealing a wide passage bordered by smooth, featureless walls.

The group's progress faltered as the aristos murmured in surprise at their surroundings. Instead of rough, undressed stone, Lukan saw, the walls were made from the same black, glasslike material as the Ebon Hand. As for the light, Lukan couldn't even guess at how it worked, or what might power it. *Some sort of alchemical globe, perhaps?*

"Look," Ashra whispered, gesturing at the smooth, black floor. "What are those marks?"

"They look like scratches," Flea replied, as she crouched and ran her fingers over them. "From an animal."

"Must have been a damned big animal," Lukan replied, as he stared at one particularly deep groove. "They're on both sides of the passage," he remarked, noting how the marks stretched away before them. "But not in the center. As if . . ."

"Something crawled along here," Ashra said. "Something big."

"Maybe it was a giant cat," Flea said, grinning as she stood.

"Whatever it was," Lady Wretzky said, with a dismissive wave of her cigarillo, "it's long dead now. Let's proceed. We're falling behind."

Lukan looked up to find she was right; the others were already moving ahead of them, their movements tentative. As he watched them, he had the sense they were being swallowed by a gigantic throat, and again felt a stirring of unease; this was not a place humans were meant to tread. But powerful forces were in play; destiny was driving Lady Marni forward, ambition doing the same for her father, while simple greed compelled the other aristos to follow at their heels. Duty urged Lady Wretzky onward, while necessity forced Lukan and his friends to follow.

Lukan took a deep breath and followed the Iron Dame, Flea, Ashra and Razin beside him.

There was no going back now.

The air grew colder as they progressed deeper into the passage. It felt heavier too, as if the group's collective anticipation and trepidation was bleeding into it and lending it weight, giving it body. Lukan felt it pressing against him, as if the air itself objected to his presence and sought to impede his progress. He realized his hand had strayed to his sword hilt, and saw that Flea was now carrying her crossbow openly, her token attempts at discretion abandoned. Not that anyone else had noticed. The others were all preoccupied by the darkness at the far end of the passage. It grew larger as they approached, but no less impenetrable. A great slab of blackness that seemed to pull them toward it. Any hope Lukan had that it might just be a dead end—and that they could all just turn round and go home—faded as they drew closer and he realized the truth.

It was a void. A yawning space that threatened to suck them in and swallow them whole. They would all disappear without a trace, and the mountain would keep their bones.

What little conversation there was died out as the group lingered on the threshold. The Volkovs were still at the front, surrounded by their guards and attendants, though the expression on Lord Volkov's face suggested his enthusiasm had fled as quickly as it had arrived. Even Lady Marni appeared hesitant as she leaned forward and peered into the darkness. General Orlova stood behind with her detachment of guards, who had spread out to form a line to stop the nobles behind from pushing to the front.

Not that there was any chance of that; the jealousy and greed that had been on full display just a short while before had vanished.

"What did Diagoras say?" Lukan asked quietly, as they joined the back of the crowd. "If you stare for too long into an abyss, so too the abyss stares into you."

"It was Dagorian," Wretzky murmured in response, "but the point is apt."

"Go on then!" someone called, with forced joviality. "Ladies first!"

The jest failed to elicit so much as a whisper of amusement. Instead the words hung in the still air, jarring and misplaced. The crowd shifted nervously, as if someone had blasphemed in a temple and risked drawing the attention of a wrathful deity. *But isn't that exactly why we're here?* Lukan mused, recalling Lady Marni's earlier words. *I want to touch the divine. To see the faces of gods.* And if there *was* a god awaiting them in the darkness beyond, then she would seek it out and worry not for the consequences.

It was that same sense of destiny and divine purpose, Lukan mused, that animated Marni now. He watched as she snatched a burning torch from a servant and strode boldly into the darkness. That same blackness swallowed her whole, her flame doing little to force it back; it was like an ocean that engulfed her, drawing her into its embrace. At any moment Lukan expected to see her torch flicker and die, snuffed out by some boundless entity that didn't care for her supplication.

Instead, a great shaft of light speared down.

Lukan gasped along with everyone else as it revealed a wide, circular pit in the floor, some fifty paces away. A small structure—some sort of dais—stood close by. He shaded his eyes, tried to look beyond the light, but could make out only the barest hint of surrounding walls rising into the darkness above. *Lady's mercy, this place is vast.*

"What is this?" Lady Wretzky breathed.

"It feels like a temple," Ashra replied, her voice tight.

"It's like no temple I've ever seen," Lukan replied, but even as he spoke he realized she was right; there was a sense of sanctity in the air. The vast space inspired awe, and the great light above—burning like a sun—almost demanded obedience. "Whatever this place is," he added, with a sudden, dread certainty, "we should never have come here."

But it was too late: Lady Marni was already striding toward the circle of light, and the great pit within it. "With me!" her father snapped at the rest of his entourage, before taking off after his daughter, the various attendants and guards following behind.

Time seemed to slow as the Volkovs crossed the darkened floor. When they were halfway toward the light—and hadn't been struck down by some sort of divine punishment—a murmur passed through the rest of the nobility. Aristos exchanged guarded looks, as if trying to read each other's intent.

"Stay where you are," Orlova warned, glaring at them.

Someone—Dragomir, Lukan realized, because of course it was—took a few steps forward. The other noble he'd been bickering with earlier quickly followed. They eyed each other warily, both tense.

"I said, stay back!" Orlova barked.

Dragomir paid her no heed at all. Instead, he broke into a run. His rival sprang after him. The rest of the group quickly followed; a tide of nobility running, walking and hobbling toward the great circle of light at the center of the chamber, as Orlova flailed around, cursing them all.

"Go on," Lady Wretzky, gesturing at Lukan. "Get over there and see what's in that bloody pit. If it's empty, we can throw Dragomir into it and go home."

"Perhaps we could just skip to the going home part," he replied.

"Do you want your key back or not?"

"Fine." He glanced at Ashra. "Let's go."

They took off at a run, Flea just behind them. Within a few heartbeats the girl raced past both of them, throwing an elbow at Lukan as she did so. Together they raced across the darkened floor.

The Volkov party had already reached the light, and the edge of the circular pit within it. Lady Marni was slowly climbing a flight of steps cut into the side of the dais, while her father paced back and forth below, waving his arms. "Stay back!" he shouted, glaring at the onrushing nobles. "This discovery belongs to the Volkovs!"

What discovery? Lukan wondered, as he struggled to keep up with Ashra and Flea. *What's in the pit?*

"Guards!" Lord Volkov shouted at the handful of men and women wearing his household's livery. "Keep them back!"

But it was hopeless: the guards were too few, and the nobles too many, and the great circular pit too large. Lukan dodged one guard's half-hearted lunge and joined Flea and Ashra at the edge of the pit. Together, they stared down into its depths. A great, uneven mound of glittering blackness lay within, its highest point some five or six feet below the rim.

"What is it?" Flea whispered, awe in her voice.

"No idea," Ashra replied. "Lukan?"

"Not a clue," he said.

"They look like black diamonds!" a noblewoman squealed.

"There's thousands of them!" Dragomir said, staring down with wide eyes.

"They're not diamonds," Lukan replied.

"How in the hells would *you* know?" the young noble retorted.

"Because the Phaeron didn't lust for jewels the way we do. They had no interest in gems." *Or so Father always said.*

"Then why lock them away like this?" someone else demanded, to a murmur of agreement.

"Because they're not jewels," Ashra said, her eyes narrowed as she stared down into the pit. "They're pieces of metal."

"Metal?" the noblewoman echoed, sounding appalled.

Voices swelled as others offered their own opinions, underscored by Lord Volkov's repeated insistence that his family owned whatever the hells they were looking at. Raised voices echoed in the cavernous space, the silence that had endured for a thousand years broken by the sound of human greed.

"You're right," Lukan told Ashra, as he squinted down at the black mass. "It *is* metal." Each individual piece was shaped like a teardrop, curving to a sharp point. "And there's a pattern," he added, feeling a ripple of unease. "They're all perfectly aligned. As if . . ."

"They've been fitted together," the thief finished. "Like chainmail. This isn't a pile of scrap metal."

"They look like scales," Flea said. "Like a fish. Or a snake." Her eyes widened. "Does that mean . . ." She stared down into the pit. "Is it *alive?*"

Lukan barely heard her question; he was thinking of the deep gouges in the passageway. The kind a gigantic creature might make.

A sudden dread stole over him. *Surely not.* He caught Ashra's gaze and saw the same horror reflected in her eyes. "We need to go," he said.

"Agreed," the thief replied.

A ragged cheer rang out.

Dragomir had jumped into the pit.

"Get out!" Lord Volkov bellowed, as the young noble scrambled across the black mass. "That's my property you're walking on! Desist at once or I'll have you shot!"

Dragomir—encouraged by the whoops of his friends—ignored Baranov and instead knelt and took a knife to one of the scales, trying to pry it loose. His idiotic grin made it clear he hadn't realized the truth—nor had any of the nobles standing around the edge of the pit.

"Surely it's long dead," Lukan whispered to Ashra. "Whatever it is, it must have been in here a thousand years or more. Nothing could have survived that long. It must have died along with the Phaeron."

"Desist, or this place will become your tomb!" Lord Volkov shouted, but his words fell on deaf ears; Dragomir continued with his attempts at prying the scale loose, a scowl replacing his grin as another aristo jumped down into the pit.

"Get out," he yelled to the newcomer. "This is mine."

"It belongs to *me*, you insolent fools!" Volkov thundered.

A fresh cacophony of raised voices echoed across the cavern, as some nobles shouted encouragement and others appealed for calm.

"And now begins the bloodletting," Lady Wretzky said, as she joined them at the edge of the pit, General Razin at her side. "It was always going to end this way." She sucked on a cigarillo as she peered down into the pit. "What in the Builder's name is this?"

"We need to leave," Lukan replied, pulling Flea away from the pit. "If this thing is still alive, then we're—"

"Alive?" Wretzky glanced at him, then back in the pit. "What do you mean alive?"

The *twang* of a crossbow sounded above the raised voices. Dragomir yelped as a bolt struck the black mass beside him.

"The next one won't miss!" Volkov shouted, as the guard beside him hurriedly reloaded a crossbow.

"Enough!" General Orlova cried, struggling to make herself heard above all the raised voices. "All of you, stop at once!"

But her command had no more effect than Volkov's warning shot; Dragomir continued to furiously jab at the scale, while his rival started trying to carve out another. Two more aristos jumped down into the pit, eager to claim their own spoils, followed by three of Orlova's soldiers, as the general desperately tried to impose order. Two of the soldiers wrestled one of the aristos to the ground, drawing laughter and jeers from the crowd, while Volkov shouted at his crossbowman to reload faster.

"Damned fools," Razin growled, still clutching Lady Wretzky's elbow. "They've all lost their damned minds."

"Not all of them," Lukan replied, pointing to where Marni stood on the dais. Despite her father's attempt to lay claim to what was rightfully hers—not to mention Dragomir and the other opportunists—the woman's expression was calm. In fact, she seemed oblivious to the chaos below her, her eyes instead focused on a pedestal standing before her. As Lukan watched, Marni reached out and touched it.

A golden glow bathed her face.

A loud chime sounded, echoing through the vast space and instantly silencing the bickering nobles, who ceased their squabbling and exchanged confused glances.

"The hells was that?" Lady Wretzky demanded.

"We need to go," Ashra said, backing away from the pit's edge.

"It's too late," Lukan replied, dread certainty churning in his stomach. *We should have gone already.*

Shouts sounded from the pit, where Dragomir and the other

aristos had ceased their struggle with Orlova's soldiers. Both factions wore panicked expressions.

It was obvious why.

The black mass was moving.

A collective gasp sounded from the watching nobles as the seven men in the pit struggled to keep their balance upon the shifting scales. All of them jolted as the movement abruptly ceased. Dragomir was first to react, dropping his dagger and scrambling to the side of the pit.

"Help me!" he pleaded, waving his arms.

But his peers merely gaped at him, their eyes wide. Some had finally come to their senses and were backing away from the pit.

Dragomir staggered as the black mass shifted again, but managed to keep his feet. The six other men in the center of the pit weren't so lucky. All of them lost their balance as the surface beneath them tilted—and suddenly they were sliding away down the scaled slope, their screams fading as they disappeared into the depths of the pit.

"Please!" Dragomir wailed. All his earlier bravado had left him, leaving nothing but panic in his eyes. Suddenly he looked very young.

"Dragomir!" someone shouted. "Here, grab hold!" Lukan realized the speaker was Lord Arima, who had removed his coat and was lowering it into the pit, while two other aristos held him fast. "Quickly now!" Arima shouted.

Dragomir leaped for the coat, which dangled just beyond his fingertips. He swore and leaped again, but the sleeve remained just out of reach. He backed away, preparing for a runup, and took a breath to steady himself. Just as he started forward, the black mass moved beneath him, forming new surfaces and contours, revealing a terrifying new shape.

"Builder's balls," Wretzky murmured, cigarillo falling from her lips. "Is that a *wing*?"

Lukan had no words, nor breath to shape them. *Lady's blood, she's right.* He could only stare in horror as a second great wing unfolded and the black mass rose, arching upward, black spikes longer than spears rising from what he now realized was a spine. Dragomir was flung aside, his scream fading as he fell into the depths of the pit.

He reappeared a moment later in a pair of gigantic jaws.

A cage of black swords—*teeth*, Lukan realized—contained Dragomir's struggling form. His screams grew fainter as the massive head rose higher, propelled by a long, powerful neck, the creature revealing itself in all its terrible glory. As Lukan stared upward in horror—at the great jaws and the huge, curved horns—he was reminded of the great skull that hung above Saphrona's waterfront gate. There were many theories about the nature of the beast the skull had belonged to, but one had always stuck in Lukan's mind. It was that word he thought of now.

Dragon.

Yet as the great head turned, Dragomir still thrashing between its teeth, Lukan saw that, where the skull's eye sockets had been empty, these were not. Two tear-shaped eyes looked down upon the stunned crowd, glowing gold.

No, Lukan realized. *Not gold, but amber.*

The dragon shook its head and opened its jaws. Dragomir screamed as he was flung through the air, flailing head over heels like a ragdoll. He arced across the vast, empty space and disappeared into shadow; Lukan didn't see him hit the far wall, but he heard the impact: a dull slap, followed a few heartbeats later by a sickening wet smack as Dragomir's body hit the floor.

Silence.

Then someone screamed, which triggered a multitude of shouts and cries and wails, followed by the sound of booted feet as the gathered nobles fled for their lives.

"Run!" General Razin shouted, waving his arms madly.

"Take my arm," Lukan urged Wretzky, and the Iron Dame didn't need to be told twice. Together they turned and hurried for the exit, Flea and Ashra racing before them, while Razin hobbled along behind, as if trying to shield them. *Not that anything could stop those jaws if they come flashing down*, Lukan thought. He glanced back over his shoulder.

Lady Marni hadn't moved.

She remained standing on the dais—still, almost regal. She didn't even flinch as the dragon turned its eyes to her.

"General!" Lukan said, releasing his hold on the Iron Dame's arm. "Get Lady Wretzky out of here."

Razin gaped at him. "Lukan? What are—"

"Go!" he shouted, and ran back toward the pit. "Marni," he called as he neared the dais, "you need to run!"

Marni gave no sign she had heard him. Instead, she remained still as the dragon loomed over her, as if transfixed by the amber glow of its eyes. Then she raised a hand and began to chant in a language Lukan didn't understand. He saw a silver flash; something was dangling from her hand, some sort of artifact—Phaeron, most likely, but he couldn't even guess at its function or purpose.

"Marni!" he shouted again, as the dragon's great head lowered toward her, teeth glinting, but the woman continued with her strange ritual, chanting the unfamiliar words as she held the artifact before her. A blue glow surrounded her hands. The dragon tilted its head, and Lukan swore its amber eyes narrowed as it watched her.

"Marni!" he called again.

"Quiet, damn you!"

Lukan turned to find her father, Lord Volkov, stalking toward him from the shadows. "Don't you see?" the man demanded, a note of awe in his voice. "She's speaking to it. *Controlling* it." The smile that played across his lips suggested he was already envisaging what such a feat would mean for his family and their influence. "All these years," he continued, speaking as if to himself, "I thought this obsession of hers was foolish, that only an idiot would worship the Phaeron as gods." He shook his head. "How wrong I was."

"You're not wrong," Lukan replied, looking back at Marni. "This sort of power is not meant for us."

"For *you*, perhaps," Volkov scoffed. "Or for anyone else. But we Volkovs have always been destined for greatness. And with this"—he pointed at the creature—"I can rule Korslakov! Forget the Frostfire Council. I can rule as a king, like the monarchs of old!"

They watched as Marni continued to chant. The dragon lowered its head further, until it hovered just before the woman in red—close enough for her to touch.

Which—to Lukan's amazement—she did, gently pressing one hand to the dragon's snout.

Finally, Lady Marni Volkova was touching the divine.

"You see?" Lord Volkov breathed. "With this sort of power, I can . . ." His voice faltered as the dragon reared, arching its spined back. "What's it doing?" he whispered, fear replacing his glee.

As if in response, the dragon threw back its head and roared, a deafening sound that reverberated around the chamber. Lukan felt it vibrate in his chest, stealing the breath from his lungs. Marni clearly felt it too; she flinched and took a step back, her regal pose broken.

"Marni!" Lukan shouted again, though his voice sounded feeble in the wake of the dragon's roar.

"Daughter!" Volkov called, a note of panic in his voice.

Marni turned, her eyes wide with horror—no longer the coy, manipulative heiress Lukan had come to know, but a terrified young woman who was only now realizing the folly of her actions.

The dragon's head snapped downward.

Amber eyes flashing.

Jaws widening.

Marni's eyes found the two men. She opened her mouth to speak.

Too late. The dragon's jaws swept down with appalling speed, teeth gleaming as they closed round her.

And bit Marni in half.

One moment she was there; the next, only her lower body stood on the platform, blood fizzing upward.

Lukan blinked, barely comprehending what he'd just seen. *Run.* The instinct sparked deep within him, but his body was frozen, unresponsive. All he could do was stand and stare, gaping stupidly as Marni's legs slowly toppled sideways.

"No," Volkov managed, falling to one knee. "No, this . . . No. No." He surged upward. "NO!" he shouted, voice thick with fury. "NO!"

And then he was running toward the dragon.

Whether he was driven by grief for his daughter, or rage at seeing his chance at kingship snatched away, Lukan couldn't say. It didn't matter. The dragon certainly didn't care.

As Volkov ran up the steps of the dais, the beast raised an arm and slashed at him with a huge talon. Volkov's head flew one way, his body the other.

The dragon's amber eyes fixed on Lukan.

Lukan ran.

39

NECESSARY QUALITIES

The chamber—already vast—seemed to grow even larger as Lukan raced for the exit. Suddenly the passage seemed impossibly far away, the pinprick of daylight at its end as distant as a star. There was surely no way he would make it.

He ran anyway.

Heart racing, blood pounding, breaths bursting from his lungs. He ran as fast as his injured leg would allow, gritting his teeth against the growing pain, but the distance to the exit only seemed to expand, the vast space yawning before him. He almost stumbled as the dragon roared behind him, loud as thunder, the bass rumble vibrating in his ribcage. *Don't look back*, a voice in his mind screamed. *Don't bloody look back.*

He looked back.

And regretted it.

The dragon was already halfway out of the pit, moving with a speed that belied its great size, amber eyes glowing and teeth gleaming.

Lukan turned back to the exit, his heart trying to escape through his mouth, as if trying to beat him to the passage. He struggled to breathe as his rising terror squeezed his lungs. And through the boom of his own blood in his ears, he heard it: the thud of heavy footsteps, the squeal of talons on stone, each one a scream.

The dragon was coming.

But Lukan's terror gave him additional strength, and he somehow found an extra burst of speed, heedless of the numbness in his leg. Suddenly the opening loomed before him, and a moment later he was through it, hurtling down the passage beyond. He could see the others ahead; the younger aristos were already emerging into the daylight, while the rest—Razin and Wretzky included— were not too far behind. Hope flared inside him. *Nearly there*, he thought, as he hurtled down the passage. *Lady's blood, I'm actually going to make it—*

Another roar from behind him silenced the thought, castrating his foolish hope. He could hear the sharp talons screeching on stone, he could feel the dragon looming behind him in all its awful immensity.

And he could sense the great jaws descending.

Lukan veered to the left and dived toward the edge of the passage where the floor met the wall. He curled into a ball, a scream piercing his ears, which some distant part of him recognized as his own. Eyes clamped shut, he felt a great rush of wind, sensed a huge mass passing over him, heard the metallic screeching of talons as they skittered past, and then . . .

Nothing.

For a moment he wondered if he was dead. But no, his heart was still pounding furiously. He looked up to see the dragon moving away from him, toward the daylight, which was barely visible beyond its gargantuan frame. *Lady's blood*, he thought, feeling light-headed as he pushed himself up, *it missed me*. The beast's momentum had taken it past him. Whether the confines of the passage meant the dragon couldn't turn about, or whether it had simply lost interest in him now that its freedom beckoned, he couldn't say, but either way the beast was now heading toward the open doorway, tail swishing from side to side as its talons traced the same grooves that Ashra had pointed out on the way in.

The elation he felt at not ending up between the dragon's jaws died as the beast neared the end of the passage, chasing after those who had already fled into the daylight beyond.

Flea. Ashra.

Lukan rose shakily to his feet and ran after it. He heard screams as the dragon emerged from the mountain, followed a few moments later by the thump of ballistas firing. He doubted they

would kill the beast, but perhaps they might wound it, or incapacitate it . . .

His faint hope was extinguished as the dragon bellowed and
surged across the open grounds toward the ramparts. As Lukan
finally reached the doorway, he saw a scene of total chaos: nobles
and servants running in all directions—most toward the gateway
and their carriages that waited beyond—while soldiers on the
ramparts raced for the stairs. He glanced around wildly, but saw
no sign of his friends.

Only one figure ran toward the dragon: a golem, though Lukan couldn't guess whether it was compelled by a command, or
whether the human soul within—like the construct that had followed Ashra through her portal—saw a chance to be freed from
its metal prison. The dragon's head turned toward the golem, its
great jaws widening. Lukan expected the beast to simply snatch
the construct in its jaws and hurl it away, but instead the dragon
hesitated. Several heartbeats passed as the beast and the golem
stared at each other. Then the dragon turned away and roared as
it crashed toward the rampart, leaving the construct unharmed.

Lukan watched helplessly as the dragon leaped onto the gatehouse. Stone exploded beneath its claws as one side of the structure collapsed, dust and masonry engulfing those who were fleeing
through the gateway beneath. Men and women—aristos and servants alike—screamed as they were buried. Others fled back into
the grounds, jostling each other in their panic, but the beast paid
them no mind from its position on the ruined wall. Instead, the
dragon's great head turned slowly, as if it was studying the surrounding valley.

Then it stilled, amber eyes gazing south.

Toward Korslakov.

A low rumble sounded from its throat as the dragon spread its
great wings, beat them twice, then launched itself into the air and
headed southward, rising higher as it flew. Within moments it was
nothing but a black shape against the steel grey sky, its distant roar
echoing across the valley.

A brittle silence fell, broken only by a chorus of wails and cries.

Lukan sank to his knees, feeling suddenly exhausted. He glanced around at others who stood and sat nearby—aristos, attendants and soldiers alike, disbelief etched into every face, horror reflected in every pair of eyes.

"What have we done?" a grey-haired lord was babbling, a shaking hand at his mouth. "What have we *done*?"

Lukan had no answer for him. No one did.

"Orlova!" a familiar voice bellowed, and Lukan's heart soared to see Razin striding out from the lee of the wall, Lady Wretzky just behind him. "Damn it, Orlova," the general shouted, his face flushed as he looked about. "Where in the blazes are you?"

"Here," Orlova replied from near the gateway. The general was covered in dust; she must have been close when the gatehouse collapsed. Lukan wondered if she'd been trying to escape rather than standing her ground, as was surely her responsibility. Still, he found it hard to blame her if she had tried to run.

"Have your men clear that rubble and look for survivors," Razin commanded, pointing at the ruined gatehouse. "Quickly!"

Lukan thought Orlova might refuse, but instead she looked relieved that someone else was taking command. She turned away and shouted orders to her remaining soldiers. Several ran to the gateway and started clearing the shattered masonry. "There's someone here," one of them shouted, pointing to an arm in a dust-covered sleeve.

Lukan wasn't one for praying, but he found himself murmuring a prayer now, pleading to the Veiled Lady that it wasn't Flea or Ashra they'd found. He hadn't seen either of them since he'd emerged from the mountain, and he couldn't see them now. Lord Arima still lived; he caught Lukan's eye before turning away, a haunted look on his face. Lukan looked around desperately, trying to ignore the growing dread in his stomach. His friends had to be alive. They *had* to be . . .

"Lukan!"

He turned to see Flea racing toward him. The girl almost

knocked him over as she reached him and hugged him fiercely. "You're all right," she murmured.

"Somehow," he replied, relief flooding through him as he hugged her back.

"Thought you were dead," Ashra said as she joined them. One corner of her mouth curled upward as she offered him a hand. Lukan managed a wan smile of his own and allowed the thief to pull him to his feet.

"Lord Gardova." Lukan looked over to see Lady Wretzky walking toward them, Razin a few paces behind. Somehow the Iron Dame had found time and composure to light a fresh cigarillo. "I'm glad to see you're still alive," she continued, her tone suggesting the alternative would only have been a minor inconvenience. "I assume Lady Marni is not?"

Lukan winced. "You assume correctly."

"And her father?"

"He lost his head. Literally."

"Builder's mercy," Wretzky swore, her expression darkening. "Still. I suppose that'll make what comes next a little easier. Fyodor did love to be contrary." She turned to Razin. "Leopold, be a dear and gather the rest of the Frostfire Council, would you? Lord Baranov had the sense to stay at home, but Lady Mirova and Lord Saburov are both here somewhere. And ask General Orlova to attend as well. We need to move quickly. Oh—and send a rider back to the city at once. Tell the Watch to spread the word that everyone is to remain in their homes. The last thing we need is panic on the streets."

Razin saluted and spun on his heel.

"So, what's the plan?" Lukan asked as the man strode away.

Lady Wretzky took a deep drag on her cigarillo. "That," she said, exhaling a cloud of smoke, "is what we need to figure out."

The Frostfire Council—what was left of it—met in a storeroom in the base of the rampart, with a couple of soldiers guarding the entrance. Some of the aristos had already departed for the city, desperate to protect their estates, though what any of them thought they could do against the dragon Lukan had no idea. Yet most remained, and Lady Wretzky was in no mood to "put up with their tiresome yipping," as she put it to the guards, before closing the door. A flickering oil lamp threw her shadow across the bare stone walls.

"Thank you for attending," she said, nodding to everyone present. "I hereby call an emergency meeting of the Frostfire Council to determine—"

"Here?" Lord Saburov stammered, glancing around as if only just realizing where he was.

"Yes. Here."

"Now?"

"Oh, is now not a good time?" Lady Wretzky's lips thinned. "Would sometime next week suit you better? I suppose we can all just sit around in the meantime and watch that dragon turn our city to rubble . . ."

"But Lord Baranov's not here!"

"We'll have to make do without him. Now, we need to—"

"And Lord Volkov," Saburov continued, glancing toward the door. "We can't proceed without him."

"Fyodor's lying in pieces beside his daughter, but, if you want to go and fetch his head so that he can have his say, be my guest."

Lord Saburov stared at the Iron Dame, mouth quivering. "Fyodor . . . he's *dead*?"

"Yes," Wretzky said, her expression softening. "I already told you. Fyodor and Marni both."

"But . . . no, that can't be right . . ."

"General Orlova, please could you escort Lord Saburov out? I think he's in need of some air."

Saburov didn't protest as Orlova steered him away. The man had clearly lost his mind in the aftermath of the afternoon's events. Lukan sympathized; he too was having trouble accepting what he'd seen with his own eyes. Every time he saw Marni's death in his mind's eye, it only felt more unreal.

"Thank you, General," Lady Wretzky said, as Orlova returned to their circle. "Now, what's the plan?"

A moment passed before Orlova realized the question had been directed at her. "Ah . . . plan, my lady?"

"Yes, General. Your plan for protecting our city from the horror we've just unleashed on it. What do you propose we do?"

Orlova could only stare at the Iron Dame in response, her mouth forming various shapes as words tried and failed to vacate her throat. "I-I don't know," she managed eventually.

"What do you mean you don't know?" Lady Wretzky snapped. "You command our military, yes?"

"I do."

"And your sole responsibility is the protection of Korslakov and its citizens from all potential threats, is it not?"

"It is," Orlova reluctantly agreed.

"Good," the Iron Dame said, plucking her cigarillo from her mouth. "I'm glad we've cleared that up. So, I'll ask again: what is your plan?" She punctuated each of her last four words with a jab of her smoke.

Orlova swallowed, nervously wetting her lips.

"I appreciate," Lady Wretzky continued, her tone droll, "that the only threat to our city in recent decades has come from hairy men in the far north with strange names and terrible hygiene, and that when you got up this morning you weren't expecting us to be attacked by a dragon. Nonetheless, that's the challenge that lies before us." The Iron Dame slid her cigarillo back between her lips. "So, how do we take the bastard down before it destroys our entire city?"

Orlova wilted under the Iron Dame's gaze. She turned her eyes to the floor, perhaps thinking if she stared at it hard enough it might do her the favor of swallowing her. Lukan wondered how much she now regretted ousting Razin and taking his place. No doubt she'd anticipated an easy life of regimental balls and the occasional foray into the Clanholds, where she'd rarely stray from the comfort of her command tent, and where the only danger she'd face would be running out of wine. Lukan felt no sympathy for her. Orlova had brought this on herself—and trampled over Razin in the process, reducing him to a shadow of the man he'd once been. Her ambition had brought her this humiliation, and it was no less than she deserved.

Ironically, it was the man she'd stabbed in the back who came to her rescue.

"Lady Wretzky," Razin ventured. "If I may?"

"You have a plan, Leopold?" the Iron Dame asked, her eyes still fixed on Orlova. "Because your successor certainly doesn't."

"I believe I do."

"Let's hear it, then."

"We gather every single barrel of black powder we can find, and line them up on the Bridge of a Thousandfold Thoughts. We lure the dragon there, and as soon as it lands . . ." He slammed a fist into his other palm. "Boom! We blow the bridge heavenwards."

"You'd blow up the Bridge of a Thousandfold Thoughts?" Lady Mirova gasped, one hand rising to her throat.

"I don't suggest this lightly," Razin replied, with a solemn bow of his head.

"Outrageous," the woman murmured to herself.

"Could it work?" Wretzky asked, ignoring the horrified look Mirova shot her. "Would such an explosion destroy this beast?"

"My lady," Razin replied, "there's not a creature alive that could withstand the blast of a hundred barrels of our black powder."

"That's the problem though," Lukan put in, deciding now was the time to voice the thought that had been bothering him. "This creature isn't alive."

The others stared at him.

"What do you mean, Gardova?" Wretzky demanded. "Of course it's alive—the damned thing just demolished half the bloody gatehouse! It killed Dragomir and the Volkovs."

"What I'm saying," Lukan said, raising a hand, "is that it's not a living creature. It's a construct."

"A construct?" Lady Mirova scoffed. "That's *preposterous*!"

"It's made from metal," Lukan replied firmly. "And what color were its eyes?"

"Amber," Flea gasped, realization dawning on her face. "Like a golem!"

"It's a Phaeron-made construct," Lukan continued, "but modeled on a real dragon." He turned to Ashra. "Did you recognize it?"

The thief nodded. "It looks like the skull mounted above the waterfront gate."

"What gate?" Wretzky demanded, glancing at each of them in turn.

"Above Saphrona's harbor," Lukan replied, "there's a huge skull, believed by many to be that of a dragon. It looks very similar to the construct we just set loose. So, my guess is twofold." He counted off one finger. "Firstly, that the Phaeron deliberately made a construct in the image of a dragon, and secondly"—he counted off another finger—"that this construct has the soul of a real dragon inside it."

"Skulls? Souls?" Lady Mirova blinked in bewilderment. "What in the Builder's name are you talking about?"

"The Phaeron could transfer a soul from a living body into an artificial construct," Lukan replied, barely keeping a leash on his impatience. "Your alchemists use the same method to create their golems, with the aid of a Phaeron artifact. All your constructs are powered by human souls. It's why they can understand spoken commands."

"What utter nonsense," Lady Mirova trilled, but her laugh faltered when she saw Wretzky's somber expression. "Olga?" she inquired tentatively. "Don't tell me all those rumors . . . surely they're not actually true . . ."

"If the Phaeron could store their own souls in receptacles," Lukan continued, "then it stands to reason that they could store those of other creatures too. I think that's what we're facing here." He shrugged. "Just my two coppers."

"So, we're up against a dragon made of metal," Lady Wretzky

said, dropping her cigarillo, "that's controlled by the soul of its real-life equivalent." She grimaced as she ground the butt beneath her heel. "Shit."

"I'd say that about sums it up."

"I suppose it's foolish to think we could somehow command it? The way we can command our golems?"

"Lady Marni tried," Lukan said, recalling her strange chanting and glowing artifact. "I saw first-hand how that went."

"Real dragon or not," Razin put in, tugging at one end of his mustache, "I still think a hundred barrels of black powder would blow this thing to pieces."

"Gardova?" the Iron Dame prompted.

Lukan shrugged as he considered the prospect. "Maybe. We don't know what the construct is made from, how strong that black metal is. But I'd say it's worth a try."

"Destroying it is only half the battle," Ashra said. "How do we lure it to the bridge in the first place?"

They considered the question in silence.

"Fireworks," Flea piped up, her eyes gleaming. "My friend Matiss has some! He lives in Emberfall with his husband, Radimir, who made Nighthawk." She patted her crossbow. "That's how I met them. I was meant to be keeping watch, but . . ." She trailed off, as Lukan made a subtle *get to the point* gesture. "If we set the fireworks off near the bridge," she continued, her eyes narrowing at Lukan, "maybe the dragon would come to watch."

"You're saying we should invite a dragon to a fireworks display," Lady Mirova said with a shrill laugh. "Blessed Builder, I must be losing my mind."

"You got a better idea, you old prune?" Flea demanded.

"I *beg* your pardon?"

"Enough," Lady Wretzky snapped. "It's not a bad idea. Who knows if it'll work, but . . ."

"It's worth a try," Razin finished for her.

"Even if it does work," Ashra put in, already focusing on the

next problem, "we'll need the creature to land on the bridge before we ignite the barrels. The explosion won't harm it if it's in
the air."

Another silence, this one longer than the one before.

"Anyone?" Wretzky said eventually, looking round at them.
"Orlova? Here's the chance to restore some of your reputation."

A shadow passed across the general's face, but she remained
silent.

"Pity," Wretzky sighed, exhaling a plume of smoke. "Well, if we
can't think of a way to bring the creature down, then I'm afraid—"

"Wait," Lukan said, the glimmer of an idea forming in his mind.
"What if there was a way to ... I mean, it probably wouldn't
work, but—"

"Out with it, Gardova," the Iron Dame snapped. "You're babbling like a priest in a brothel."

"The Inventors' Parade the other day," Lukan offered, glancing
around the circle. "Do you remember the artificer that Lord Arima
sponsored?"

"I remember. What of him?"

"That machine of his was able to hold a golem in place. But
what if there was a way to make the effect much stronger, so that
it could trap something far larger?"

"Like our dragon." The Iron Dame's brow furrowed and she
turned to Orlova. "General, make yourself useful and fetch Lord
Arima, if he's still here."

Orlova made no protest as she strode from the room.

"Fireworks," Lady Mirova muttered, fussing with a button on
her coat. "Souls and skulls and dragons and black powder." She
tittered again and shook her head. "This is madness."

No one replied. *What's the use in denying it?* Lukan wondered.
She's not wrong.

"Ah, Shiro," Lady Wretzky said, as Orlova returned with Lord
Arima. "Good. I feared you might have returned to the city."

"No, I thought I'd watch its destruction from here," the man replied, without a trace of humor. "The view's far better." His shoulders sagged. "I had no idea about . . . if I'd known that *thing* was beyond the door, I'd never have tried to open it."

"Save your self-pity. It was Lady Marni who opened the door, not you." Wretzky's eyes twinkled. "Just be glad that my agents successfully sabotaged your formula."

Arima blinked at her. "Agents? Wait, what do you mean, 'sabotaged my—'"

"Never mind that. Marni's actions may have condemned our city, but you might just have the chance to save it. Lord Gardova, please explain."

"Your artisan, Hulio Arcardi," Lukan ventured. "His contraption has the power to trap a golem and hold it still."

"That's right," Arima agreed hesitantly. "What of it?"

"We believe this creature is a Phaeron construct—like Korslakov's golems, but fashioned in the image of a dragon."

"I had wondered the same," Arima replied, nodding to himself. "Scales that look like metal. Eyes that glow amber, like our own golems."

"And it's got the soul of a real dragon inside it," Lukan continued, raising a hand as Arima—his eyes widening—tried to interrupt. "I'll explain later. What we need to know is whether Hulio's machine could hold this dragon in place the same way it can hold a golem."

"You mean to try and trap it," Arima replied, catching on immediately. He chewed his lip as he considered the question. "You'd need more than one machine. I'm not sure how many Hulio has. In any case, the key component is the iron disc—that's the part that becomes magnetized and holds the subject in place. A small disc can trap a golem, but to hold a creature of this size . . ." He shook his head. "You'd need a massive piece of iron."

"Like the Medallion of Remembrance?" General Razin put in, tugging at his mustache. "That's made of iron."

Arima's eyes widened. "Of course! I'd completely forgotten."

"We'll fill the Square of Sacred Memories with as many barrels of powder as we can," Razin continued eagerly. "And once the dragon's trapped on the medallion, all we need to do is light the fuse and *boom*!"

Lady Mirova jumped as Razin shouted the last word. "You cannot be serious!" she snapped at him. "You would blow up the Square of Sacred Memories? Where the Builder himself laid the first stone of our great city? That's *sacrilege*! And the medallion—it's our entire *history*!"

"Better to destroy our past than our future," Razin said gravely.

"No!" Lady Mirova shrieked. "I'll have no part of this!" With those words she swept out of the storeroom and slammed the door behind her.

"Blow up?" Arima asked, into the silence that followed. "What exactly are you proposing?"

"Could it work?" Lady Wretzky asked, ignoring the question. "Could we create a force powerful enough to trap the dragon on the medallion?"

"In theory, yes. We could." Arima frowned. "But only if we have enough machines to power it. To create the necessary magnetic strength, we'd probably need at least a dozen. Maybe more. I'm not sure if Hulio has that many."

"He'd better," the Iron Dame said grimly, "because right now, he's our only hope."

"Even if he does, we don't know what metal this creature is made from," Arima continued. "It might not possess the necessary qualities."

"What qualities?"

"I don't fully understand the science, but it's the type of metal that dictates the magnetism of an object, and . . ." He trailed off as the Iron Dame raised a hand.

"Please, Lord Arima," she said wearily, "speak in terms I can understand."

"My apologies. What I mean is that Hulio's machine trapped the golem, because the golem was made of steel, which reacts to the invisible force the machine creates. But it wouldn't work on a golem that was made of brass or copper. Those metals don't react in the same way."

"And we don't know what this dragon is made from," Wretzky murmured, understanding dawning in her eyes. "So we won't know if this plan will work until your pet machinist throws the switch."

"Exactly."

"Damn it."

"If we had a scale from the dragon, we could test it to see if it has the required properties," Arima said, "but without one there's no way to know."

"Would this do?" Flea asked, reaching into a pocket.

"Where the hells did you get that?" Lukan asked, as she held up a sleek, black scale, which glinted in the light.

"Found it outside," the girl replied, with a shrug. "It must have fallen off the dragon when it landed on the wall or something."

"Well?" Wretzky asked, glancing at Arima. "Will this do?"

"It will," he replied, reaching out to take the scale. "I'll get this to Hulio immediately."

"I want it back," Flea warned.

"If this plan works," Lady Wretzky replied, with a bleak smile, "you'll have all the scales you want."

40

MORE BAD NEWS

Lukan stood at the great bay windows in the Frostfire Council chamber, looking down at the frenzied activity below. Preparations were already at an advanced stage, with dozens of barrels of black powder lined up in the Square of Sacred Memories. A detachment of soldiers—supported by three golems—labored to move more barrels into place, with General Razin in the thick of the action, gesturing furiously and bellowing at anyone who didn't move fast enough. *The old man's in his element*, Lukan mused, and it gladdened his heart to see the general moving with such vim and vigor, a far cry from the diminished figure he'd come to know. Lord Arima was also down in the square, watching as the inventor Hulio Arcardi waved his arms at a group of bemused soldiers, who had been tasked with moving the eccentric artificer's machines into place around the great medallion. Lukan had asked Arima how the machines actually worked, but the explanation had mostly escaped him—something about burning a certain substance (the name of which he couldn't remember) to activate the metallic bands (whatever that meant) in order to greatly increase the lodestone's natural magnetism, which in turn would be passed to the great seal to turn it into a giant magnet.

Or something.

Truth was, he didn't have much of a clue how the process worked, and even less as to whether it *would* work. To everyone's relief, Arima had reported that the construct's scale did possess the necessary properties for their plan, but, as Lukan watched Arcardi directing the placement of his machines at the edges of the seal, it seemed absurd that such a ploy could trap the creature they'd unleashed. Yet he'd seen that golem held fast by the same scientific principles. It made sense that by increasing the power, if that was even the right word, you could trap something bigger. *Either way, we'll find out soon enough.*

The preparations in the square below weren't the only source of frantic activity; various stewards were bustling around the large council chamber behind him, removing portraits from the walls and ornaments from pedestals, and arguing over whether the wooden chairs were worth saving. One individual managed to drop a marble bust on the wooden floor, the thud of its impact momentarily silencing the room. Then the arguing started again.

"Builder's bloody teeth," Lady Wretzky snapped, not even turning from the window. "Leave the damned chairs!"

They left the chairs.

"What about him?" Flea asked, pointing at the skeletal form of the last king of Korslakov, who still sat on his throne in one corner of the room. The dagger that had ended both his reign and his life was still embedded between his ribs.

"He can stay as well," Wretzky replied. "Given the atrocities he committed, being blown to dust is the least he deserves."

The Iron Dame continued staring out of the window as the stewards continued bustling around behind her, but Lukan knew she wasn't watching the activity below. She was eyeing the dragon as it soared above Korslakov, its black mass increasingly hard to discern against the darkening skies as twilight set in. The Iron Dame's fear had been that they would return to find half the city already in ruins, and she had even berated the coach driver for not going fast enough. Lukan had shared her concerns—as did Razin, judging by his expression—but they'd clattered back through the north gate to find the dragon merely gliding in circles high above. The general's belief was that it was merely selecting its first target, but Arima had suggested the possibility that it was disorientated and unsure what it was looking at. If there was a dragon's soul in there, he argued, then it was hardly surprising the creature had reacted the way it had. Having been roused from a thousand-year slumber, only to find its masters gone and a strange people in their place, it was little wonder the creature had lashed out. He even ventured that the dragon was likely the greatest marvel of Phaeron engineering in the known world, and as such it deserved to be studied rather than destroyed. Lady Wretzky's stony expression made it clear what she thought of that. Lukan, for his part, could only think of the shock on Marni's face, the blood fizzing upward from her severed waist, and of her father being torn in two like a piece of old parchment. *The dragon's already destroyed one family*, he thought now, as he watched the creature gliding above the city. *How many will soon follow?*

"Why doesn't it attack?" Ashra said quietly.

"Maybe it won't," Flea replied. "Maybe it will fly away across the sea."

"And be someone else's problem," Wretzky said, with a snort. "Wouldn't that be nice."

"My lady!"

All of them turned, the Iron Dame included; the urgent tone of the newcomer's voice was unmistakable.

"Captain," Wretzky replied, acknowledging the approaching woman with a brusque nod. "Report."

"We have sixty barrels of powder secured in the square," the captain replied, saluting as she spoke. "Some of the deliveries were delayed by crowds in the streets. Most citizens have obeyed the order to stay indoors, but others are panicking and trying to leave by the south gate."

"So there's another forty barrels to come—"

"Begging your pardon, ma'am," the captain interrupted, with a pained expression, "but we're only expecting another dozen or so. One of our storage cellars has been flooded by meltwater, and our engineers claim the powder's no use."

"Builder's balls," the Iron Dame muttered. "We'll just have to hope that we've got enough."

"Um . . ." The captain shifted uneasily.

"More bad news?" Wretzky asked, giving her a hard stare. "Out with it."

"We've had difficulty obtaining the fireworks," the woman admitted with a wince.

"By 'difficulty,' am I to assume you mean you've failed?"

"The purveyor is refusing to cooperate."

"You told him we'd pay him twice what they're worth?"

"I did."

"You made it clear that failure to comply would be considered a crime?"

"I did."

"And when that failed you and your men attempted to take the fireworks by force?"

"We did."

"And?"

"He threatened to set fire to his workshop and give us the best damned fireworks display this city has ever seen. Um, those were his words, not mine—"

"Builder's bloody teeth," the Iron Dame hissed, turning back to the window. "We need those fireworks, otherwise all this"—she flung a hand at the activity below—"is for nothing."

"I can get them," Flea offered. "Matiss will listen to me." She chewed her lip. "I think."

"You *think*?" Wretzky echoed, her expression strained. "Fine. We've nothing to lose. Captain, escort this young lady to—"

"No," Lukan interrupted, "this is too dangerous. The dragon's out there."

"You can stay here if you're too scared," Flea said over her shoulder as she made for the door. The captain glanced uncertainly between Lukan and Wretzky, but departed at a nod from the latter.

"Lady's blood," Lukan swore, glancing at Ashra. "This is a terrible idea."

"You have a better one?" the thief replied, already striding after Flea.

"No." Lukan swore under his breath and followed.

41

UP IN FLAMES

As they raced toward Emberfall—and as his knuckles turned white from gripping the side of the cart, his injured leg feeling every shudder of the axles as they bumped over endless cobbles—Lukan wondered how in the hells they'd ended up in such a bizarre scenario. Paying a visit to a fireworks merchant, while the construct of a dragon soared menacingly overhead, was like something out of a second-rate play or a two-copper serial. *Except the heroes always survive in those stories*, he thought, wincing as one of the cart's wheels struck a pothole.

He wished he could be as optimistic about their own chances.

"Make way!" General Orlova cried, and her command was echoed by the two mounted guards who flanked her. A crowd of people scattered before the riders; Lukan caught a glimpse of terrified faces in the lantern light as the cart hurtled past, before they were lost in the gloom. They weren't the first he'd seen, and likely wouldn't be the last. Lady Wretzky's order to remain indoors appeared to have been heeded by most of Korslakov's citizens, but there were plenty who had decided to flee. But in the darkened streets, they were more at risk of being struck by a horse or cart than snatched by a dragon. They turned a corner, passing a wagon where a man was trying to balance a mounted bear's head atop a pile of possessions, then suddenly they were racing across the Bridge of a Thousandfold Thoughts toward Emberfall.

The purple flame atop the alchemists' tower burned brightly on the other side of the water, no more than a quarter-mile upriver, but Lukan only had eyes for the darkened sky above them. He watched for a hint of movement, a black mass blocking out the distant stars. Nothing. He felt a desperate flicker of hope. *Perhaps it's gone*, he thought. *Flown away across the ocean, like Flea said, never to be seen again.* He swore under his breath. *Some chance.* The dragon was here somewhere. The only question was where.

"Builder's balls!" one of Orlova's riders cried. "Look out!"

Lukan was thrown against the inside of the cart as it shuddered to a halt. Flea's elbow connected with his chin as she fell across him. He winced, tasting blood in his mouth. Numbness spread through his jaw.

"Shit!" someone exclaimed. Orlova, he thought.

"Are you all right?" he mumbled at Flea, even though he'd clearly come off worse in their collision. The girl didn't answer as she found her feet. Instead she stared ahead, her eyes wide.

"What in the hells . . ." Lukan forced himself onto his knees. "Why have we stopped?"

No one replied. They didn't need to.

The dragon was perched atop the alchemists' tower, its great black form gleaming in the light of the frostfire, which flickered harmlessly against its metal skin.

"We need to turn back," one of the riders whispered, his voice hoarse with fear. "If it sees us here—"

The dragon threw back its head and roared, drowning out the man's words. Even from a quarter-mile away, Lukan could feel the violent sound in his bones. His insides clenched with renewed fear.

"Lukan," Flea murmured.

"It's okay," he replied, pulling the girl to him, knowing it wasn't okay at all; the huge construct was going to swoop down and snatch them up in its talons the same way it had snatched Dragomir. They needed to get away, but panic had broken out among the horses; Orlova was struggling to control her rearing mount, while the carthorses were whinnying in fear and not responding to the driver's desperate entreaties. *There's no time*, Lukan thought hopelessly, as he looked back at the creature, expecting to see it spreading its wings as it launched itself toward them, great jaws open wide . . .

But the dragon didn't even seem to have noticed them.

Instead its amber eyes were fixed on the violet flame. With a slow movement it raised a clawed foot and placed it on the rim of the bronze bowl.

And pushed.

"Lady's blood," Lukan whispered, as the great bowl rose—slowly at first, then faster as the dragon exerted more force. Violet coals spilled from within the bowl as it tipped over.

And then it was falling, purple flame trailing as it plummeted toward the roofs and chimneys of Emberfall.

The crash that followed was even louder than the beast's roar.

Orlova swore as her horse reared again. She managed to stay in her saddle, but one of the other riders wasn't so lucky and his horse unseated him in its panic. The man cried out as he landed awkwardly on his arm, only to fall silent when his horse clipped his skull with a hoof as it turned and bolted.

"Turn the cart," Lukan yelled. "We need to go."

"I can't," the driver shouted back, flailing an arm toward the prone rider. "He's in the way. You'll have to move him."

"Shit." Lukan scrambled off the cart and knelt beside the man. "Flea," he called, "give me a hand here." For once the girl didn't complain. Together they managed to haul the rider back to the cart. "He's in," Lukan shouted, as blood oozed from the man's head to stain the boards. "Now let's get the hells out of here before that damned thing sees us."

"It's too late!" Flea shouted. "Look!"

Lukan glanced up, and his eyes widened in horror as the dragon spread its wings and launched itself from the tower. He pulled Flea to him and tried to say something, he wasn't even sure what, but terror stilled his tongue. He could only watch helplessly as the beast swept downward . . .

And veered away from them.

Lukan stared in disbelief as it headed toward the Cinders, blotting out the stars as it flew.

"You can let go now," Flea muttered.

He released the girl. "You all right?"

"Better without you crushing me."

"Yah!" the driver called to his horses, flicking the reins. "Move yourselves!"

"No," Lukan called, placing a hand on the man's shoulder. "Wait."

"For what? That bloody monster to come back?"

"We need to go on."

"Have you lost your mind? Look!" The driver pointed to a purple glow in the distance. "Half of Emberfall is on fire!"

Lukan turned to Orlova, who was staring at the distant flames. "General," he called. "We need to keep going. The dragon's gone. This is our only chance. We need those fireworks."

"Ma'am," the other rider urged, "it's too dangerous."

"She's right," the driver piped up, shrugging off Lukan's hand. "The horses are terrified enough already. The fire will only—"

"Enough," Orlova snapped, turning her horse round. "Gardova's right. We go on."

"But General—"

"That's a damned *order*, soldier." She flicked her reins. "With me. Quickly." *About time you showed some backbone*, Lukan thought, as the driver swore under his breath and urged his horses on.

They crossed the bridge in a silence broken only by distant screams.

42

RUNNING THE GAUNTLET

Frostfire had engulfed a large part of Emberfall. Chaos had engulfed the rest.

Screaming horses, screaming people. Some running, others standing still, shaking, eyes wide with shock. More screams carried on the wind, as if borne by the violet embers that rose above the district. Some of the inhabitants were fleeing the ravenous flames, but more still were running toward them with pails of water in hand. As he watched the machinists and artificers battling to save their home, he felt a stab of guilt at the part he'd unwittingly played in the unfolding events.

The cart shuddered to a halt at a crossroads.

"Which way?" Orlova shouted over her shoulder, as she struggled to control her horse. Her subordinate didn't seem to have a clue. Nor did Lukan; he'd barely paid attention on his one previous visit, and now, with ravenous purple flames devouring the district, he felt like he was somewhere else entirely. One of the hells, maybe. He shook his head hopelessly as he glanced about. They were drawing dangerously close to the fire, and this entire mission was feeling increasingly like a fool's errand. *As if that hasn't been obvious from the start.*

"Turn right," Flea shouted back.

"Are you sure?" Orlova demanded.

"Yes!"

"*Are* you sure?" Lukan asked her as the cart started moving again.

"Nope."

"Great."

"I don't see you leading the way," the girl retorted, elbowing him in the ribs. "Anyway, I've just got a feeling . . . yeah, look! There's Zelenko's workshop!"

Lukan followed her pointing finger and saw the familiar sign—VIKTOR ZELENKO, MASTER ARTISAN—as they rumbled past.

"It's just a bit further!" Flea called. "There, that's it!"

The girl hopped off the cart before it had even stopped moving. Lukan swore and struggled after her.

"Make haste!" Orlova barked.

"The hells does it look like I'm doing?" he yelled back as he ran after Flea, who had raced up to the front door of a large workshop. Light glowed behind the shutters. A promising sign.

"Matiss!" Flea called, rapping on the door. "Radimir!"

Silence, save for the screams and cries on the wind.

"Matiss!" the girl called again, pounding her small fist against the wood. "It's me, Flea!"

No one stirred within.

"Stand back," Lukan said, picking up a length of iron from a nearby pile. "Matiss!" he yelled, swinging the bar against the wood with a loud crunch. "Open the bloody door!"

He was just readying for a second strike when a small grille slid back and a shadowed face peered out, sharp features lined with anger. "Who are you?" the man demanded.

"Matiss!" Flea shouted, stepping back up to the door. "It's me!"

The green eyes swung to the girl. Blinked. "Flea? What are you doing here?"

"We need your fireworks to stop the dragon! We're going to lure it to the square with that big metal disc, and there's a machine that's going to trap it or something, I dunno how it works, and then we're gonna blow it all up! But we need your fireworks to make it happen!"

The man just stared.

"What Flea is trying to say," Lukan said, leaning closer to the grille, "is that we're working with Lady Wretzky and the Frostfire Council to destroy the dragon that's set fire to half your district. We've got a plan, and it requires your fireworks. All of them."

"And you are?"

"This is Lukan," Flea piped up. "He's my friend."

Matiss's gaze narrowed. "Some Sparks came by earlier and gave us the same story. I didn't think . . ." His eyes met Lukan's again. "*Why* do you need them? I don't understand."

"We need to attract the dragon to the Square of Sacred Memories so we can destroy it." He raised a hand to forestall the man's next question. "There's no time to explain. Will you help or not?"

"What of the cost?" the man replied. "I spent a considerable amount of coin on these fireworks; I can't just give them away."

"You'll be reimbursed. Wretzky said so."

Matiss's lip curled. "The promise of an aristocrat is—"

"Worth less than shit, I know. For what it's worth, I trust her."

"I don't know you," the man pointed out. "Your trust means nothing to me."

"You can trust me," Flea put in. "And *I* trust Lady Wretzky. She's quite scary and eats cigarillos, but she'll pay you what she promised."

Matiss eyed Flea dubiously.

"You'll get your money," Lukan said. He glanced down the street, toward the black shape of the tower and the purple fire that roared behind it. "Or you can keep your fireworks," he added, turning back to the grille, "and lose them anyway when the fire reaches you. Your choice."

"Wait here." The grille snapped shut before Lukan could reply. He swore under his breath and glanced at the sky. No sign of the dragon, but it would be almost impossible to spot against the night sky. He looked back to where Orlova and the other rider waited with the cart. It could be swooping down for them right now and they wouldn't even know until it was too late. Still, at least the creature didn't breathe fire, like its living counterparts were said to have done. Small mercies.

The sound of bolts being pulled back drew him from his thoughts. A soft light spilled forth as the door opened. "Quick," Matiss said, beckoning. "Come in." They stepped through into a workshop where half-made crossbows lay on workbenches and the finished articles hung from the walls. Another man stood nearby, eyeing Lukan with hostility. His features softened when he saw Flea, and he returned the girl's wave of greeting.

"This creature," Matiss said, not bothering to introduce the other man, who Lukan assumed was Radimir. "You called it a dragon." He closed the door and regarded Lukan intently, doubt in his gaze.

"I did," Lukan replied wearily. "Look, I know what you're thinking—"

"I'm thinking that, if it *was* a real dragon, the entire city would be on fire by now."

"It's not a real dragon—"

"Of course not. So, what is it?"

"A Phaeron construct made in the image of a dragon. And we think it has a dragon's soul inside it."

Matiss's eyes widened. "A dragon's *soul*?"

"That's right." Lukan waved away the question forming on the man's lips. "There's no time. We need these fireworks. I can explain everything later. If we're still alive."

Radimir suddenly made a rapid series of signs with his hands, a questioning look on his face. Matiss replied with his own series of gestures, to which Radimir responded with a sharp motion.

"My husband thinks you're full of shit," Matiss told Lukan.

"Good to know," Lukan replied. "A pleasure to meet him, too."

A smile flickered across Matiss's lips. "We moved the fireworks down into the cellar when the fire broke out. Follow me."

It took them a quarter-hour to load the fireworks onto the wagon, which, judging by Orlova's increasingly curdled expression, was far too long. Even so, as they raced back toward the river, Lukan wished they'd taken a little bit longer to secure their cargo. One of the ropes they'd used had already snapped, and it was all he and Matiss could do to stop the uppermost crates from toppling off the cart. Worse, the tarpaulin they'd soaked with water and thrown over the crates was slipping more and more with each lurch of the cart, leaving several of them exposed. The fire that was sweeping through the district was mercifully to their backs, but the air was full of violet embers. It would only take one to ignite their cargo—and them along with it. *Best not think of that*, Lukan mused, straining to hold the crates in place as they hurtled round another corner. Not that the other thoughts clamoring for his attention were any better. He kept seeing the dragon in his mind's eye, swooping down from the alchemists' tower. With any luck they wouldn't see it again. Not until they *wanted* to see it, at any rate, and when that time came they would just have to hope the fireworks did the trick. But even if they did, there was no guarantee Arima's machine would be able to trap the creature . . .

Lukan was jolted from his thoughts as the cart struck a rut in the road, and for a panicked moment he thought he was going to pitch over the side of the wagon. He might have, too, if Matiss hadn't grabbed his arm. Lukan nodded his thanks, glad the man had insisted on accompanying them. He didn't trust anyone else with his fireworks, he claimed. Orlova hadn't bothered to argue, and Lukan could scarcely object, since he'd never lit anything more significant than the occasional cigarillo. Best to leave the lighting of fireworks to the experts, especially when the stakes were so high. Matiss, for his part, seemed unperturbed—if bemused—by the whole episode, and, while his countenance was drawn with concern, Lukan fancied it wasn't for the task before him, but for Radimir, who had remained behind to help fight the frostfire. The men's embrace had been brief, but fierce.

"Make way!" Orlova bellowed as the cart rattled toward the bridge.

A crowd of people scattered before them, and suddenly they were out of Emberfall and racing back across the Bridge of a Thousandfold Thoughts, the lights of the Mantle glittering high in the distance, as if urging them to greater speed. Lukan felt a flash of elation, subtle as a whisper. *We're going to make it.*

Then he felt something far less subtle.

A presence. A shadow.

Descending.

"Orlova," he yelled, his words drowned out by a mighty rush of air. "Look out!"

But Orlova was gone. The other rider too.

Lukan blinked at the empty bridge that stretched before them. *What in the hells* . . . He twisted round, thinking they'd somehow overtaken the two riders, but there was nothing but empty space behind them.

"They were taken," Matiss said, his voice barely above a whisper. He looked terrified. "It . . . it just swooped down and . . . and . . ."

"Lady's blood," Lukan swore, giving the sky a panicked glance, before scrambling round to Flea. "You all right?" he asked her, gripping her shoulder. The girl didn't reply, just stared back at him, her eyes wide with a fear he'd never seen in her before. "We'll be fine," he told her, giving her shoulder a squeeze. "Just sit tight." As if she was going to do anything else. Then again, he couldn't deny that leaping into the chill waters of the river was rapidly looking like a better option. *We need to get off this damned bridge.*

"It's coming back," Flea suddenly said.

Lukan felt a stab of panic as he scanned the sky. "Where? I don't see it . . ."

"She's right," Matiss said, a note of despair in his voice. "There," he added, raising a hand. "To the southeast."

Lukan's insides turned to ice as he saw the distant black mass blotting out the stars. *Shit.* He scrambled toward the front of the cart. "Hey," he called to the driver, "we need to go faster!"

"The hells do you think I'm trying to do?" the man yelled back, thrashing his horse's reins.

Lukan glanced back at the distant black mass—bigger than before—and then at the end of the bridge.

It seemed very far away.

"Lukan," Flea said softly.

"We're going to make it," he replied, knowing it was a lie. The dragon was moving too fast and they were moving too slow. He caught Matiss's gaze and could tell the other man knew it too. Lukan shrugged, a hopeless gesture that was part apology, part resignation. Matiss turned away, his gaze lowered, no doubt thinking of the husband he wouldn't see again.

"Lukan," Flea said again.

"I'm here," he replied, crawling beside her and pulling her to him.

"I'm scared," she whispered.

"So am I."

The black shape of the dragon was close enough for Lukan to see the span of its great wings, light glinting on its metallic body.

Lukan closed his eyes. *Any moment now*, he thought, gritting his teeth as he waited for that looming presence, that terrible rush of wind. A series of images flashed through his mind: his mother, his father, Amicia, his old friend Jaques, the old willow tree by the river. They twirled in his mind, gilded with gold. "Do it," he hissed through gritted teeth, to the dragon that even now was surely swooping down for them. *Just bloody do it—*

A shout snapped him from his thoughts.

Lukan opened his eyes to see the driver furiously punching the air. For a panicked moment he thought the dragon had them, only to realize the man's cry was of jubilation, his gesture one of celebration.

Because they were across the river, the buildings of Hearthside closing around them like a protective fist.

They'd made it.

Lukan looked back in time to see the shape of the dragon rising into the sky.

Then Flea started shouting too, and Matiss, and finally Lukan joined in, howling like an idiot, giddy with relief. The most dangerous task of all still lay ahead, but for now, as their cries of elation echoed through the empty streets, still being alive was enough.

43

An Unresolved Element

Lukan's elation had faded by the time the cart rattled into the Square of Sacred Memories, and was replaced by a growing unease at what was to come—at whether this ludicrous plan would work, or whether Orlova's death, and that of the other rider, would prove to be in vain. More pressingly, he worried about whether Lady Wretzky had managed to solve their one remaining problem. *If she hasn't*, he thought, his gaze passing over the dozens of barrels lined up in the square, *all of this will be for nothing. Unless . . .* He clenched his jaw. *No, why should I? Surely I've done enough already.*

"Gardova," Lady Wretzky said, jolting him from his thoughts. Lukan looked up to see the Iron Dame striding toward the cart, with General Razin at her back. "You made it. Good." Her eyes flicked to the crates. "I hope those are what I think they are."

"They're fireworks," Flea replied, squeezing out from under the unconscious guard and sliding off the end of the cart. "Just as I promised."

"Not just any fireworks," Matiss said pointedly, as he disembarked. "But the finest illuminations this side of the Mourning Sea." He folded his arms, his gaze on Wretzky. "And you would waste them on a dragon—not even a real one."

"And you are?" the Iron Dame replied, entirely unruffled.

"I am Matiss, the purveyor of those same fireworks. And I expect to be compensated at least three times over. Especially after I almost died bringing them to you."

"You have the look of the Clanholds about you," Razin said, his gaze hardening. "If I didn't know better, I'd say you were a clansman."

"Half-clansman, actually." Matiss shrugged. "But if the matter of my birth is an issue for you, I'm more than happy to take these fireworks back."

"We shouldn't put our trust in a clansman," Razin urged Orlova.

But the Iron Dame wasn't listening. Instead she was staring at the slumped body of the soldier in the cart. "Orlova?" she asked, turning to Lukan.

"Gone," he replied. "The dragon took her and the other rider as we returned across the Bridge of a Thousandfold Thoughts. They had no chance."

"Then they died as heroes," Razin intoned, placing a fist across his chest. "We will remember them as such." Lukan thought the news of his nemesis's demise might have brought a smile to the old man's face, but his expression was grave.

Wretzky swore under her breath and pressed two fingers to her lips, only to look surprised at the lack of a cigarillo between them. She swore again and let her arm fall. "Leopold," she said, turning to Razin. "As acting leader of the Frostfire Council, I hereby restore you to your former rank of general, and all the responsibilities that entails. Do you accept?"

"I do," he replied, bowing his head, this time with the hint of a smile on his lips.

"Good. Now, back to business." Wretzky turned to Matiss. "You will be fully compensated for your fireworks. And, if you agree to stay and light them according to our instructions, I will pay you triple their worth." She glanced around the square, again raising a hand halfway to her lips before she realized her mistake. "And if this ridiculous scheme somehow works," she added, "then I'll pay you four times the amount." Her gaze found Matiss's. "Agreed?"

"Agreed," Matiss said quickly, with a satisfied smile. "Just tell me where to go."

"Leopold, would you please escort this gentleman and his fireworks to the Garden of Golden Roses? Explain what we require and ensure he gets whatever he needs. We can't afford to fall at the first obstacle."

Razin gave Matiss another dubious look, but duty won out over doubt. "Of course," he said to Wretzky, before turning and bellowing to a couple of nearby soldiers. The men ran over and snapped off salutes. "Climb on, lads," the general said jovially, ushering them onto the cart. "You've got front row seats to the most extraordinary firework display this city has ever seen."

"Good luck, Matiss!" Flea called, as the man climbed on after them.

Matiss smiled and waved as the cart jolted into motion and rattled toward the square's eastern exit.

"Builder's balls," Wretzky muttered, her fingers twitching. "I'd kill for a cigarillo."

"I'd do the same for a drink," Lukan replied.

"Have one," the Iron Dame replied, with a shrug. "A tipple won't accidentally blow this square to the heavens."

"I don't know. I once drank some Talassian liquor that I think might do the trick."

"Are you sure you didn't misread the label and drink horse piss by accident?" a dry voice said from behind him.

Lukan turned to find the artificer, Hulio Arcardi, striding toward them, Lord Arima at his shoulder.

"Artificer Arcardi," Wretzky said by way of greeting, one finger twitching as if tapping off ash from an imaginary cigarillo. "Lord Arima. How go your preparations?"

"We're ready," Arima replied, with a note in his voice that fell somewhere between excitement and apprehension. "Everything's in place. All that's left is to pull the lever."

"And hope it works," Lukan added.

"It'll work," Hulio snapped back, his sharp eyebrows angling downward like blades.

"A dragon's a lot bigger than a golem."

"And my intellect is much bigger than yours." He turned and strode back toward his machine. "It'll work," he fired back over her shoulder.

I hope for both our sakes it does, Lukan thought, his gaze moving to the array of pedestals and green crystals that were placed round the great metal disc, and the lengths of copper wire that connected them like the outer ring of a spider's web. The ramshackle appearance of it didn't fill him with confidence. But he'd seen it work on a smaller scale, saw the golem held fast by invisible forces he barely understood. It made sense that a bigger disc of iron and more of the machines could immobilize a bigger construct, but could they really constrain the dragon? Hulio seemed to think so.

"Lady Wretzky," Arima said, "it appears to me that we're almost ready. Hulio's machine is primed. The fireworks are being prepared. That just leaves one element unresolved."

"Indeed," the Iron Dame replied, and the thin line of her lips told Lukan all he needed to know.

"You've not found a volunteer," he said, with a grimace.

"No," Wretzky agreed, her fingers fluttering again. "I've not."

Somehow, Lukan had known it would come to this. After all, it was hardly surprising. Who in their right mind would want to act as bait to lure a dragon? *Especially one that's just set half of Emberfall on fire.* "I'm surprised Razin didn't offer to do it," he said.

"Oh, he did. I refused. I told him I'll need him if"—Wretzky lowered her voice, glanced surreptitiously at Hulio—"this doesn't work out. Besides, whoever takes this role is going to have to run like the hells as soon as the dragon is trapped. Leopold's got many qualities, but he's not going to beat anyone in a sprint."

"Nor am I," Arima said ruefully, "I'd gladly volunteer, but . . ." He shrugged and gestured at his cane.

"You have nothing to prove to anyone," Wretzky replied. "Not with Dragomir dead, at least." She eyed Lukan. "Lord Gardova, are you sure we can't use a golem as bait?"

"I just don't think it'll work," Lukan replied, recalling the way the dragon had ignored the golem that had rushed toward it, shortly before the beast had laid waste to the gatehouse. Had the dragon somehow sensed another soul, similarly imprisoned? He wasn't sure, but something seemed to have passed between the two constructs. "We can't be certain the sight of a golem would encourage it to land."

"But a person would," Lady Wretzky said, with a sigh.

Lukan shrugged. "Probably. We know it has a penchant for slicing off heads."

"Then there's nothing for it. I'll have to ask Leopold to order every soldier we can find into a room and then tell them no one's leaving until we have a volunteer. And that while we dither, that bloody dragon is laying waste to our—"

"I'll do it," Lukan said, wincing at his own words.

"—city, and if . . ." Wretzky blinked, looking at him sharply. "What did you say?"

"I'll do it."

"No!" Flea objected, her eyes wide. "Lukan, you *can't*."

"Someone has to." He forced a rueful smile and patted his leg. "Besides, this injury hasn't slowed me down *that* badly. I can make it. And I've already escaped the dragon once." He didn't mention that the dragon had very nearly caught him back inside the mountain, nor did he admit to the growing ache in his leg since that desperate flight—an ache only made worse by their trip to Emberfall. He wasn't going to shirk the responsibility just because of a bit of pain.

"No," Flea repeated. "I'm faster." She steeled herself. "*I* should do it."

"If it's a question of speed," Ashra put in, "then I'm quicker than both of you." Her gaze flicked to the circle of machines. "It should be me."

"No!" Flea cried for a third time, grabbing the thief's arm. "It can't be."

"Someone has to do it, *majin*."

"Tell her, Lukan!" the girl implored, her eyes pleading.

"Flea's right," he told the thief. "It should be me."

"That's not what I meant!"

Lukan dodged the kick the girl aimed at his shin. "If I hadn't been careless and lost my key," he said, "none of this would have happened." He gestured toward the purple fire in the distance, visible from the western edge of the square.

"It's Marni's obsession that caused all this, not you," Wretzky replied. "She was the one who opened the Crimson Door."

"With the formula I gave her. Some of the responsibility is mine."

"Ours," Ashra said firmly. "*We* brought it back. All three of us."

"If this is about your key," the Iron Dame said, "you can have the bloody thing. You've already done more than I asked for."

"I'm not doing it for the key." Lukan thought back to that moment in the cell, when he told himself that if he got another chance he'd try to do better. Face the consequences of his actions rather than run from them. Take responsibility. "Besides," he added, forcing lightness into his tone, "I've stood before the Faceless and lived to tell the tale. This is no different."

"No different?" Ashra replied. "You could talk to the Faceless. Make them see sense. How do you reason with the soul of a dragon?"

"I don't need to," Lukan replied. "I just need to convince it to land on that medallion. And hope this machine works."

"It'll work!" Hulio shouted from where he was fiddling with a green crystal.

"Lukan, a word." Ashra turned and walked for a few paces. "Stay there, *majin*," she warned Flea, who was already following. The girl scowled but stayed where she was.

"What is it?" Lukan asked as he joined her.

"I will do this," the thief replied, in a low voice. "I will stand before the dragon."

"But—"

"No. Listen to me. Flea needs you. You're her rock. Her anchor. And she is yours." The thief raised a warning finger as Lukan tried to interrupt. "I never got the closure I needed. I've learned to live with that. But you still have a chance. An opportunity to find out what happened to you father. To find justice for him. I won't take that from you."

"Ashra—"

"What did I tell you about listening to others? This is my choice. Respect it."

"But . . . Are you sure?"

"I'm sure." The thief turned and walked back to the others before he could reply. Lukan followed behind, relief and guilt warring inside him. "I will do it," Ashra told Wretzky.

"Ashra, *please*," Flea begged.

"Courage, *majin*."

"Laverne was right about you, Lady Midnight," Wretzky said, a note of admiration in her voice.

"Ashra," the thief replied. "My name is Ashra."

The Iron Dame favored her with the first genuine smile Lukan had seen cross her lips. "Well, Ashra, know that you do us a great service. You remember the plan?"

"I remember."

"Good. Then get ready and watch for the fireworks. That's your cue." The Iron Dame glanced at Flea and Lukan. "I'll leave you to say your farewells. Until you all meet again, of course." With those final words, she turned and walked away.

"Good luck," Arima said to Ashra, before following Wretzky.

Lukan, Flea and Ashra stood alone.

"Promise me you'll run the fastest you've ever run," Flea said, furiously wiping away a tear. Lukan reached out to the girl but she shoved his arm away.

"I promise, *majin*."

Flea embraced Ashra, hugging her fiercely.

When they finally parted, Lukan looked the thief in the eyes and held out his hand. Ashra clasped it, holding his gaze.

There was nothing more to say.

44

TOGETHER OR NOT AT ALL

Ashra stood a few yards from the medallion.

If Lukan was here, he'd be pacing back and forth, muttering under his breath. If Flea was present, she'd be masking her nerves with chatter. But they were both standing at a safe distance with everyone else, halfway down the avenue on the square's southern side. She felt their absence keenly. Wished they were with her. Was glad they weren't. That they were safe.

Ashra shivered. Not from the cold. Dread squeezed her chest. She tried to tame it, but the slower she breathed the faster her heart seemed to beat. It didn't help that she was standing there like a sacrifice. Just like the prisoners in the Bone Pit, back home in Saphrona. She'd only seen the spectacle once, but that had been enough. She'd never forget Gargantua rising out of her pit, and the gleamers forcing her back down into it with their sorcery. If only they had a couple of gleamers here now. They'd have this dragon snared without so much as breaking a sweat.

Instead, she was placing her life in the hands of Hulio Arcardi's machine.

Despite Lord Arima's confirmation that the machine was ready, Arcardi was still fussing over it, prodding at copper wires and tapping the green crystals with some sort of stylus. Ashra could only hope this activity was driven by the artificer's own anxiousness and wasn't the result of a sudden malfunction.

Ashra looked to the sky. Full darkness had now descended and the moon was partially hidden behind clouds. She could barely see any stars. Had hardly seen any since she'd arrived. The night sky here was nothing like Saphrona's, where the stars were so numerous

you couldn't count them all. Alphonse had known the names of all
the constellations. He was a sly one. A simple soldier on the surface,
but that was only a facade that hid a keen intellect. Still waters ran
deep. Another of his sayings. She felt a rush of affection for him.
How she missed him. How she hoped to see him again.

One day, perhaps.

As Ashra watched the sky, she saw a flicker of light. A faint
spark, moving quickly. It faded from sight. A moment later a vivid
shower of green sparks exploded against the black, accompanied
by a loud bang.

Ashra's dread squeezed tighter.

It was time.

More explosions followed, showers of scarlet, gold and silver.
Their detonations echoed across the square. Matiss was right; these
were good fireworks. If they didn't attract the dragon's attention,
nothing would.

"You ready?" Arcardi called.

Ashra lowered her gaze to where the artificer stood at some
sort of podium, a few yards from his invention. His hand was on
a lever that Ashra presumed would start the machine. Hopefully.
She raised a hand in the affirmative, wincing at the falsity of the
gesture. She wasn't ready. How could she be?

Ashra turned her eyes back to the sky as the fireworks continued. Perhaps the dragon wouldn't come. She gritted her teeth at
the traitorous thought.

There.

Her heart skipped a beat as an obsidian shape moved against
the black.

"It's coming," Arcardi called. He sounded almost excited. "You
see it?"

"I see it," she replied, forcing the words past the tightness in
her throat.

Ashra took a breath and raised her arms, waving them above
her head.

The dragon drew closer.

Respect the odds, and don't be afraid to quit if they're not in your favor. Ashra's seventeenth rule of thievery. A rule she'd followed many times over the years.

A rule she was now determined to break.

Even so, she nearly ran as the dragon filled the sky, great wings beating as it hovered over the square. Nearly. But she clenched her jaw, forced down her rising terror and stood her ground. "Come on," she hissed, through gritted teeth, as she waved her arms. "Come on."

The dragon stayed where it was. It had seen her, no doubt. Its amber eyes glowed as it stared down at her. She could feel its gaze like a physical weight. From what Lukan had told her, it had regarded Marni much the same way. Before it tore her apart.

Rapid footsteps sounded.

Ashra glanced over her shoulder. Someone was running toward her. Her heart plummeted when she saw who it was.

"Ashra!" Flea cried, panting as she closed the final distance.

"Flea? What are you doing here?"

The girl took a moment to catch her breath. "I'm not letting . . . you do this . . . on your own."

"Oh, *majin* . . ." Ashra glanced up at the sound of more footsteps.

"And neither is Lukan," Flea panted.

"Lady's blood, Flea," Lukan stormed as he limped toward them. "What in the hells are you doing?"

"Passion before reason," the girl said defiantly. "Ashra's not doing this on her own. We do it together or not at all."

Lukan shook his head helplessly, his breathing heavy. "I tried to stop her," he said, meeting Ashra's gaze. "But . . ." He shrugged.

Ashra managed a smile. "When has she ever listened to you?"

"Exactly." He looked up at the dragon, still beating its wings above them. "But I really wish she had."

"Together then," Ashra said, a sudden warmth stirring inside her as she raised her arms again. "Or not all."

"Together or not at all," Flea echoed, raising her own hands.

"You two will be the death of me," Lukan muttered, but he was smiling as he raised his own hands.

"Hey, dragon!" Flea yelled up into the sky, as the three of them waved their arms furiously. "Why don't you fly down and get us, you big, ugly—"

The dragon came.

With one beat of its wings, it descended toward the square. Fast.

"Steady," Ashra said, as Flea took a step back, her eyes wide, her taunt dead on her lips. "We don't run until it's down." She glanced at Arcardi. The artificer was hunched over his podium, watching intently, hand still gripped round his lever.

The ground shook as the dragon landed near the center of the medallion, a great rush of air accompanying its arrival, rattling the cables and wires of the machine.

"Arcardi!" Lukan yelled, his voice coming out as a strangled croak. "Now!"

But the artificer had already thrown the lever. The green crystals glowed on their pedestals as they hummed with whatever energy it was that now powered them.

Time slowed.

Ashra saw the dragon's great head, the light of its amber eyes, the gleam of its teeth as its great jaws opened . . . and descended toward them.

"Run!" she yelled, trying to shove Flea to safety. "Lukan, take her!"

The man grabbed the girl and hauled her away.

Ashra dove and rolled, the dragon's great jaw snapping closed on the empty air where she'd just been standing.

"Ashra!" Flea cried.

Ashra scrabbled backward. Tried to rise, fell back down again. Heart racing, blood thrumming, she watched helplessly as the dragon's great head rose again. Jaws widening for the killing blow.

Ashra closed her eyes.

Felt a rush of air. Heard the snap of teeth closing.

But not on her.

She opened her eyes.

The dragon's jaws were working furiously, opening and closing on empty space. No closer than before. Elation rushed through her as she realized the rest of the creature's body was immobile within the circle of glowing green crystals, held fast by an invisible force.

"Seven shadows!" Lukan exclaimed, from somewhere behind her. "It worked! It actually bloody worked!"

"Of course it worked," Arcardi yelled back as he raced past. "Now run!"

Ashra felt arms round her, pulling her up. "Come on," Lukan said in her ear. "You heard the man."

Ashra didn't need to be told twice.

Together they raced across the square behind Arcardi, toward the avenue, where a horse and cart were waiting. Lukan fell behind, teeth bared against the pain in his leg, but when Ashra dropped back he waved her away.

"Go on!" he said between breaths.

She pressed on, and reached the cart at the same time as Arcardi. Flea was already onboard, urging them on. Ashra clambered on behind the artificer, then turned to help Lukan scramble up.

"Go!" Flea yelled to the driver.

The man didn't need to be told twice. With a lurch the cart started forward, a roar from the dragon chasing them out of the square and into the avenue beyond. Ashra watched the dragon's head thrash while the rest of its body remained still, before she turned her gaze to the road and the line of powder on the right side of it. Once they were halfway down the avenue, someone would light the fuse, and that would be the end of it. But only if the dragon remained trapped.

An orange glow caught her attention: the flame at the end of the fuse, which was heading in the opposite direction to the cart, burning up the line of powder, all the way to the hundred barrels in the square. As impressive as Matiss's fireworks had been, the impending explosion promised to be far more memorable.

They could only hope it worked.

Moments later the cart lurched to a halt. Twenty or so figures stood close by, transfixed by the distant sight of the dragon in the square. Its head still thrashed, its jaws still snapped, but the rest of it was still held fast by Arcardi's machine. Wretzky approached the cart as they climbed down, Arima and Razin at her heels.

"Excellent work," the Iron Dame said, a lit cigarillo dangling from her lips. "All of you have done this city a great service."

"I knew it!" Lord Arima exclaimed, grabbing Arcardi's hand and pumping it. "I knew the science was sound!"

"Of course it was," the artificer replied, with a shrug.

"Now let's just hope those barrels are enough to blow this damned dragon to pieces," Razin said, tugging at his mustache.

They watched in silence as the tiny glow of the burning fuse neared the square. Soon it disappeared, too distant to be seen with the naked eye.

"Oh," a soldier breathed as she peered through an eyeglass. "Oh, *no* . . ."

"What?" Wretzky demanded. "What's happened?"

"The fuse." The soldier looked at the Iron Dame, her face stricken. "It's gone out."

"What?" Razin replied, striding over to the woman. "Let me see." He fussed with the eyeglass. "Builder's balls, it *has* gone out."

Ashra exchanged a glance with Lukan, saw the same despair in his eyes that she felt in her gut. All that effort. All that risk. And all for nothing.

"We need to relight the fuse," the Iron Dame said.

"It's too close to the square," General Razin replied, snapping the eyeglass closed. "Whoever lights it won't be able to get away before the barrels explode."

Silence. Nervous glances and whispers as everyone digested that statement.

"Then let's send a construct with a burning torch," Wretzky suggested, glancing around. "Where's the nearest golem?" When the only responses were shrugs and head-shakes, she snapped, "Someone find me one *now*."

"It's too late," Lord Arima said, as several people hurried away,

General Razin among them. "I'm not sure the machine can hold the dragon for much longer." He looked to Arcardi. "Hulio? What do you think?"

"Probably not," the machinist agreed with a shrug.

"Damn it all!" Wretzky spat, dropping her cigarillo to the ground and grinding it beneath a heel. "Then I'm afraid *someone* is going to have to—"

Clattering hooves cut her off as a figure rode past, greatcoat flapping in the breeze, burning torch held aloft in one hand.

"For Korslakov!" General Razin bellowed, riding as hard as he'd surely ever ridden in his life. "For the Builder's glory!"

Ashra could only stare in shock with everyone else.

"Leopold," the Iron Dame whispered.

Ashra expected Razin's heroism to be in vain, that the general's bumbling manner would be his undoing. She waited for him to fall. For his torch to sputter out. But instead he rode hard, leaning over his horse, his torch bright against the darkness. His war cry echoing down the avenue on the breeze.

The dragon roared in response and bared its teeth as Razin rode into the square. The general didn't falter. Instead he pulled his horse to the left and disappeared from view.

Ashra held her breath. Everyone did.

Silence.

Then a great roar shook the world. It started loud and only grew louder, carried on wings of orange flame that turned night to day. Ashra closed her eyes. Felt Flea hug her tight. A rush of hot wind followed, bitter and acrid like the breath of the hells themselves. Ashra opened her eyes and glanced upward, saw clouds of billowing smoke rising into the sky, and movement within them. For a moment she thought it was the dragon surging free in the midst of chaos. But no: it was countless chunks of stone and splinters of wood, all rising in concert, arcing up and outward, before falling back toward the ground.

A stunned silence fell. Ashra glanced at the faces around her. All were tight and drawn. Everyone staring at the distant smoke.

No doubt pondering the same question that was at the front of her own mind. It was Flea who finally put the thought into words.

"Did it work?" she asked, as a thousand embers were borne upward. "Is the dragon dead?"

"I don't know," Lukan replied, his voice hoarse. "I suppose we better go and find out."

45

A FITTING END

The Square of Sacred Memories was a ruin.

Just moments before it had been a celebration of Korslakov's storied history. Now it only held one memory—not a recollection forged in iron, but one reflected by shattered stones and splintered wood. By the gaping, broken facades of buildings, and a crater in which darkness pooled like a black lake.

"Builder have mercy," Lady Wretzky murmured, as the lights from the soldiers' lanterns revealed the devastation around them. "Nothing could survive this."

"I wouldn't be so sure," Lord Arima replied gravely, pointing to where a large black shape lay half-buried in a mound of rubble that had once been the front of the Artificer's Guildhall. *A fitting end*, Lukan thought, *given it was an artificer who helped bring it down. Assuming the damned thing's actually dead.* He had no doubt that question was on everyone's minds as they slowly moved toward the construct. One of the soldiers drew a sword, as if that would be any use if the dragon suddenly stirred.

"Builder's might," Arima whispered, as their lanterns illuminated the dragon's tail and right hind leg. "It's not damaged at all. There's not so much as a scale out of place."

"We ought to retreat," one of the guards urged, fear writ large across his face. "My lady, if this thing isn't dead, then—"

"If it's not dead," the Iron Dame snapped, snatching the man's lantern, "then we might as well be. Enough pussyfooting around." She strode forward, and the rest of the group had little choice but to follow.

As they moved around the bulk of the dragon, Arima's words

echoed in Lukan's mind. The more he saw of the construct, the louder they became. The dragon might have been motionless and half-buried by fallen stone, but what Lukan could see of its body was entirely undamaged. *Of course it is*, he thought bitterly. *As if black powder could unmake a Phaeron alloy. We were stupid to even think it might.*

"Seventy barrels of black powder," Arima said, wonderingly. "Seventy barrels, and it's not taken so much as a scratch." He turned to Lady Wretzky. "Perhaps we *should* withdraw," he added. "We can't be certain it's dead."

"We can," Lukan replied. "There's a way to know for sure."

"How?"

"The eyes!" Flea piped up. "We need to see if its eyes are glowing."

"Exactly," Lukan confirmed. "So, let's find its damned head and be done with it." He waved away the questioning looks directed at him. "I'll explain later."

They continued along the side of the dragon, round a great forearm and along the curve of its neck. *Any moment now*, Lukan thought, his heart racing as they neared the great head. *Any moment now those jaws will suddenly whip round and tear us apart.* But they didn't, and within moments they assembled before the dragon's open jaws. It was only then that Lukan's fear finally left him.

The eyes were dark.

One of the soldiers found her courage and stepped forward. She raised her lantern to reveal the dragon's swordlike teeth, and above the gaping maw and angular snout . . . two black eyeholes, lined with shards of amber.

Everyone stared in silence.

"The black powder," Lukan finally managed, "it didn't harm the dragon's body. But it shattered the amber receptacle in its head. The receptacle that held the dragon's soul."

"So the soul escaped," Arima remarked, realization dawning. "Which means . . ."

"It's no longer inside the dragon," Lukan finished. "It's gone. This is just an empty husk." To prove his point, he bent down and picked up a chunk of stone, weighted it in his hand, and then hurled it. The stone clanged off the side of the dragon's metal skull, but the creature didn't move. No amber fury glowed in the hollows of its eyes.

"It's dead, then," Lady Wretzky said.

"For all intents and purposes," Lukan replied, "yes."

That brought no more than a sigh of relief from several lips, along with one or two fleeting smiles. The cost was too high for anything else.

"Then Leopold's sacrifice was not in vain," the Iron Dame murmured, as if to herself. "Nor was all this," she added, glancing around at the ruined square. The darkness hid the true extent of the devastation, but dawn would reveal that soon enough.

"He died a hero," Lukan said. "It was the least he deserved."

"It was," the Iron Dame agreed. "And we will honor him. Orlova too. She played her part, in the end." She sighed and shook her head. "So much to do. What a bloody mess. Still, your part in this is over, Lord Gardova. You have my deepest thanks." She reached into a pocket and pulled out his key. "And you can have this," she added, the garnet and amethyst gleaming as she offered it to him.

Lukan felt no elation as he reached out and took it.

Only relief, and a strange sense of loss.

46

THE LAST LEGACY

The Blackfire Bank remained closed for five days.

Lukan spent the first two at Razin's house, working his way through what remained of the drinks cabinet (he was sure he would have had the general's blessing). But the house felt cold and empty without Razin's bluff presence, and Lukan found himself slipping into a sullen mood. He realized he'd come to hold a good deal of affection for the man, and his death weighed on him. The fact that Razin had briefly regained the rank that had been so unfairly stripped from him was the only crumb of comfort he could take. Lukan thought often of the smile that had twitched the general's mustache the moment Lady Wretzky reappointed him, the quiet satisfaction of a man who'd finally found the redemption he'd sought for years. Perhaps that was why he was willing to sacrifice himself barely an hour later. It was ironic, he thought, that the man who had been humiliated and ridiculed by his city—and who, in his blacker moments, had ranted about razing the whole place to the ground—would be the one to save it.

On the third day, he took to wandering Korslakov, preferring the bitter chill of the streets to the cloying emptiness of the general's house. He returned once to the Square of Sacred Memories, the extent of its ruin finally revealed by the winter light, only for a soldier to bar his way—no civilians allowed, apparently. Lukan couldn't be bothered to explain his own role in the recent events, and so merely watched from the edge of the square as red-faced soldiers heaved at huge chunks of masonry, and stonemasons and carpenters did a lot of frowning and pointing and head-shaking.

That same afternoon, he visited Emberfall with Flea, who had been strangely quiet, though not so quiet that she hadn't asked half a dozen times if they could adopt Ivan. She regained some of her usual vim when they found that Radimir's workshop had survived the frostfire, and they spent an enjoyable hour with him and Matiss, who Lady Wretzky had already reimbursed four times over, as promised. Much of Emberfall had been reduced to blackened ruins, but repair efforts were already well under way, and Matiss had every confidence that the artisans' district would be back on its feet in no time.

Razin's funeral was held the following day, and was a grand affair, Lady Wretzky seemingly sparing no expense. Word had spread about the general's heroic sacrifice, as not only did the entire nobility turn out for the occasion, but many commoners did as well—so many that the crowd spilled out of the Builder's temple and into the street outside. Thanks to a contraption provided by Grand Artificer Vilkas, all those present heard Lady Wretzky's declaration that General Leopold Razin would always be remembered as a hero of Korslakov. Lukan suspected that Razin, wherever his soul was, would be rather happy about that.

The Frostfire Council, Timur told them that night over dinner, had admitted Lord Arima to its ranks to replace Lord Volkov, and had elected Lady Wretzky as its official leader—a move that surprised none of them. What *was* surprising was a rumor Timur had heard that the construction of golems might be banned, which led Lukan to wonder if his heartfelt words on the subject might have carried more weight than he realized. Regardless, as Timur pointed out, with inept figures like Lord Saburov and Lady Mirova on the council, change would be slow in coming, if it came at all.

Finally—after what felt like an age—the Blackfire Bank reopened its doors, and Lukan, despite the early hour, was first in line, Ashra and Flea right behind him. Ashra had thoughtfully asked whether he'd prefer to enter his father's vault alone, only for Flea to make it perfectly clear that she was not missing out on this particular adventure. So it was that all three of them came to be following Zarubin, the head banker, into the depths of the Blackfire Bank, and Lukan was perfectly happy with that. Now that the moment had finally arrived he felt a peculiar sense of unease, and was glad for his friends' presence.

"Here we are," Zarubin said, as he stopped before an iron door that looked no different to the dozens they'd already passed. "Vault thirty-three." His gaze had been positively icy when he'd laid eyes on Lukan that morning, but his frostiness had melted as soon as Lukan had held up his key. Now Zarubin couldn't seem to do enough for him, to the point where it felt a little unnerving. "I'll leave you the light," he said, hanging his lantern on a hook by the door. "There's a bell-pull inside the vault if you need further assistance." With those words, he spun on his heel and strode away.

"The moment of truth," Ashra commented.

Lukan blew out his cheeks. "I guess it is." The key suddenly felt heavy in his hand.

"Well go on, then," Flea urged, practically hopping from one foot to another. "Open it!"

Lukan's heart drummed in his chest as he slowly inserted the key, and turned it clockwise.

Click.

He took a steadying breath, his mouth dry, and pushed the door open.

Nothing but darkness beyond.

Flea sagged a little, as if disappointed a mountain of gold hadn't spilled out and buried him. As if he hadn't told her a dozen times there wouldn't be any coin in the vault. Lukan unhooked the lantern, stepped into the vault and swept the lantern around to reveal . . .

Bare surfaces and dusty shelves.

Shadows lingering in corners, as if taunting him.

Emptiness.

"Of course," he spat, unable to keep his rising bitterness inside him. "Of *course* there's nothing bloody in . . ." He trailed off, his heart skipping a beat as the light illuminated a far corner.

There *was* something there.

"Look!" Flea exclaimed, but Lukan was already moving toward the slender object, which lay on a stone plinth. A sword, he realized, as the light revealed a blade that was unlike any he'd seen before. The pommel and handle were unremarkable, but the quillons of the cross guard formed a heptagon enclosing the base of the blade, where a gem was set at its center. *Amber*, he realized. *Of course it is.* The blade itself was double-sided, faintly leaf-shaped, and cast from the same bluish-silver alloy as the circlets Marni had possessed. The entire blade was no longer than the distance from his elbow to the tip of his longest finger—a short sword, really—but it was exquisitely forged, and he had no doubt as to its makers. *Phaeron*, he thought, noting the geometric patterns running down the length of the blade on either side of the fuller. *It has to be.* Only that lost race could have fashioned something as elegant as it was deadly.

But why had his father left it in a vault? He looked around for a note, a letter, anything that might offer explanation, but there was nothing. Fighting his rising frustration, Lukan reached out for the sword. His fingers closed round its grip.

The gem flared with amber light.

And the world vanished.

The vaults, Ashra, Flea—gone, snuffed out like a candle flame.

All was darkness.

He turned round, his heart racing.

Nothing.

Then suddenly there was color and light, shapes and detail. Lukan blinked, trying to take in the sight before him.

He was standing in a room.

There had been no transition; one moment all had been darkness, the next he was here, wherever *here* was, surrounded by bookcases filled with leather-bound tomes. More books were piled on the floor; some of them lay open, their pages covered in script. A door stood before him, but it was the framed map mounted to its left that caught his eye. He found himself stepping toward it, as if drawn by an unseen force. As his gaze passed over the familiar

brushstrokes and calligraphy that depicted the geography of the
Old Empire, he felt a rush of familiarity. His eyes fixed on Parva,
nestled in the Heartlands, then tracked north, past the lakeside city
of Seldarine, over the barrows and haunted hills to where Volstav
huddled before the sweep of the Gloomshroud Forest, then further
north still to where Korslakov lay in the shadow of the Wolfclaw
Mountains. Finally, his eyes settled on the words that he knew
he'd find, the northernmost notation on the map, the sentence he'd
stared at so many times.

> *These be the unmapped lands of men that look like beasts
> and beasts that walk like men.*

He backed away, his eyes wide.

This was his father's map; the same one he'd spent hours studying when he'd been a child. He looked around at the bookshelves,
the curtained door, the books on the floor. All achingly familiar.

Surely not, he thought, struck dumb by disbelief. *This is impossible.* But the more he stared, the more familiar details he found. The
pair of worn leather boots by the door. The vase on a side table that
his mother had insisted on filling with fresh flowers every week—
empty now, as it had been for years. The crack in the glass of the
closest window, which Lukan himself had caused the last time he'd
been here, when he'd hurled a goblet in rage.

There was no denying it.

He was in his father's study.

"Hello, my boy."

Lukan felt a sense of vertigo, as if the floor were tilting beneath
him. For a moment he couldn't breathe. Could only hear the rush
of blood in his ears. But even that couldn't drown out the echo
of the voice he'd just heard. A voice he'd thought he'd never hear
again. He drew a shaky breath.

And turned.

His father was leaning against his desk, which was covered in
books and papers and various knick-knacks. The curtains behind

him were drawn against the daylight, a variety of lamps and candles providing illumination. A fire crackled in the small grate. It was as if he'd stepped back in time, with everything exactly as he remembered.

Except his father.

Conrad Gardova was older than when Lukan had last seen him. The lines on his face were deeper, his eyes more sunken, his hair almost entirely grey. Yet there was a vigor to him that Lukan hadn't seen since before his mother died, and a gleam in his eyes that had replaced the grief that had so often lingered there.

But most surprising of all was his father's expression.

Lukan couldn't remember the last time his father had looked at him with anything other than a frown, when he'd even looked at him at all. But now Conrad Gardova regarded his son with a smile that Lukan could best describe as wistful.

"Father?" he replied uncertainly, his mind racing. Had Shafia somehow been mistaken when she told him his father was dead, all those weeks ago? His heart soared at the thought that maybe it had all been some sort of mistake. That his father might actually still be alive. That he wasn't too late to say all the things he needed to say.

But then he realized his father wasn't looking at him; he was looking *through* him. As if he wasn't really there.

Because I'm not, he realized, despair gripping him as he glanced around the room. *This is just an illusion.*

"Impressive, don't you think?" the elder Gardova said, his smile widening as he swept a hand at their surroundings. "I imagine my study's exactly as you remember, though I can't say the same for myself." One corner of his mouth twitched with what might have been regret. "It's nothing but an illusion, of course. Well, for you at least. Go on, see for yourself. Take my hand."

Lukan stared at his father's outstretched hand. It looked utterly real. So did everything in the room; it was as if he really was standing there in his father's study. How many times since he'd left home had he imagined this moment? Being back in this place, ready to bury the hatchet, to bridge the gap that had grown between them? How many times since his father's death had he regretted not having done so when he had the chance? And now he was here—wherever *here* really was—and his father was right there. So close Lukan could touch him. And yet he couldn't. The distance between them remained. A different kind of distance, but a distance nonetheless.

"Go on, lad," his father said, somehow predicting his son's hesitation.

Lukan stepped forward and reluctantly reached out. His heart skipped a beat as his fingers passed through his father's hand. He didn't feel anything, nor did his father react. Instead the man remained still, his gaze directed over Lukan's right shoulder.

"You see?" his father said eventually, as he lowered his arm. "Nothing but a living painting of a moment in time. Incredible, don't you think? The Phaeron used such methods to relay important messages. No pen and quill for them. I'd offer you a seat, my boy, but you'd only fall right through it. So, you'll have to stand while I say what I need to say." He stepped forward and passed right through Lukan, who watched as the older man opened the door to his study and peered through the crack. Then he closed the door and turned the key. When he turned back his smile was gone. "There's so much I want to say to you, Lukan," he said, his voice lower, his expression pained. "So much it pains me. But I need to be brief. The more I reveal now, the more risk there is for all of us. And I can't trust anyone any more, not even Shafia. I don't doubt her loyalty, but if *they* found out she knew . . . I'm getting ahead of myself. But where to even start?"

Lukan had never seen his father so agitated. His memory was of disapproving glares and cold silences, but now the elder Gardova was pacing back and forth, glancing at the windows and the door, worrying at a button on his jacket.

"What are you so afraid of?" Lukan murmured.

"The Phaeron," his father said suddenly, as if in reply. "We were right, you know: it *was* a war that caused the downfall of their civilization, over a thousand years ago. But some of them still live. They've endured into our time." He wetted his lips nervously. "And they've brought their war with them."

Lukan could only stare at his father—or this simulacrum of him—in disbelief.

"They've told me everything," the elder Gardova continued, a note of wonder in his voice. "Things you wouldn't believe." He shook his head, as if irritated at himself. "No time," he muttered, glancing at the locked door again before turning his gaze to the center of the room where he imagined Lukan would be standing. Lukan moved in to his line of sight so his father was looking right at him. For a moment they looked into each other's eyes.

"The Phaeron are split into two factions," Conrad continued, his gaze moving away again. "Their true names in the Phaeron language will tie your tongue in knots, so I won't trouble you with them now—no doubt you'll learn them soon enough."

Lukan didn't like the sound of that one bit.

"We always called them the Loyalists and the Apostates," his father continued. "I suppose you would say the loyalist Phaeron are on the side of virtue. More so than the Apostates, at any rate. Regardless, I say *we* because I was part of a network of scholars who worked for the Loyalists." He shook his head in apparent wonder. "I'll never forget the day they recruited me. I was standing there"—he pointed to the window—"watching you playing in the garden. You would have been . . . oh, eight or nine, I think. I turned back to my desk, and there she was. A living, breathing Phaeron, just standing in the middle of my study. I knew instantly what she was, even as my mind told me I must be mistaken." His expression darkened. "And if I'd known why she was there—if I'd known where it would all lead, I never—*never*—would have . . ." He sighed and waved his own words away. "What you need to know is that both the Loyalists and the Apostates are searching for an artifact. A device of their own making, lost since their downfall. I don't fully understand its function, only that it holds the key to victory for both sides. The Loyalists had me and my comrades scouring old books and codices for any mention of this artifact. They were desperate to find it before their enemies."

A bird cawed loudly outside. His father moved to the curtains and peered through.

"One of my comrades defected to the Apostates," Conrad said, turning back to the room. "He tried to convince me to do the same. When I refused, he warned me there would be consequences. I told the Loyalist Phaeron, of course, but they told me not to worry. They promised me I was safe. That you and your mother were safe." His expression darkened. "But they were wrong."

Lukan felt dread twist inside him.

"I don't know how they did it," his father said, his tone pained. "But your mother took sick, and it wasn't a mere fever like I told you. It was something much worse, a vile disease the Apostates had created, and the Loyalists couldn't cure it. I could do nothing but watch as your mother faded away. The day she finally passed . . ." His father set his jaw, as if trying to hold off a sob. "That day I lost a part of myself. I loved her, Lukan. Loved her like you wouldn't believe. And it was my fault she was dead. I can't describe how terrible that felt." He bowed his head and was silent for a long moment. "I was so lost in my own grief and guilt," he continued, "that I wasn't able to help you work through your own struggle. And I'm so sorry for that, Lukan. I'm so sorry. You were just a boy and I wasn't there when you needed me. I will carry that regret to my grave."

You already have, Lukan thought, feeling a stab of anguish.

"I told the Loyalists I was done with them. That I wanted no part of their war. I thought that if I just turned my back on them, the whole business would go away. I wanted that for your sake even more than mine. I couldn't risk anything happening to you too. And to my surprise, they left me alone. But the Apostates didn't.

"They told me to continue my research, and that if I didn't there would be further consequences. As much as I hated the notion of working for the Phaeron who killed your mother, I feared the thought of losing you more. So, I resumed my work. I did just enough to avoid suspicion, but not so much that I made any real contribution to the Apostates" pursuit of the artifact. I realized that this was my life now. There was no escape from it. Which meant there was no escape for you, either. Not unless I fashioned one for you. I spent so many sleepless nights thinking about how I could free you from this nightmare that I'd inflicted on us.

"Eventually I realized I had no choice but to distance myself from you. The greater the gap between us, the safer you'd be. So, I suffered the hurt in your eyes every time I pushed you away. I let the rift between us grow over the months and years. And I hated myself for doing so. Countless times I nearly broke and told you everything, but I knew that, if I did, you would insist on staying and trying to help. You've got a good heart, Lukan—your mother's heart. And you've got my stubbornness. Perhaps that's why you never entirely gave up on me, no matter how bad our relationship became in those final days. I knew I needed a way to cut that final thread that still bound us together. Your duel with that Castori boy gave me my chance. I believed you when you said you acted in self-defense. And I didn't want to give them a copper of our money. But I knew that by doing so I'd kill the last shred of hope you had in me. In *us*."

His father shook his head and looked down at the floor.

"The day you left was one of the worst of my life. I wept for hours after you'd gone. I felt I was grieving all over again. And yet I felt relief as well, because I knew you were as safe as I could make you. The Apostates couldn't hurt you if they didn't know where you were. Nor were they likely to bother searching for you when they have far greater concerns.

"Eventually, my anguish gave way to a burning desire to avenge your mother's death. I came to realize this was the only way I'd ever find a measure of peace. So, I resumed my work, desperate to find any mention at all of the artifact the Phaeron sought. I knew that only by helping the Loyalists defeat the Apostates would I find the vengeance I sought. The closure."

His father glanced around, then lowered his voice. "And would you believe it? I only bloody found it. The location of the arti-fact." He raised a hand, a look of intent on his face. "Listen to me, Lukan, because now we arrive at the point of"—he gestured at the illusionary room around them—"all this. I have a plan to try and make contact with the Loyalists, but it carries great risk. I don't care for my own safety, but it's vital that the information I've uncovered reaches them. This isn't just about my desire for vengeance; it's so much bigger than that. The fate of our whole world . . ." He trailed off as he strode to one corner of his study, where a sword rested against the wall—an identical blade, Lukan realized, to the one he'd found in the vault. "I need a failsafe in case my plan fails," his father said, snatching up the weapon. "A way to get my information to the Loyalists in the event of my death. This sword"—he raised the weapon—"is that failsafe." He eyed the blade, a glint of admiration in his eyes. "They gave this to me when I agreed to work for them. The Loyalists. Beautiful, isn't it? Would you believe, there's the soul of a Phaeron contained in this amber gem? It means the weapon's almost sentient. That's how I'll be able to store this message for you inside it, and . . ." He sighed and lowered the weapon. "Never mind," he said, his expression rueful. "I expect this all sounds ridiculous to you."

"Far from it," Lukan replied, managing a smile of his own. *If only you knew, Father.*

"Anyway," Conrad continued, "in a few days I will travel to Korslakov and deposit this blade in the Blackfire Bank, where only you will be able to find it. I have to be sure this information doesn't fall into the wrong hands. I will dispose of my vault key for the same reason. My dear friend Zandrusa has the only other key, which I entrusted to her after your mother died. I think even then I realized one day something like this might be necessary." His brow furrowed. "I've not yet figured out how to tell you to retrieve it from her, but I'm working on it." He smiled faintly. "If you're lis-tening to this message, then I obviously succeeded. I do hope she's well. And that you enjoyed your time in Saphrona."

"She is," Lukan murmured, "and no, I did not."

"Now, here's what you need to do. Go to somewhere safe—the more remote the better. You don't want to attract undue attention. Then, you need to press your finger to the gem." He held the blade up and pointed to the amber set in its cross guard. "The sword will do the rest. I don't know how it works, but it can connect to others of its kind. So stay where you are, for the Loyalists will come and find you. It might take days, even weeks, but they'll come. And when they do, you need to tell them . . ." Conrad wetted his lips and glanced again toward the door. "You need to tell them that the artifact they seek is in the archives of the University of Tantalon."

He lowered the blade. Lowered his gaze.

"I hate to involve you in this, Lukan. Especially after all the efforts I made to keep you safe. And all the pain I suffered as a result, not to mention that which I inflicted on you. Would that I could turn back time and reject the Loyalists when they first asked me to join their network. I will never forgive my own folly. This is not the last legacy I wanted to leave you." He sighed and ran a hand over his face. "I sincerely hope that you never hear this message. That I can save you the trouble of being involved in this business at all. And that once I've had my vengeance, once I've helped the Loyalists defeat their enemy—those same Phaeron bastards that killed your mother—you and I can start again." His father looked up, and Lukan was startled to see tears in his eyes.

"I know that's asking a lot," Conrad continued, his voice thick with emotion. "I hope you realize now, if you are listening, that I'm so proud of you, Lukan. I always was. I always will be. And if we do meet again, that's the first thing I'll tell you. Go now, my boy. Go with . . ." Conrad's voice cracked, and he drew a deep breath, his eyes shining. "Go with all my love, Lukan. Always." His father raised a hand in farewell, a tear rolling down his cheek—

And the world collapsed.

Conrad Gardova, and his study with its books and curiosities, all vanished as if they had never been, and Lukan found himself back in the dimly lit vault. He felt a rush of blood to his head; he staggered, nearly fell. Ashra grabbed his arm.

"You all right?" she asked.

"Fine," he managed, realizing he was blinking back tears. He thumbed them away, his mind still reeling from what he'd seen. What he'd heard. "I just need a moment."

"What happened?" Flea asked, as Lukan leaned against a wall and waited for his dizziness to subside.

"I could ask you the same question," he replied, his mind racing. "Did either of you see anything?"

"Just you almost falling over."

"Did you hear anything?"

Flea and Ashra exchanged glances.

"Like what?" the thief asked.

"Like . . ." He struggled to find the words. How could he explain what had happened when he barely understood it himself? He realized he was still holding the sword, and he glanced down at the gem in the cross guard. *Stay where you are, for the Loyalists will come and find you.* His mind reeled at the impossibility of it all.

"Lukan?" Ashra prompted, her eyes revealing her concern. "What did you see?"

"My father. And he said . . ." He sighed, pushed himself off the wall. Glanced down at the blade in his hand. "There's something I need to do."

47

A Burning Desire
for Vengeance

Lukan had never seen so many stars.

They lay strewn across the night sky, like diamonds cast aside by a careless celestial hand, left to glitter in the endless dark. The moon—determined not to be outdone, perhaps—had revealed itself in full, bathing the Winterglade Woods in a spectral light that lent the snow-laden trees a fey, ghostly quality.

Silence reigned over the clearing.

Not the fleeting silence between a sleeper's breaths, nor the fragile silence of a nocturnal city street that might be broken at any moment. No, Lukan thought, this was a true silence, the kind he'd only ever found far away from the hustle and bustle of humanity. A silence deeper than the ocean, a silence so profound it felt almost like a presence—one you dared not disturb.

Thunk.

Unless you were Flea, of course.

"Lady's blood," he swore, glancing at the girl. "Must you?"

"Must I what?"

"Must you keep firing those damned bolts at that fence?"

"I can fire them at your head if you like." The girl's tongue poked out as she closed one eye and aimed her crossbow.

"Can you even see where you're aiming?"

Flea's crossbow string snapped in response, a second *thunk* sounding as the bolt struck a fence post—right beside the first bolt. "Does that answer your question?"

"It's not my questions you need to worry about," Lukan shot

back. "I'm sure Lady Wretzky will want to know why her family's cabin is covered in holes."

"Reckon she's got"—Flea grimaced as she tugged her bolts free—"bigger things to worry about."

"True enough," Lukan conceded, thinking back to the devastation caused by the dragon and the explosion that had destroyed it along with the Square of Sacred Memories. "Still, perhaps you could give it a rest? I'm trying to think."

"About what?"

"Everything."

Four days had passed since he opened his father's vault; three since they'd arrived at Lady Wretzky's cabin; and yet his mind was still awhirl. His father's revelation about the secret Phaeron war was astonishing, but it was the admission that his coldness was merely a ruse—a deliberate act to drive Lukan away—that had really stunned him. At first he'd felt a mix of anger and frustration—why hadn't his father just said something? Seven years he'd spent on the road, drifting aimlessly, too afraid to return home to try to close the rift that had grown between them. Seven years of anger and sorrow and frustration and fear.

All for nothing.

For Conrad's plan had failed and now Lukan found himself in the midst of his father's war regardless. Then again, if he'd never left home, the likelihood was that he'd be dead now too. So perhaps his father's sacrifice—forcing his own son away, fanning the flames of the enmity between them—had saved Lukan's life after all.

Lukan's only regret was that he'd never get the chance to thank him. He wanted nothing more than to tell his father that he understood, to tell him that he was sorry for everything he'd said. To tell him that he loved him, and that he always had. But his father was dead, likely murdered by the same bastards who had killed his mother. The Apostate Phaeron—or their human agents—had murdered them both. And now that Lukan's fury and sorrow were spent, all he was left with was a burning desire for vengeance.

The Phaeron war had become his father's war.

Now it was his.

Or it will be, he thought, *if the Phaeron ever show up.*

He turned his gaze to the treeline, hoping to see a shadow approaching beneath the snow-lined branches.

Nothing.

It didn't matter. He'd wait as long as he had to.

"I'm going inside," Flea announced, making for the door. "Cold as a mother-in-law's kiss out here."

Lukan snorted. "Where'd you hear that phrase?"

"From a dockworker in Korslakov," the girl replied. "While I was dipping a hand into his pocket."

"I told you not to do that."

"I know."

Lukan tensed as Flea passed behind him, expecting to receive a handful of snow shoved down the collar of his coat. Instead the girl's arm wrapped round him as she hugged him.

"Call if you get scared on your own," she murmured.

"I will." He patted her arm. "Go and annoy Ashra."

Flea's arm released him. Her only reply was the creaking of the cabin's door as it opened and closed behind her, briefly spilling light across the snow.

Peace at last, he thought.

He watched the treeline for a time, enjoying the silence and beauty of the night, before his thoughts drifted back through the years. He recalled summer days in the garden, playing with wooden swords as his mother sat in the shade of the old oak tree. He thought of winter nights before the hearth, listening to his father spin old tales. He thought of Jaques, his old friend, and his lost love Amicia, and wondered where they both were.

And his heart ached.

Finally, Lukan rose stiffly from the bench, the lure of the fire inside the cabin—and the company of his friends—proving too strong. *Lady's mercy*, he thought, rubbing his hands as he glanced once more at the treeline, *it's so bloody cold—*

His mind froze along with his body.

A figure stood barely five yards away.

It was tall; somehow that realization registered amidst the shock that paralyzed him. Lukan watched as the stranger drew a sword, the blade sleek and elegant, the gem in its cross guard glowing with an amber light that nonetheless failed to penetrate the darkness within the figure's hood.

Lukan tried to move, tried to think.

All he could do was stare.

The stranger stared back.

The stars glittered overhead, uncaring.

Then the figure raised its sword and pointed it at Lukan.

"Who," the stranger said, in a voice that seethed like cracking ice, "are *you*?"

ACKNOWLEDGMENTS

The problem with writing a novel and declaring it to be the first in a series is that you then have to write another one. Except this time, you have a deadline, and, if you're anything like me, you also have a voice in your head whispering "Hey, psst . . . what if your first book was a total fluke and you don't actually know what you're doing? Huh? What then?" All of which is to say that writing The Blackfire Blade wasn't always the smoothest of experiences.

Fortunately, as with the last book, I've not been walking this road alone. So, a raise of the glass and a tip of the hat to the following wonderful people:

Emma Swift, my partner in life and literary crimes, for helping me find the emotional heart of this novel, and for always being a safe harbor in stormy seas.

My family—my parents Ian and Liz, and brothers Matthew and Richard—for their support, and for cheering me on every step of the way. Love to you all.

My brilliant editors Anne C. Perry and Stephanie Stein, for their editorial expertise, support and enthusiasm. (Anne—I'm sorry Lukan didn't bang his head enough for you in this book, but there's always next time, right?) Thanks as well to Gaby Puleston-Vaudrey, Ayo Okojie and the rest of the team at Arcadia/Quercus, and to Desirae Friesen, Emily Honer, Peter Lutjen and everyone else at Tor US.

Jeff Brown for another amazing cover. (And for the maggot in the liquor! No, I haven't drunk it yet.)

Jacqui Lewis for the excellent copyedit, and for once again facing the assorted grammatical horrors I left throughout the manuscript.

At the time of writing, it's been nearly a year since The Silver-blood Promise was published, and I owe a lot of thanks to many people for contributing to the success of that book:

All the booksellers—especially Ash (formerly of Waterstones Piccadilly), Anya at Waterstones Covent Garden, and the team at Foyles Waterloo—who showed such amazing support and enthusiasm for the book. I'm hugely grateful.

All the authors who kindly provided endorsements, and the many YouTubers, Instagrammers and podcasters who shouted about the book (or invited me on their show to shout about it myself), especially Petrik Leo, Andy Peloquin, Weston Warnock, Adrian M. Gibson and M. J. Kuhn.

Matt and the team at the Broken Binding for producing such a beautiful special edition.

Brenock O'Connor for the wonderful narration for the audiobook, and for bringing my characters to life with such verve and vigor.

Finally, a special thanks to everyone who bought or borrowed the book, and to all the readers who contacted me to say how much they loved it. Those kinds of messages always make my day. You guys are the real MVPs.

Right, onward. This story still has some way to go—to places old and new, with faces both familiar and unknown. There are still secrets to be revealed and scores to be settled.

Passion before reason.

James Logan
London
21st February 2025

ABOUT THE AUTHOR

Ella Kemp

JAMES LOGAN was born in the southeast of England where he grew up on a diet of Commodore 64 computer games, Fighting Fantasy gamebooks, and classic eighties cartoons, which left him with a love of all things fantastical. He lives in London and works in publishing. *The Silverblood Promise* is his first novel.